Honor's Reward

KRISTEN HEITZMANN

◆◆◆◆◆◆◆◆◆◆◆◆◆◆◆◆◆◆◆

Honor's Reward

BETHANY HOUSE PUBLISHERS
MINNEAPOLIS, MINNESOTA 55438

Honor's Reward
Copyright © 2000
Kristen Heitzmann

Cover illustration by Joe Nordstrom
Cover design by Dan Thornberg

Unless otherwise identified, Scripture quotations are from the King James Version of
the Bible.

Published by Bethany House Publishers
A Ministry of Bethany Fellowship International
11400 Hampshire Avenue South
Minneapolis, Minnesota 55438
www.bethanyhouse.com

Printed in the United States of America by
Bethany Press International, Minneapolis, Minnesota 55438

Library of Congress Cataloging-in-Publication Data

Heitzmann, Kristen.
    Honor's reward / by Kristen Heitzmann.
        p.   cm. — (Rocky mountain legacy ; 5)
    ISBN 0–7642–2204–X
    . Title.
PS3558.E468 H68   2000
813'.54—dc21   99–006867
                                                                          CIP

To Stevie,
may your joy be complete.

With closest custody guard your heart
for in it are the sources of life.

Prov. 4:23
New American Bible

Rocky Mountain Legacy

◆◆◆◆◆◆◆◆◆◆◆◆◆◆

KRISTEN HEITZMANN was raised on five acres of ponderosa pine at the base of the Rocky Mountains in Colorado, where she still lives with her husband and four children. A music minister and artist, Kristen delights in sharing the traditions of our heritage, both through one-on-one interaction and now through her bestselling series, ROCKY MOUNTAIN LEGACY.

Prologue

The crack of gunshots smote the rugged crags above the pine-clad slopes, shattering the pristine quiet. Foam-flecked horses strained against the harness as the coach careened along the narrow bend of mountainside road. The iron-banded wheels flew up and slammed down as the road cut back on itself.

Earth and rocks crumbled away down the steep embankment. New shots sounded from the woods ahead, and the stage driver jerked back in the seat, stunned by the impact that bloodied his chest. The horses plunged on, but the weight of the Concord carried it over the side, yanking the horses down from behind. Over and over the coach and horses tumbled, before one final plunge shattered them among the pines at the base of the cliff.

Crete Marlowe reined in and peered through the clearing dust to the wreckage below. The smell of the carnage rose up to him as he watched for movement, however unlikely.

Beside him, Jackson Finn dismounted and followed his gaze. "Think they're dead?"

Crete held his piece, waiting as another man rode up from behind and climbed down off his saddle.

"Whooee. That be one nasty bend in the road."

Crete scowled at the large half-breed Sioux. "Suppose you leg it down there, Washington, and see what's left." Crete jabbed his chin toward Finn. "Go with him and bring the box."

"What if they ain't dead?"

"Just get the box." Crete watched them skid down the rutted slope. He rubbed a hand through his gray hair. It was standing out like a bush at the sides but thinning on top.

Too many years of grubbing and bad luck had left him hungry in ways he couldn't satisfy. He'd started out honestly enough—trapping, then buffalo hunting, then trading with the redskins. And now this. But what choice did he have with a warrant out on him . . . for murder. The murder of Auralee Dubois, a stinking saloon prostitute. He scowled again.

Cole Jasper. Cole Jasper had changed his luck, given him a bad name, and derned near killed him. And Jasper had much as caused that woman's death as if he'd done it himself. Crete figured he should have slit his gullet when he had the chance. He could still picture Cole half-dead, beaten and bleeding from the bullet in his shoulder.

Crete felt his hands clench and shook his head. That was the last time he'd let the law see to his personal business. When he and Cole Jasper met again, the trail would end for one of them.

One

That ain't a real wedding ring. It hasn't any jewels." Seven-year-old Jenny tossed her brown braids to emphasize her disdain.

Across the table, Abbie looked down at the gold band with rose gold tracery glittering on her ring finger. Jewels? What did she need with jewels when Cole Jasper now sat beside her at the end of the long cherrywood table?

She glanced up at his rugged face, clean-shaven except for his thick mustache. It was darker blond than his unruly curls, cropped close except at the neck where they grew just long enough to touch the knotted kerchief about his throat. His green eyes met hers, amused, and he wore a hint of his sideways grin.

"It is too a wedding ring. Mama said so." Four-year-old Elliot's face was earnest in her defense, and Abbie felt a surge of love for her small son and his valiant effort.

"No, it ain't. Real wedding rings have lots and lots of jewels."

"Jenny, don't say 'ain't.'" Abbie sat back for James to clear her plate.

"Why not? Pa says it." Jenny raised her pert chin.

"Don't sass your aunt, Jenny."

The child turned her large brown eyes to Cole. "Well, you do say it."

"Only when I ain't thinkin'."

Abbie frowned. He did that on purpose, she could tell, to ease the correction he'd given in the breath before. She would have to nip that if they were going to keep her niece in hand at all.

And it jarred her to hear Jenny call Cole "Pa." It seemed to ally

11

them unfairly. It was Abbie and her late husband, Monte, who had first taken the child into their care, though it seemed so long ago now. The trip to Charleston after the death of Monte's sister, Monte's grief, the miracle of learning Abbie would bear his son, Elliot . . .

She looked across the table at the dark-haired boy so like his pa. His features, his elegance of motion, the quirk of his eyebrow . . . all so like Montgomery Farrel, except for his cerulean blue eyes, the color of hers with equally thick, dark lashes.

Elliot turned them to her in appeal. "It is a real wedding ring, isn't it, Mama?"

She hated to side with one against the other, but Jenny lorded it over him so often that Abbie spoke up now. "Yes, it is. Cole married me with this ring." And with those words she felt the wonder of it still, though they'd had little enough time to themselves.

Beside her son, the young woman, Birdie, stood abruptly and walked out, her narrow oval face a mask of scorn. It was on Abbie's lips to correct her bad manners, but she caught Cole's shake of the head and accepted his wisdom. After all, he knew more about the girl they'd rescued from an El Paso saloon than she did.

What Abbie knew was bad enough. As Cole had said, Birdie may be young and small, but she was wily as an oiled snake. Abbie had seen firsthand how conniving she could be, extorting money for the truth about Auralee's murder. Would Birdie have let Cole hang?

Abbie almost wished Pablo Montoya had recaptured the girl from them. But it was unchristian to wish that on anyone. God's hand had saved them all, though Abbie wished He could have parted the Rio Grande like the Red Sea instead of Cole swimming her across under fire. They'd had a long ride home, with no time for romance and certainly no privacy.

She glanced at her husband again. Husband. She was almost as disbelieving as Jenny. On the trail he'd prayed for their marriage, and she'd felt hopeful. At home it was harder to juggle the memories and emotions.

Last night was their first night home, the first they would spend together as man and wife. But they had scarcely finished dinner when Matt brought word of the colicky horse. The expression on Cole's face had been thunder and lightning, but he'd spent most of the night in the stable and the rest in the bunkhouse so he wouldn't disturb her.

Abbie had lain awake until the wee hours, but Cole hadn't come in until morning. Then he'd bluntly informed the ranch hands they would take their meals in the kitchen from now on, instead of in the dining room as they had done since old Charlie, the chuck-wagon cook, passed on. Cole's brother, Sam, had taken that avenue as well, though Cole hadn't intended to exclude him. Abbie wished Birdie could be joined to their number, but she knew better. Birdie was trouble from head to toe where men were concerned.

Jenny spread her fingers dramatically. "I'm going to have big sparkling jewels on my wedding ring. Emeralds and rubies and diamonds."

Cole chuckled. "You'll have to marry a rich man, Jenny."

"Marry a good man, Jenny." Abbie's soft admonition had little effect. Jenny only had ears for Cole's words, and her eyes never left him. By his return expression, he seemed in a remarkably good humor, all things considered.

"Are you rich, Pa?"

"No, I ain't. . . . I'm . . . not."

Abbie bit her lip against the smile. If she once laughed at his efforts, Cole Jasper would speak like a hard-riding cowboy the rest of his days. He was that stubborn.

Jenny looked pained. Clearly it was a battle between jewels and the adoration she felt for Cole. It still amazed Abbie that her niece opened up to him as to no one else. And that Cole not only allowed, but encouraged it.

He truly loved that little girl who was no blood of his. But then, that was Cole—a soft heart for any lady in need. Abbie tried not to think where that had gotten him with the saloon girl, Auralee Dubois, though had he not been accused of her murder and taken by bounty hunters, things might be different now.

She might not have come to know what he meant to her, might not have seen that she would risk her life for him as he had for her so many times. If not for that business with Auralee, they might not be married now. Abbie reached for his hand, her eyes revealing her choice over jewels for the man who had encouraged her to love again.

Cole closed her fingers in his. He'd loved her so long, she had nearly worn out his hope. He had told her as much down in El Paso. If she had said one more time she couldn't love him, he would have walked away.

Abbie's chest tightened as she realized how close she had come to losing him through fear—fear of loving, fear of losing those she loved, fear of grieving as she'd grieved Monte. There was still sorrow. Perhaps that would be with her always, especially as she watched Elliot grow. Sensing Cole's awareness, she pushed the thoughts aside. He knew her heart too well.

"They could be little jewels. Could you buy little jewels, Pa?"

He gave Jenny the smile he kept for her alone. "I reckon I could, if I worked real hard. But that kind of work ai . . . isn't easy for an old man like me."

"You're not old, Pa!" Jenny jumped up from her chair, rushed to his place, and threw her arms around his neck. "You haven't even one gray hair."

He laughed. "Well, I'm too old for bustin' broncs, and a good sight too wise."

Elliot pursed his lips. "Jenny, you didn't say, 'May I be excused.' "

Jenny ignored him. "Will you take me riding today, Pa? Can we see the cattle? Will you show me how to rope one?"

"I want to rope one." Elliot slipped from his chair unexcused and put his hand on Cole's knee.

Abbie held her tongue. She must allow the children to welcome Cole in their own way. Elliot's advances were few enough.

"You're too little." Jenny pressed in closer, edging him out.

Cole hooked an arm around Elliot. "You're never too young to learn. But I've got work to do, checkin' the livestock and cleanin' up the mess from that fire."

Jenny's eyes narrowed, turning up at the corners with a look of perfect spite. "Those were very bad men."

Cole nodded. "Yup."

Abbie cringed. Somewhere out there, Crete Marlowe and Jackson Finn still rode, though there was a warrant out on Crete for the murder of Auralee. It infuriated her that Crete had hunted Cole down for the crime he committed himself. And he'd had the gall to try to burn her house as Cole had once burned his. Bad blood like that didn't go away.

Cole tugged Jenny's braid and sent Elliot scurrying with a pat to the seat of his pants.

Abbie clicked her tongue. "Jenny. Elliot."

Both children stopped at the doorway and spoke almost in unison. "May I be excused?"

Abbie nodded. "Yes, you may."

"Sheez." Cole rubbed his chin, chagrined by his error, and she laughed. He caught her hands up together. "You want jewels?"

"I have all the jewels I need."

"Reckon I have Mr. Farrel to thank for that."

"I wasn't meaning those." Abbie pictured the emerald bracelet and the pearl and garnet earrings Monte had given her.

"What then?"

"Elliot and Jenny . . . and you." She leaned close, and he kissed her.

Coming in from the kitchen, Pearl puffed out her lips and muttered, then took the plate of remaining hot cakes from the table and bustled back out of the room.

Cole grinned. "Reckon it's my turn to win her over now."

Abbie shook her head. "She's been on your side for years. You should have heard her go on the day I dismissed you."

"That right?"

"Yes, it is." Abbie made a close imitation of Pearl's voice. " 'Mistuh Jazzper, he a good man. He done his best by you. Ain' right you sendin' him off, ain' right.' "

Cole laughed. "Then what's she puffin' about?"

"She doesn't approve of our lack of decorum. She and James are from Monte's plantation—complete with all the rules of southern etiquette."

The green of his eyes deepened. "Yeah, I don't reckon Mr. Farrel kissed you at the dinner table."

Abbie tried to hide the pang his words caused her.

Cole didn't miss it. His hands tightened. "I'm sorry."

She shook her head. "It's better to talk about it. I went too long keeping silent. Silence sinks it deep."

Cole pressed her fingers to his lips. His mustache was incongruously soft, and she suddenly yearned to kiss him again, long and lingeringly. But he drew a deep breath. "I reckon I'd better get after it. That's a piece of work we got, building the portico back with those great big pillars."

"Cole . . ." Abbie kept his hands in hers. "What if we don't do it that way? Could we make it look right with, say, a wrapping porch?"

He eyed her. "I figured you'd want the entrance as it was."

She licked her lips that felt suddenly dry. "It doesn't have to be. We could . . . do something different."

"Is that what you want?"

She looked down at their clasped hands. The tall portico with massive white pillars had been so southern, so like the places she'd seen in Charleston with Monte, so like his own plantation house had been. "I thought something more western . . ."

"Let me have a look at it. I'll see what we can do."

She smiled. Cole was capable, reliable, and willing . . . more so than she deserved. She caught his face between her hands and kissed him.

Pearl clicked her tongue loudly, descending on the table like a ship in full sail. With a scrape of his chair, Cole stood and put on his black Stetson. He gave Pearl a cowardly smile and beat his retreat. When it came to the servants, he was as out of his ken as she'd been as Monte's new bride. As soon as the door closed behind him, Abbie steeled herself.

"Mizz Abbie, you ain' got no cause to carry on like that. Mistuh Jazzper, he don' know no better, but you . . . you's a lady."

Abbie wanted to stand up and kiss Pearl's broad, mahogany cheek. She had despaired of ever reaching that status in Pearl's eyes. It now sent such warmth and pride through her, she'd have to confess it come Sunday.

◆◆◆◆◆◆◆

Cole strode to the stable. He'd already set the men to their tasks for the day, and his own would keep him plenty busy. Deciding he'd have one more look at the mare he'd nursed through the night, he stopped outside the stall and eyed the sleek chestnut.

The treatment appeared to have worked fine, meaning the horse's impaction might not have been as serious as it seemed. Some animals were like that. They made more of it than it was. Some people, too. He stepped in and gave the mare a pat on the withers.

"You put a crimp in my plans last night, Lady Belle. I trust you'll stay fit now, so I can get to know my wife."

He turned his head at the sound behind him and looked into the coffee-colored depths of Birdie's eyes. On the outside she looked like a child, but he knew better. He'd spent time enough in the public rooms of La Paloma Blanca to know Birdie had been part of that scene since she was far too young. He'd caught her picking his pockets more times than he wanted to think, all the while nestling close with those same eyes she was giving him now.

Cole respected Abbie's crusade to rescue the girl, but he reckoned she hadn't thought it through too clearly. In fact, as he recalled, it was Will's doing. Abbie had gone along in order to get the truth about Auralee's murder, but she seemed none too happy about it. And while he was grateful for the efforts that saved his neck from the noose, he reckoned maybe it wasn't so safe now after all.

"What're you doin' here, Birdie?"

"Waiting for you." Her eyes blinked with the languor of a well-fed cat.

"You ought to be at the house, seein' how you can be helpful."

"Is that what the lady expects?" She tossed back her hair, and it shimmered like crow's feathers in the sun streaming through the loft window. She was too fair to be pure Mexican, but enough to make her exotic . . . to another man.

He felt only pity for her. He was twice her age and married, though there'd been enough interference so far to make him wonder. But he'd said his vows—twice, in fact. Once for the circuit rider, Brother Lewis, so Abbie wouldn't change her mind, and again for the Irish priest to satisfy Abbie's Catholic sensibilities.

His own faith was too new to figure yet. It wasn't quite a gallows conversion, but something near. At any rate, Brother Lewis had set his feet straight and brought him to a faith that would make his ma proud. And Cole figured he could use a little supernatural help just now. He looked hard at Birdie and spoke low. "Mrs. Jasper don't expect more than common courtesy."

Birdie's eyes flickered at his use of Abbie's title. She took a step into the stall. "I can be courteous." She reached her small, well-shaped fingers to his arm.

He closed them in his hand, but only long enough to remove them from his arm. "I think you'd best put those ways behind you, Birdie. You've got a second chance here, and you owe it to Mrs. Jasper."

Her eyes turned like jet. "What did *you* owe her? Did you marry in return for your freedom? It was I who got you free."

"Sure it was. And if there wasn't somethin' in it for you, you'd have watched me hang." To his surprise, her eyes teared up and her lips quivered. Even if it was a trick, it was effective. "Aw, c'mon. No hard feelin's."

Birdie dropped her face to her hands. "I would not have. I would have told before they . . . You didn't need her. I . . ."

"That's enough, Birdie. And just so you don't get the wrong idea, I've been in love with Abbie more than half your life."

She looked at him with tight-pressed lips that puckered her chin. The hard rage he recognized in her eyes gave him pause. What had he done to merit her hatred?

Birdie's voice was low and venomous. "The great Cole Jasper. Untouchable, uncompromising. Auralee died for you." She spit the words and turned on her heel.

Cole let her go, feeling as though she'd kicked him. He didn't know the particulars of Auralee's death, but he did recall the state he'd left her in after refusing her love. She'd fallen for him hard, though God only knew why. He'd likely been the only man in town, save Sam, who never availed himself of her services.

Maybe that was it. Maybe no matter how fallen a woman was, she still longed for a decent man. Then why hadn't she accepted Sam? Cole dropped his head, still smarting from the pain he'd caused his brother. How could he have been fool enough not to see? He'd trifled with the woman Sam had buried in his heart. He'd done it to forget Abbie.

Cole rubbed the back of his hand across his jaw. He should have known there was no forgetting. He should never have encouraged Auralee or any other when his heart was gone on Abbie. Though Mr. Farrel had married his first wife for honor, he'd loved only Abbie and accepted that torment as a sort of penance for the sorrow between them. Cole had seen it clear as day in both of their faces.

He scowled, knowing he'd have to quit comparing himself to Abbie's late husband. But it was powerful hard now that Cole was living in Farrel's house, working his ranch, and loving his wife. Provided, of course, he ever got the opportunity.

◆◆◆◆◆◆◆

Will Stoddard watched Birdie stalk out of the stable. Her every step spoke of anger and disappointment, and he couldn't help but feel glad. Cole must have set her straight again. She didn't know Cole Jasper one bit if she thought she'd catch him where Mrs. Farrel—Mrs. Jasper—was concerned.

He saw the wind take Birdie's hair and toss it like shining black silk. What would it feel like in his fingers? His throat thickened and his heart stampeded within his chest. He couldn't take his eyes off her.

Will knew that hard look on Birdie's face. He'd seen it in his ma, felt it in her slap if he interfered when she sold herself to feed them after his no-good pa was killed in a fight. But Mr. Farrel had taken him in, given him a position, and brought him out West. He hadn't looked back, seldom wondered where his ma was. If she lived . . . or not.

Birdie had churned up feelings and thoughts he wasn't used to. In a way, Will figured, he'd been helping his ma when he took Birdie out of that place. In a way he was making up for the past, for the things he didn't do. Never mind that he was only eight years old, cold and sickly, when Mr. Farrel took him in.

Will swallowed hard. *Birdie.* He had tried talking to her that first day when they rode alone. He'd felt green as a pasture and awkward as two left feet. But she hadn't helped him out any. She had been everything cruel and heartless. In fact, he'd been relieved when Cole and

Mrs. Jasper caught up to them, though from that minute, Birdie saw no one but Cole.

Will sighed. What did Cole Jasper have over him? Age, experience, confidence, the kind of looks girls went soft over . . . and a good heart underneath his gruff ways. Will supposed girls liked that, too. He'd seen the kindness himself, even when Cole was rough-mouthing him like belt leather on bare skin.

He reckoned it was that kindness that drew Birdie. Will's heart fluttered. Maybe if he was kind to her, she'd respond to him the same way. He liked the thought of her looking to him for protection and comfort, even though a single glance from her made him stammer, causing the hard look on her face.

Will shook his head. He wouldn't talk to her now. Not after Cole. But sometime . . . sometime soon.

Two

Abbie pulled open the door with a smile to greet Nora Mc-
Connel, but Nora gripped her tightly, the strength in her hands reflected in her tall Irish frame and riotous red curls. "I dinna think you
had it in you." Her pale blue eyes sparkled with the accusation, and a
grin played on the corners of her lips.

Abbie looked past her shoulder. "What, no Davy?"

"Och! You think I'd bring him along when it's news I'm wantin'?"
She screwed up her face in mock imitation of her new husband.
" 'Dinna be pryin', Nora. It's not seemly.' "

Abbie laughed and hooked her arm through Nora's, pulling her
inside. "I know what you want to hear, but first you have to tell me
how Davy finally won out. The man has the patience of Job."

"Patience! He's Irish stubborn is all. He wore me out."

Abbie smiled knowingly. Four years of courting was definitely one
or the other. But then, hadn't Cole waited twice that for her? But that
was different, of course. She'd been in love with Monte.

"But you, now. Aren't you the secretive one. It's hurt, I am, that
you dinna tell me. Not one word about this Cole Jasper who's now
your husband." Nora flashed a truly condemning look.

"That's not true. I told you the man who had been Monte's foreman was back."

"Oh aye . . ." Nora waved her hand sarcastically. "And he helped ye
drive the cattle and was stayin' on to run the ranch. I could say as
much for the cow that gives us milk each mornin'."

Abbie motioned toward the settee in the parlor, and Nora sat.
Abbie took her place beside her and nodded to Pearl, who arrived with

the tea tray in perfect timing, as always.

"G' mornin', Mizz Nora."

"Good mornin', Pearl. You best plan on me for dinner and supper, too, and be makin' up a room. I've a feelin' it'll take that long to get the truth from this 'un." She waved at Abbie as though she were an errant schoolgirl instead of a twenty-six-year-old widow.

Then Abbie realized with a start, once again, that she was no longer the widow of Montgomery Farrel, but the wife of Cole Jasper. No wonder Nora was surprised. It was nothing compared to her own amazement.

Pearl nodded with a look of full agreement, then swept her wide bulk from the room. Abbie reached primly for the pot and poured the steaming tea into the fine china cups sitting on saucers that used to belong to Monte's first wife, her own dear friend Sharlyn. Were they together now? The thought stopped her in midpour.

"Well?"

She looked up at Nora. "It's not such a mystery, Nora. I've known Cole for years."

"Aye, and ye sent him packin' the week after Elliot's birth, blamin' him for Mr. Farrel's death."

Abbie's mouth dropped open in surprised dismay. "Where did you hear that?"

"From Davy. And I had to pry it, I assure ye. He got it from his ma, who learned it from yours. I canna say where she got it, but I'd be thinkin' from yourself."

"Well, then, since you already know it all . . ."

Nora gripped her hand. "Dinna think I blame ye, Abbie. You know my own darkness and the hateful things I did on account of it."

Abbie felt the stirring of shame. "I wasn't hateful. I . . . I just couldn't have him near. He'd been too close to it all, too close to both of us. He was with Monte when . . . I thought he could have stopped it. I blamed him wrongly."

"Aye. I know the way of that."

Abbie let Nora's words soothe her. She sat back and sipped the hot tea. "Cole was helping the whole time, sending money to my head man during the four years he was gone. Behind my back, of course."

Nora hid her smile behind her cup.

"You can well imagine my fury when I found out." Abbie still felt a twinge.

Nora nodded dutifully.

"But when things got so bad, with the men dying from the typhoid and no money without the sale of the herd . . . I had to turn to Cole. Who else was there?"

Nora shrugged her sympathy.

Abbie brushed a strand of hair from her cheek and tucked it behind her ear. "It was only natural to keep him on. I had learned the truth about Monte's death, and Cole . . . well, he helped me to grieve."

"Aye." Nora's murmur came from her own depths.

Abbie waved her hand abruptly. "Then this business with Auralee, and the bounty hunters coming for Cole, and his thinking it was Sam . . ."

"Wait a minute. You're spinnin' words like a crazy quilt, all patched up and twisted. I'll tell ye what I've heard and you tell me if it's so."

Abbie cupped her forehead with her palm. "How much of my life is being discussed without me?"

"Most of it, ye can be sure. You canna ride off after bounty hunters with a Comanche guide, then return married to the man ye spurned without an eyebrow or two raised in surprise."

Abbie had to laugh at Nora's frank depiction. "Well, when that varmint Crete Marlowe came after Cole for a murder I knew he could have no part in, I had to do something. Gray Wolf was an answer to prayer, and between him and Will we did get Cole free."

Abbie sipped her now warm tea, remembering Gray Wolf's rage at learning the man he rescued was none other than Death Rider, as Cole was known to the Comanches. She shook her head. "But Cole was determined to stand trial in Sam's place, and if it hadn't been for Birdie . . ."

Nora pressed her palms to her face. "I'm losin' me mind. Start from the beginning, ye daft thing."

With a resigned breath, Abbie settled into the corner of the settee and told Nora how she and Will had set out and all the things that had followed. When she came to Cole's marriage proposal outside the rundown Texas shack that had been his childhood home, Nora's cheeks were streaming.

"Och, Abbie. He was meant for ye."

Abbie raised her eyes to Nora's and studied her friend's urn-shaped countenance sprinkled with freckles, eyes the pale blue of mountain lupine. "Do you believe that? I thought . . . I thought only Monte . . ."

"I know. And I thought only Jaime. But ye love him, lass. I see it in your face and hear it in your voice. Ye canna speak of him without it showin'."

Abbie nodded mutely. Yes, she loved Cole. But things were still so topsy-turvy. She had yet to spend one night alone with him as her husband. And at the thought, she felt all sixes and sevens. It was worse not knowing what to expect, and knowing what had been once—in another lifetime, it seemed—when she was young and Monte . . .

She shook her head. It had to be sinful to still think of him in that way. Abbie had pledged herself to Cole. And he loved her with a love so fierce it burned. She quickened at the thought. Yes, she just had to give it time to settle. They'd only been home from the long, stressful ride one night. She couldn't expect things to be easy yet.

◆◆◆◆◆◆◆

With her small boots turned out and her shin against the post, Jenny balanced on the top split rail of the corral behind the bunkhouse. The wind caught the brown strands of her hair and tossed them, but she ignored them in her eagerness to watch Cole work. "Why are you doing that, Pa?"

Cole crooked his head sideways while he hunched over the horse's back hoof, which was gripped between his knees, and pried the shoe loose. "It ain't settin' right."

Jenny noticed he said "ain't," but didn't point it out. She liked how he talked. It didn't sound ignorant, just daring. He was like a dime-novel hero, only really, truly real. And he was hers. Her pa.

The board on which she balanced suddenly shook, and as she worked her arms like a windmill to catch her balance, she saw Elliot clambering up. He straddled the rail and smiled at her with his knowing eyes, as though he saw inside her. She felt as though she'd been caught, but at what she didn't know.

Most times she included Elliot. She liked being with him, liked the way he looked up to her, the way he believed the things she said. They were almost always true, except when she was make-believing. But she guessed he could tell when it was pretend. Sometimes he even said as much, and though it spoiled the mood, she admitted it.

He kicked his boot against the rail below. "What are you doing, Jenny?"

"Watching Pa." She returned her attention to Cole . . . to Pa. There shouldn't be a distinction even in her thoughts. If he'd been born her pa, she wouldn't think of him as Cole.

Elliot wrapped his arms around his middle and shrugged. He could be very quiet and patient for a little boy. He could hold still far longer than Emily Elizabeth, who thought she was so prim. But just now he fidgeted. Jenny felt it along the rail and stepped down, resting her knees against the upper rail, but still not using hands.

She wanted Pa to notice how well she balanced. Maybe he'd teach her how to be a stunt rider. She'd seen him clowning with Will once. Will was too big and slow, but Pa had been exciting, leaping from the ground over the saddle to the ground on the other side while the horse circled the corral.

Pa did not often play like that. Or she didn't think so. That memory was an old one, from before. She saved her memories that way. "Before" meant before Aunt Abbie sent him away when Uncle Monte died. She'd been only three years old, and she didn't have many clear memories of then—at least not ones she was sure she hadn't improved.

But she remembered perching on the fence as she was now and watching Pa play. And she itched to have him invite her in now, but he'd kept her out. He was busy. He was busy yesterday when he'd come home married to Aunt Abbie and he was busy again today. It was better before, when she had him to herself.

Elliot squirmed. "Why're you watching Pa?"

Jenny turned with her sternest expression. "Cole is not your pa. You have your own."

Elliot screwed up his forehead. "I do?"

Jenny felt a shiver down her spine. She wasn't supposed to say that. She wasn't supposed to speak of Uncle Monte, especially to Elliot. It was Aunt Abbie's rule. She glanced over her shoulder with the uneasy feeling that something was waiting to get her.

"Jenny?" Elliot shook her arm.

"Yes, you do. His name is Montgomery Farrel. So you can't have Cole." She watched Elliot's face heat and knew her wickedness would be discovered. Even if she begged him not to tell, it would show in his face. Everything showed in Elliot's face. And once again she had done the wrong thing.

◆◆◆◆◆◆◆

After Nora left, Abbie sat in the blue room off the master bedroom and helped Zena let out the hems of Jenny's skirts. She'd never enjoyed using a needle, but she was adept enough, especially after the intricate work Monte's sister, Frances, had overseen with gloating delight.

Poor Frances. Abbie sighed. The sorrow of Frances's death had been eased by Elliot's conception, even for Monte, though he hadn't lived to see his son born. The pang that accompanied such a thought, however, didn't plunge her into the dark place. And Abbie knew that was Cole's doing. What she had told Nora was true: He had allowed her, forced her even, to face the grief. And it had loosed its terrible grip.

"Lawd, that chile's growin' like buckwheat in July."

Abbie smiled at Zena, who at twenty-five was as vivacious as she'd been at eighteen. She worked as hard as Pearl and James, yet seemed more comfortable having Abbie join her in her tasks. Maybe she'd been young enough when slavery ended to adjust more easily. Or maybe they were near enough in age to bridge the gap Pearl would never consider crossing.

Pearl knew her place. Though freed by Monte's father, she came West with Monte and ran his home with meticulous order. Even Monte had been cowed on occasion by Pearl's opinion. And now she ruled, taking it upon herself to see that things ran according to expectation—even if Abbie knew little about what southern hospitality demanded. It made no difference that this southern household was centered in the new state of Colorado.

Abbie nodded to Zena. "Good healthy growth. We can be thankful for that." There were too many diseases, such as the typhoid last fall, that had taken four of her men but spared her children. And there was always the threat of accident and injury, things unlooked for that came unawares, injuries such as Monte's. . . .

Abbie closed her eyes against the memory of his horrible goring by the crazed bull. The images would always remain, distorting the happy memories. It just took one wrong move, one careless intention . . . A flicker of fear stirred within her. She would do everything in her power to keep the children safe. But would it be enough?

"Mama!" Elliot rushed in, red-faced, and threw himself into her arms, narrowly avoiding the point of her needle.

She held him tightly. "What is it, Elliot?"

"Jenny says Cole can't be my pa. She says I have another pa. Montgomery Farrel."

Abbie's heart contracted. Not since Monte's death had she spoken his name to her son. She'd kept silent so Elliot would never know what he was missing, and she insisted everyone else do the same.

She hadn't wanted people speaking of Monte's honor and integrity, his handsome looks and handsome ways. Yet Abbie realized it was more for her own protection than for her son's. Would he have the yearning in his eyes now, if she'd told him of Monte all along?

"Jenny has a pa, too, Elliot. Her pa's . . . in heaven . . . with yours." Perhaps that was true, though Kendal wasn't half the man Monte'd been.

"But why can she have a new pa, and I can't?"

His focus hadn't shifted at all with that revelation. Abbie settled him into her lap with a sigh. How could she answer that? "Elliot, Cole isn't really Jenny's pa. He wants to help me take care of you and Jenny, but he—"

"May I call him Pa like Jenny does?"

Abbie's chest tightened. Why did that hurt so? Was it that Elliot was all she had of Monte? She stroked his damp head and kissed its crown. How had Cole so captured the children's hearts, filling a need she hadn't known existed? "I think . . . we should think about it."

"If I ask Jesus, He'll tell me I may."

Oh, Lord. "How does He tell you, Elliot?"

"He just makes me know." He scrambled out of her arms. "I'm going to ask Him right now if Cole can be my pa, too." He walked out the door with such dignity, Abbie smiled in spite of the ache.

But her heart sank. If he came back with the answer she expected, how could she argue with Jesus?

Three

The smell of Pearl's cooking greeted Cole as soon as he walked in the door. He hung his Stetson on the mahogany hook and his duster next to it, then ran his hand over the woodwork. Even the coatrack in the cloakroom was made of hardwoods freighted out from the East and finished as finely as the carved trim, chair rails, and moldings all through the house.

Mr. Farrel had spared no expense, but he'd done it so tastefully it wasn't garish or crass like some of the houses and hotels. He reckoned it was southern charm and elegance and good taste. Cole caressed the smooth wood under his palm. Well, he had set things in motion today. He felt a keen appreciation for these walls and ceilings.

He turned, nearly trampling Abbie. His heart jack-rabbited in his chest. For a man who heard a Comanche at twenty feet, he was getting awfully careless. But howdy, she looked sweet standing there. He took her in his arms and kissed her, and not the chaste kiss he'd intended. "Do you know what you do to me?"

She gave him a look that watered his knees.

He took her hand and placed the palm against his chest. "See there? I ain't likely to survive it."

Abbie laughed. "You don't fool me, Cole Jasper. You're strong as an ox and twice as stubborn."

"That may be, but I ain't contended yet with a mischievous female with designs of her own."

"Oh, come. A little flutter of the heart is nothing to wild bucking broncos and outlaws' bullets." She slid her palm to his shoulder, where he'd taken Crete Marlowe's bullet and had it cut brutally from the bone and sinew.

He still felt tender there, but now it was more from the warmth of her touch than the wound. *Lord, what have you done?* Only given him the woman he'd loved since almost the first time he'd seen her. "Abbie . . ." His voice came thick. Dern it. She knew exactly what she was doing.

She stretched and kissed his chin. "Wash now. Supper's ready."

He nodded like a schoolboy, then caught himself. If once he let her take control, God help him. Catching her to him, Cole gripped her elbows and kissed her soundly. Then he set her back with a grin. "I'll wash now." It was right satisfying to note the racing of her pulse in that milky throat of hers. He walked out while he still had the upper hand.

◆◆◆◆◆◆

Pearl had outdone herself. Abbie watched, amused, as Cole shoveled in the glazed chicken, scalloped potatoes, and stewed apples. His fork clinked and scraped the white china plate. Where did he put it all? There wasn't a fleshy inch on him anywhere. He was spare and lean and muscular—she knew from the times she'd nursed him without his shirt.

But, then, he worked hard. And constantly. She'd heard him chopping and dragging and calling commands while she sewed and mended with Zena. Where had he gone after pulling down the portico debris? After finishing Jenny's hems she'd gone looking, but had not found him.

Cole glanced up and caught her gaze. She saw the instant chagrin. He'd misread her attention and become self-conscious about his table manners. He wiped his mouth slowly and sat back. She sent him a smile she hoped would ease his tension.

He'd been on the trail and in the bunkhouse since he was twelve years old, so he couldn't be expected to eat like a southern gentleman. Abbie recalled the first stilted meal she'd shared with Monte at this table. She'd felt as out of place as Cole must now.

Her smile deepened. "Pearl's going to spoil us." She dipped her chunk of chicken through the glaze. "I can hardly keep from bringing the plate to my chin and scooping, as we did the beans at the campfire."

Cole frowned, glancing at the children. "That ain't . . . isn't likely with the young'uns here learnin' their manners." He cupped Elliot's head in his palm. "You two watch your ma, not me."

Abbie tensed. Had he intentionally used "ma" to refer to both children? She was always careful for Jenny's sake.

"Your manners are fine, Pa." Jenny dabbed her mouth. "I think cowboys are better than gentlemen any day."

Elliot's face colored, and Abbie's chest constricted. She could only imagine what Jenny had been telling him about Monte. She forced her breath to come. "Any cowboy worth knowing is a gentleman, Jenny."

Birdie snickered with a sidelong glance at Cole.

Abbie ignored her. "It's not how you dress or eat, but how you live your life." Jenny's own pa was proof of that. He'd been immaculate in dress and etiquette, but a scoundrel nonetheless.

And Cole ... Abbie hated to think how she'd jumped to conclusions. Not that he'd gone to great lengths to set her straight, not until he thought they'd part ways without her knowing the truth. But she had surely thought the worst of him. That he was thirty-six years old and had not wrongfully known a woman was commendable, especially with the rough cowboy's life he'd led.

He was a true gentleman, manners or no. Her heart surged, then plunged when she saw Birdie looking at him with nearly the same hunger. She cleared the dryness from her throat. "Have you given any thought to what you might do now, Birdie?"

"Do?"

"To make your way. Have you any skills?"

Birdie's laugh was immediate, and Abbie flushed fiercely. She prayed Birdie would not elaborate in the children's presence and silently kicked herself for giving her the edge. Abbie was not up to the girl's wickedness.

She'd leave her to Cole. No, not to Cole. Abbie glanced his way and found him reading her thoughts. His gaze was inscrutable. Birdie's presence obviously disturbed him, but there was something more.

She hid her frown and pushed away her plate, the delicious glaze on the chicken suddenly thick and tasteless. Immediately James cleared it, wheezing slightly as he bent beside her. The gnarled fingers on the plate showed his age more than his smooth, dark skin. But the grizzled hair and brownish flecks in the whites of his eyes confirmed his years. How many exactly, she didn't know.

Abbie tried again. "Zena could teach you some sewing, if you've a mind to learn, Birdie. She makes up the children's clothes."

Birdie looked bored.

"Perhaps Pearl could teach you to cook."

Birdie refused to comment.

"Well, think about it."

Birdie's glance showed her disdain.

Abbie controlled her anger. She'd taken the girl into their home and treated her as a guest, but all she got in return was insolence. Birdie left the table and headed for the lower guest room that had housed the mission orphans not so long ago. Abbie heard her close the door with a slam to express her feelings, though why Birdie felt she had a right to be angry was beyond her.

"Zena, take the children for their baths and see them to bed, please. I'll be up for prayers."

"And stories." Elliot sent her his earnest look.

"One story."

"Each." Jenny negotiated with the confidence of a horse trader.

Abbie smiled. "One each if you mind Zena."

Cole stood when they'd gone and pulled out her chair. Then he took her hand and led her outside into the frosty night. They stood on the remains of the stone steps, the pillars and portico now completely removed. He leaned his hip to the wall with all his old swagger. "Purty night." His breath came white in the light of the lantern beside the door.

Abbie looked into the cold, clear sky shot with stars. It would drop near to freezing, she guessed. Already the cold made her shiver.

Cole seemed unfazed by it. "You worried about Birdie?"

How did he mean? Worried for her welfare, worried by her venomous ways, or worried about her attraction to him? Abbie crossed her arms for warmth. "Well, I ... I think we should all give some thought to what happens next."

"If you turn her loose, she'll go to workin' in town. It's all she's known."

"She can't be more than sixteen years old. She could go to school."

He cocked his head with a skeptical look. "You don't rightly believe that."

"Well, she could. No one here knows—"

"Abbie, it's written all over her. It's in her soul." Cole's green eyes were like the emeralds in her bracelet, sharp cut and faceted, beneath his pointed brows that angled down to the weathered creases at their sides.

"Are you saying she can't change? That just because she started out wrong—"

"She didn't start out wrong. She was done wrong."

Abbie heard an edge to his voice. "What do you mean?"

"I mean Birdie was sold when she was just a bitty thing to keep her family fed."

Abbie's heart quavered. "How do you know?"

"She's half one, half the other. A Mexican ma without a man to keep her. Her pa was likely a gringo passin' through. Pablo saw a bargain and made it. Cain't hardly blame Birdie for that."

She wasn't surprised he jumped to Birdie's defense, but there was something else. "What is it, Cole?"

"Nothin'."

She reached a hand to his slightly stubbled cheek. "I know better."

"A'right, I'm kickin' myself."

"What for?"

He stared out to where the land met the starry expanse of sky. "I got to lookin' at Jenny at the table and thinkin' that Birdie was little like that once. I don't reckon she had someone like you teachin' her right an' wrong."

"It's never too late to learn."

"That ain't the point. Birdie was at that saloon some years. At least four. I reckon she lost her innocence before she was done losin' teeth."

Abbie stared.

"That's the way it is, Abbie, cuz men like me go there."

"Not like you."

"Maybe not in that way, but I spent money on drink there, enough to keep Pablo Montoya lookin' fer young'uns like Birdie to train up. I should've never set foot in the place."

Abbie released a slow breath. "You didn't know."

"I do now. It seems I see a lot of things different now. Prayin' with

Brother Lewis may not have made a saint of me, but it made me see my shortfallin's."

"What are you saying?"

Cole faced her directly. "I don't wanna turn her out." He jammed his fingers through his hair. "I feel a responsibility."

Abbie stood frozen, her mouth caught between speech and breath. The inevitability of his words, his feelings in this situation struck down her arguments. She made a weak attempt at humor. "Cole Jasper, champion to the downtrodden, luckless ladies of the world."

"Not to mention the stubborn, headstrong, trouble-seekin' one I call my wife."

Abbie held out her hands.

He clasped them warmly. "It wasn't my idea to bring her up here, but now that she's here I reckon we oughta keep her. At least until she's learned another way."

"I guess you're right, but it boils my blood the way she looks at you."

He didn't deny it, merely tightened his hold. "You got no worries, Abbie."

"I know that." She sighed. "Before we freeze out here, there's something else we should discuss."

"What's that?"

"Elliot and Jenny."

He cocked his head. "What about?"

"It's confusing Elliot to have Jenny call you Pa. He came to me asking if he could as well. He—"

"It's all right by me."

Abbie shook her head. "I don't know if it's right to confuse things. I mean . . ." What did she mean? What was the right thing?

"What if I adopted them?"

Abbie's heart froze. Adopted? Monte's son? She stared into Cole's frank, honest eyes. He was not just saying it. He'd obviously considered it, maybe for some time. He wanted it. It was there in the green depths, spoken as clearly as words.

His voice came softly. "What if we both did, you with your niece, and me the two of them? Make us a family like it should be. No Aunt Abbie, no Cole—just Ma and Pa, with these young'uns and the ones to come."

His words penetrated somewhere deep. Why did they hurt? What secreted grief did they violate? Abbie shivered.

He drew her close and kissed the crown of her head. "Think about it."

Her own words, the ones she'd given Birdie. But the warmth and gentleness of his voice soothed her. She turned up her face. "Are you sleeping in the stable tonight?"

"Heck no."

"What if Lady Belle has another attack?"

"I'll shoot her myself."

Abbie punched her fists into his chest. "You will not."

"Try me." Cole grinned and cupped her hands with his.

She shook her head. "Where were you today?"

"The bank."

"Why?"

He shrugged. "Had my money sent in from San Antonio. It arrived this afternoon, so I went in and I paid off your debts."

Her thoughts went numb. "You what?"

"Paid off the loan on the Lucky Star." He reached inside his vest.

Abbie watched as he unfolded the deed. Her heart pounded. "How?"

"When you retire the debt you regain title."

"But Mr. Driscoll rolled all the debts into one. The loan on the Lucky Star and the money Kendal—"

"It's all covered. The railroad stock certificates are in a safe box at the bank."

She could hardly believe her ears. All the years she'd felt crushed by the debt, living in fear that Mr. Driscoll would foreclose and turn them out, that she would lose the valuable railroad stocks she had foolishly risked on Kendal . . . It had all been such a crushing weight of concern, driving her decisions, her prayers. Cole was not handing her a deed, he was giving her freedom.

"The only thing is, with us married now and my paying off the loan, my name's been added to the deed. I hope you don't mind. It's a legal detail your brother felt was important."

Her mind spun again. Cole's name on the Lucky Star? Monte's ranch, his dream . . . his lucky star. She swallowed the tightness in her throat. How could she object? Cole had worked the land, worked the herd, worked the horses. Cole had paid the debt. And he was her husband.

He pressed her hands between his. "It's awful cold out here. You got prayers to hear and stories to read. And I ain't nursin' a horse tonight." His eyes were solemn and deep, trying her, telling her he at last intended to know her as his wife.

Sudden tears stung her eyes as she reached up and kissed him. "Thank you." She blinked back the tears. She was thankful, more so than her heart yet recognized.

She went upstairs and saw to the children, scarcely knowing what she read. She dumbly took the third book Jenny handed her and was halfway through before she realized she'd been duped by her wily niece. She kissed them and tucked them into their beds after hearing the prayers they whispered on their knees.

Then Abbie went to her room, let down her hair, and changed into a white batiste nightgown. Looking into the mirror, she caught sight of the twin framed photographs on the bureau behind her. Her image and Monte's, taken on their trip to Charleston shortly before his death.

She turned and studied the picture over her shoulder. How many nights had she clung to that picture to keep his image clear, terrified she might forget? But now... Hearing Cole on the stairs, Abbie crossed the room and lifted the pictures joined by silver hinges. Gently she closed them and slipped them into the drawer with her handkerchiefs. She turned as Cole's knock came at the door.

✦✦✦✦✦✦✦

"Aw, Abbie." Cole lay in the dark and stroked her hair as she pressed into his chest and soaked him with her tears. It wasn't the reaction to their intimacy he'd hoped for. He knew she'd kept the tears bottled up too long, but it did make a man wonder.

"I'm sorry, Cole. It isn't you."

He touched his lips to the crown of her head and tightened his arms. "I ain't takin' it personal."

"It's just ... I ..."

He raised his chin obligingly as she once again sobbed on his chest.

He stroked her back gently, slowly. It was better for her to let it out. She'd had a powerful love for Montgomery Farrel, a love so encompassing she'd refused all others, including him.

He'd seen the love between them when they'd married after Sharlyn Farrel's death. For Abbie it was the answer to her dreams—for Mr. Farrel, too, he surmised. But they hadn't had much time together, and she'd put off her grieving too long.

Cole remembered the day he'd held Mr. Farrel, gored by the Durham bull. He recalled the promise he'd made the man to look after Abbie and his child. He remembered bringing the body home in the wagon and the look on Abbie's face. He'd never forget that look.

He still felt the guilt of not saving Montgomery Farrel. He should have refused to try capturing the bull in its loco state; he should have stood up to Mr. Farrel and said they couldn't do it. He should have been quicker, smarter, stronger.

Cole drew a long, slow breath. He'd lost a good friend, the best he'd had since his brother, Sam. But Abbie had lost the father of her unborn child and, with him, the light in her eyes. Only now was it starting to come back. Sometimes when she looked at him, it nearly made him soft.

Then there were times like this when he thought the well of her tears would never run dry. Why his loving should bring it on, he didn't know. But she was his wife now. If it meant holding her every night while she cried to sleep, he could do that.

At least she didn't turn away from him, didn't shut him out as she once had. He wasn't sure how he'd handle that if she did. He'd just keep being there, he guessed, as he had year after year.

He felt her sobs ease and her breathing deepen. Maybe in time he'd love her this way, and she'd sleep in his arms without the tears. Maybe in time.

Four

Abbie woke with Cole's arms still around her. The air in the room was chilly, but warmth spilled from the covers when she stirred. It was strange and awkward to be here in her room with Cole. Last night's passion and tears had left her confused and shaken. She turned tentatively.

His eyes were open already, and he smiled. "Awake now?"

"Were you waiting?"

"That's why I'm still abed." He gave her his crooked grin. "A man who won't learn from his mistakes makes himself a heap of trouble."

She quizzed him with her eyes, then realized where his thoughts were. "I presume you're referring to that morning on the trail."

"Yes, ma'am."

"Well, I've no intention of repeating that childishness." Even as she spoke, a shadow of the fear she had experienced passed over her. After wakening from a dreadful nightmare to find Cole's blankets empty in the half-light before dawn, she could hardly be blamed for lashing out, then cold-shouldering him all day.

"Is that what it was?" There was amusement in both his eyes and tone.

Abbie frowned. He'd told her once that he woke meaner than a grizzly in spring, but here he was calm and good-humored, and she was the one feeling fractious and uneasy. She ignored his taunt. "What are you doing today?"

"Buildin' you a porch."

She raised her head. "Really?"

"Actually, I'm ridin' out to the pinery to chop and drag logs. I'll have 'em sawed at the mill and start buildin' by the end of the week."

"Have you drawn the plans?"

"Yup."

"May I see them?"

"I'd rather surprise you. If you don't like it, I'll pull it off and start over."

Her heart quickened. She'd have thought him too pragmatic to waste his efforts surprising her. "I'll like it, Cole."

He brushed her cheek with his thumb. "I'll know if you don't."

"How?"

"It ain't too hard seein' everything you feel right here." He cupped her cheek with his palm.

"So I'm an open book to you?"

"Better. I cain't make heads or tails of the scratchings on a page, but I can read you."

"Then what am I feeling now?"

"A little tense, a little hopeful, a little crazy for hookin' up with me."

She drew a breath to contradict him, then realized he'd summed up her emotions exactly. She sat up. "How do you do that?"

"Well, Abbie, I got ten and a half years on you. Every day you learn a little more by watchin' if you keep your eyes open and your mind alert."

She smiled softly. "I guess I should deny it, especially the crazy part."

"Wouldn't do you any good. I know what you're dealin' with. It's something we'll just have to take a day at a time."

The warmth of his words spread through her like a tonic. "I love you, Cole."

"I know you do. But not so much as you will tomorrow, and not so much as the next day. That's how it works. At least how it'll be for us."

"Is that a revelation?"

"Nope. Observation." He swung his legs to the side and pulled on his jeans. "We've already plumbed the dark depths. Now we'll climb up together."

Abbie stared at him, amazed. "I believe you're waxing philosophical."

"I ain't stupid, Abbie. Unschooled maybe." Cole pulled on his boot. "But I understand a sight more than you'd think."

"I've never thought you stupid."

"Then don't look so surprised if I say somethin' intelligent."

With his back to her, she couldn't read his mood. Had she offended him, or was he merely stating the score? She guessed he'd keep it to himself if she had injured him. He'd said his piece and now pulled on his other boot as though they'd just discussed the weather.

She swung her legs onto the braided rug on the cool wood floor and smoothed her gown. "After I take Jenny to school, I think I'll ride out and see Nora. Elliot would like that."

Cole stood and buckled his belt. "I thought I'd take him along to the pinery."

Abbie turned. "You did?" The sudden pounding of her heart was unexpected.

"Yeah. He might enjoy watchin' us cut and haul the trees." He took his shirt from the chairback.

"It's dangerous."

He slipped his arm into the sleeve. "I'll keep him out of harm's way."

Her breath came short and tight. The image of Monte in the wagon, of Cole standing hat in hand unable to meet her eye . . . Cole, who had taken Monte, but had brought him back . . . still and silent.

Elliot. She started to tremble.

"What's the matter, Abbie?"

"I don't want you to take him."

He stopped dressing and eyed her. "Why not? You let me take Jenny."

"That's different."

His expression darkened like a Rocky Mountain thunderstorm. "Why? Because she ain't Monte's?"

His words stabbed her. She choked back the tears. "Elliot's too small." It sounded feeble even to her. She willed him to understand. Understand what? That she didn't trust him with her son, Monte's son, the son he wanted to adopt as his own?

He cocked his jaw to the side, and she watched the realization of her thoughts register in his face. He grabbed his vest from the chair and walked out of the room. Abbie wanted to call him back, wanted to undo the hurt, but she couldn't. The fear for Elliot had paralyzed her.

Cole stalked through the yard to the bunkhouse. He pulled open the door and surveyed the room. Matt sat on the edge of his bunk looking groggy. Curtis's bunk was empty. Sam was up and washing.

Will stood up beside his bunk, snapped his suspenders over his shoulders, and turned. "Mornin', Cole." At twenty-one and six foot three, Will was looking manly and taking his place in the bunkhouse instead of the stable.

"Will, I want a remuda of four horses, and harness a pair to the wagon. Matt, we'll need axes and rope enough to drag logs. Where's Curtis?"

"Out back." Will indicated the outhouse.

"Matt, you and Curtis saddle up. Will, you'll drive the wagon. Meet me in the yard." He might have been talking to the wall. "What are y'all standin' there for?"

"Wull," Matt cleared his throat. "We ain't had breakfast yet."

Cole realized he hadn't, either. "You got jerky in your packs?"

"Yeah, but . . ."

"Then you can chaw that. We got a long day's work ahead. Now git." He glanced at Sam. They hadn't worked out the details of his stay, and Cole wasn't used to giving his older brother orders. "You can come along if you like."

He didn't wait for an answer but stalked back across the yard. Inside the stable, he shouldered saddle and blanket, took the bridle from the wall, and hung a length of rope over his other shoulder. He caught Birdie's scent and motion behind him and spun furiously. She recoiled, but that only kindled his anger worse.

"What do you want, Birdie?" Then before she could answer, he pushed past. "Whatever it is, see Mrs. Jasper. She's runnin' things."

Her sudden spiteful laughter followed him out, and he almost turned back to set her straight. But now was not the time.

Reining in his tongue, he headed for the pasture and whistled for Whitesock. He didn't see the gelding, but from the corner of his eye, he saw the sorrel Arabian's ears perk up. He turned. Most likely that stallion had hardly been ridden since Mr. Farrel's death. He was no good as a cutter, though fine blood for racing. Maybe Mr. Farrel had figured that out, and that was why he'd dismounted that very horse to take the bull squarely on his feet. He eyed Sirocco, noted his unkempt coat, his wary gaze. Had anyone tended him since the accident four years ago? Surely so, but he was obviously not a first choice for the men. Maybe they were reluctant to use the animal that had been Mr. Farrel's undoing.

Cole set down the saddle and bridle and slipped the rope from his shoulder. With a motion as natural as taking a breath, he swung the rope over his head and tossed. It looped the stallion easily, and Cole pulled him in.

The horse showed his temper and neglect. If he'd been worked, it hadn't been much. Cole spoke low and brought the head close, then worked the bridle on. He tossed the blanket over the stallion's back and settled the saddle in place.

He fastened the cinch, kneed the air from the horse's belly, and tightened the strap. He tried not to picture Mr. Farrel astride this same horse, though he was plenty sure that's who Abbie was thinking on at this moment. He felt his gall rise as he swung onto the saddle.

The fiery tempered stallion sidestepped and flared its nostrils, but Cole had mastered too many horses to be put off. This one would learn who was boss. He brought the horse around and rode for the yard. He reined in abruptly and the stallion reared.

Matt stood uncertainly with Curtis. Sam eyed him without speaking, though if anyone could read his distress it was his brother. He obviously planned to go along, and had his own horse saddled and ready beside the wagon. The wagon was loaded with rope, axes, and canvas sacking. Will hadn't come yet with the spare horses.

Cole reached inside his coat, felt his shirt pocket, and scowled. Quitting tobacco was a fool thing to do. Why in the blazes had he thought it necessary? To prove he was a new creation after the dunking Brother Lewis gave him in the Rio Grande. Cole scowled. At the moment he felt anything but pure.

The minute Will strode up with the four-horse remuda, Cole gave the word to head out. He heard Matt murmur under his breath, "Meaner than a rattler with a toothache." Well, let them mutter.

He didn't feel mean. He felt a burning need to drive himself, to work his body to the limits of his strength, to close off his thoughts and emotions. He had dared to hope Abbie no longer blamed him for her husband's death. He'd reasoned that she wouldn't love him if she still thought him responsible.

But he was wrong. She not only blamed him, she didn't trust him. She certainly didn't trust him with Montgomery Farrel's boy. Cole fairly shook with the knowledge. Had she married him for convenience? To have someone to run the ranch? Or someone to hold her when she cried, to ease away the nightmares?

She'd never seemed fearful before. But she was obsessed with fears for Elliot. Abbie kept him under her thumb so deep he'd never grow to be a man. Cole had thought to open the boy's world some, take him along and get to know him—without Abbie hovering. Obviously that wasn't her plan for them.

He supposed he was pretty near the mark when he drew the line between Jenny and Elliot. He reckoned Jenny, being the orphaned daughter of Mr. Farrel's sister and her crooked husband, Kendal, didn't rate Abbie's concern. Not the same as the boy she'd borne from the man she'd loved.

His gut wrenched with jealousy, and he urged the stallion to a quicker pace. The horse's breath came white in the chill of the morning. It was more than four years now. He thought she'd be past it. Why had she claimed to love him if she still clung to the hallowed memories of Montgomery Farrel? So he wouldn't walk away?

He had told her he'd go and not come back if she couldn't love him. Had she only said what he wanted to hear? Had she seen it as her only way to keep his services? Was that why she cried when he took her in his arms and loved her as a man loves his wife?

Cole spurred the stallion, and the horse bolted forward with a racing gait. He wouldn't keep it up for long, but right now it cooled his blood. Thirty-six wasn't so old, after all. He still felt the powerful need to conquer and control, same as he had since he was twelve. Even then he'd had a way with horses. When he and Sam had signed on at the Crooked T, he'd worked as a wrangler. But he'd learned within the year to bust the broncs as well as the men who outweighed him double.

He was tall and wiry with his pa's strength and his ma's nature. The horses knew he could wear them out, but they sensed there was nothing mean in it. He just matched his body to theirs and went along for the ride until their bodies matched his and went where he wanted.

Cole reined the horse down to a walk. Had he tried to do that with Abbie? Tried to match his body to hers and bring her along where he wanted to be? Had he assumed she wanted him because he'd wanted her so long? A cold desperation filled him. *In the world ye shall have tribulation: but be of good cheer, I have overcome the world.*

Brother Lewis had spoken that. And things had gone right in El Paso. But one thing Cole knew. The heart of a woman had nothing to do with the natural law of the world. It was a domain wholly and completely baffling.

He reached the outskirts of the pines that sprang from the snowy ground. He automatically began measuring them in his mind's eye for the purpose he had. He dismounted and marked one with a gouge of his knife, then walked the horse in deeper. He wanted straight trunks of medium girth with minimal knotting.

His boots crunched the crisp snow. He'd marked four trees by the time the others joined him. They looked hangdog enough to kindle his blood. What did they think this was, a picnic? He frowned as Sam dismounted and stepped up beside him.

"Should've let 'em eat," he murmured low.

Cole nodded curtly. Sam was right. But the truth was, if he'd let them set up in the kitchen with Pearl laying out hot cakes and buttered grits and bacon and eggs, he'd have had to sit at the fine, long dining room table with Abbie and the children and choke down the same.

He strode to the wagon and opened the bed, then took out an ax and hefted it. It would do. Heading toward the farthest tree, Cole sank the ax into the wood with a satisfying thud. The others set to work as well, no doubt figuring the sooner they finished, the sooner they'd get some decent grub. He worked up a sweat and more, pushing his muscles until they throbbed.

Eventually he shed his duster and worked in his shirtsleeves, seeing Matt do the same. With the logs piling up, they rested long enough to chug water from the canteen and chew the jerked beef. The men stayed sullen, and Cole suspected he set the mood. He looked up to the tall, straight trees with hardly any branches until their scraggly tops.

Pine was softer wood than some, but it was easy to work with. And for what he had in mind, it would finish off real nice. He picked up a chunk and ran his hand over it, then took out his knife. While the others jawed and rested, he worked the wood, slicing off curls and slivers. The image of a short-legged pony took shape in his hands. He had a promise to keep.

The little pony took on life as he worked. Will stood and went off to the tree he'd started. Matt and Curtis followed suit, then Sam as well. Cole sheathed his knife and pocketed the little horse, then grabbed his ax and joined them.

Five

Abbie left Birdie in Zena's charge. The girl might not be interested in sewing and housekeeping, but she'd learn it anyway. And it would keep her occupied and under Zena's watchful eye while she was gone.

She bundled the children into the buggy and drove toward town as the sun rose pale and dispassionate in the winter sky. The cottonwoods along the frozen stream bed cracked and popped in the cold, and a single magpie took wing beside them. Jenny held her books primly to her chest, her lips tightly sealed.

Abbie guessed she knew what disturbed the child, laying odds ninety to one it concerned Cole. She couldn't bring herself to ask, but she had watched Jenny droop throughout the quiet breakfast they'd had without him. Well, Cole was his own man, and they would have to realize that. If he wanted an early start ... It sounded foolish even to herself, and she dropped the thought.

After leaving Jenny at the schoolhouse, she turned about and headed for Nora's. It seemed strange not to go to the mission where Nora had kept house for Father O'Brien and her younger sister Maggie. Instead, she drove to the new house Davy McConnel had built for them midway between Rocky Bluffs and the Irish homesteads.

How surprised she'd been to learn that Nora had married just days before Brother Lewis joined her and Cole down in El Paso. Abbie shook her head. She and Nora were more like sisters than friends, and after opening up yesterday and telling Nora the facts, Abbie now felt the need to share her fears. She reined in outside the house, set the brake and tethered the horse, then reached for Elliot.

He squirmed out of her gloved hands and jumped down. "I can do it myself, Mama. See?"

She did see, but she could only manage a halfhearted smile. His new independence sent a pang to her heart. What did she expect after being gone these last months? If only need hadn't driven her, she would have never left his side. Then maybe he'd be her baby still.

She watched him scamper up the stairs and hammer the door with his small mittened fist. The door opened, and he looked up directly. "Where are the children?"

Nora raised her brows. "Can it be Elliot accostin' me? You must have rocks in your shoes to be standin' so tall."

Elliot looked down at his small leather boots. "I don't have rocks. It's all me."

"Och. Ye've eaten your taties and good Lucky Star beef, then."

Elliot nodded. "Pa says to finish what's on my plate."

Abbie startled. Elliot must have decided on his own what to call Cole. No doubt Jesus had given the permission he wanted.

Nora glanced up briefly. "Indeed. It's good food makes you grow." She pushed wide the door. "Come in, now, before you catch your death. It's a cold snap sure, and it'll mean snow."

Abbie climbed the three low stairs. "I don't think so. It's a dry cold."

"Aye, maybe. You'd know better."

"Where are the children?" Elliot looked inside the small room behind Nora's skirts.

"If it's Glenna's bairns ye're after, you'll be disappointed. I've nary a one today."

Elliot's face fell, and Abbie felt a twinge of guilt. He wouldn't be looking so glum if Cole had him along. No doubt his eyes would be shining with glee at the wonders Cole performed.

She sighed. "I hope you don't mind our dropping in."

"Mind? It's that glad I am." Nora looked down at Elliot. "Have a look in the chest there. It's the playthings for Glenna's bairns." She slipped her arm through Abbie's. "Will you have a cup with me?"

"Thank you. It was a cold drive." She tried not to think of Cole out at the pinery working hard in the January chill. Such work might be all it took to affect his lungs again. His bout of pnuemonia had taken its toll.

Abbie remembered the sound of his coughing when she and Will and Gray Wolf had rescued Cole from the bounty hunters, more dead than alive. Strange, but she'd hardly known him to have a sick day before that—and he had seemed hale enough since. She mustn't borrow trouble.

She followed Nora into the kitchen. Mariah McConnel, Davy's sister, jumped up beside the stove when they entered. She wrapped herself in her arms and shifted from one foot to the other.

"Hello, Mariah."

Mariah snatched her coat and muffler from the hook. "I have to check the sheep."

Abbie watched her go, saddened. When had Mariah come to fear her? They'd been friends, or at least more than simple acquaintances. But these last years she'd had less and less to do with the McConnels. With Blake's death and the events of her own life, she had neglected Mariah the same as most of the town had.

Nora took the kettle from the stove and poured the tea. "She's a mite queer, ye know."

Abbie took the cup Nora extended. She recalled Monte saying Mariah wasn't right. She hadn't wanted to believe it, tried to think she was just shy, but it was more distinguishable now, more evident with each passing year. Yet Nora had taken her in with her marriage to Davy.

Davy had always been tender to his sister. Mack had been busy and Blake had been too wild. Davy was the one with a soft spot for Mariah. Abbie sipped the warmth of her tea gratefully but felt a pang of remorse at Cole's missing breakfast or even coffee. None of the men had come in for Pearl's cooking. She was certain Cole had rushed them off before she could gainsay him.

"So." Nora sat and wrapped her cup with her hands. "How is your husband?" She smiled.

Abbie was amazed how pretty Nora's smile was. Without it she looked too stern for her blue eyes and red curls. She wished she could tell Nora that Cole was fine, he was wonderful, he was kind and loving and honest and true. But her throat tightened over those sentiments.

Just now he was angry and hurt and justified in both. And Nora had cut to the quick of things.

"He's out at the pinery cutting logs. He's going to build a porch in place of the pillared portico that burned."

Nora tipped her head. "And that's *what* he's doin', but ye haven't said *how*."

Abbie stared into her tea. "Nora, do you ever fear things?"

"What sort of things?"

"Well, something happening to the ones you love?"

"Beyond what's already happened to those I love?" Her voice was low and flat.

Abbie felt tears burning. "Sometimes I think I'm losing my mind. I get so afraid for Elliot . . ." She looked up.

"He's a bonny lad, Abbie, and smart. He has a wit about him of one much older. He's strong and well. And he has a champion now."

"A champion?"

"His da. Or didn't ya hear the pride with which he spoke of your Cole Jasper?"

His da. Abbie's heart stung. She had heard it. Cole seemed a hero in Elliot's eyes, a man strong and wise and capable, who had a way with animals and children that drew them irresistibly.

She was thrilled that Jenny loved him. She should be thrilled for Elliot, too. She wanted him to know and love Cole, but . . . he was Monte's son. She hadn't wanted him to know about Monte, but now—now she desperately wanted him to know.

What if Elliot never knew who his father was? What if Cole adopted him as his own? His name would not even be Farrel. It would be Jasper. Elliot Montgomery Jasper. What if he grew up like Cole?

She was startled by the thought. Cole was exceptional. He had risen over tragedy and betrayal and become a man others looked to, a natural leader, a man of compassion and courage. Anyone would be proud to call him Pa.

But Cole was unlearned in his speech, unread and uneducated except by life. Whereas Elliot had the same eager, questing mind as Monte. He asked more questions than she could answer in a day. Already he was learning his letters and scribing his name.

But it was Cole he looked to now for his example. Cole who would instill in him the character he would take into manhood. Had she made a mistake? Something inside said no. Who had better character than Cole? He recognized his shortcomings. He was not polished or well-bred. But he ran deep.

"It's harder adjustin' than ye thought. Is that it?"

Abbie sighed. "Oh, Nora, how is it for you?"

Nora smiled. "Och, you know Davy. He's impossible now that he's had his way. Not a day passes he doesn't bring me some foolishness, even if it's a wee rhyme he put together in his head. He's a bard, that one, in a warrior's body."

Abbie returned the smile. "He always was the studious McConnel. Mack was bored and Blake plain stubborn. But Blake had a way with nature. Cole's like him there. Do you suppose some men are meant to live wild?"

"Aye. For some it's a wildness inside themselves."

"Jaime?"

"Aye."

"Do you think of him still?"

Nora shrugged. "What are thoughts? This is real." She swept her arm around the room, the house Davy built. "And I'll admit to you, I love Davy. And more: He's right for me. More right maybe than any other."

Abbie closed her eyes. Could she say the same? She hadn't intended to marry Cole, hadn't intended to love again. But she did love him. She couldn't deny that, even to herself. She loved him with an intensity that amazed her. But there were parts of her mind, of her heart that held back. And one dark place of fear that held her captive.

◆◆◆◆◆◆◆

With her fingers gripping the slate, Jenny read in clipped tones the verb tenses she now conjugated and used in sentences. It was nothing difficult, but this morning her thoughts were so scattered, she couldn't recall even the easiest things.

"No." Mr. Ernst rapped the ruler on his desk.

"Has swum," Jenny amended, picturing a giant wave carrying Mr.

Ernst away. "Mr. Ernst has swum away."

A quick burst of laughter circled her, then died in choking gasps. Jenny looked up in time to see the teacher's mouth open and close like a fish. Then his lips settled together in a thin line.

"Since it is your intention to be amusing, Jenny Stevens, you may sit and write ten limericks, and you may continue to write throughout recess."

"Yes, sir." Jenny sat down primly, laid her slate exactly in the middle of her desk, and folded her hands atop. Already her mind spun to the task. *There once was a very bad teacher, with eyes like a reptile creature. He couldn't be nice, because he had lice* . . . She couldn't stop the snicker, and again Mr. Ernst turned his cinnamon-colored eyes on her.

She swallowed hard and tried to look repentant. Mr. Ernst cleared his throat and turned to the towheaded boy on the next bench to her right. "Billy Peel. Conjugate the verb 'to rise.'"

Jenny dropped her gaze to her slate. With a smooth stroke of her cloth, she cleared the gray surface and, licking her chalk, began to write. Writing was really not a punishment. Words came easily, faster than she could catch them with her chalk. *There once was a boy named Billy, who always acted silly* . . .

She discreetly wiped the words off. It wouldn't do to provoke Mr. Ernst further. Thoughts of his temper only made her think of Cole, of Pa. Why had he stomped past as though he hadn't seen her? Why was he angry? And worse—did it mean he would leave again?

But he couldn't leave if he was married to Aunt Abbie, could he? A large hollow grew inside her. She would follow him if he went. She would go with him wherever he wandered. She would not let him out of her sight. He needed her.

There once was a man named Cole, who was a sad and lonely soul . . . She felt her stomach get tight, a hard little knot. Why couldn't Aunt Abbie see? Didn't she know Cole loved her? Pa . . . loved her. It was harder to call him Pa when she thought of him leaving.

Well, she wouldn't think it. No, she wouldn't think it ever again. Her worst thoughts had a way of coming true. Jenny glanced up at Mr. Ernst. He was half-turned from her, listening to Melinda recite. She sighed. Sitting inside with him through recess would ruin whatever chance her day had to improve.

◆◆◆◆◆◆◆

Cole heaved the last log from the wagon bed onto the floor of the lumberyard, his arms stiff with the effort. His back ached. He'd out-worked his men and then some, but the saws were quiet now with the workers gone home and the night heavy with storm. He'd had to get Hank Thorne from his home to open up the mill and let him unload.

Cole wiped his forehead with his sleeve and told Hank how he wanted the wood cut. Hank took down the order and quoted the price. It wasn't exactly usury, so Cole nodded. With careful deliberation, he signed the work order. He could write his name and cipher numbers well enough to get by.

He handed the board back. "You'll deliver 'em Friday?"

Hank nodded. "Looks like you brought some good wood."

"I reckon so." Cole put on his Stetson and shrugged into his duster, then nodded to his men. They stepped out together into the cold night.

They weren't exactly surly anymore, but he'd sure seen them in better spirits. He took out his wallet and handed each man a bill. "Why don't y'all get a meal in town."

Curtis grinned. "Is this out of wages?"

"Bonus. Since you missed breakfast." He glanced at Sam as the men took off with a whoop. "Thanks for your help."

Sam nodded. "Worked it out yet?"

"What?"

"Your temper."

Cole rubbed his chin. Sam would know.

"Come on, I'll buy you a drink."

Cole shook his head. "Thanks, but I've kinda sworn off those places."

Sam hooked his thumbs into his belt. "Since when?"

"Since my activity there almost got me hung."

"Havin' a drink ain't what almost hung you."

Cole nodded slowly. "No. But I cain't rightly justify supportin' that traffic. Not after . . ."

"Auralee?"

Cole winced at the bitterness in his brother's voice. He was going to say after Brother Lewis got hold of him, but he reckoned it had all sort of started with Auralee, the saloon girl Sam had loved. "Sam . . ."

Sam turned his head away.

"I ain't makin' excuses, though I could say you never warned me off. What I did was wrong. I should never have led her on. Maybe if I hadn't . . ." He saw the color leave his brother's face. Cole kicked the dirt. "What I'm askin', you might not want to give. But I'm . . . I'm askin' your pardon."

In all their scraps, Cole had never said those words, never asked to be forgiven. On occasion he'd admitted he was out of line, but he'd never asked Sam to pardon him. Nor had Sam ever begged his that he could recall. He waited in silence.

A thin vapor showed the release of Sam's breath. "I'll consider it, Cole. It just ain't in me yet."

Cole nodded. "I understand." He reached into his pocket. "How are you set for funds?"

"Set enough. Maybe Lady Luck'll smile on me tonight."

"I hope so. I'll see you back at the ranch." He stated it, but meant it as a question.

Sam didn't gainsay him, only turned and strolled toward the town's night life, such as it was. Cole watched him go. Maybe he should have taken the offer of a drink. But he couldn't stomach the thought of laying down good money to prosper the Pablo Montoyas of the world.

Some establishments were different. Some served drinks to men who had nowhere else to go and provided solid camaraderie for the lonely. But just now, Cole couldn't separate them. Not after considering Birdie as a child, not after recalling Auralee's temptations.

The Lord Jesus might have made wine for the wedding and drunk his share with the sinners, but He never wooed the barmaids and broke His brother's heart. No sir, until Cole could see his way clear, he'd avoid those places like the plague.

Cole checked the ropes that tied the spare horses to the wagon, then climbed up. He took the reins and rode out of town without looking back. It was close to half past nine when the ranch came into sight. The clouds hid the stars, but the moonlight glowed behind the veil. The white walls of the house reflected it, and a yellow splash poured out from the lamp in the upstairs window.

So Abbie was still up. He let the spare horses loose to pasture, then parked the wagon and unhitched Hickory and Star. Once he'd seen to their needs, he stepped back into the cold night air. He rubbed his jaw, rough with the day's growth. Lately he'd taken to shaving twice a day, but he didn't feel inclined tonight.

He stood and stared up at the glowing window until he saw a shadow pass before it, and then it went dark. He went inside, hung his coat on the hook in the cloakroom, and made his way up without a lamp. Cole didn't want to rouse the servants or the children, but he slipped into Elliot's room and walked softly to the bed.

The child's cheek was like new milk in the muted moonlight. One hand was cupped under his head, the other lay curled on the pillow. Cole reached into his pocket, took out the little wooden pony, and tucked it into the warm, plump fingers.

He went down the hall to the room he shared with Abbie, hesitated, then went in. He could see her hair spread over the pillow and hear her soft breath. Her eyes were closed, and the lashes made dark shaded moons against her skin. He swallowed over the tightness in his throat and took off his clothes. He washed as quietly as possible, then climbed into bed.

Abbie stirred. "Cole?" Her fingers were warm on his shoulder.

He stiffened and rolled. "I'm tired, Abbie. It's been a long day's work."

❖❖❖❖❖❖❖

Abbie stood at the jagged edge of the cliff, its surface made of glass or black obsidian. She couldn't see the bottom, but she felt the deadly cold that seeped up from the depths. The silence hung heavy like the pause before thunder.

The air was charged with an oppressive primacy of waiting, but not anticipating—rather waiting with dread. She wanted to step away from the edge, but her legs were fixed there. As hard as she tried, she couldn't lift her feet. It was as though they were grafted to the black, glassy surface.

The gray mist that filled the chasm swirled, and her attention was drawn there against her will. Something moved inside the mist. Faces. Faces without features, and hands . . . groping. She tried to step back. Her legs refused. The faces took form. She recognized the boy rustler, the boy she'd killed unknowingly. Fear shot up her spine as he rose from the hole and she looked into his chest.

Then there was Blake beside him. But that was wrong. Blake's chest had not been torn open. Another came near. She tried not to look, but her gaze was fixed. She moaned. *No, Monte, no.*

He took shape beside Blake, coming up as though riding the mist from the hole. Her beloved. His eyes were blank, his chest gaped, and she knew if she touched him he'd be cold. She cried out and staggered. The edge fell away, and she plunged down, screaming, screaming.

"Abbie!"

She clenched something solid, something warm. The terrible cold released its grip. She opened her eyes and buried her face in Cole's neck. He held her tight. Her breath came in shallow gasps, but she didn't cry. She wouldn't cry, though she couldn't stop shaking.

His voice was deep, slow, and soothing. "A'right . . . a'right now. You got the whole house up an' runnin'."

She heard Pearl and Zena open the door and felt like a child.

"Mizz Abbie—Mizz Abbie, you all right?"

"She's a'right, Pearl. Had a scare in her sleep, is all."

Abbie closed her eyes against his chest as the women shut the door behind them.

He rubbed the knotted muscles of her back. "You wanna talk about it?"

She shook her head without lifting it. How could she voice the horror? How could she tell Cole the agony behind the images? How could he understand? If he would just hold her it would pass.

His warmth was real, solid. Her breath eased until Abbie no longer fought for air. He stroked her hair, her neck, then with one arm securely around her, he eased her back into the pillows.

In the glow from the coals in the brazier, she looked at the angles and planes of his face, his shadowed eyes, and whiskered jaw. She saw his concern, his compassion . . . but something was different.

"Please don't be angry, Cole."

He brushed her damp hair from the side of her forehead. "I ain't angry."

She fit so well in the crook of his arm, resting her head on his shoulder. He brushed his rough chin against her forehead. He hadn't shaved, and she knew why. She raised her face, but he didn't kiss her.

"I'll just hold you, Abbie." He settled her head into the crook of his neck. "I'll just hold you."

Long after she went back to sleep, Cole watched the glowing embers. He was bone tired, but sleep wouldn't come. Abbie was warm and soft against him, and he could almost imagine she'd meant it when she raised her face so sweet and willing . . . until he recalled it was Monte's name she'd screamed again and again.

✦✦✦✦✦✦✦✦✦✦✦✦✦

Six

✦✦✦✦✦✦✦✦✦✦✦✦✦

Mama!" Elliot's stage whisper startled Abbie awake, and for the first time she saw Cole's eyes still closed. Poor man, she'd spoiled his sleep. His arm was draped over her and she tried to ease free without . . .

But Cole jumped awake when Elliot pressed a knee into his thigh as he crawled over to her.

"Look!" Elliot held up a carved pony. "Angels came last night."

Abbie looked from the pony to Elliot's shining eyes, to Cole. She recognized his workmanship.

Cole rose up on one elbow. "Angels? What makes you think that?"

"I prayed for animals like Jenny's. And look—it was on my pillow this morning. It's my pony. It's Ralph." He sobered. "You were going to make it. Do you mind if angels brought it instead?"

Cole hooked an arm around Elliot. "I don't mind. Here, let's have a look."

Abbie's heart jumped. Another man would have laughed, would have told Elliot the truth. Another man would have taken credit for his own beautiful efforts.

"I'd say that's a right fair likeness." There was an amused sparkle in Cole's eye.

"I'm going to pray for a rabbit tonight." Elliot's eyes were wide and serious, and Abbie bit her lip at his simple faith.

Cole cleared his throat. "You know, Elliot, I reckon I could make you a rabbit."

"Will you?"

"Yup."

57

"And a coyote and a bear and an elephant—"

"Hold on, now." Cole's smile was gentle. "I got other business, too."

"What business?"

"Ranch business."

"Are you roping?"

Cole shifted on his elbow. "I might some."

"Can I watch?"

"May I," Abbie corrected, but neither of them noticed.

"No, I reckon you'd better stay close to the house. It was smellin' like snow last night, and your mama needs you."

Abbie's breath caught, but he never looked her way.

Cole climbed out of the bed and pulled his pants on. "I'm goin' down to wash. Want a ride?"

Elliot leaped for the strong back, and Cole heaved him up. They walked out of the room without a backward look. Cole had not kissed or even acknowledged her, and she felt a heavy weight settle on her heart.

Cole was silent through breakfast while Elliot prattled on about his pony and the angels. Jenny looked subdued. She eyed the pony, and Abbie prayed she wouldn't recognize it as Cole's work and spill the beans.

Jenny tossed her head. "I'd rather have Pa's animals than any others. I don't think angels carve as well as Pa does. And I have lots of animals."

Elliot put up his chin. "Pa's going to make me some, too."

Jenny turned her eyes on Cole, but he drained his cup and stood, then put on his Stetson and walked out. Abbie guessed this was one of those "grizzly in spring" mornings.

❖❖❖❖❖❖❖

From her vantage in the gazebo outside the breakfast room, Abbie watched Birdie carry the large pail of slop water from her bath out the back door. She could have reached through the slats and touched the girl's hair, but Birdie didn't notice her there. She was too busy mocking Zena's instructions, "Don't dump it near the door or the stoop will freeze."

Setting her jaw, Birdie stalked two steps from the house and raised it to pour. A sound to her right made her jump, and Will rounded the corner. Abbie knew she should make her presence known, but she trusted Birdie so little and worried about Will. If he saw her, she would wave, even speak. But he didn't. His eyes were for Birdie alone.

"Let me help you with that, Birdie." The look on his face was so obviously besotted, Abbie cringed.

But Birdie ignored him and stepped onto the stone border beside the walk.

He stumbled after. "It's slick and . . . too cold without your coat."

Oh, Will, don't abase yourself for her. You're too upstanding, Abbie silently urged.

Birdie stopped, and Abbie clearly read her expression before she turned toward Will. "I have to carry it to the stream."

"All the way to the stream?" His brow puckered.

"*Sí.* And fill it again with ice."

He straightened. "Well, you can't do that with your little hands. Wait here, and I'll get it. All the way full?"

She nodded.

"I won't be two shakes." He hoisted the bucket from her hands and started for the stream bed.

Birdie watched him go, then turned a malicious smile directly to Abbie. She'd been aware of her presence through it all. She then made a sound in her throat that might have been laughter and went inside.

Irked, Abbie almost called to Will to point out Birdie's cruel ploy, but then perhaps it was best to let him see for himself.

It was natural he should feel protective after saving Birdie from Pablo. And, she supposed, it was inevitable that he would notice and respond to Birdie's beauty. But, God willing, he'd see the blackness of her soul before it was too late.

What was she to do with the girl? The sooner they found a place for her, the better. But where? Abbie shook her head. That worry only added to her Jonah day. First Cole, now Birdie . . . She sighed. Could life never be easy?

✦✦✦✦✦✦✦

Cole crouched next to the steer thrashing weakly on the frozen ground. He worked his gloves through its hair and inspected the hide.

The ulcerated lesion confirmed his suspicion, and he noted the number of wounds, eyeing an especially bad patch just above the open star brand.

He'd changed the brand from Mr. Farrel's original, which had been a closed star. A closed circle of any sort on a brand caused the hide to fester and die away inside it. Opening the star had prevented that. But the brand had nothing to do with this animal's problems. It was disease, plain and simple. And the steer's infection was too advanced to treat.

He looked up at the approaching horse and rider. Abbie. Her hair was scarcely contained by her hat, and her breath and Zephyr's hung in the air. She reined in and slid down from the saddle. "What is it, Cole?"

"Keep back."

"It's contagious?"

"Anthrax. And yeah, it's contagious. But only by contact, so keep back." He stood.

She had already looked pale and tired, but now she showed fresh concern. "Is there a treatment?"

"There's a vaccine, but it's too late for this one."

"Are you putting him down?"

"Got to."

"Then go ahead. I've seen it before."

Cole eyed her, then took out his revolver and shot the steer in the head.

Abbie jumped from the report, but didn't flinch when the blood ran from the hole. "Now what?"

"Now we'll burn it so it don't spread. Then I've got to check the others. We'll likely need the vaccine anyhow. If one picked it up, others prob'ly got it. How long's it been since someone inspected the herd?"

"I don't know. With losing the men to the typhoid, and then driving the beef herd to Kansas, and then El Paso . . ."

He frowned. "Well, we'll need to round 'em up."

She took a step toward him. "I brought you lunch. The men came in, but you didn't, so . . ."

"I got work to do." He turned away from the appeal in her eyes. Didn't she know he was giving her what she wanted?

"But you have to eat."

He turned. "Abbie, I'm thirty-six years old. I don't need a ma." He saw the hurt in her face. He hadn't meant to say it so gruffly, but it was easier to do things as they had before. "I'll eat when I need to. Don't expect me at the table."

She stood a long moment, then dropped her gaze and turned away. She swung easily into the saddle and kicked in her heels. The mare had the same speed as Sirocco. Had she noticed he rode Mr. Farrel's stallion? Cole turned to the horse. It was a fine animal. Mr. Farrel had intended to breed him with Zephyr once the mare matured and tamed down.

He reckoned now was as good a time as any. Abbie could ride Lady Belle while Zephyr foaled. But his first order of business was to deal with the cattle disease. If he was going to build the herd back to what it should be, he'd need to take things in hand right now.

He'd already used a chunk of change to pay off Abbie's debts and take back the Lucky Star deed. He hadn't ever really anticipated owning the Lucky Star, but now that he did, he meant to make it work. And he'd do it with his own hands and sweat just as he had when the place belonged to Montgomery Farrel.

The cold wind bit her face as Abbie rode, urging Zephyr to more speed. Cole hadn't used that tone with her in a long while, but it irked her as much as ever. A ma, indeed. She looked at the sack holding his lunch that hung over the saddle. Well, let him starve.

He'd said he wasn't angry, but he was. So let him be. If he couldn't accept her apology—well—she hadn't actually said she was sorry, hadn't asked his forgiveness. But he must have seen, understood . . . Fire rose to her cheeks.

How much clearer could she be than what she'd offered in the night? And he'd refused her. Well, she wouldn't make that mistake again. Cole might be her husband, but she'd have some say in things. She slid from the horse's back and ran. The ground was unyielding beneath her feet, hard and crisp and brown.

She was tired of the brown, tired of the cold. And there would be months of it yet. It wasn't so bad when it snowed. Then the land had a fairy-tale beauty. But now it was just brown and hard and dry. Exactly as Monte had claimed. He was right. The land that stretched around her was ugly.

Abbie kicked the frozen turf of the Lucky Star ranch. It was Cole Jasper's ranch now. She'd given it away. "Well, you can have it, Cole Jasper!" she yelled into the wind, then dropped her face to her hands. He was the most exasperating man.

She stalked back to the mare and rode home. Inside, Zena was polishing the silver, Pearl oiling the wood, James scraping the ashes from the braziers, and even Birdie was wielding the feather duster, however haphazardly. What was there left to do? Abbie had taken Jenny to school in the morning, but Grant had offered to bring her home with something he had for Cole.

Elliot. Where was Elliot? She swept past Pearl in the hall and entered the library. He was there, sprawled on the floor with the picture book his great-grandpa Martin had sent the year before he died. Abbie dropped to the floor beside him, heedless of her dress.

"Mama, see this elephant. Do you think Pa can make me one like this?"

Grudgingly, Abbie nodded. "Cole can make anything." It was true. Cole had an artist's eye and a steady hand. The carving that he'd made of Sirocco for her to give Monte still stood on the desk in the study. It was a magnificent piece of work for hands so rough . . . and so tender.

Abbie felt a pang. Hadn't he the right to be angry? She had insulted and hurt him. She'd shown her distrust, her doubt. He'd seen the blame that was still lodged in her heart, even though her mind knew better. Yet he had held her through the fear in the night. He'd been there, strong and sure, asking nothing in return.

"What's the matter, Mama?"

Abbie looked into Elliot's troubled face, then scooped him into her arms. "Nothing's the matter, Elliot. Nothing I can't figure out." He curled his head over her shoulder and wrapped his arms around her neck, then scrambled loose and went back to his book.

Abbie wandered out. She trudged to the kitchen and leaned her hip on the board. Pie. She'd bake him a pie. It always cheered Pa when Mama made him apple pie. Abbie marched to the pantry and dug out two handfuls of dried apples. These she set to boil with water and sugar and cinnamon.

Then she measured flour and salt into a bowl and cut in the lard.

She spooned in enough water to make the dough follow the fork, then turned it onto the floured board and formed two balls of pastry. She rolled the two balls into thin circles and lined the pan with one. She'd forgotten how much she liked to cook, forgotten how well she cooked.

It was Pearl's kitchen. She had given up that fight, but today ... this effort was her own, to show Cole she cared. Abbie thought of him taking that first bite, the look of pure appreciation he'd wear. She brushed a strand of hair back and felt the flour on her forehead. She smiled. Mama always sported flour when she baked.

Abbie spooned the filling into the bottom crust, then cut butter over it and laid the other pastry circle on top. She folded and pinched the edge all around, then pierced the center with marks in the shape of a heart. Her heart given to Cole. She did love him. Things just got too complicated.

She had just put the pie in to bake when Pearl descended. "Whatchu doin', Mizz Abbie?"

She knew well enough to use Pearl's fondness for Cole in her defense. "Making a pie for Cole. It's a peace offering for waking him up last night and spoiling his sleep."

Pearl's annoyance left. "I'll watch it now. You go on."

But Abbie saw she approved. Pearl understood the power of food over a man's heart.

Abbie took a long, drowsy bath and scented her hair with honey-suckle, then donned the blue dress that Cole had said turned her eyes to mountain lakes. Then she brushed her hair until the curls danced like skeins of silken thread on her shoulders.

As she went downstairs, she heard James at the door and Grant. She hurried to greet her brother, smiling already. She hadn't seen him since she'd gone off with Will and Gray Wolf to rescue Cole, and that had been a hasty and disappointing meeting. She swept into the entry.

Grant stood in the doorway with Jenny beside him. His handsome smile was Pa's, but his coloring was their mama's all over, warm brown eyes and hair. Jenny looked piqued, and when Grant stepped in, Abbie saw why. Her own smile faded when it landed on Grant's wife, Marcy, great with child and holding five-year-old Emily Elizabeth by the hand.

Though she hadn't expected him to bring the whole family, Abbie bolstered herself. "Come in." She extended both hands to Grant, and he squeezed them, then she reached a hand to his wife, making her best effort. "Marcy, you're positively glowing. Hello, Emily." She stooped to hug her niece.

"It's Emily Elizabeth, Aunt Abbie." When she said it, the child looked exactly like Abbie's memories of Marcy as a child, right down to the angle of her nose.

"Of course it is. I'm sorry, Emily Elizabeth." She could not see why Marcy insisted on such a mouthful for the little blond waif. She returned her attention to Grant. "I'm so happy you've come. Will you stay for supper?" The need for hospitality was ingrained in her, though she might have wished otherwise tonight.

"Twist my arm." Grant grinned.

James took their coats and went off to the cloakroom. Abbie showed them into the drawing room, as the parlor was decimated by the fire. She could see Marcy's annoyance and knew she was comparing her home to this extravagantly beautiful room. Abbie tried not to gloat.

The status and elegance of her home didn't matter to her nearly as much as to Marcy. She'd have been happy living in a small, comfortable farmhouse like Mama and Pa's, but Monte had already built this beautiful house before they met. Still, the wicked side of her enjoyed Marcy's irritation. Pearl brought a tray with steaming cups of chocolate—a rare delight for them these days—but Marcy acted as though it was only her due.

Grant leaned on the mantel. "Where's Cole?"

"Working. The cattle have an illness. He's inspecting the herd." Or so she assumed.

"Nothing bad, I hope."

"Bad enough. Anthrax. But he says it's treatable."

"Cole would know. Sometimes I think he has more stored in his head than I do for all my Harvard education."

Abbie didn't miss Marcy's huff and the roll of her eyes as she fanned herself, though the room was hardly stuffy, except maybe the air just around where she sat. Abbie bristled. She knew exactly what Marcy thought of Cole Jasper. She made no secret of it, which was one reason Jenny could not tolerate her. Cole didn't deserve the disdain of a featherbrain like Marcy.

"And by the way, congratulations." Grant's eyes were shining mischievously. "If I'd known you meant to marry the man, I'd have advised you differently when you came seeking my opinion."

Abbie sent him a careless smile. "Well, I ignored you anyway."

Grant threw back his head and laughed. "So you did. You should hear the tales going around about your hijinks."

"Hijinks? Hardly. That was serious business taking on those bounty hunters."

Grant sobered. "I know that too well. I think Pa aged ten years when he heard."

"He's already scolded me, so you needn't bother. I'm hardly a child. Besides, I didn't mean for any of you to hear until we were back."

"Well, with the fire and all—any word on that pair?"

Abbie shuddered, picturing Crete Marlowe and Jackson Finn as she'd left them: without their boots or weapons or horses and fit to be tied. "No. I only hope they're long gone from Colorado. Though I don't expect they'll be heading back to Texas."

"Not likely, with warrants out for them dead or alive."

"I'm just glad we got Cole away in time." She remembered him weak, beaten, coughing, and gunshot. One thing was certain. Crete Marlowe hadn't an ounce of compassion, at least where Cole was concerned.

Abbie felt the fight rise up within her. What an enigma she was, one moment blaming and doubting Cole, the next ready to scratch out eyes to defend him. If only he'd come in so she could repent properly.

Seven

Abbie heard the commotion of the men entering the kitchen. Her heart jumped. Now was her chance to make up to Cole with the flaky, golden pie. "Will you excuse me?" She stood up and set her cup on the table. She'd also better warn him of Marcy's presence. Those two came together like flint and steel.

Matt, Will, Curtis, and Sam were all seated, having washed in the yard, and Pearl was setting bowls of good hearty pot roast before them. Will tucked his napkin into his shirt and looked as though he'd eat the whole pot.

Abbie glanced around the room and through the door to the washroom. "Where's Cole?"

Matt took up his fork. "Workin', ma'am."

"In the dark?"

"Yes, ma'am. He's totin' a lantern and goin' over the cattle one by one."

"Isn't he coming in for supper?"

"I don't know. He's kinda grumpy if you ask questions."

Her heart sank. Cole was still angry. She'd never known him to carry a grudge this far. She sighed, eyeing the pie on the board, then turned to Pearl. "When the men are through, serve Birdie and the children here also. My guests and I will wait, but if Cole's not in when the children are through, we'll go ahead without him."

She returned to Grant and Marcy, putting on a cheerful face over her disappointment. If Grant had come alone, she might have asked him for advice, though Grant and Cole were as different as men came. Still, they were both men, which gave Grant an edge over her. How could she mend a fence when Cole wouldn't allow her on the property?

In the drawing room, Elliot was showing off his wooden pony, and for once Jenny didn't bring up her animals. Abbie guessed she didn't find Emily Elizabeth worthy of seeing them.

"I don't believe angels brought it." Emily shoved the pony back at Elliot.

"It was angels."

"Was not."

From her perch in the wing chair, Jenny raised her chin. "It most certainly was angels. I saw them. Or rather, I saw one." Abbie raised her brows in surprise, not that Jenny would come to Elliot's defense—she already knew of their devotion when pitted against Emily—but that Jenny would fabricate a tale, no matter how well meaning.

Emily had her eyes glued to Jenny, and Jenny matter-of-factly smoothed her skirt over her knees. "He was tall with great big wings that brushed all the way to the floor. And he walked without any sound at all but a kind of rushing—like wind in his feathers. He glowed like the moon on a cloudy night, all white and golden, and when he passed my room he smiled. Then he took the pony to Elliot." She folded her hands and pertly closed her mouth.

Elliot stood with eyes like hen's eggs, and Abbie saw his little fingers close around the pony with near reverence. How could she scold Jenny for fibbing when she'd done it so wonderfully?

Zena came in and bustled the children off to eat. Marcy prattled on about Emily Elizabeth, but Abbie scarcely listened, constantly watching the door for Cole. Surely he must be hungry. He hadn't taken the lunch she'd brought, but he was stubborn enough to live on jerky rather than give in. A short time later James entered, walking with dignity, though his rheumatism bent his back now more noticeably. "Mizz Abbie, dinner is served."

"Thank you, James."

"No Cole?" Grant dropped his elbow from the mantel.

"He's still with the herd. We'll start without him. I'm sure he'll come when he can." She saw Marcy's smug look. No doubt Grant would never dare be late for supper, even if she scarcely put herself out to feed him anything decent.

Abbie walked stiffly to the dining room and took her place after her guests. All the rules of etiquette Monte's sister, Frances, had drummed into her head were still there, known but not adhered to completely. She did her best, for the children's sake, breaking only the rule that said little ones must be silent if allowed to be present at all.

She liked them to talk, as long as they didn't interrupt or quarrel. All the same, she felt better eating separately tonight. The children were prone to bring up things she didn't want discussed. And Abbie was not about to give Marcy a single look at Birdie. The less anyone knew about that one the better.

James ladled out cold creamy potato soup, then cleared those bowls and served steamed greens and chives with crusty bread on the side. He had just spooned hearty helpings of pot roast when Abbie saw Cole in the doorway. He looked tired and raw from the cold.

He removed his hat and nodded to their guests, but he didn't join them. "Abbie, I ain't dressed for company. I'll wash and eat in the kitchen." He turned and went out.

Abbie sat a moment, fighting surprise and dismay, then turned to Grant and Marcy. "Will you excuse me, please?"

The kitchen was empty except for Pearl. Zena must have taken the children to the nursery. She passed through to the washroom and found Cole. He had his back to her as he hung his hat on the hook, then pulled off his shirt and long johns to the waist. She watched the lean muscles of his back ripple as he plunged his arms into the tub and reached for the soap. He lathered not only his arms, but his chest and neck, as well.

"Cole."

He spun. "Doggone it, Abbie. Don't sneak up on me."

"I didn't sneak." She looked at the hair of his chest, sudsy and dripping, the bullet wound puckering his shoulder, his hard, lean torso. She could sense his animosity like a wolf's ferocity and felt small and tentative. "I'm sorry we started without you. I didn't know when you'd be in and . . . I didn't want our guests to wait."

He splashed his arms into the tub and rinsed his chest and neck, then rubbed his face and reached for the towel. "I told you not to expect me."

"Will you come now?"

"I ain't in the mood to dine with your sister-in-law."

Neither was she, but she had to face her anyway. For a moment she wished she could hide in the kitchen with Cole, but the look on his face was as formidable as anything Marcy could dish out. She took a step toward him. "Grant brought something for you."

"A'right. I'll see him after."

"Cole . . ."

He fixed her with a scowl that made her mute. Tears stung behind her eyes and her throat felt full of alum. Couldn't he see she was trying?

"I baked you a pie," she blurted.

His expression softened as he gave his chest one last rub. "Thank you, Abbie. That's real nice."

"Don't you want to know what kind?" She wanted to reach for him, wanted him to reach for her.

He hung the towel. "I'm sure whatever kind it is, it's fine."

She bit back her frustration. She would not beg. She would go back and face Marcy and Grant alone and endure Marcy's gloat and Grant's concern. She would make excuses for Cole that sounded weak even to her, but it was the best she could do. She turned.

"Abbie."

She glanced back over her shoulder.

"I reckon I can join you."

It felt as though he'd given her the sunrise. And it must have shown because he took her arms and pulled her close in a brief embrace. "I'm sorry."

She looked up to argue, but he released her and directed her into the kitchen. Pearl was at the stove.

Cole nodded. "Just pot roast, Pearl."

"Yessuh." From the look on Pearl's round face, she'd heard enough to believe things were on the mend. Abbie wished she felt as confident.

Grant stood when they entered and shook Cole's hand. "Evening, Cole. I brought the papers for you to sign."

Papers? Abbie looked from one man to the other as Cole seated her.

"All right." He took his chair at the head of the table, barely acknowledging Marcy with a nod and a curt, "Ma'am."

Marcy sent him a sugar-coated smile. Abbie felt Cole's defiance. It was just under the surface, but she saw the danger signs. Marcy had better button her lip, though she knew from experience that was hardly likely.

Grant refolded his napkin in his lap. "You took care of the other business?"

"That's right."

"Grant." Marcy pouted.

"Pardon me, dear." Grant patted her hand. "You're right. No business at the table."

Marcy had a point. It was inconsiderate to discuss something that excluded the rest of them, but Abbie suspected Marcy only said it because she couldn't bear not knowing what business Grant could possibly have with a trail boss like Cole Jasper.

For that matter, what was their business? Grant had brought a folder and set it on the mantel, but he hadn't told her a thing about it. A thought crept into her mind. Adoption papers? Had Cole gone ahead without her agreement? Could he?

Cole applied himself to his meal with dogged determination. As the rest of them were nearly finished, Grant spoke about town matters that involved him as a new member of the town council. Marcy had plenty to say on each topic, and relayed it as though she were the one sitting on the council.

Abbie scarcely noticed. Her mind was on the folder in the drawing room. What did it hold? Change, betrayal … She glanced at Cole. What had he set in motion beyond joining her ownership of the ranch? That much was his due, she acknowledged. But he was demonstrating an adept working knowledge of things she would not have suspected.

Had Grant advised him? Had they gone behind her back to give Cole legal charge of things, including the children? What was she thinking? Cole was her husband. He had a right to everything, didn't he? For better or worse, till death do them part.

Pearl brought the pie and served it without a word as to its maker.

But Cole caught her eye and sent his approval. Abbie wished it mattered now as much as it had when she made it. Her stomach was twisting with worry, and she could scarcely get it down.

Marcy ate with greater gusto than she might had she known Abbie baked it. No doubt she would have picked at it as though it were contaminated. Even with all the years they'd been sisters-in-law, even though she and Grant were Elliot's godparents, even though Abbie had seen her through Emily's traumatic birth, Marcy could not let go of the rivalry.

In all fairness, Abbie's own efforts were less than wholehearted. She was impatient with Marcy's whining, intolerant of her badgering Grant, and infuriated by her cutting remarks regarding Cole and her children. Right now, she just wished they would leave.

As though reading her thoughts, Cole and Grant excused themselves, stood, and went to the drawing room. Marcy fixed her with a stare. "What's their business, do you suppose?"

"I'm sure they'd say if we needed to know." Abbie was amazed by the detached tone she managed, though her heart was racing. She wanted to jump up from her chair and run after them, stomp her foot, and demand answers.

"Since we're alone, I must say I was stunned to learn you'd married Cole Jasper."

Abbie stared. That was bold even for Marcy.

"He's certainly no Montgomery Farrel. How you could even consider—but then, you must have been desperate with the ranch going down and—"

"I was not desperate." Abbie felt the hairs rise at the back of her neck. "Cole is a fine man and a good husband."

"But, Abbie, he was wanted for the murder of a . . . a woman of ill repute." Marcy said it as though the very taste of the words repelled her.

"He was falsely accused and cleared of that."

"Nevertheless . . ."

"I'll not have you speak ill of my husband, Marcy."

Marcy shrugged. "You needn't be so touchy. I'm only warning you what everyone is saying."

"Everyone?"

"The ladies in town, Abbie. You've damaged your reputation immeasurably—not that it could stand much damaging. At least as Monte's wife—"

"That's enough, Marcy." Just hearing his name on Marcy's lips sent fire through Abbie's veins.

"As your sister-in-law, I walk a fine line. For Grant's sake, I can't afford to let your indiscretions affect our standing. Though, of course, I defend you when I can."

"I just bet you do."

Marcy looked grieved. "Abbie, we are sisters, no matter how ruefully. It's my duty—"

"Oh, please. In what way has my marriage to Cole compromised anything?"

Marcy's eyes gleamed, and Abbie knew she'd been caught exactly where Marcy wanted her. "Well, there is speculation, you know."

Abbie's throat constricted. She ought to drop it right now, ought to tell Marcy to keep the gossip to herself, but she couldn't. "Speculation?"

Marcy tried to look dismayed. "Of course it's a dreadful lie, and I've done all I could to dispel it, but ... your own actions and Cole's ..."

"What on earth are you talking about?"

Marcy raised an eyebrow with diabolical glee, though her mouth maintained its pained line. "There's talk that you and Cole were close even before Monte's death. That he might have ... welcomed the 'accident.'"

Abbie felt such a rush of horror she thought she might faint, something she'd done only once in her entire life. But her head cleared suddenly and pounded with fury. Her voice was deadly calm. "How dare you."

That was clearly not the reaction Marcy hoped for. She paled and sank into her seat. Her hand fluttered to her throat. "I never said it, of course."

Abbie had a keen sense that she was lying. How could she? Even with all their differences, how could Marcy voice something so horrid?

Abbie's skin burned with a flush that had nothing to do with chagrin. She could no more stop her words than a rushing train. "I've never expected kindness from you. But I did believe you had some decency, even though your jealousy rarely allowed it to show."

Marcy flushed crimson. "Jealousy?"

"Oh yes, Marcy. Jealousy that Monte chose me, though you threw yourself at his feet, jealousy that I have a grander home, jealousy that another man would want me enough to wait years for my love, though Lord only knows if Grant hadn't pitied you, you'd be a bitter spinster yet."

Marcy went completely white. Abbie hadn't meant to stoop so low, but it felt desperately good. She was in the grip of wickedness and didn't care.

A choking sound came from Marcy's throat, and she suddenly heaved herself up and snatched Abbie's dress by the collar. "You vile little witch!" She shook her.

Though easily the stronger of the two, Abbie fought back only with words. "Sometimes the truth hurts, doesn't it, Marcy? But you wouldn't know that, since you specialize in lies. Well, go ahead and tell your lies if it makes you feel important. No one would notice you otherwise."

Even as she said it, Abbie saw her words sink deeply into Marcy's spirit. With a deep, growling rage, Marcy grasped for Abbie's neck and squeezed. Abbie clamped Marcy's wrists and wrenched them free. She could feel the animosity coursing through Marcy's nerves and was suddenly afraid for her in her stage of pregnancy. What if . . .

But no, she must calm her, is all. Abbie had no desire to force another of Marcy's children into the world. Her own fury dried like sweat on her skin, sticky and uncomfortable, but no longer virulent. She kept her grip on Marcy's wrists. "Stop it, Marcy."

But Marcy lunged again, then froze. With a gasp, Marcy doubled, and Abbie's fears were realized. *Not again, dear Lord. Oh, not again.* Marcy's knuckles whitened as she gripped the back of the chair.

Abbie held her shoulders. "Try to sit, Marcy. Breathe slowly." But she saw the fluid running across the floor from under Marcy's skirts. She tried not to panic as she saw it go red. *Please, God, please.*

Eight

Abbie eased Marcy into the chair. "I'll get Grant." She rushed for the drawing room and found him already heading for the door. Had he heard them, or had they merely concluded their business?

"Grant, it's Marcy. The baby's coming."

His brow lowered. "Good heavens. She has three weeks yet. Will she make it home?"

Abbie tried not to show her panic. "I think we'd better get Doctor Barrow."

"I'll go." Cole headed for the door.

Abbie followed him. "Go quickly, Cole. If it's like last time..."

He nodded.

Abbie rushed for the kitchen. "Heat water, Pearl, and make up a bed for Marcy. She's birthing."

"Lawd save us."

"Have Zena put the children down. Emily can sleep with Jenny. And keep Birdie occupied." Abbie gripped her hands together. "Cole's gone for the doctor." There was nothing to do now but to go back to Marcy.

Marcy was hysterical, crying on Grant's sleeve. For once Abbie couldn't blame her. Why, oh, why had she said those terrible things? Between them, she and Grant got Marcy to the bed. Abbie helped her into a gown and swabbed the blood from the floor.

She had prayed Marcy would have a safe, gentle delivery this time, but then she had provoked this terror. What was wrong with her? Shame weighed like lead on her heart, matched only by her fear. She

74

glanced at Grant's strained face. *Please, God. Please protect Grant's child and his wife.*

Pearl brought a basin of water and cloths, and Abbie mopped Marcy's head.

"Leave me alone," Marcy shrieked. "I can't stand the sight of you. Go away."

Grant shook his head, desperate for her to stay.

Abbie smoothed the cloth over Marcy's forehead. "Be calm, Marcy. Everything's going to be all right. You'll see. Lie still now."

Marcy slapped at her hand. "Don't touch me. I hate you. I've always hated you."

"There now." Abbie stroked her fingers through Marcy's damp hair. She broke a sweat of her own as Marcy's pains came and went and she continued to rave. The room seemed alternately hot and cold. Grant paced.

Marcy tossed her head from side to side. She glared at Abbie. "You did this! You—" She shrieked with pain and thrashed.

"Don't fight it." Abbie looked with horror at the blood seeping into the sheets. It was too much. How long had it been? Why wasn't Cole back? Grant looked as though he'd pass out himself. She ordered Pearl to bring him coffee.

Cole, where are you? As though in answer to her thoughts, he filled the doorway. Relief washed over Abbie until she realized he stood alone. She met his eyes with stark terror, then stood and went swiftly to his side.

He drew her out of the room. "He's deliverin' the Epperson twins. It'll be a long spell there. But he'll come when he can."

"But Cole, if this baby's breech like the last one . . ."

"How close is she?"

"I don't know."

"What does Pearl know?"

"I'll fetch her." Abbie felt woefully ignorant. She'd been delirious with grief and then laudanum with her own delivery and had only vague, distorted memories. She found Pearl at the stove and pressed her for answers.

Pearl's old face contorted with alarm and distress. "No'm. Old Esther, she midwifed the births. I never gave birth, nor attended one till yours. And Doctor Barrow and yo' mama saw to you 'cept what I'm doin' now."

Mama. Abbie accosted James. "Fetch Mrs. Martin as fast as you can. Tell her Marcy's having her baby."

"Yezzum." He shuffled off.

"And hurry, James, hurry."

He pressed his hat on his head and went. Abbie composed herself and headed back to the room. Cole stood in the hall, thumbs hooked in his belt, hip against the wall.

He straightened. "Well?"

Abbie shook her head. "Pearl knows as little as I do, but Mama's coming. I sent James for her."

Cole brushed her arm with his hand. "You all right?"

The tenderness in his voice almost undid her. No, she wasn't all right. She'd caused all this just as she had the last time. She'd lost her temper and said things she should never have said. Though Marcy had provoked her, she should have held her tongue. But she nodded gamely.

"You'd better get on in there. Grant ain't lookin' too good."

Abbie hesitated. She suddenly longed to stay close to Cole. He was so calm and level-headed. But she could hear Marcy screaming through the door. She drew a long breath and reached for the knob.

He touched her hand. "I'll be out here if you need me."

His words bolstered her, and she went in. She could tell with one look that things were bad. Grant crouched beside the bed, looking harried, but it was Marcy she fixed her gaze upon. She was so pale her lips looked gray. Her eyes were wide and unfocused and she writhed, drawing her knees up in agony.

Abbie rushed to the bedside and felt beneath the sheets. The hard knob at the top of Marcy's belly had to be the baby's head. It was completely breech, as Emily had been. She tried to recall what Doctor Barrow had done, but her focus had been on holding Marcy still while he turned the baby. She did recall his arm bloody to the elbow.

She could try, but what if she made it worse? What if one of them died at her hand? She met Grant's agonized eyes.

His voice was hoarse. "The doctor?"

"Not yet. Mama's coming."

Marcy screamed and clung to Grant's hand. "Take it out! Take it out of me!"

Abbie's throat constricted as the fresh blood gushed. She rushed out and gripped Cole's arms. "The baby's breech, Cole, and Marcy's bleeding terribly. Can't you make the doctor come?"

"He's over his head with the others. They're tangled or some such. He nearly threw me out."

"But she'll die. I know it. She can't hang on much longer."

He frowned at the door, then released a slow breath. "Let me look." He went into the room.

If Marcy was aware of him, she made no sign. With her last scream she had crumpled and lay panting and delirious, scarcely cognizant and beyond caring.

With both hands on the sheets Cole felt her abdomen, then checked the pulse in her neck. "I'll need to wash."

Abbie stared, incredulous.

"She's near the end. We cain't wait for the doc or your ma." He strode out and returned with his sleeves rolled and his arms red from scrubbing. "Grant, you keep her still, and I mean still. Abbie, hold her leg like so."

Abbie obeyed and watched with mingled horror and amazement as Cole reached in and turned the baby in Marcy's womb. Blood gushed. Marcy's screams were shrill, but before she knew it Cole had the baby's head between his hands. He eased the tiny shoulders free and took Grant's son into his strong, bloody arms.

With shaky fingers Abbie tied off and cut the cord. She handed the mewling baby to Pearl and stayed beside Cole, who kept hold of the cord and waited for the rest to pass. When it did, he checked the mass over and nodded. "Now rub her belly—hard. Keep rubbin' even if she hollers."

Abbie obeyed, but Marcy was beyond hollering. Her breathing was shallow and she'd lost consciousness. Tears streaked Grant's cheeks as he pressed his face to Marcy's head, and Abbie rubbed, feeling the muscles contract as she forced them. The bleeding slowed and Abbie's chest heaved. "Will she be all right, Cole?"

"I don't know. This part's up to God."

Abbie dropped to her knees beside the bed and closed her eyes. She folded her trembling hands and felt Cole's palm rest atop her head, despite his bloody fingers. Her voice came out in a hoarse whisper. "Dear Lord, Marcy's life is in your hands. Spare her, we pray. Give her strength, help her fight, help her . . ." The tears rushed upon her. "Oh God, forgive me for provoking her."

Cole's hand slid to the back of her neck, and its warmth comforted her. But she didn't deserve it. How would she live with herself if Marcy died? She clutched her sister-in-law's limp, cold hand in her own. *Please live, Marcy. Please live.*

Cole stepped aside as Selena Martin pressed in. He saw the relief on Abbie's tear-streaked face. He'd done all he could. The women would take it from there. He went to the washroom and stripped off his bloody clothes, then bathed in the predawn light.

His heart settled back into a standard rhythm, but he couldn't get over the feel of that tiny body in his hands. Marcy's agony was horrific enough, but that little babe all twisted up and turned backwards . . . He shook his head.

No one ought to enter the world so limp and troubled. He'd seen bum calves stronger than that, and they'd died in the night. That little one's fight was just beginning. He was lucky to be alive with the afterbirth partly blocking his exit as it had been. For that matter, so was Marcy.

He rubbed the weariness from his eyes, dried himself, and dressed in a clean pair of pants and a shirt from the mending shelf. As he neared the hall, he heard the banging on the door. James admitted the doctor, and Cole showed him to the room.

Cole listened while Abbie described the ordeal with a good deal more emphasis on his own efforts than need be, then Doctor Barrow shooed them all out to the hall. Grant stood with his head leaned back to the molding, eyes to the ceiling. Cole watched the sweat trickle from his neck to his stiff collar.

Usually he would have ordered a shot of whiskey to bolster the man. But Crete Marlowe had cleaned out Mr. Farrel's stock and he hadn't replenished it, so he just waited in silence like the rest of them. When the door opened, he turned.

The doctor emerged. He shook his head. "I won't say she's in the clear, but she's holding on. Barring complications and fever, I believe she'll make it."

Abbie quivered visibly. "And the baby?"

Cole wondered what she thought herself guilty of. Whatever it was hadn't kept her from a cool head and more compassion than he'd imagined she had for her sister-in-law.

"The baby's small and immature. It's too early to say, but just now he's holding his own." The doctor looked pointedly at Grant. "Young man, you have a daughter and a son. I wouldn't press your luck." He turned. "Cole, fine work."

Cole nodded. It wasn't something he'd want to repeat, but the feel of that baby's head in his hands had been some kind of powerful. He saw Abbie's eyes shining with pride through her weariness.

He reached for her hand, and she came to him. His heart swelled. The others could manage now. Abbie's ma was already taking charge, and Pearl would see them all bedded down for what little was left of the night. He led Abbie up the stairs to their room and took her in his arms. She pressed into his chest, and he held her, smelling the sweet scent of her hair even though the back was clotted with blood from the hand he'd rested there.

"Here." He leaned her back, rinsed her hair clean with the pitcher and toweled it dry. Then he dipped a cloth and gently rubbed it over her face, wiping away the sweat and tears. She stretched her arms up over his neck, and he met her kiss with his own. It was sweet and searching, and he realized she was crying again. He closed her in his arms.

She drew a shaky breath. "Are you still angry?"

"No."

She pulled back to search his face. "But you were."

"I reckon so."

"I'm sorry. I should have let you take Elliot. I should have realized . . ."

"What?"

"That he'd be safe with you."

It seemed petty, now, that he'd taken offense at her doubts. Life was derned fragile and nothing was certain. How would it be to bring Abbie's son to her as he'd brought her first husband? How would it be to see again the agony in her eyes and know he'd caused it?

"It's all right."

Her lips trembled. "Cole, I'll sign the papers downstairs."

He set her back. "What papers?"

"The adoption papers."

His eyes went over her features trying to figure what she meant. "You got them?"

"No, I thought that's what Grant brought to you tonight. I thought..."

Cole frowned. "You thought I was doin' it on my own? I don't work that way."

She looked so surprised it annoyed him. Doggone if she wasn't the most vexatious creature. "Abbie, let's get somethin' straight. I ain't tryin' to take your kids. I just thought—"

She put her fingers to his lips. "Please don't get riled again. You're awfully hard to live with in a temper."

"A temper!" He gripped her upper arms. "Can you hardly blame me?"

To his utter annoyance, she laughed and kept laughing until he silenced her with his lips. She must be dern near hysterical to carry on so.

Abbie caught his face between her hands. "I love you, Cole. I want to be a family as you said."

He felt a powerful warmth sink deep within him. Family. Isn't that what he'd missed all those years in the saddle, thinking he'd never settle down, never have the woman he loved, never hold a child of his own? "Then I'll see your brother again, soon as he's back to work."

She raised her face to him. "What was he here about tonight, then?"

Cole looked away. "I had him make up my will. I figured with y'all and the ranch, I wanted things settled in case ... well, just settled.

Now, Abbie, don't look so stricken. Doggone..." He pulled her against him. "I hardly needed to wash, seein' as how you're doin' it for me."

"I don't want to think of something happening to you."

"Then don't. I'm too stubborn anyhow." He kissed the damp crown of her head.

She held up her face, eyes glowing. "You were wonderful tonight. How did you know what to do, how to do it?"

"I didn't exactly. I've done it for cows and horses both, but never on a woman. I ain't likely to do it again."

"You saved them, Cole. You saved Marcy and the baby."

He stroked her hair, wondering. That babe was awfully weak, and Marcy was likely not out of the woods yet. But he needn't say it now.

"I'll never stop being amazed by you."

"Good. I gotta manage a whip hand somehow."

She pushed against him. "A whip hand, indeed. You're tender as a mother hen."

He chuckled. "Don't blab it around."

Nine

Abbie crept into the room where Marcy slept in the dim light of early morning. Grant was sprawled in the chair beside the bed, and the baby lay tucked into the cradle Elliot had slept in as an infant. Abbie gazed with wonder at the tiny, downy head and recalled it clasped between Cole's strong, sure hands. He hadn't hesitated one moment once he saw what needed to be done.

She brought her eyes to Marcy, lying limp and bedraggled, her blond hair in strings, her skin still pale. Abbie didn't want to think how it had been for her last night. To go through that pain and terror was bad enough without having the emotional trauma on top of it.

She stepped to the bedside and knelt down. She dropped her forehead to her steepled fingers and closed her eyes. *Lord, thank you for sparing her through the night. Thank you for seeing us through, for giving Cole the wisdom and ability to bring her child into the world. Thank you for Mama and Doctor Barrow. And most of all, thank you for your mercy.*

She glanced at Marcy's face. In sleep she looked soft and vulnerable. Abbie remembered the inadequacy she'd seen in her eyes when Marcy spoke of her parents' disappointment in having only a girl. Abbie guessed their adoption of the orphan, Michael, last year had been another blow to Marcy's fragile selfhood, though she was grown and married already.

She hadn't deserved the cruel words Abbie threw at her. Even if they were true, even if Marcy had betrayed her to the townswomen with her horrid speculations . . . even so, she hadn't deserved it. Marcy couldn't help her meanness. Maybe that's why Grant could love her.

And he did. That had been painfully obvious in his tears last night.

Abbie couldn't remember if she'd ever seen her brother cry before. She reached for Marcy's hand that lay above the covers. It was cool, though the air in the room was warm from the coals in the brazier.

Marcy stirred but didn't waken. Abbie warmed the hand between hers, then slipped it under the cover and went out. Three hours sleep wasn't enough, but she couldn't rest. She had left Cole sleeping like the bear he claimed to be.

It amused her to slip out without his notice. If they were out in the wild, she'd scarcely breathe without him knowing, and the least disturbance would bring him instantly awake. She had learned that lesson when she'd wakened him from a dead sleep and he had gripped her wrist faster than a rattler could strike.

She wandered down to the kitchen and put the percolator on to boil. She reached for the coffee beans and grinder. From the washroom a motion caught her eye, and she spun. "Who's there?"

Birdie stepped into the open wearing Abbie's coat, but her feet were bare inside her house slippers.

Abbie stared. "Where are you going, Birdie?"

"Out." The girl's eyes went like flint. "To practice my skills."

Abbie hoped she didn't mean what she guessed. "Where?"

The mouth turned up just perceptibly, and her pointed chin set. "The bunkhouse. Where else?"

Abbie felt sick at the thought of Birdie creeping in and finding Will and Matt and Curtis in their bunks. Was this the first morning she'd been so bold?

"I'll get a week's wages off Will like that." She snapped her delicate fingers, looking anything but fragile.

Abbie stayed calm. "I didn't bring you here to work, Birdie."

"No? Then why do I clean and sew and iron as one of your slaves?"

Abbie felt her ire rise. "Everyone works here, Birdie."

"Sí. Then I will do what I do best."

"I reckon you won't." Cole spoke from the kitchen doorway.

Abbie turned with a rush of relief as he joined her.

His gaze was squarely on the girl. "Birdie, the business you know is no good."

Birdie frowned, looking more like a sixteen-year-old than she did a moment ago, but then her expression changed. She gave Cole such a blatant invitation, Abbie caught her breath.

"Sit down." Cole's voice was low, but there was no denying the command.

As she sat, Birdie looked smugly pleased to have his attention.

Cole spun a chair and straddled it. "Let's talk straight. You asked Mrs. Jasper to take you out of La Paloma Blanca, and she did. She saved your neck in more ways than one. That was her part, now you're gonna do yours."

Birdie's eyes blazed, but she said nothing.

Cole leaned closer, emphasizing his words. "You know why? Cuz if you don't, I'll haul you back down there so quick Pablo won't know you were gone."

Abbie started to protest, but he silenced her with a look.

"You got you a chance at a new start. I reckon you'd better take it." He held Birdie's now sullen eyes until she looked away. "And you can start right now by respectin' Mrs. Jasper."

Birdie refused to look at her, but softly mumbled. "I am sorry I offended you."

By his expression Abbie wondered if Cole had intended for Birdie to apologize. If he believed her apology sincere, he didn't consider it enough. "And here's rule number one. Keep away from the men. You ain't here to ply your trade."

"What then?" She glared at him.

"To learn a better way."

"I like my way."

"No, you don't, Birdie. I know that well enough."

"How? You never saw me at my best."

Abbie felt her anger ignite. How did she dare? What made a young girl so brash?

Cole never flinched. "You got a lot to learn, and folks here are willin' to help you. I hope you'll let us."

Abbie expected a sarcastic response, but Birdie merely sat there. She gave away nothing by her sullen silence.

Cole stood. "Coffee ready?"

Abbie shook her head. "The water's boiled, but I haven't added the grounds."

Cole spoke over his shoulder. "Go get dressed, Birdie."

She stood and left without a word.

As she ground the coffee beans, Abbie anticipated Cole's embrace, and the next moment his arms wrapped her from behind. He kissed the curve of her neck. "How'd you get up without me knowin'?"

"You were hibernating."

He laughed, then turned her in his arms, sobering. "I got a thought to share that you ain . . . are not gonna like."

"What?"

"Has to do with Birdie."

Abbie's heart sank. "Then you're right. Any thought concerning that minx—"

He put a finger gently to her lips. "It's just this. As long as we're adoptin' the others . . ."

The air in her lungs dispelled in a rush. "Oh, Cole! You don't mean . . . Cole, I can't." It was one thing to be knit together with him and the children—but Birdie?

"I'm not sayin' it'd be easy or even right. Just . . . you don't know what home and family can mean when you ain't had it."

Abbie's heart sank further. Hadn't she been the one to champion the mission orphans, to find every one of them a home and loving care? But . . . but Birdie didn't want a home or loving care. She resisted every effort. Her animosity was tangible. It poisoned the very air around her.

What about the children? What would they learn from her? She had never meant to keep Birdie with them, not even in the same capacity as Zena or Pearl or James or the men—much less as her daughter. It was impossible.

There weren't enough years between them to accord any sort of respect. It was different for Cole. He could almost be her pa, and he'd certainly handled her a moment ago. Abbie looked up at him, and she knew her eyes were pleading.

He stroked her cheek with his thumb. "Just think on it."

She shook her head. "My thoughts will never come to that. It'll take an act of God."

Cole gave her a crooked grin. "God help us."

After being shooed from the kitchen by Pearl, Cole pulled on his hat and duster and went out. Small flakes of snow flurried into his face as he crossed the yard to the bunkhouse. It was early yet, and the men would still be sleeping. But the sooner he saw to this, the better.

He pulled open the door and stepped in. Three of the bunks were filled. Sam was not among them, but Cole couldn't think on that now. He tugged on the window shade and it flapped open noisily. "Mornin', men."

Curtis rolled over and groaned. Cole suspected he'd done some hearty drinking by the red of his eyes and the sag of his jaw. They'd most likely played some cards, as well, and Curtis was a notorious loser. Cole recalled the nights he'd spent fleecing Breck and Skeeter and Curtis in this very bunkhouse.

Breck and Skeeter were gone now, victims of the typhoid. Cole shook his head. Two strong men brought low by bad water and a wanderer. He nudged Matt with his knee. "Y'all wake up. I got somethin' to say."

Will rose to one elbow. "Is it mornin'?"

Cole shrugged. "Close to. I got somethin' to discuss, and it can't wait. Give Curtis a boot there, Matt."

Curtis raised a bleary head. "I'm up. You gotta talk so loud?"

"Clear your head, cuz I wanna be heard good."

Curtis sat, then hunched over with his face in his hands. "So talk a'ready."

Cole leaned a hip to the table. "Y'all know we brought home a young woman with us. Birdie. I reckon Will's told you where from."

The men shared a few awkward glances.

"I want you to keep your distance. I don't care what she offers or even if it's free. No man here takes advantage. Got it?"

Curtis rubbed his face. "Yeah, we got it. What's the point?"

"The point is, she might come offerin', and she can be mighty persuasive."

He saw Will flush. The kid was bit already, but he'd be the least inclined to use her, Cole reckoned. They were all good men, though Curtis was a bit of a hothead and braggart. He was also the best looking of the bunch. He reckoned that's where the trouble would lie if it were coming.

Matt slid his suspenders over his shoulders and stood. He gave Curtis a slow grin. "After last night, Curt can't afford anything anyway."

Cole frowned. That was the sort of thing they didn't need. "All right, then. Pearl's got breakfast on. Curtis, wash out your mouth before she gets downwind of you."

Curtis scowled. "I reckon I'll just sleep through breakfast."

"Do what you like, but be ready to work in an hour. We got a sickly herd to see to." Cole went out. That was a little like stopping a stampede with a tumbleweed, but he reckoned they'd listen. He wished he felt as confident that Birdie would.

It rattled him she'd shown her hand in front of Abbie. He'd wanted to shake her something fierce when she came on to him like that, with Abbie watching it all. He had more reasons than one for hoping Abbie would consider his suggestion. Maybe if he was her pa, Birdie would quit with the eyes.

He sent a rock skipping with his boot. Not that he'd ever take her up on it, but he didn't need Abbie wondering. Especially after last night when he'd loved her so thoroughly she hadn't cried a tear.

◆◆◆◆◆◆◆

After she and Cole breakfasted, Abbie sent Grant downstairs to eat and took his place beside Marcy's bed. She was pale and her breathing short and shallow. Sweat beaded her forehead, and she hadn't yet awakened. Mama came in and they exchanged a glance. Abbie shook her head. "She's worn out."

Mama sighed. "I hope that's all. Thank God Cole didn't wait."

Abbie's heart swelled. "He was so calm, Mama. You should have seen it. He just took over and . . . brought the baby out."

"He's a good man, Abbie. I saw that the first time he brought you home in his arms."

Abbie smiled faintly. She had no memory of that. It was the day she learned Monte had married Sharlyn, and she'd ridden so heedlessly she'd been thrown. Cole had found her unconscious and half-frozen. It was the first of many times he'd played the hero throughout the years she'd loved Monte.

She felt something ease inside. Maybe Cole wasn't just a second chance at love. Maybe he, too, was intended for her from the start, just as Nora said. Was that possible? Had God planned all this?

Marcy stirred, and Abbie leaned close as her eyes fluttered open. Marcy looked from Abbie to Mama. The tip of her tongue ran over her dry lips, and they parted. "Is it over?" Her voice was thick and groggy. It seemed Doctor Barrow had given her laudanum.

Abbie pressed her hand, amazed by the compassion she felt. "You have a beautiful son, Marcy."

Marcy turned slowly as Mama lifted the baby from the cradle and laid him in the crook of Marcy's arm. Marcy's face kindled with amazement.

Her lips trembled. "I was sure he died. I thought . . ." Tears came to her eyes. "How. . . ?"

Abbie didn't want to tell her how her son had come into the world. How would Marcy feel about Cole delivering her child? But Marcy was lost in her baby's face. If she had expected an answer, she forgot it now.

Mama dabbed Marcy's lips with a damp cloth, then swabbed her brow. "How do you feel?"

"Tired and . . . slow."

Pearl brought a tray with steaming grits and hot cakes, coffee and cream, and stewed plums. Mama lifted the sleeping baby while Abbie helped Marcy to sit. Marcy whimpered, but Abbie only looked on with compassion.

She was beginning to see things differently. Everyone had their trials, their weaknesses. She had plenty of her own. Her cruelty had caused Marcy's terrible ordeal. There was no excuse, and the most she could hope was that Marcy could forgive.

But now was not the time to pursue it, not even to ease her conscience. She waited on Marcy while she ate, then washed and brushed her hair. Did Marcy resent her touch? She seemed oblivious. Did she even remember last night's pain and Abbie's part in it?

The baby woke with a pitiful mewling, and Marcy fed him. He was underweight and suckled weakly, but again Marcy scarcely noticed. A flush came to her cheeks, and Abbie was amazed how pretty she looked. With her blond hair drying in bright wisps and her eyes alight, it was easy to see how Grant had been swept off his feet. Not even a Harvard lawyer learned to withstand that kind of trap.

Abbie toyed with Marcy's curls. They were more of a honey blond than Sharlyn's nearly white strands had been. She recalled plaiting and threading Sharlyn's hair with flowers. Sharlyn had been like a sister, but here she *had* a sister. Could she learn to love Marcy? Was it even possible with all the hurt between them?

Grant tapped the door and came in. When he saw Marcy sitting up with their child in her arms, his face took on a look of wonder and delight.

Abbie smiled. "Has your son a name?"

Grant's chest swelled. "Wendel Timothy Wilson Martin."

Abbie fought her dismay. "Don't tell me he'll go by all four."

Grant tugged her hair and glanced nervously at Marcy, who was forming a pout. "I imagine we'll call him Wendel." Grant stroked the baby's head with one finger. "He sure brought his mama trouble for such a little mite. If it wasn't for Cole . . ." He shook his head. "Where is he anyway? I never thanked him properly for bringing my son safely into the world."

Abbie cringed. Well, there it was. And by the look on Marcy's face, she wasn't as benumbed as she had seemed.

Abbie tried to catch Grant's eye and urge him to silence, but the best she could do was answer. "He's out with the herd."

"Then I'll catch him when he's back. That's a debt I won't easily repay."

Marcy's color was up, and Abbie recognized the fever in her eyes.

Grant seemed oblivious. He sat on the side of the bed and tucked his finger into Wendel's fist. "I thought I'd lost you both until Cole took charge."

Marcy went white as the pillow behind her head.

"We'll let her rest now." Mama's voice cut through the tension.

Grant nodded as he settled in with the baby's head cupped in his palm. Abbie was only too glad to slip away. She wouldn't be in Grant's shoes at this moment for all the gold in the Rocky Mountains.

Ten

Cole sat astride Whitesock, watching Matt rope in a steer. For the first time he saw Mr. Farrel's wisdom in fencing his piece of the open range. It was change, but change was inevitable. The days of the open range and the cattle drives were ending. Mr. Farrel's vision had been more accurate.

For two days now, they'd been checking and treating the herd for disease. The work went much quicker and easier when they didn't have unlimited miles to cover. Not that you'd know it to look at it. Mr. Farrel's property—Cole's property now—covered all the land in clear sight. But if only this herd was affected, the fences might keep the anthrax from spreading to neighboring stock.

Cole saw Matt hobble the steer, then check the hide for disease. That one must have been clear since it was released. Cole turned the gelding and urged it to a canter. He eyed a cow and calf pair, the calf almost grown by now. With an easy motion he scooped the rope from the saddle horn, circled it overhead, and threw.

The cow tugged, but he held steady and dismounted. Cole approached the animal and examined her hide, then checked her eyes and tongue. If she'd been a longhorn, he'd likely be skewered by now. They'd have had to corral her and immobilize her head, but these Herefords were more docile if you handled them right.

Cole felt a pang for the old days, then shook his head. He was thirty-six years old. He didn't need to be busting broncs and running down stampedes of skittish longhorns too stupid to stop before they injured themselves. He grinned sideways to himself. But it sure had been fun while it lasted.

He and Sam had taken a couple of drives together before he worked his way to trail boss and Sam moved to another operation. Had Sam been jealous he'd risen so quick? Far as he knew, Sam had never bossed a drive, but that wasn't his style. He was sure, steady, and dependable, but he didn't need to be in charge.

Still, it had to be hard for him to be here now. Even without the personal score between them, playing second fiddle to the younger brother he'd mostly raised must irk a man something fierce. So why had he come? After helping them get Birdie clear of Pablo, he could have taken off anywhere. Why had he come all the way here? And where was Sam now? He hadn't seen him since the night in town.

Maybe he shouldn't have asked his pardon. Maybe it was too much to expect. If it had been Abbie . . . Could he ever forgive someone who harmed her? Even if it was Sam? What if the tables were turned—what if Sam had caused Abbie's death? It sent ice through his innards.

No, Sam was right. He couldn't expect pardon. From God, maybe. But not from a man. Not from Sam. Cole released the cow and moved toward the calf. This would be trickier if the offspring were new. But hopefully this mother was not too protective still.

Cole returned to his thoughts. Would God pardon him? Brother Lewis had said every sin he'd committed and every one he might commit were covered by the blood of the lamb. Nothing he could do was bad enough God wouldn't forgive.

You'd think that would give a man great license to have at it in all sorts of ways. But it didn't work that way. The more he knew he was forgiven, the worse he felt about needing it. Maybe it was a good thing Sam wouldn't forgive. He already felt terrible about Auralee.

Cole rubbed a glove over the calf's bony skull, then checked its hide carefully. These two were clean, thankfully. Clean. Just as he'd been when he came out of the Rio Grande in Brother Lewis's hands. And not just washed of the trail's dust either, but washed of every bad thought and every wrong, stupid thing he'd done. And that included Auralee.

But it didn't change circumstances. It didn't take away the fact that he'd incited her temper and she'd taken it out on the wrong man. Crete Marlowe. Cole shook his head. That man had been connected to most of the worst events of his life. The memory of his ma's charred body hanging from the tree flashed in Cole's mind.

Crete Marlowe, his pa's friend, who had imbibed with Pa out on the porch while Ma cried inside. Crete Marlowe, who'd made Ma's life miserable after Pa took off, ogling and insinuating. Crete Marlowe, who'd sold the whiskey to the Comanches who killed her.

No, some things were beyond pardon. Only God could forgive them. Only God.

◆◆◆◆◆◆◆

As she went downstairs, Abbie heard wheels in the yard. She went to the door as the ox-drawn wagon rumbled in. She recognized Hank Thorne and Burton Wells on the seat and saw the bed filled with fresh smelling pine. The wood for the porch. She hurried down the steps.

Hank Thorne tipped his hat. "Mornin', Mrs. Jasper. Is Cole around?"

"No, I'm sorry. He and the men are doctoring an ailing herd."

He rubbed his chin with the bristly brown beard jutting out unattractively. "Well, he ordered this here lumber delivered today."

"I'm sure if you stacked it right there, that would be fine."

He rested his hands on his thighs and worked over the wad of tobacco in his cheek.

"Is there a problem, Mr. Thorne?"

"It's like this. There'll be a fee for us to unload it."

Abbie met his steely gray eyes. So that was it. She knew Hank Thorne for the skinflint he was. She had no idea what arrangement he'd made with Cole, but she knew he'd take advantage of anyone he could. Well, he'd have none here as long as she was able-bodied.

"If you'll wait just a moment, please." She stalked inside. "James! Pearl! Zena! Birdie!" She waited impatiently. "I need your help, please. We have lumber to unload."

Pearl wiped her hands on her apron and muttered. James put a hand to his back but followed her out. Zena and Birdie came behind.

"You may water your horses and fetch yourselves a drink at the pump while you wait, gentlemen." That was the most hospitality Hank Thorne would receive. And Burton Wells hung on his heels like a well-trained hound. Abbie stalked past them and opened the back of the wagon.

The lumber was piled high. Cole must be planning a large porch indeed. Unloading it all would be a formidable task. She turned. "Birdie, can you climb up in there and slide them off to us?"

Birdie looked up at the stacked wood with her usual sullen expression. Abbie prayed she wouldn't make a scene, but the girl merely flicked her hair over her shoulder and hiked up her skirts, no doubt fully aware of Hank Thorne's attention.

He frowned. "You be careful, now. I won't be responsible."

Birdie gave him a scornful glance and, with her skirts still clutched, walked the length of the top board like a daredevil rope walker. Abbie suppressed a smile. There might be a little bit of herself in the girl after all.

One by one Birdie slid the boards, then the rest of them paired off and carried the wood to the edge of the stairs. Abbie caught her breath as a wicked splinter pierced her flesh. Without a word, she set the end of the board down and pulled the splinter out. Blood ran across her palm, but she ignored it. If that was the worst any of them suffered, they'd be lucky.

Across the yard, Hank Thorne and Burton Wells drank from the tin cup at the pump and watched. Hank paced the yard and hollered for them not to bang the wagon. He slumped against the wheel and eyed them. He looked as perplexed as he was surly.

The boards got broader and heavier as they worked their way down. It was all Abbie and Zena could do to haul one between them. Abbie's arms were shaking, but she wouldn't give Mr. Thorne the satisfaction of seeing her slacken. James and Pearl, though, were too old for this, and she ordered them to rest. If only Grant and Mama hadn't left for the morning.

Abbie looked at the bottom of the bed, which held a double layer of logs, smoothed and routed. They must be the posts, she guessed, but they were heavier than anything yet. She tugged and Birdie pushed, but they scarcely budged one.

Abbie swiped her forehead with her sleeve. "Climb up and help her push, Zena. I'll catch it, and we can roll it to the stack."

"Them posts could crush you, Mizz Abbie."

"Nonsense."

They pushed, and the log came slowly forward. Abbie gripped the end, shaking with the effort. It was heavier than she had imagined. She held her breath and strained against the weight.

"Aw, gimme that." Hank Thorne tried to push her aside.

Abbie held tight and set her jaw. "No, thank you, Mr. Thorne. We can manage without you." She sent Birdie a purely conspiratorial look and saw a flicker in return. Zena jumped down and caught the log just above Abbie's grip. Between them, and with Birdie guiding the high end, they eased the log to the ground, then rolled it to the pile. Abbie's back ached with the effort.

Hank Thorne blocked her way back. "I see marriage and mother-hood haven't tamed you down any."

Abbie straightened. "If you mean I'm not likely to let you cheat my husband, you're right." She heard Birdie snicker.

Hank Thorne's face purpled. He set his jaw and turned. "You, girl, get outa there." He stomped to the wagon and nearly hauled Birdie off her feet. Abbie caught her from stumbling and hushed the Spanish curse that sprang from the girl's lips. Hank barked an order to Burton Wells, who came running.

From under the seat Hank Thorne pulled some sort of belted contraption. He fastened it to a log and the two men tugged it down from the bed. As soon as he loosed it, Abbie and Zena rolled it to the stack. When they had finished, there were eighteen posts in all, lying together beside the sawn lumber.

Abbie rubbed her bloody palms on her skirt and faced the two men. "What do I owe you?"

"Not a dern thing." Hank Thorne scowled and climbed into the wagon. The dust from its wheels rose in a cloud.

Abbie watched him go with mingled resentment and satisfaction. She noticed Birdie's gaze, and for once it was not poisonous.

"I have never seen a lady talk down a man that way."

Abbie brushed the grimy hair from her forehead, thinking that a "lady" probably wouldn't have. "Well, I've never seen anyone walk a board as you did on the top of the stack. I thought Mr. Thorne might drop his jaw right there in the yard."

Birdie shrugged. "I've been dropping men's jaws for years." She turned and started across the yard.

Abbie let her go. They'd shared a moment, which was more than she'd expected. James was obviously in pain with his rheumatic back. He leaned heavily on Pearl as they walked inside. Pearl would nurse it with linament, but Abbie felt a guilty pang as she observed his pained gait.

She should never have made him work so. Maybe she should have paid Mr. Thorne. He made it look easy with whatever that contraption was. He could have unloaded it himself in less time than he waited for them. But it was the principle of it.

Abbie sighed. She'd be feeling her principles tonight.

◆◆◆◆◆◆◆

"Here?" Cole worked his thumbs into the small of Abbie's back, feeling the knots and seeing her wince. She nodded, her face pressed into the pillows.

"How about here?" He moved his hands upward and eased the pressure a little.

"I don't think you'll find a spot that doesn't hurt."

"Doggone it, Abbie."

She rolled to her side and tugged the lace-edged sleeve of her flannel gown. She gave him a look both saucy and pert. "What was I supposed to do? Pay him?"

"You might've considered it."

"I'm used to watching every cent. Besides, I didn't want him cheating you. Delivery ought to include unloading. Why else did he have that strap contraption and a man with him?"

Cole stroked a finger over her flushed cheek. Her skin was like the petal of a rose, soft and scented, though her palms were now sliced and bruised. He kicked himself for not remembering the delivery. "To my mind, it was included. But without me handy, he probably saw an opportunity and thought to seize it."

"Well, he'll think twice the next time."

"Boy, won't he." Cole stroked the hair from her forehead. "I'd like to've seen his face."

"He looked as though he were choking on something."

"His pride, most likely." He chuckled. "You have a way of doin' that to a man."

"Have I?" She laughed back. "How lucky I found a man with pride enough to spare."

"Don't you start." But man, if he wouldn't shed every ounce of pride he had for that look in her eyes.

She sobered. "How bad is the herd?"

"We vaccinated just over a dozen. Had to put down three more. And we're still combin' the range for strays." He idly twisted a long spiraling curl around his finger. He loved the color of her hair, like molasses when it drizzled from the spoon with the light shining through. He loved the way it tumbled around her in a soft curling mass and the small curls she'd cut around her forehead. They sprang from his touch with a life of their own.

"Are you worried?" Her voice was low and a little sleepy.

"Hmm?"

"Are you worried about the cattle?" Abbie raised herself onto her elbow. "What were you thinking about?"

He grinned. "It sure wasn't the herd."

"Cole Jasper." Her mouth formed a pout. "I happen to take personal interest in those cattle. I've raised them myself enough years, you know."

"Yeah, I know. But just now we've done what we can for them. The strong will survive, the rest, well . . . Speaking of which, how's the little coot—what's his name?"

"Wendel. Wendel Timothy Wilson Martin." Her eyes clouded. "He seems . . . puny still. He doesn't cry as he should, just makes weak little bleats. And he doesn't seem to feed well. He falls asleep too soon."

"He came a tad before time. And he was tangled up inside. I had to get the cord off his neck before he could turn."

"Oh, Cole." Her brows came together with concern. "He's going to be all right, isn't he?"

He smoothed the worry from her face with his thumb. "I don't know. I've had strong, healthy calves die in the night, and miserable bum ones hang on against all odds. I reckon the most we can do is wait and pray. How's Marcy?"

Abbie sighed. "Doctor Barrow spent a long while with her today.

He's still giving her laudanum, so I'm not sure how aware she is of the concern. She lights up like an angel whenever she sees her son."

"I reckon you know how that is."

She reached up and ran her fingers along his jaw. "Yes, I do. More than you know. I had begun to think I'd never bear a child. Elliot was a miracle."

He rested his hand on her belly, feeling the firm muscled flesh through her soft flannel gown. "Well, God willing, he won't be the only one." He bent and kissed her. "But as Doc Barrow said, we have a daughter and a son. Better count our blessings, too."

✦✦✦✦✦✦✦

Sitting beside Cole in the small adobe chapel early Sunday morning, Abbie could hardly stop counting her blessings. The mission chapel held so many memories: her school days there with Blake, Father Dominic's healing words after her shooting the boy, Brother José and Brother Thomas and all the orphan children, many of them mostly grown now in the families where she'd placed them.

And then there were the times Monte had come with her, though not many. He had kept his day of rest in a more private way or on occasion attended the church in town where Reverend Winthrop Shields presided. But she did recall him sitting beside her as Cole did now, his smooth baritone voice singing out the Latin chants. And little Jenny, so impossible to keep still . . .

Abbie glanced at her now, sitting picture perfect on Cole's other side. She was obviously on her best behavior for his benefit. She always behaved best for him. Elliot snuggled against her, and Abbie rested her hand on his small thigh and felt the swinging of his leg from the knee.

In his hands Elliot held the pony Cole had carved. He had argued it be permitted on account that the angel had brought the pony, so it must be okay with God. Abbie smiled to herself. Angel. That wasn't a description of Cole she would have come to easily. But in a way it fit. Especially Jenny's description.

Abbie returned her focus to Father Paddy O'Brien. How differently he said the Mass, compared to Father Dominic's austere manner. Father Paddy's good humor and delight in serving his God came through all but the most solemn parts. But in a way it was the same, too. Both men giving their lives in service to God, even as the circuit-riding preacher Brother Lewis did.

Around them sat Mama and Pa and little Tucker—though he wasn't so little anymore—Grant with Emily Elizabeth, and Nora and Davy. Nearby were all the Irish and the McConnels and several families from town. The chapel was fuller than it had ever been, even when the orphans had lived there.

Now the pews were filled with redheaded children by the dozen and a smattering of dark-haired Irish, as well. There were an Italian and two German families and a young couple from Baltimore. The church, like the town, was outgrowing its boundaries—as was Reverend Shields' church, she knew. God must be pleased these Sunday mornings to hear the hymns and praises raised to Him.

Abbie flashed a glance at Cole to see how he was taking the experience. His face looked calm, even reverent when they knelt. His new-found devotion to his Savior ran deep, and neither circumstance nor situation hindered it. Here in this place, he honored God with his presence and with his being. Her heart swelled.

Abbie gazed at the heavy carved wooden crucifix, the symbol of Christ's ultimate gift, His own life. She felt small and unworthy, but humbled and awed that Jesus had died for her and for Cole and the children and for everyone who would believe in Him and allow Him to transform their lives. Even lives wounded by grief and bitter loss. She allowed His love to wash over her with a sense of peace. She was healing at last.

Stepping out into the cold air, Abbie drew a deep breath and released it, forming a cloud of white. Already a few scattered flakes toyed with the frigid breeze. Nora gripped her hand, and even Davy was cordial. His happiness with Nora was evident in his blunt, frank face.

As frantic swirling small bodies surrounded her, Abbie laughed and greeted the children by name. Cole cut through and made his escape, speaking briefly with Davy before fetching the buggy.

Enjoying the chance to socialize, Abbie laughed with Nora's sister, Glenna, and touched her friend's burgeoning belly. She hugged Mama and assured her Marcy was holding her own and they had plenty of help. Though she agreed that it was too bad Marcy's own mama had passed away last winter and wasn't there to help, Abbie secretly believed Marcy would recover more swiftly without Darla Wilson enumerating her many ills.

Too soon, Cole pulled up the buggy and jumped down. With a swift thrust, he extricated Elliot from the crowd and hoisted him onto the seat. Then he reached down for Jenny and added her with only slightly more decorum. Holding his hand out for Abbie, he gave her a no-nonsense smile and helped her in. He knew only too well she'd linger and talk until the snow came in earnest and their noses were red from cold.

But though he meant business, the early hour at which they had embarked for the mission did not seem to have damaged his mood. She scooted in toward the children on the seat, and he climbed up beside her.

His nicker to the horses started them off, and they cut out from the yard. Other wagons and conveyances were moving out around them as they started down the rutted track toward home. Cole whistled a tune, which Elliot tried to imitate, and Jenny plaited the ribbons on her coat.

Abbie sat in silence until she couldn't stand it one more minute. "Well?"

Cole turned to her. "Well, what?"

"What did you think of church at the mission?"

He flicked the reins and guided the horse around a hole in the track. Then he cocked his head and considered a moment. "Aside from the fact that everyone spoke a foreign language, it was . . . well, it was a little like comin' home. Like it don't matter where you been or how long you been away, there's always a welcome from above."

He met her gaze. "I reckon Brother Lewis would have a word or two on the doctrines and all, but to me worshipin' God can be done just as good wherever you are. And I imagine some of the most fervent prayers have gone up from places where angels fear to tread."

Abbie smiled and clutched his arm with hers. "My wise man."

"And don't you forget it."

Eleven

After a right satisfying supper and a few evening chores, Cole went upstairs to clean up and change. It was Monday night, and the Stockmen's meeting was scheduled in just over an hour, the first he'd attend as owner of the Lucky Star. With a full week of holding title to the ranch under his belt, he figured it was time to make his presence known. He'd spruce up a little and head into town early.

Upstairs, he stopped in the doorway, paused by Abbie's silent presence beside the bed. He glanced down at the quilted coverlet where a long coat, vest, and trousers lay. She hadn't heard him come up, and the unguarded look on her face was a queer combination of bondage and release.

He recognized Mr. Farrel's clothes easily enough, but her purpose was murkier. Did she hold court with Monte's duds to recall him? Was this some grieving ritual he'd happened on unfortunately?

She must have sensed him there. Abbie turned, and he expected to see some false, compensating smile thrown his way. Instead her eyes took on that deep water look, and she drew a sharp, shaky breath. "I was just going to find you."

He stepped in, feeling like a trespasser. "Guess I saved you the trouble."

Now she did smile, but it was neither false nor particularly compensating.

"What's all this?" He nodded toward the bed.

Her smile faded as she surveyed the clothes. "You're nearly Monte's size. I let down the cuffs of the trousers a little, but beyond that, you'll have to try it for fit."

He kept his eyes squarely on his wife. "What exactly are you sayin'?"

"For the Stockmen's meeting tonight."

So that was it. He felt the tension ease in his neck. "Abbie, I appreciate the gesture. I expect it wasn't easy takin' those out and recollectin'. But I ain't much for fancy duds."

"You're not accustomed to dressing this way, but like it or not, you're a rancher, not a foreman now, and this suit of clothes is appropriate dress for the Association meeting." Her voice had an edge to it that belied her calm gaze. She was hurting after all.

"Abbie." He reached for her shoulders and turned her to him. "This isn't necessary."

"The others will be dressed accordingly. So unless you'd rather spend the money on a new suit . . ."

He sized up the fine clothing with a glance. He'd feel like a fool in it, a grouse in pheasant feathers. He'd never been inclined to duding up. But then, he'd never filled a station that required it. Whereas Mr. Farrel had been a gentleman of the first degree, and born to it.

There it was again, smacking him broadside in the face—he was comparing himself to Montgomery Farrel and coming up wanting. But Abbie was likely right. The Stockmen's Association was a gentlemen's group, and poorly as he might fit the bill, he'd have to try to look it. She stood waiting, as taut as new leather.

He gave her a grim smile. "I ain't sure I'll clean up as nice as you'd wish."

The corners at the sides of her mouth deepened, and a slight dimple marked her cheek. "I think you'll clean up fine, Cole."

He ran his hand across the back of his neck. "I'll feel downright uncomfortable."

"Oh, you'll forget what you're wearing once you get down to business."

Maybe he would . . . if they were any but Mr. Farrel's clothes. "Well, let me wash, and you can do your worst by me."

She laughed. It would have been convincing if her eyes had matched its mirth.

Lord in heaven, won't it ever let her loose?

Cole strode down to the washroom, scrubbed up, and shaved. He'd planned on wearing the six dollar broadcloth suit he'd purchased in El Paso for his wedding. But next to Mr. Farrel's things, it seemed a cheap attempt at frippery.

Resigned but not eager, he went back upstairs and put on the clothes. It surprised him how well they fit, but then, they were cut to Mr. Farrel's build, not just the basic cut of the general store's goods. Abbie was right about his matching Mr. Farrel's size. She'd given him extra length in the leg and the shoulders were a mite snug in the coat, but she'd have never managed it if he'd gotten the extra four inches his pa and Sam sported. At six foot one inch, he'd barely topped Mr. Farrel at all.

He looked himself over in the tall oval-shaped looking glass. It was not a sight he ever expected to see. He glanced behind him at Abbie, scrutinizing his reflection as well, and raised his eyebrows for her opinion. She lifted her chin slightly and drew a long breath, then walked to the bureau and removed a small box. She crossed in front of him, set the box on the vanity, and lifted out the gold watch and fob.

He started to shake his head, but Abbie ignored him and clipped it inside his vest, then dropped it in the pocket provided for that purpose. "This was Monte's father's, and it'll be Elliot's one day. But until then, I want you to have it." Her voice was strained, and he caught and raised her face.

"Abbie, what are you doin'?" Cole couldn't fathom her motives. How could they be so close one day and have all the ghosts between them the next? "I don't need all this. I ain't—"

"Humor me, Cole."

What was she saying? Was she trying to dress him up and pretend it was Mr. Farrel returned? What did he want with the man's watch? What did he want with any of it? Cole swallowed back his rising anger. He could do it for one night. As she said, he could humor her. After all, he was representing her tonight as much as himself.

It was her ranch and her herd before it was his. Hadn't she reminded him of that? Four years she'd run it alone after Mr. Farrel's passing. Four years she'd attended the meetings herself with Breck to speak for her. Did she resent his going in her place now?

"Abbie . . ."

She ran her hand over the quilted vest across his chest with a be-mused expression. Was she seeing another man there? Recalling Mr. Farrel?

"Do you want to come along?"

She raised her face. "To the meeting?"

He nodded.

"No." She took a step back, shaking her head. She gave him a thin smile. "They tolerated me, but . . . it'll be better for you to take over."

He took her answer at face value. "Anything particular you want me to address?"

"No." She shook her head again, folded her hands before her, and sighed. "I guess you're ready."

"Yeah."

"You look . . . fine." Her smile had a hint of warmth in it this time.

"Too fine."

"No. Just fine." She reached up and kissed his cheek.

Well, he was dressed to play the part; he may as well play it. He headed out, throwing his own duster across his shoulders as he closed the massive front door behind him.

Abbie stood for a long moment in the bedroom after Cole left. She felt a dull throbbing in her right temple and her throat was tight, but she was glad she had done it. They were clothes, not relics. Across the room, an armoire, not a shrine.

She walked slowly to the bureau, took out the photographs, and gazed at them. Monte stood in the very suit she'd laid out for Cole. Had she done that intentionally? Monte looked so poised and elegant. But Cole had looked vital and . . . fine. The soft gray of the vest had heightened the green of his eyes, and the fit of the slightly darker coat accented his lean, muscular build.

She looked again at Monte's likeness. The dull sienna hues muted his coloring and softened his features. But even so, what a handsome man he'd been. She swallowed the lump in her throat and drew a jag-ged breath. And what a handsome man was Cole Jasper. Different, yes. Rugged, not refined. But handsome—as handsome as Monte—in his own way.

Abbie closed her eyes and shut the frame. She considered putting it in the trunk on the shelf of the wardrobe, then slipped it back into the drawer. Soon, maybe, she could put it where she would not need to see it so often. Soon.

Her eyes glanced over the box on the bureau that held her jewels, as Jenny called them. Tenderly she opened the box and watched the light glance off the amethyst brooch given her by Mama and Pa on her twentieth birthday. Then she eyed the pearl and garnet earrings Monte had given her the same night, the night his hands were burned in the fire.

She closed her eyes against the painful memory. But he had overcome the injury. He had learned to compensate, to go on. Abbie looked at the emerald bracelet he had given her their first Christmas as man and wife. She had felt so . . . cherished.

With a slow breath, Abbie closed the box. She hadn't worn either the earrings or the bracelet since Monte's death. She had spent last Christmas on the road from El Paso, hardly even aware of the day, but for the aching pain of not spending it with her children. And now with Cole's reluctance to wear Monte's finery . . . would she ever have occasion to wear them again?

Shaking her head, she went out and made her way down to Marcy's room. Mama had left earlier that day when Pa came for her. He and Tucker had need of her, and he held a valid point—Marcy and the baby had all the help they needed. Grant, too, had gone into town for changes of clothing and for the baby things they had compiled at the house.

Doctor Barrow insisted Marcy not be moved, so Grant was also bringing his saddle stock to the ranch and seeing to countless other things he'd neglected in these days of worry. Abbie pushed open the door and gazed at Marcy sleeping, propped up in the bed with a half dozen down pillows.

Perspiration sparkled on her brow, and Abbie crossed to the water bowl on the stand beside the bed. She dipped the cloth and swabbed Marcy's forehead and hands. The childbed fever held her in its grip, and Marcy scarcely stirred. Abbie stroked her hair and smoothed it from her face, then rested her hand on Marcy's head and prayed again for her healing. Not to assuage her own guilt, but for Marcy's sake alone.

Then she left her to sleep and went to the kitchen. As she expected, she found Pearl there, rocking baby Wendel near the stove's warmth. She held a cloth dipped in sugar water to his lips, and he sucked in his sleep. He looked the picture of contentment.

It was when he was awake that it troubled Abbie to see him. The way his eyes didn't follow and his little mouth hung limp. And his movements were so feeble and halfhearted. Some of that could be the early birth—maybe even all of it. No one else made mention of it at all, not even Doctor Barrow.

Abbie then went to find the children. Zena had them in the nursery, and Abbie smiled at the normal playful noises that greeted her the moment she opened the door. Even Emily Elizabeth seemed undaunted by the tumult in her life. But then, maybe this was a welcome change.

Abbie felt a flicker of disloyalty at the thought, but admitted it anyway. It had to be happier for the child to be here playing with her cousins than dressed up and fussed at alone in her own home. Abbie watched the lively game of leapfrog they were playing around the perimeter of the room and laughed when Elliot tumbled over Jenny's head. He landed on his hands, then tucked his head and rolled with the ease of motion Monte, too, had possessed.

Emily clapped her hands and laughed, then imitated him on her own. Soon they were all rolling somersaults on the hard floor covered only with a thin woven rug. From the looks of Emily's rolls, this might be the first time she'd been allowed that diversion.

Of course, it messed up her curls and rumpled her dress. Again, Abbie silently chastised herself. Even in her thoughts she was unkind to Marcy. She sighed and squatted down to tickle Elliot, who rolled against her skirts. He'd done it intentionally and giggled with delight at his accomplishment.

Abbie scooped him into her arms and covered his neck with kisses. To her surprise, Emily Elizabeth came forward for kisses of her own. Abbie closed the child into her embrace and kissed her soft cheek again and again while the little girl squeezed with all the strength in her chubby arms.

Looking up over Emily's head, Abbie reached out a hand to Jenny who came near willingly, but with less abandon than the younger ones. Abbie craned her neck up and kissed Jenny's cheek. "I see you're handling the entertainment as usual."

Jenny nodded. "Elliot wanted leapfrog and Emily Elizabeth wanted dolls, so once we put the dollies to bed we leaped."

Abbie laughed. "So I see." She glanced at Zena asleep in the chair. She had sat up with Marcy last night and the children had clearly worn her out. For all Abbie's arguments against needing a nanny for the children, she was awfully glad to have Zena at times like this.

Though how it had worked out that way, she wasn't sure. Being Pearl's niece, Zena had started out as a housemaid for Monte shortly before Abbie married him. She had also dressed Abbie and done her hair.

But since the children came, Zena had proved herself a natural with them, and Abbie had little need of the fancy hairstyles and the corset that required another woman's strength to fasten properly. She had gone back to wearing her hair down or pulled back in a simple manner. At the moment it was almost as unkempt as Emily Elizabeth's.

Abbie released the little ones and stood. "Come on, now. It's time to wash and change for bed."

"Not yet . . ." Elliot whined.

Abbie held up a finger. "You know the rules. No story if you whine."

He pouted but refrained from whining. "What story?" He looked as though that would determine whether he complied or not.

She fought her smile at his naughtiness. "Tonight I'm going to tell you one."

Jenny's curiosity was piqued. "You mean you're not reading it?"

"Nope. Tonight I'm going to make one up for you."

"May it be about an ice fairy?" Jenny's eyes were already shining.

"No, a dragon." Elliot clawed his fingers and pretended to shoot flames from his mouth.

"An ice fairy and a dragon both." Abbie turned to Emily Elizabeth. "And what would you like to have in the story, Emily Elizabeth?"

Emily puckered her face with thought. "I'd like a princess that looks just like me."

"Then she's a very messy princess," Jenny pronounced and gave vent to a gale of laughter.

Emily Elizabeth stomped her foot and shouted, "I'm not messy! I'm not messy!"

"Oh yes, you are." Jenny gripped her middle and kept laughing.

Abbie scooped up Emily with a warning glare for Jenny. "Nothing a little cleaning up won't help. Jenny, why don't you see to your own messes."

"Ice fairies are always messy. They never have to wash because it's so cold where they live that the water is all frozen."

"I see. Perhaps you should tell the story tonight."

"Me too," Elliot piped.

"All of you." Abbie smiled at the three eager faces. "After you've washed and changed. Now run along."

❖❖❖❖❖❖❖

She had just finished tucking them all in for the night when Cole returned. Abbie swept down the stairs and met him emerging from the cloakroom. He had unfastened the stiff celluloid collar, but the rest of him was impeccable, and her heart caught unevenly. He looked wonderful. Maybe together they would bring back some cheer and elegance to this house.

She leaned on the post of the banister, one arm wrapped around the knob. "Oh, Cole. Tomorrow I'll get out the rest of the clothes for you, and Zena and I will let out the hems."

He gave her a queer look, but didn't answer.

She stepped toward him. "How was the meeting?"

"Fine. I've been elected vice chairman, which is probably fittin' since I know more about cattle than any man there. But as for Robert's rules of order, it's the silliest means of communicating I ever did hear."

Abbie caught his hands as he joined her at the base of the stairs. "They keep men like you from causing total anarchy."

"Well, I ain't sure what anarchy means, but I'll take your word for it. Now if you don't mind, I'll get out of these duds and get back to normal." He squeezed her hands and let go.

She felt a quiver of disappointment. Couldn't he at least show his gratitude? After all, sharing Monte's things with him had been a big step for her.

He looked back over his shoulder. "You're welcome to join me, if you like. I'll be turnin' in promptly."

With the best smile she could muster, she followed him up.

◆◆◆◆◆◆◆

Sam Jasper stood on the balcony of the same hotel room he'd rented the last time he lingered in Rocky Bluffs. That time he'd been waiting to avenge himself on Cole. He looked out at the night. After sitting holed up in the small, plain room for over a week, having his meals sent up and basically lost in a fit of melancholy, it seemed he still was waiting.

He shook his head slowly. Why did getting back mean so much? Sure, he'd heard their pa rail about it often enough. He was always getting back at someone. Burning the store that wouldn't give him credit, shooting the dog that barked, beating the son who failed.

But pardon? Sam wasn't sure he knew what that meant. All this month he'd chewed on it after sleeping off each night's excess. Funny that this little burg should be the place where he'd finally given in to the drink once again.

Yes, he'd followed his old man's example and swallowed enough rotgut to forget Cole's plea. But each day it had been there when he woke, and it was still there now. Maybe it just wasn't in his nature to do it. He couldn't imagine saying the words.

He recalled the time Cole had apologized to their pa. He'd been probably five or six when he'd messed with Pa's watch and broken it. He could picture Cole's eyes as big as green marbles, his hands clasped up at his chest and his voice as small as a new chick's.

"I'm sorry, Pa."

"What's that you say? You're sorry? What kinda words is that?" Then the

smack of his fist on Cole's face. *"Sorry? I'll show you sorry. Don't you ever let me hear sorry again."*

And he'd beaten him senseless.

Sam dropped his chin to his chest. No, he didn't reckon there was much room for pardon in their house. But here Cole was, still asking. The kid had some kind of mettle, never turning hateful as he might have. Instead, he just seemed to care more. Not for the old man, though. No one could go that far. But for others, unfortunates and the like.

Even as an adult Cole was fighting for the misfits: the Mexican mule driver who'd become the town's whipping boy, the kid who lost his hands in a wagon accident, the widow who sold her pitiful wares on the boardwalk. And he was fire from heaven when he saw a bully acting up.

Sam rubbed the back of his neck. It wasn't that he didn't love Cole. He probably loved him more than most brothers, though he didn't often think on it. It was just that . . . well, pardon wasn't in him.

Then why had he gone back to the ranch with Cole and his new wife? Was he trying to make up for almost letting Cole hang? Was he trying to show without words that they were brothers still? Of course they were. But that didn't undo the wrong.

Sam closed his eyes. No, it didn't undo the wrong.

Twelve

In the thin mountain sunshine, Crete Marlowe leaned on the pillar of the Leadville Bank. He was sixty-three years old and felt every day of it. Even mid-March was cold in the Colorado mountains—cold and unfamiliar. He ought to be in San Antone, in the hill country, where the air was thick enough to breathe. Or in El Paso, where the women were warm and the whiskey cheap.

But things hadn't gone right. He hadn't seen Cole Jasper hang. Instead it was *his* face the posters sported. If he ever got his hands on that little Birdie's throat . . . He took a chaw of tobacco, slid it around to his cheek, and turned slightly when Finn came back out. They stepped off the walk together and headed down the muddy street.

"Well?"

Finn shook his head. "Two guards. Safe's in a back room with an office at one side. Windows in clear view of the street on both sides. Too much traffic. Folks're runnin' through there like cattle."

"You deposit your poke?"

"By name of Spencer Jackson." He grinned briefly. "In honor of the poor bloke what supplied it."

Crete scowled. "That was stupid. So far we ain't connected to Henry Spencer's murder."

"We still ain't. That clerk treated me right respectable."

"You think Washington can handle the guards?"

"Not alone."

"Then we'll have to tie the horses out front. Dooley can take one guard and Washington the other." They'd picked up the kid, Dooley, after the stage job.

"I don't like it, Crete. Too many folks comin' and goin'."

Crete shrugged callously. "Anyone comin' in can join the party."

"It's too risky. Why don't we move on to some place less jumpin'?"

"Cuz I'm tired of small change."

Finn shook his head, and the skin under his chin wobbled. He'd put on substantial weight since they'd been on the lam. How was that? How did a man get fat on the run? Crete glanced down at his own gut. No more than the usual paunch of age.

And Finn was getting skittish, too. Well, they'd had a couple of close calls. And the worst was that Injun jumping him in the dark. Crete's mood soured. An Injun, a woman, and a kid. Now, there was a story for a dime novel.

Cole's woman. Who would have thought that pretty little thing . . . He shook his head. Well, she'd get her due soon, too. No one crossed him like that, leaving him without his boots, unless they were willing to pay the price. Man or woman, made no difference to him.

Crete stepped off the sidewalk and felt Finn follow. Finn was more like a shadow than flesh and blood. They'd been together close on twenty-five years now, Finn being the nearest thing to a son he had. Which was lucky for Finn, since lately he'd been annoying enough to part ways.

Crete found Washington and Dooley in the Silver Emporium where he'd left them. Dooley was trying his luck with the faro dealer, and on account of his size and the scar on his neck, Washington was being served at the bar. Crete nodded for Finn to keep an eye on Dooley, then sidled up beside Washington.

He raised his eyebrows at Washington, a half white, half Sioux, as he ordered, but neither man spoke. Crete swallowed down his whiskey and walked away. A short time later, Washington, too, stepped away from the bar and followed him outside. They stopped at the corner.

"What do you say, white chief? Is there money for us here in this den of iniquity?" Washington questioned.

"There's money, all right. Enough to see us a good while."

"And will the spirits smile on us?"

"They'll be downright jovial." Crete glanced up as a man in a bear-skin coat jostled him, then passed on by.

"When?"

Crete lowered his voice. "I'd say right about closin' time. That way if they panic and close the safe, you'll have time to open her up again."

Washington grinned. "Yes, my friend, there is good medicine in my fingers."

"Don't I know it. But you keep clear of the firewater, General."

Waiting out the next hours was the worst part. Crete watched Dooley make a fool of himself at a handful of games before he pulled him clear and set him to watching the street, just to get a feel for the flow of things. And keep him out of trouble.

Washington sat on his rolled Navajo blanket against the wall of the dry goods store, his ten-gallon hat down over his eyes, his knees forming a shelf for his arms. If he didn't sleep he was a better actor than any Crete had seen onstage. But how the man could sleep with the tension growing in their guts was beyond him.

Crete wandered the town like a man newly arrived. No one paid him any mind. New men arrived twice daily on the stage line and by all manner of other conveyance, including one riding an old steer. All of them looking to make their fortune.

Crete shrugged. Himself included, he supposed. But he wasn't trying his luck on any hole in the ground. Grubbing around the black dirt of this place for some percentage of gold and lead and silver was not his style. Nope, he'd have his from the bank, thank you.

Finn shouldered up to him with the heavy shuffle he was developing with his weight gain. "Where to after this one, Crete?"

Crete didn't answer. He never thought past the job at hand. It made for mistakes if one's focus wasn't steady.

"I say we leave Colorado," Finn added.

"We ain't leavin' Colorado."

"Why?" Finn's wattle shook with the sudden turn of his head.

"I got business in Colorado."

Finn screwed up his face. "Oh, you ain't still stewin' about Cole Jasper?"

Again Crete didn't answer.

"He's bad medicine to you, Crete."

Crete glanced up the street, then stepped off the walk. "You've been talkin' to Washington."

"I think the breed's got somethin' to that business. He says it like a joke sometimes, but have you noticed every time he says it'll snow, it does?"

"That ain't medicine."

"What, then?" Finn scratched his ear.

"Sense. Plain common sense. Go tell Dooley to fetch the horses."

While Finn hustled away, Crete went to wake Washington. The man opened his eyes before he could nudge his boot. "I heard you coming, chief. You walk like a herd of buffalo."

"Well, thank you, General."

"It is time?"

"It is."

Crete entered first and waited while a man emptied his poke onto the scale, then signed for the amount deposited. "Thank you, sir," the clerk said.

And thank you. Crete stepped aside for the man to pass, then approached the counter. From the corner of his eye he saw Dooley and Washington come in and position themselves between him and the guards. Dooley's hands were in his pockets and he looked up and around at the ceiling as though he'd never been inside a bank before. Washington looked straight ahead.

Outside the door, Finn would have taken his place, and the moment Crete reached the transaction window, Finn stepped inside and turned the lock on the door. He flipped the sign to Closed just as Crete's army-issue revolver met the startled clerk's nose.

"In case you ain't done this before, fill the bags in the vault and lay them here on the counter."

Both guards jumped to the alert. Both found themselves covered by guns to their chests. Washington raised his slowly with an animal look on his face. "Drop your weapon."

The guard unstrapped his gun and laid it on the floor. Dooley waved his gun and the other guard did likewise.

Washington flashed his teeth. "Close the shades, white man."

The guard turned and began pulling the shades. Did he have a belly gun? Crete watched the guard for any sign of such as the clerk and manager both filled the bags with gold dust and currency from the vault. One shade went down, then flew up, noisily banging the roller and flapping around. A signal? The guard pulled it again, looking contrite.

Crete and Washington shared a glance. "Leave the door." Washington motioned the man past the shade on the door to the window beside. They needed to see that the horses remained tied out front. If the guard had signaled someone, it would be the obvious thing to remove their means of escape.

Finn searched the street. "No one."

Did Crete imagine the guard's disappointment? The man pulled the last blind, and Dooley waved his gun for him to join the other against the wall. Washington picked up both guns and shoved them into his belt. The last bag nestled the others on the counter.

"Tie them together." Crete waited while the clerk and manager tied the ends of the bags in pairs, then he began distributing them.

Each of his men hooked the bags over one shoulder and kept his gun hand free. Together they backed to the door. "Now?" Finn murmured.

"Go." Crete spun and they plunged through the door to the horses.

Washington saw it first, the flash of light on the rifle barrel on the roof across the street. He lunged for his horse and clung to its side, Sioux fashion, as it galloped down the street. Crete mounted with the speed of a younger man and ducked low as Dooley took a bullet in the shoulder.

Crete returned fire as Finn dragged the kid, then he reached down to yank Dooley into the saddle. The law hadn't had time to organize, or they'd all be shot dead by now. Crete splintered the wood that hid the shooter.

It seemed to be a lone gunman. Maybe a third guard they hadn't known about. Maybe one who caught the signal. Another bullet whizzed past and Crete kicked his horse into action. He felt a thump, but the bullet had lodged in the saddlebag.

Crete's heart thundered in his chest like the horses' hooves as Finn and Dooley galloped behind him. The town seemed to explode with gunmen, but as he ran the gauntlet, head pressed down to the horse's neck, Crete felt invincible. Without a backward glance, he rounded the corner and followed Washington's path. They left behind the tents and wooden shacks, and after several hard miles, they left behind the road.

That was the first bank they'd hit, and Crete felt the sheer terror evaporating into euphoria. He reined in at the line of spare mounts they'd left in the woods, and with fresh speed he leaped down from his spent horse and mounted the black one.

Finn and Washington dragged Dooley from one saddle to the next, and Crete saw that he was bleeding badly. "Tie him on." Crete tossed a rope, and Finn wrapped it around Dooley's belly, then anchored it to the saddle horn. They left behind the wrecked getaway horses and started out again.

The mountains were an endless void, and it was likely the sheriff had little skill in tracking. One thing Crete had learned aforehand was that the law in Leadville neither knew much, nor lived long. It was a thankless position foisted on anyone desperate enough to take the job.

Once they'd put some miles behind them, it wasn't likely they'd encounter serious pursuit. Except perhaps the infuriated depositors of the Leadville Bank themselves. He figured they could handle that. In fact, it amazed him how easy a life of crime could be.

If folks actually took the plunge and saw how quick things happened, no one would want to scrabble for a living no more. It was the fear of getting caught that held them back. But once you looked that fear in the eye, it turned out to be no more real than the bogeyman. Besides, at sixty-three, taking a bullet in the street was no worse than hacking your last days out feeble and dim-witted.

✦✦✦✦✦✦✦

Cole planed the sawn edge of a board to fit perfectly against the last, then pressed it in place and nailed it there. The porch was coming along nicely, and truth be told, he thought it fit the house better than the overstated portico with the giant southern pillars. Abbie would be pleased.

He ran his hand along the smooth board, checking for imperfections, same as he would any carved piece he made. There was one thing he and Mr. Farrel agreed on. Things were worth doing well. And now that this house, this land, the whole ranch was deeded in his name, too, he felt even more strongly about keeping it up.

It was one thing to work for someone and do your best because it was right. It was another altogether to work for yourself. Not that he really worked now for himself. It was Abbie that made it matter. Abbie and the young'uns.

Would it be the same if he had all this without them? Not a chance. What good was settling down alone? Again he thought of Sam. He must have hit the road, his leaving town evidence enough that pardon wasn't possible. Sam hadn't any roots here, not like the ones Cole had found in Abbie.

Her roots were deep enough to reach bedrock. And she seemed willing to let him grab hold. More willing than he'd like in some ways. He pictured himself in Mr. Farrel's fine clothes. He had looked fine, as she said. The fit was good, the clothes better made and more comfortable than anything he'd worn yet.

But it worried him that she was upstairs taking down the legs and some of the sleeves and letting out the shoulders of more suits and pleated shirts and frock coats than he'd wear in a lifetime. It wasn't him. Leastwise, it wasn't him the way he wanted to be.

Was she trying to make him into someone he wasn't? Someone he'd never be? Was she trying to recreate what she had with Mr. Farrel? Couldn't she love him as he was? Cole shook his head and fitted the next board.

In his thirty-six years he'd grown accustomed to his faults. He didn't talk fancy, didn't dress fancy. He lived plain and honest, worked hard and loved hard. He'd loved Abbie so long that even when she wasn't his, she'd become his roots. No matter where he strayed when she cut him loose, part of him had stayed here.

But that didn't mean he could grow into a different tree. An oak was an oak, not a birch or an aspen. God knew he wasn't perfect, and there were plenty of things he could improve on. He allowed that without argument. As an oak, he had a heap of knots and wormholes. But the wood was hard and solid.

Cole hammered the nails in place and felt the joining with his fingers. Smooth and tight. He stood and carried the next board. So how would he explain all that to Abbie, who'd looked at him with stars in her eyes when he put on the ruffled shirt and satin vest? How would he tell her he didn't want that?

◆◆◆◆◆◆◆

As soon as she saw Cole come in for lunch, Abbie tugged him from the washbowl and led him upstairs by the hand to the sewing room where Zena still sat with striped trousers across her knees. "Look, Cole." Abbie crossed to the rack that held an assortment of shirts, coats, and pants. "We've done all these. If you'll just try them for a final fitting, we'll have them finished in no time."

It had been cathartic to handle each piece that morning, lowering the pant hems and cuffs and adjusting the shoulders that she had noticed pulled a little in the coat he wore to the Stockmen's meeting. With each vest and shirt that she had taken from the armoire, she had released a little of the tightness that had seized her chest at the very thought of Cole in Monte's things.

Now she not only felt willing, but eager for him to have them. He cut such a handsome figure in clothing that did him justice. And he deserved it. Hadn't he freed her from the choking debt that had worried her for years? Hadn't he won her heart when she thought it could never be healed?

She turned, anticipating his approval. But the look on his face was anything but approving. He brushed a drop of water from his sideburn that he'd missed with the towel. "Well, it looks like you've been busy. And I am, too. Let's eat so I can finish up out there while I still got daylight."

She stood for a moment, uncertain she'd heard him correctly. Then she tried again. "Isn't it nice to have all these choices and ... well, you won't need a new suit for some time."

Cole glanced at Zena, then hooked his thumbs in his belt. The loops were frayed, she noticed, and the denim knees worn. "No, I reckon I won't. I don't imagine there'll be too many occasions to wear such as these."

Now she saw what he was doing. He was rejecting her gift. He had no intention of wearing the clothes she was presenting him. She felt her cheeks flame and knew her tongue wasn't far behind. But with Zena there as a witness, Abbie kept it reined. Instead, she swept past him and headed into her own room across the hall. She turned the lock with such decision, he couldn't help but hear.

Cole stood a moment outside Abbie's door. He heard her crying, and he could tell they were angry tears. He'd handled that poorly. But doggone if he was going to allow her to dress him up like a doll and play house. She had to realize he was what he was.

He raised his hand to knock, then thought better of it and went downstairs. Pearl would have a hot meal waiting, and he'd worked up a powerful hunger. As he headed for the dining room, Jenny and Elliot stormed him from behind with war whoops and captured his legs.

"You're our captive now. Don't try to get away." Elliot waved a wooden stick that Cole guessed was either a knife or gun.

Cole stooped swiftly and caught them up, one in each arm. "Now who's captured who?"

Elliot wiggled, but Jenny squeezed his neck. "I like when you capture me, Pa."

He gave them both a hug and set them down. "Where's your little cousin?"

"She wouldn't play Indians." Jenny spoke with true disdain. "She says she could never pretend to be a savage. I think I'd like to be one. Would you like to be an Indian, Pa? A Comanche like Gray Wolf?"

Cole felt his gut twist. A Comanche like the ones who hung and burned his ma, who ravaged the settlers of Texas and wakened the wrath of Death Rider, as he'd become known to them?

He looked at Jenny with her dark braids hanging Indian fashion and her eyes some kind of wild. His throat constricted. "No, Jenny, I don't reckon I would."

She frowned, obviously having anticipated his agreement. "Why not? You could talk to the spirits."

"There's only one spirit I need to talk to, and that's God."

She looked decidedly disappointed. "You could be a war chief."

He stooped down to one knee and got eye level with her. "Do you know what war chiefs do to little girls like you?"

She shook her head uncertainly, and he saw Elliot's eyes go wide.

"Well, you don't want to know. But if you want to play Indians, you ought to play the sort who mind their own business, like the Pueblos or the Navajo."

"What do *they* do?" Her brow furrowed dubiously.

"Well, they grow maize and grind it into meal, and they make baskets and pottery and weave blankets and such."

"Do they take captives?" Elliot held his stick ready.

Cole ruffled the boy's hair. "I don't reckon so."

"Then I'll be a Comanche. I'm going to scalp you." He ran the stick back and forth over Cole's head.

Cole stood up with a dull ache inside. He supposed he should be grateful their innocence allowed them to make a game of things he knew were more terrible than they comprehended. But it conjured memories too deep for him to appreciate their sport.

"Come on, let's eat."

"Where's Mama?" Elliot looked up the stairs behind him.

"She's not herself just now. I reckon Pearl will take her a tray."

✦✦✦✦✦✦✦

Abbie went down to supper that evening dry eyed and nearly serene. She had declined the lunch tray Pearl brought and wallowed in her self-pity. Who did Cole think he was, refusing to wear the quality clothing available to him? But little by little, it had crept in that maybe he had his reasons.

She and Zena could finish the job, and he could wear them or not as he liked. If it was pride that kept him from accepting, perhaps it would wear thin with the knees and elbows of his current collection. If it was something else, well, he'd tell her in his own time.

When she took her place at the table, he gave her a look that said he was sorry he'd caused her grief. And for now, that was enough.

Thirteen

Birdie crept into the upstairs room, telling herself she wasn't sneaking. She had never been forbidden there, though in her two weeks in this house she had not before ventured in. She brushed the feather duster across her chin, feeling the soft fibers that had once carried a bird through the air. Zena had ordered her to dust.

Birdie felt her lip curl. Even at Pablo's she had never cleaned. Now, though she was called a guest, she was treated like a slave. She looked around the room, finer in every way than the one she slept in. Though hers was neat and practical, with care given to her comfort, this room was sumptuous.

The walls were papered in soft greens and roses, the windows adorned with lace and chintz. The large bed was finely crafted of polished wood in a dark reddish hue, rich and inviting like the thick downy coverlets. The brazier still glowed warm and the oval looking glass reflected the coals. The vanity, bureau, and armoire did not crowd the spacious walls, nor did the high molded ceiling dwarf the floor.

Birdie trailed the duster along the edge of the trunk at the side of the door as she advanced into the room and closed the door behind her. This was Mrs. Jasper's place. A room for a lady, though what was done within its walls was no different than what Birdie had known for three years now.

She felt the bitter tightening in her throat. Except for one thing. Mrs. Jasper chose. Birdie ran the duster along the footboard of the bed and sauntered to the bureau. She pulled open one drawer and then

120

another and ran her hand through the fine clothing nestled there. Everything neat, everything fine.

Her fingers touched a hard, smooth contour among the silk and linen handkerchiefs. She pulled it free and opened the picture frame. The dark man who stood in the photograph opposite Mrs. Jasper's must be her late husband. He was striking and genteel, but that was only on the surface. Underneath he was like any other.

She replaced the picture frame and brushed the duster across the bureau and the small silver box sitting alone on its broad expanse. The box was filigreed and ornamented, but the silver was flawed and blackened as though by fire. Birdie felt a flickering curiosity. Why would a rich woman keep something that had been spoiled?

She laid down the duster, and with her left hand, she opened the box and looked inside. Her eyes widened of their own accord. She had seen cheap imitations of cut stones, but until this moment she had never seen actual gems. The clear sparkling stones on the fine gold bracelet could not be otherwise.

The earrings and brooch were beautiful, but the bracelet ... Birdie's breath came sharp and tight. All those nights she had scrabbled men's pockets, dug for loose change, and secreted it in her bodice in the hope that one day she would fly ... All those nights Pablo had searched her and taken from her the small amounts she had won ...

Yet here, hidden away in a box, not even worn, was more wealth than she had ever imagined. Her chest ached for air, and she realized she had stopped breathing altogether. Green stones. *Verde*. Like Auralee's eyes. How the men had carried on about Auralee's emerald eyes.

Now Birdie saw. Now she knew. Before she had only imagined the color of emeralds. They were indeed as pale and cold as Auralee's eyes. But they, dead stones though they were, caught the light and danced in her fingers. They were life. They were freedom.

She felt an annoying twinge. Where would she go? How long would the stones last? What if they came after her? What if Cole ... She had a flash of herself on the end of a rope, Cole Jasper waiting to see her hang.

No. She would have stopped them. Cole had always been kind, even when he caught her filching. She would have stopped them from hanging him. Wouldn't she? If Mrs. Jasper had not come offering escape, would she have defied Pablo and Crete Marlowe to save Cole?

Birdie clasped the bracelet into her palm, felt its sharpness cutting into her skin. It did not matter. Cole had caused Auralee's death. She spoke truly when she said so. Auralee had loved him. And for a saloon girl, love was death. Birdie closed the small box, then with her hand gripped into a fist, she left the room.

◆◆◆◆◆◆◆

On the floor of the library, Jenny sat cutting paper dolls with small, sharp embroidery scissors. Abbie nestled Elliot close as she read from the *McGuffey Primer*. She glanced up when Cole came in and perched against the end of the settee. He looked too long and manly for the fine velvet piece with the carved cherrywood fans. Maybe he felt that way, too. He never sat in it, just perched against the side.

Jenny jumped up. "Look, Pa. I made a dress for Maribella. I colored it myself."

"It's right purty, Jenny."

Abbie smiled with her eyes while she kept reading. She turned the page and pointed. "What's this word, Elliot?"

"*A*. That's too easy. It's only one letter. Ask me a harder one."

Abbie pointed again.

Elliot moved his lips silently, then pronounced, "That word says 'and,' *a-n-d*."

"That's right."

He pressed his finger to the page. "And that's 'be.' 'Cept it's not the kind that stings, 'cause there's only one *e*."

"Very good."

Elliot squirmed loose and ran to Cole. "Did you make my rabbit?"

Abbie bit her lip. He'd asked Cole every night, but with the sickness in the cattle, Marcy's baby coming, and working on the porch, Cole had hardly had time to catch his breath. He hoisted Elliot to his hip.

"I don't know. Seems to me I had a bit of wood I was shavin' on some." He shoved his hand into his pocket and pulled out the rabbit.

Abbie smiled at the long foot the rabbit had raised to its ear in a very realistic scratch. Elliot took it and examined it with serious eyes, turning it around and around in his hands. He looked solemn and troubled.

Cole cocked his head. "What's the matter? Don't you like it?"

"I like it. But it makes me kind of sad."

"Why?"

Elliot shrugged his small shoulders. "Jenny's right. You do carve better than the angels."

The corner of Cole's mouth twitched.

"Did you make me one, Pa?" Jenny's dark eyes held him fast.

"Now, Jenny, I made you a passel of 'em already." At her pout, he tweaked her chin. "You be patient while I get Elliot caught up, then I'll make you somethin' special."

Her face immediately lit. "What?"

"I ai . . . I'm not tellin'. It's a surprise."

She clasped his hand between hers. "But I'll like it. I know I will. Oh, thank you, Pa."

Cole grinned self-consciously. "You haven't got it yet."

"But it'll be soon, I know. You won't make me wait long."

Abbie almost spoke up. Jenny was shamelessly manipulating him. But, then, Cole had to learn how to handle that himself. Especially if he did indeed adopt the children as his own.

Elliot shifted on Cole's hip. "Did you hear me read? I can read words now."

"I heard."

"I can a'most read like Jenny."

"I reckon so."

Zena tapped the door and retrieved Jenny and Elliot for their baths. Abbie stood to put away the primer.

Cole nodded toward the bookshelves. "I didn't know you were learnin' him a'ready."

"Teaching him."

"Seems kinda young, don't it?"

She caught something in his tone, an edge or defensiveness. "He's ready. Age doesn't really matter."

"I reckon not."

Abbie stood at the shelf and fingered the primer. What was bothering him? Did he feel self-conscious, even shown up? She turned. "I could teach you, too."

He cocked his jaw to the side. "What for? I know what I need to know."

"Reading is more than necessity. It's . . ."

He frowned. "I got no use for it. I can cipher numbers well enough and write my name. Sam taught me that much."

"Show me."

"What?"

"Your name."

He pushed off from the settee and took a sheet of vellum from the escritoire.

Abbie watched as he dipped the pen and wrote. The letters were a near enough semblance, but . . . She tipped her head. "I could show you how to make it right."

"I don't need extra strokes and curlicues. It's 'Cole Jasper' plain enough. Anyone can read that."

"You can't." She said it softly, unsure why she pushed an obviously tender area.

He shoved his finger to the paper. "Cole Jasper."

"But you don't know why it says that, what the letters do to make it so."

"I don't need to."

Abbie took the pen and wrote three words beneath his name, then held the paper out to him.

He frowned. "Abbie, I ain't gonna . . ."

"Don't you want to know what it says, Cole?"

He hooked his thumbs in his belt and looked away.

Abbie smiled and tugged his sleeve. "Here, I'll show you."

He looked, but the frown became a scowl.

She ignored his bad humor. "The first letter is a word by itself. 'I.' The second word says 'love'—*l-o-v-e*." She took a step toward him. "The third is 'you.' It says 'I love you.'"

The hard line of his mouth softened.

"See how easy it is?"

"I got no use for it." He took her in his arms. "I can say that easy enough without writin' or readin' it." He kissed her soundly.

She pressed against his chest, unwilling to give in to the rushing inside that his kiss created. "Have you always been this stubborn?"

"I reckon so."

Abbie wrapped her arms around his neck and felt his tension ease. "I'm not sure I caught the whole drift of your message. Could you tell me again?"

Cole kissed her long and slow to make his point. What did the scratching of a pen on paper possess, compared to the actions that made clear what you wanted to say? He caught Abbie's hair in his fingers, then jumped at the opening of the door. Birdie stood there, dark and sullen, but her eyes flickered knowingly.

Cole's ire rose. "Ain't you ever heard of knockin'?"

"I thought this was done in the upstairs rooms." She jerked her chin at Abbie, who flushed with either shame or fury.

Cole ignited. He felt Abbie touch his arm, but advanced on the girl anyhow. "Well, let me teach you a thing or two about common courtesy. In this house a closed door means keep out."

Birdie's eyes flashed. "Then you won't need to know that Mrs. Martin is thrashing and delirious."

Abbie gasped and rushed past him, and Cole felt as foolish as Birdie had intended him to. "Listen, Birdie . . ."

"I heard already. A closed door means keep out." She turned on her heel and stalked away.

Cole ran his fingers through his hair. Women. Meddling, conniving, self-satisfied women. What he needed was simple male companionship. He scooped up his hat and headed for the bunkhouse.

Abbie called to Pearl as she hurried to Marcy's room. Since it was directly beside Birdie's, it was understandable the girl had been the first to hear Marcy's distress. Abbie blanched at the sight of her sister-in-law curled up and mumbling. She felt Pearl behind her. "Send someone for Doctor Barrow, Pearl, then bring me fresh water and some broth."

"Yessum." Pearl hurried out.

Abbie dropped to the chair beside the bed and took Marcy's hand. She had seemed better today, lucid for minutes at a time and stronger than she'd been since the fever started. The doctor had checked in that morning and seemed pleased with her progress.

Baby Wendel seemed stronger, too. He suckled what milk Marcy had for him and took the thin goat's milk Doctor Barrow provided, as well. With them both recovering, Grant had gone to spend the night in town, hoping to catch up tomorrow on his work. Abbie wondered for a moment if she should send for him as well, then decided to wait for the doctor's orders.

When Pearl brought the bowl of fresh water, Abbie dipped the cloth and stroked it over Marcy's forehead. She heard Pearl leave to warm the broth, then a fresh rustling caught her ear, and Abbie turned. Birdie stood in the doorway.

Abbie felt herself flinch. She didn't want to deal with Birdie's mood just now. But Birdie moved into the room like a dark shadow and stood, silent, against the wall. Her shapely hands were loosely clasped at her waist, and her face revealed nothing.

Abbie swabbed the cloth over Marcy's arm, trying to cool the burning flesh. She drew a slow breath. "Thank you for getting me so swiftly, Birdie."

Birdie didn't answer.

Abbie cooled Marcy's throat and cheeks. "I don't understand why she's burning up again."

"Childbed fever."

"Yes. But I thought she was better."

Birdie came to stand on the other side of the bed. "It comes and goes. We should light a candle."

Abbie glanced up. "Why?"

"To guide the angels to her bed. To watch over her."

Abbie hid her amazement. "There's a candle behind you in the drawer. The stand is on the shelf." She bit her lip as Birdie rummaged for what she needed. What would Birdie know of angels? She watched the girl light the candle and set it on the windowsill, then stare out into the night.

Abbie felt her breath catch at the bitter longing that passed over

Birdie's face, so acute it hurt to see it. She wanted to speak, but the words clogged in her throat. How could she reach out to Birdie? She looked at the small, flickering flame and cleared the emotion from her voice. "How do you know the candle guides the angels?"

Birdie kept her gaze at the window. "*Mi mamá* told me so. When she birthed my fourth brother, she took the fever. She told me then how to light the candle for the *ángeles.*"

Abbie could scarcely believe Birdie was sharing something so personal. Her voice even sounded like a child's, high pitched, without the hard edge.

"Every night I lit the candle and watched for them to come. The day the baby died, I buried him."

Abbie's heart softened. "And su mamá?"

Birdie's eyes went flat, replaced by two black iron plates in her oval face. She turned slowly, the window outlining her lovely profile against the dark night. The candlelight warmed her skin, but her expression was lifeless. "I do not know. That night I was sold to the devil."

Abbie couldn't take her eyes from the child, for so she was. Sixteen, yes, and on the cusp of womanhood. Woman already in some ways, terrible ways. But her heart went out to Birdie as it never had before. *Oh Lord, I don't know what to do for her.*

Birdie raised her chin and the tendons in her slender neck stood out taut. She looked to have royal Spanish and Indian blood coursing through her veins, yet her family's condition had been so pitiful they sold her into the worst slavery possible. With a languid blink of her eyes, Birdie walked from the room.

Abbie released her trapped breath and, with an effort, returned her attention to Marcy. She had stopped muttering and seemed to be sleeping peacefully. Abbie dipped the cloth and wrung it, then smoothed it over the pale arm once again. She could not undo the pain and hardship of the world, but she could relieve some small measure of the suffering.

Pearl came with the broth, but Abbie sent her away. "She's sleeping now. If the doctor says to wake her, we'll feed her then."

Alone in the room, she closed her eyes, still holding Marcy's hand. *Oh Lord, if I can be your instrument, use me. In whatever way, even . . . even if it means mothering Birdie as my own. And Father, I forgive whatever poisonous things Marcy has said about me to others. You will be my shield of truth.*

Abbie opened her eyes and glanced at the light in the window, then squeezed Marcy's hand. "May the angels guard and watch over you." She got up quietly and left her to sleep.

Alone in the dark, Birdie stood like stone in the center of her room. Cold seemed to fill her chest and spread out into her limbs. What was she doing here where she didn't belong? Why had she thought Mrs. Jasper—Cole's wife—could make any difference in her life?

And why had she told Mrs. Jasper about the angels? Why had she thought of it herself? She recalled Cole's words. A closed door means keep out. And doors had been closed to her a long time now. Even the doors of heaven. Her course was set, chosen for her, destined. She had danced with *El Diablo*.

Slowly, as in a dream, Birdie walked to the wardrobe and pulled open the doors.

◆◆◆◆◆◆◆

Sam shook his head, tossed to his other side, then threw off the covers and sat up. He couldn't sleep, that was plain, though for what reason he didn't know. Maybe lack of activity and physical labor, maybe the uncertainty. Tomorrow he would leave. No more hanging around wondering.

He stood and pulled on his jeans, then walked in his socks to the window. The moon shone, though it was nigh on dawn. Down below the street was empty and quiet, something most frontier towns couldn't boast of. But Rocky Bluffs wasn't a boomtown. It was a settlement, an established town with upright citizens. It was a nice place, a place a man could settle, if he was a settling man.

Sam rubbed his face and leaned forward to search the sky. Clear and cold. He could feel the cold through the window glass. It was a lonely sort of cold, the sort that sank into your bones. A movement below caught his eye, and he looked up the street a ways.

Just passing under the lamp was a person on foot, a small form—either woman or child, not tall enough for a man. He craned closer to the glass. Black hair, long and silky, like . . . Birdie. He saw her outlined in the next lamp's glow. What in tarnation?

Had Cole and Abbie booted her out? Not likely. Most likely she'd run off on her own. She looked like a forlorn waif down there alone in the darkness. Like a stranger who'd lost her way. And he figured that wasn't far off the mark.

Oh, he knew well enough the kind of poison that ran in her veins and belied the purity of her beauty and youth. But something urged him, and he reached for his boots. He took one more look out the window, and as he turned away he saw something else. Something hovering. Some large white bird or . . . But when he looked directly, there was nothing. Only Birdie.

Must have been an owl or some such and a trick of the light to make it so large. He pulled on his second boot and started down. She wouldn't come with him but one way. He felt his pocket that held his savings. Well, no rule said he had to pay for more than company. And she must be half-froze.

Fourteen

Abbie?" Marcy's voice was tentative in the early morning light.

"I'm here." Abbie lifted her head from its dozing slant.

"I had a dream."

Abbie felt Marcy's forehead with the back of her hand. It was substantially cooler, though not normal yet. She folded the damp cloth and laid it across her brow.

"It was you."

"Hush now, Marcy. Don't strain yourself." Abbie smoothed the limp hair from her face and brushed it gently back with her fingers.

Marcy closed her eyes. "They were so beautiful. Colors like . . . like none I've ever seen, only bright, brighter than . . . light."

Abbie dipped a fresh cloth in the cool water and dabbed Marcy's lips. "Can you drink a little?" She lifted Marcy's head and spooned a small amount of water between her lips. Marcy swallowed, and she spooned it again.

"At first I thought you were one of them. But then I saw they stood behind you, their wings like . . . swans' down."

Abbie stopped, the spoon midway to the cup. Could Marcy be saying what she thought she was? She looked quickly to the window where the candle had burned to a stub, then back to Marcy. Had she heard Birdie's tale through her delirium and imagined angels coming? In truth, Abbie had never given Marcy much credit for imagination. But what she described, as though she'd really seen it . . .

Abbie recalled how sweetly Marcy had drifted off. Had angels come to minister peace and comfort? If so, it had been Birdie's doing, not her own. Strange as it seemed, it was possible. Abbie suddenly felt up-

130

lifted at the very thought. She must tell Birdie, tell her the angels came.

Zena arrived with beef broth and a soft-boiled egg on a tray. "Let me feed her now, Mizz Abbie. Your breakfast is gettin' cold, and Mr. Jazzper, he's waitin'."

"All right." Abbie stroked Marcy's hand once, then stood. She saw the soft smile on Marcy's face and thought again how lovely she was. She was glad they hadn't worried Grant last night. He needed to rest, and likely to work, and by the time Doctor Barrow had arrived, Marcy was peaceful enough. Now Grant would see her like this and be saved the aching worry.

Abbie entered the dining room and glanced around the table. Cole stood to seat her, but she refrained. "Where's Birdie?"

"I haven't seen her."

Abbie looked at the bright faces of Jenny and Elliot, and even Emily Elizabeth. Maybe she would tell Birdie of the angels in front of everyone. Then they could all share the wonder, even if it was only speculation. "I'll just see if she's still asleep."

She swept from the room, then hurried down the hall and turned left to the guest rooms she'd just left. Abbie hadn't heard anything from Birdie's room while tending to Marcy and presumed she was still asleep. She tapped on the door. No answer.

Quietly she turned the knob and pushed the door ajar. The bed was empty and made up as Zena always did after they rose for the day. But Zena couldn't have been in there already this morning. Abbie bit her lip and went inside. The dresses she had shortened for Birdie were gone from the wardrobe.

Her heart plummeted with the dismayed release of her breath. Birdie had flown. Abbie turned and rushed back to the dining room where Cole stood waiting. "She's gone, Cole."

"What?" His brows drew together in a furrow.

"She never slept in her bed."

"Doggone." He turned angrily.

She caught his arm. "It's not what you think."

He resisted her tug. "I'm checkin' the bunkhouse."

"She's not there. She took—"

"Look, Abbie, this ain't somethin' to discuss here and now."

Abbie swallowed her protest and let him go. He wouldn't find her, she knew. She recalled the look of Birdie's eyes when she spoke the words that had so chilled her. As though she had heard another call ... and followed. *Oh, Birdie.*

She saw the children watching her and smoothed her face. "Don't worry. I'm sure we'll find her. She was upset last night and ... she doesn't know she belongs here."

"Why is Pa angry?" Jenny didn't miss a trick.

"He's not really." Or he wouldn't be when he saw that she was right. "He's just concerned." She stroked Elliot's head. "Go ahead and eat. I know you're hungry."

Jenny unfolded her napkin and laid it in her lap. "Pa hasn't said the blessing."

"Then Elliot will." Abbie rested her hands on Elliot's shoulders as he said his small grace. Then she helped him with his napkin. "I'll wait to eat with your pa." She caught Jenny's suddenly raised eyes. Well, it was time she acknowledged what the little ones had already accepted. They were a family.

Abbie drew a deep breath, smiled, and left them to Pearl's ministrations. She found Cole returning and met him halfway across the yard.

He spread his hands. "So what were you trying to say?"

"She took her clothes, the things I had made over for her. I think she's gone to town."

He cocked his jaw to the side. "You s'pose it's cuz I came down on her?"

Abbie had forgotten that. "No." She quickly told him the things Birdie had said in Marcy's room. "I think there's some ... dark hold on her."

He mulled that a moment. "So what do you want to do?"

"I want to find her."

His eyes probed, then he rubbed his jaw with the back of his hand. "Findin' her could be the easy part. Talkin' any sort of sense into her ..."

"We have to try."

He hooked his thumbs into his belt. "I reckon we do." Cole reached out and took her hands. "Seems to me your heart's changed some-what."

Abbie met his eyes and heard again Marcy's words, picturing in her mind the shining angels with wings of swans' down. "Well . . . God acted."

Cole's throat moved, but he didn't speak. He released a sharp breath and looked down the drive. "I don't know if she got there, but I reckon you're right that she headed for town."

"Where will she go?"

"Any one of them places. It's not blatantly obvious in Rocky Bluffs, thanks to the council's strictures, but if she wants work, she'll find it."

Abbie licked the dryness from her lips. She knew he didn't mean honest work but the only kind Birdie knew. "Then we need to hurry."

"I'll saddle us up."

"I'll help." Together they went to the stable, and while Cole saddled Sirocco, Abbie bridled the stallion, Zephyr.

Abbie had noticed Cole taking Monte's mount more and more often, when he wasn't working the herd. The Arabian pureblood no longer looked neglected and unkempt, and Sirocco's allegiance seemed to have shifted, as well, as he nuzzled Cole.

For a moment Abbie pictured Monte astride the stunning sorrel with black mane and tail. He had cut a dazzling figure the first time she'd seen him thus. But after his death she couldn't bear the sight of Sirocco without him.

Cole had seen the horse's temper and neglect and taken him in hand. As with everything else, he had succeeded admirably. She moved to Zephyr and, speaking gently, slipped the bridle behind her teeth. The mare had been her wedding gift from Monte. Her gift from Cole had been time, time to adjust to the promise of life again. She stepped toward him.

He cupped her cheek, reading her thoughts. "Do you mind if I use Sirocco?"

"No." She said it with all the sincerity in her. "He's yours."

Cole kissed her gently, then swung her into the saddle with the strength and power of muscles hardened by long, honest work. Her fingers lingered in his, but at last he drew away and mounted Sirocco.

They headed for town at a good clip. Both horses were young and strong and had speed in their blood. As they entered the town limits, Abbie looked around. It was a sleepy little village at this hour, as it used to be before the railroad brought the saloons, dance halls, and gambling halls. Yes, they were limited, their hours curtailed, but they had come.

She sighed. "Where do we start?"

Cole reined in and rested his forearms across the saddle horn. He scanned the town in silence for a moment, then straightened. "Well, I guess we ought to tie up at the hotel there."

Abbie nodded. The old hotel was centrally located, and had a restaurant as well as rooms to sleep in. She remembered the time she'd dined there with Carolina Diamond, the great dramatic singer and actress. The night she saw inside the woman's mystique. The night Monte asked her to be his bride.

How different were the circumstances of Cole's asking. But in a way, it had been more fitting. He had taken her to his roots, to the core of who he was. So had Monte, eventually, but she had never fit his aristocratic origin. She never would.

Cole took Zephyr's reins from her and fastened the mare beside Sirocco at the hitching bar. He ran his hand through his hair. "Well, I reckon . . ."

The hotel door opened, and Sam stepped out. Abbie turned in surprise and Cole with her. She didn't know what had passed between them, but she thought Sam had left town. Cole had indicated as much—or had she simply made the assumption? Abbie glanced from her husband to his brother.

Sam drew the morning air in through his nose, then let it out slowly. "I suppose you're lookin' for Birdie."

Abbie stirred in surprise.

"She's up in my room. Sleepin' still." Sam turned at Abbie's sound of dismay and faced her directly. "No, it ain't what you think. I paid her to come in from the cold when she hobbled into town near dawn, footsore and half-froze, draggin' a parcel of dresses and whatnot."

He shook his head. "Even then, she almost wouldn't come up. Thought it was a trap. Thought I'd run her back out to y'all." The disdain in Sam's tone was probably a close match to what Birdie's had been.

Cole leaned on the post. "I reckon she's lucky it was you who found her."

Sam nodded slowly. "Question is, what happens now?"

"Let me go up." Abbie spoke softly, her voice gentle yet impassioned with an urge and desire she couldn't suppress.

Cole touched her arm with a look that said he wasn't at all sure about that, but Sam handed her the key, and she slipped inside like a shadow. The door closed behind her, and she was alone at the base of the stairs. In the room at the top, Birdie slept. But of what did she dream? And why had she run away? Again Abbie pictured the haunted look the girl had worn.

She shuddered, then crept up the stairs and past the room where years ago she had found and rescued Patricia from Kendal's grasp. Stopping before she reached the room in which Grant had lived before he married Marcy, Abbie inserted the key and went in.

Birdie nestled under the covers, her black hair strewn across the pillows. Abbie saw the blanket in the corner of the floor where Sam had likely slept sitting, just as Cole had, once, outside her own door. There was honor in the Jasper men. She smiled slightly, then moved toward the bed.

Abbie dropped to her knees beside the young woman sleeping there. In unguarded slumber, Birdie was more beautiful than Abbie had realized, but it was more than her physical attractiveness. It was the tender, peaceful look on her face that never appeared in waking.

Gently, she clasped Birdie's hand, and for an instant when the eyes fluttered open, Abbie caught the look of longing she'd seen the night before. But just as swiftly, the shutters slammed closed, making Birdie's eyes like black glass.

Birdie shrank back against the headboard. "What are you doing here? I won't go back."

Abbie ignored her outburst and spoke gently. "They came, Birdie. Your candle guided them."

Surely Birdie would feel the joy . . . But the girl searched the room fearfully, her fingers clawing at the coverlet. What did she fear? Abbie tried to touch her, but Birdie narrowed her eyes like a cougar backed against a cliff. Abbie half expected her to spring, clawing and spitting. But as she watched, confusion, then wonder, then dismay filled Birdie's countenance.

The girl burst into tears. Her sobs seemed to come from depths of human angst that no child should know. She writhed, then curled into a ball. "All those years I waited . . ." Her face screwed into a mask of agony. "All the times I prayed! They never came for me."

The lump in her throat made it hard to speak, but Abbie reached again for the girl's hand. "They have now."

"No. They came for her."

"Yes. But for you also." Abbie willed Birdie to believe. "They kept you from what you meant to do last night. They brought you to Sam, and he guarded you." She pointed to the blanket in the corner, where it looked indeed like Sam had kept watch over her.

Birdie wept. "It's too late for me."

"It's never too late. God's mercy is everlasting. He knows what's been done to you. He wants to heal and make you new. I know. I've experienced the pits of sorrow."

"You cannot know."

Abbie tightened her hold on Birdie's hand. "You're right that I don't know what you've suffered. Every person's pain is different. But it's true that I've needed God's mercy and forgiveness. Birdie, I killed a man. A boy not much older than you."

Abbie winced at the look of shocked amazement that crossed Birdie's face, then nodded slowly. "And I felt that I could never be clean again. But Jesus died so that I could. Believe in Him, Birdie, and He won't fail you."

Birdie's lips hung softly open. Her dark eyes roved between Abbie's as she fought for words. "Mi mamá, she sold me. She let him take me." Her voice rose to a plaintive wail, then she added with despair, "When I first saw Pablo, I knew. I knew he was El Diablo himself."

"Not the devil himself; only one who serves him. You're free of him now, Birdie. The darkness has no hold on you unless you let it."

"I do not know how to stop."

"Let me help you."

Birdie turned her face to the wall. "I hated you."

"I know." She pressed Birdie's hands together between hers. "Come home, Birdie."

Birdie started to cry again, but Abbie kept her hold. Here was another orphan, a child without the love and care she needed, and Abbie would not allow it. "Come." She stood and pulled Birdie to her feet.

●●●●●●●

Standing with his back to the bunkhouse wall, Will watched Cole ride in. Behind him, Mrs. Jasper and Birdie rode together on the gray mare, Birdie's thin arms around Mrs. Jasper's waist. Birdie looked tousled and worn, as though the air had been let out of her. But she didn't look as though she'd been forced to return.

He tried to catch her eye when they passed, hoping for just a glance in which he could send her his thoughts. But her head bobbed limply on her spindly neck, and her eyes were lost to him. Still, he might have some chance to reach her now that she was back.

It hadn't taken long for the word to go around that she'd run off. Curtis had smirked and said Cole should've let them keep her happy. Will's anger flared now just thinking of it. He'd wanted to tear Curtis's head off. He could have, too. Curtis was more mouth than muscle.

But Cole had taught him to keep his head, so he'd sucked in his anger. Will didn't say it to the others, but if Cole had come back without her, he meant to get her himself. He'd done it before, taken her right out from under Pablo's nose. But she had come willingly.

Since their first ride together, Birdie hadn't had one kind word for him or anyone else. And her tricks—sending him off on wild goose chases for her own amusement, ignoring every kindness . . . If he had any sense he'd let her alone.

But every bit of sense had left him when he first saw her standing there in that bawdy house like a dark jewel. It wasn't lust—not like Curtis, or Matt even. It was a crusade, a noble endeavor like Mrs. Jasper had had him read in Tennyson's *Idylls of the King*.

And besides that, he cared for Birdie. He had to, or why else would his belly get all seized up whenever she walked by? He watched Cole reach up for her and ease her from the saddle. He wished it were him.

Would she have rested her hands like so on his shoulders?

Cole lifted his wife down, and the three of them went inside. Will expelled his breath and leaned his head back on the wall. What was he even thinking? Birdie didn't know he was alive.

Abbie took Birdie straight inside and drew her a hot bath. The girl's feet were swollen and bruised from walking so far in her flimsy slippers. First thing, she'd have a pair of boots made up for her. She poured the scalding water from the stove into the tub, adding cold water from the pump before she tested it.

Abbie nodded to Birdie. "It's ready now. Have a soak, and tonight I'll treat your heels with a balm for the blisters."

Birdie said nothing, and Abbie left her to herself. She had not spoken since Abbie led her down the stairs of the hotel and outside where Cole and Sam waited. They had looked tense and uncomfortable out there on the porch together, and Sam did not return with them to the ranch. Instead, she suspected he would head off for good.

But just now it was Birdie who concerned her. Why had the girl's silence returned? Would she run again? Was she simply worn out? *Lord God, give me wisdom.* Should she tell Birdie of Cole's desire to adopt her as their own? Should they tell her together? Would Birdie even want that?

Abbie pressed her palm to her forehead as a wave of dizziness passed over her. She was wearing thin herself with so many to care for. With one last glance at the closed door behind her, she went to find Cole. It felt amazingly good to have a man to depend on. What a relief to know he was there. God certainly knew what He was about when He ordered things.

Fifteen

Cole looked along the rail of the newly completed porch and across its length. The wood was smooth and firm under his hand, and the porch held together with strength and elegant simplicity. He breathed the scent of the fresh paint that sealed the wood against the elements. It was a satisfying sight.

He had completed it last night, but with the excitement this morning, he doubted Abbie had even noticed. She had hustled Birdie up the steps and inside without even a glance around her, her thoughts understandably elsewhere. This whole business with Birdie had interrupted his surprise. And truth to tell, he had mixed feelings about it.

Birdie's running off had confirmed his doubts about the success they'd have with her, but then, Abbie seemed to have gotten through to her. Maybe, just maybe . . . Cole turned as Abbie came through the front door, framed by the huge mahogany molding.

The look on her face—a little triumphant, a little insecure—made him smile. Her return smile was like the sunshine itself. It was coming true, what he'd said. Each day they climbed a little higher, grew a little closer. Sure they took their spills. But it was worth it.

"Come 'ere and take a look." He wanted to please and impress her, then felt foolish for wanting her admiration.

She swept across the porch to him, and he led her down the stairs and across the yard a dozen steps. Cole then turned her around and faced her toward her fine house, now wrapped in a truly western porch. Abbie clasped her hands at her chest and gazed.

"If it ain't what you imagined . . ."

"It is. Oh, Cole, it's just what I imagined."

His satisfaction grew. He'd have torn it board from board if it didn't please her, but he'd felt the rightness of the design with the rest of the architecture and used the best of his skills to form it, almost like when he carved. Just bigger.

She spun in his arms. "How could I have walked through it this morning and not notice it was finished?"

"You were occupied."

"But it's beautiful, Cole. And you worked so hard. Forgive me?"

He smiled. Those words came so easily to her. Even over little things like this. What if he said no? What if he said it just wasn't in him? That was tomfoolery, but even so, the words were hard. He shrugged uncomfortably. "It's all right."

"It's not, though. I don't want to take anything for granted, not one thing you do. I want no regrets." Her eyes darkened with her remorse.

"It's just a porch, Abbie."

"It's a work of art, a work of your hands." She clasped his hands and kissed his palms.

Her words sent a wave of emotion through him. Had he ever in his life been afforded such admiration and esteem? And it came now— over a porch? "Stop it, Abbie. You're makin' a fuss for nothin'."

"It's not nothing, and I feel like fussing." The flush of her cheeks showed it was better not to press it.

"How's Birdie?"

"I'm not sure. I thought certain I'd made some headway, but now I don't know."

"You've made a difference—she wouldn't have come with you otherwise. But that's just the start. It'll take a heap of changin' on her part and just as much waitin' on ours to see it finished."

Abbie raised her face and searched the sky, her hair falling like a glossy mane in the still, cold air. "Do you believe in angels, Cole? I mean do you believe they help people in answer to prayers?"

"Abbie, I wouldn't know. What I know about God I either learned recently from Brother Lewis or dimly recall from my ma. I never studied on the trimmings."

"You could, though." She brought her eyes to him, so blue they looked like they'd taken some of the sky with them. "If you could read, you could study the Bible for yourself."

She'd caught him squarely, and it irked him that she'd worked the talk back around to that subject. "I reckon I could, if I'd a mind to." He hadn't thought how that might help his understanding. But that was neither here nor there. He couldn't read, and he was a sight too old to learn it now. "I'll be thirty-seven years old next month. I don't reckon that makes me a schoolboy."

Again she charged him with that overeager look and he dug his heels to argue, but she snatched his hands in hers. "What day is your birthday?"

He groaned inside. How many twists was she going to take? "It don't matter. It comes and goes like any other day."

She was clearly in no mood to let it pass. "Tell me the day."

Cole hung his head to the side. "April ninth, but—"

"Did you think you'd have a birthday without my noticing?"

"I would've, if I'd had the sense to keep my trap shut."

"I'm glad you didn't. If you'd slipped it by me, I'd—"

"You'd what?" He couldn't stop his grin.

She punched his chest with her fists. "Well, I don't know what. But now we'll have a party. Oh, Cole . . ."

He caught her elbows before she could wax enthusiastic. "I don't want a fuss."

She raised her chin primly. "Well, there's a rule in this house that no one's birthday goes by without a fuss."

He hung his head, annoyed. "It could've been last week or last month . . ."

"But it wasn't."

"Maybe it was. Maybe I was just sayin' that cuz—"

She cocked her head with a look that was purely skeptical. "Yes, Cole? Because. . . ?"

"Cuz I am what I am, and no amount of your fussin' and wishin' it otherwise is gonna change that. A man's got a right to his ways, Abbie. So you can get it into your head right now that I ain't learnin' to read, and I ain't wearin' fancy clothes, and I ain't havin' no birthday parties!" His voice had raised to a holler that drifted off into silence.

Abbie's head remained perched to the side, but her smile was gone and one eyebrow flickered. "Anything else?"

Hooking his thumbs into his belt, he expelled his breath. "No, I reckon that about covers it."

"Well, then if it *ain't* too much trouble, kindly saddle Zephyr again. I feel the need of a ride."

And he knew why. She was irked and meant to work it off on horseback. She sure had a way of taking it to him. But heaven knew there was only so much change a man could make.

"It's no trouble at all," he said and headed with relief for the barn.

Astride Zephyr, Abbie wondered how she had ever thought it a relief to have wed Cole Jasper. A blessing she'd allow, even a pleasure at times. But just now he tried her more sorely than a saddle bur. Why must he be so stubborn and cantankerous? Couldn't he see she thought only of him?

No, he had to get his dander up and holler as though she were one of the men. Oh, he could get under her skin and fire her blood like no one else. Why? Because she cared? Because she loved him? Because she wanted so much for him? And there he was like a mule, digging in his heels and braying. Cole Jasper was nothing if not infuriating.

◆◆◆◆◆◆◆

Cole put on his hat, hitched the team, and headed for town. He had wire, nails, and pig iron to fetch. And the more distance he put between himself and his vexatious wife, the safer he'd be. What did she want from him?

A birthday party? He shook his head in dismay. But he did recall the parties Abbie had put on with Mr. Farrel, when the house had been all done up and the guests had filled the place with laughter and merrymaking. And Abbie herself . . . she'd fairly glittered.

He felt a twinge at the memory. He'd enjoyed cutting the rug with the ladies, and with none so much as Abbie. Truth to tell, he'd stolen those moments and lived on them alone on the range and in the bunkhouse. Now that he had her to dance with whenever he liked, had he danced with her? Only the one time out on the prairie with no real music but the tune of his mouth organ.

Doggone. He hated to make a spectacle. But on the other hand, he sure would like to sweep her around the room again and see her all done up and shining just like the angels that had started the whole conversation. Maybe he'd been a tad unreasonable. He seemed to get his back up too easily these days, but then, she'd always had that effect on him. Even so, he sure didn't need to throw it all at her at once.

Cole shook his head. He was coming to think winning Abbie, as hard as it'd been, was nothing compared to keeping her. So far they'd spent more time fuming at each other than being the comfort they ought to be. He sighed. Maybe he'd see about lining up some music for her party.

Reining in at the general store, Cole decided he'd just see if Sam was still about, then get after business. As he strode past the jail, he shook his head at the hollering inside—old Sebastian demanding his breakfast. How the man could think of eating after the amount of alcohol he consumed was a mystery.

But it never failed that Sheriff Davis got an earful bright and early if that breakfast tray wasn't there when Sebastian woke. The door opened as the sheriff escaped the noise with a hasty lumber. Ever since Abbie had pointed it out, Cole couldn't help but notice how much Davis resembled a bear, with his hulking shoulders and dull brown sideburns and the loping way he moved. And just now he was clearing ground like a grizzly with a scorched tail. Cole gave the man a rueful grin.

Sheriff Davis returned it. "Not only does he want it quick, he expects it hot and tasty. I think he tries to end up in there just to get a free breakfast. I oughta boot him out at daybreak and send him off."

"Likely. But I'd worry for the old guy."

"Sentiment ain't got no place in law."

Cole dropped his chin. "Maybe not." He turned to head off, but the sheriff raised his hand.

"Say, Cole. Ain't this the feller that mixed you up in that murder down El Paso way?" He held up a fresh poster he had tacked to hang on the wall.

Cole eyed the likeness on the sheet. It wasn't a good one, but like enough to boil his blood. "Yes, sir. That's Crete Marlowe. Don't you have him posted a'ready?"

"I do. But this is fresh out. Seems he robbed a bank up in Leadville about a week and a half ago. Got off with a lot of miners' dust and currency."

Cole frowned. "Leadville, Colorado?"

"Yep. Not far enough for my likes."

"Nor mine." Cole pulled his lower lip. What was Crete doing in the Colorado mountains? Besides robbing and plundering. That he'd crossed over from swindling to thieving was no surprise. Even if Auralee's murder had been a loss of control, an act of rage, that sort of thing lived in a man and festered. Thieving was small in comparison.

But why Colorado? He must know that at least one man here would recognize him on the spot. Or was that what he intended? The hairs on the back of Cole's neck rose. Did Crete mean to cause him more trouble? If so, that endangered Abbie and the children, as well.

He caught sight of Sam outside the hotel. From the looks of the saddlebags on the horse, Sam was setting out for a long ride. Old Sebastian hollered again, and Sheriff Davis swore. He jammed the poster tacks into the wall and loped off.

Cole made a straight line for Sam. He stopped beside the horse as Sam tied the saddlebag shut with only a glance over the saddle. Cole felt the distance between them in miles. "So you're takin' off."

"Yup."

"Know where you're headin'?"

"South."

Cole nodded. And he was leaving with the wrong between them still. There still seemed so much to say. "Picture of Crete Marlowe on the wall there."

"Yeah?" Sam followed Cole's jerked thumb.

Cole looked up to Sam, the extra four inches Sam carried seeming more somehow. Maybe it was the slightly gaunt look to Sam's face. Maybe just the knowledge of all his brother had done for him in years past. "Crete's here in Colorado."

Sam adjusted the stirrup. Cole removed his hat, smoothed his hair, then replaced the Stetson with care. Sam's grip on his shoulder surprised him. "Don't look for trouble, Cole. You got a family now."

"I ain't lookin'. But I ain't runnin' from it either." He met Sam's eyes and found there a measure of concern and something else, something that wouldn't be put into words, that couldn't.

Sam tipped the brim of his hat. "Take care of yourself."

Cole nodded, ignoring the tightening of his throat. "You too." He watched Sam mount and wheel the horse in a slow arc of neck and swish of tail. Then he watched him ride out at an easy canter. *I'm sorry, Sam.*

As he neared the boundary of the ranch, Cole caught sight of Abbie riding hard, harder than he'd expect from temper alone. He reined in the team as she galloped close and halted Zephyr sharply enough to raise the mare's forelegs.

"Cole, come quickly! There's something happening in the draw."

Cole jumped down and mounted the mare behind her. She brought the head around and urged the horse to a lope. What had her so stirred up, he couldn't say. But it had saved the apologies he'd intended. Actions always did speak louder than words.

Ahead he heard noise and saw the dust and scuffle. Someone or something was getting the worst of it. As they drew closer to the commotion, Cole stiffened. A group of men were hoisting a weight up onto a shaggy pony beneath a tall ponderosa. As they backed away, he saw an Indian brave slumped astride a mustang.

Before him Abbie's breath caught. He heard her gasp, "Gray Wolf . . ."

But it wasn't. This man was younger, smaller—a Ute most likely, certainly not Commanche. He was roughly used all right, but by the looks of it, they weren't satisfied with that. One man threw a rope over the tree branch. The other end was around the brave's neck.

Abbie grasped his arm. "Cole, do something."

Even with her touch, his chest felt like stone. "It ain't our business."

She turned in the saddle, and her incredulous look shamed him. "Cole . . ."

Yet not even the power of her gaze penetrated the coldness within. "Abbie . . ."

She looked stricken, as though she'd suffered a blow, as though he'd struck her himself. He caught her hands on the reins as she tried to rush forward, realizing she'd not let it go. If he didn't do something, she would. Why was it this woman had to champion every Indian she met?

"All right, I'll handle it. Get down and stay here." He made certain with a look that she obeyed him, then urged Zephyr to a swift clip down the slope. Heads turned as he reined in.

"Afternoon, men." Cole tipped his hat. He recognized Geech and Miller and Stokes from the Lazy Y. Miller held the rope.

Geech stepped forward. "Howdy, Cole."

Cole nodded toward the brave. "What's this?"

"Caught the stinkin' redskin filchin'. Makin' sure it don't happen again."

Cole looked at the Indian on the end of the rope, followed the line of the rope over the branch, and felt his throat go dry. In his mind, his ma's body dangled there clear as day, charred and lifeless, an object of sport for filthy savages like the one in her place now. His heart hammered against his ribs, rushing blood like liquid iron through his veins.

He had thought he'd vanquished his demons, but now he felt their frenzy, their bloodlust. It had been a lot of years, but he still felt it as a living thing inside him, that desire to watch the Indian die. He wanted to feel the justice of taking one more savage life. An eye for an eye . . .

A small, still voice silenced the clamor in his heart. *Forgive, and ye shall be forgiven.* Cole shuddered without showing it. Hadn't Brother Lewis driven home the sin each man was capable of? Didn't Cole know his own well enough? He had slaughtered the braves who murdered his ma, unleashed the demons till he hardly knew himself.

Now he looked at the redskin on the horse and groaned. He was a man like the rest of them. Flesh and blood and likely a soul. He couldn't give the man life, so who was he to take it? But he knew the looks in the cowboys' eyes.

Cole kept his own face blank. "What'd he steal?"

"A flank of beef and a rifle. He was too stupid to get the cartridges what went to it."

He saw the fear in the brave's eyes. Most likely he understood some of their words, and he certainly had no doubt as to their intentions. His wrists were bound, his neck firmly attached to the rope, his face bruised and bleeding.

"This here brave's a friend of mine." Cole would have bitten his tongue on the words if he'd known they were coming. A friend? To an Indian? He swallowed hard against taking back the words, and realized that it wasn't so far from the truth as he imagined. Weren't they all men? All flesh, all mankind.

He saw the scowls and confusion his words caused. In his weakness he half hoped they'd argue, hoped they'd find it as hard to believe as it was. He wasn't disappointed.

"You gotta be joshin'." It was Stokes who spoke, one hand on the grip of his revolver.

Cole kept his voice even. "I'd thank you to cut him down."

"We'll cut him down when he's kicked his last. This dirty Injun ain't stealin' again."

"Stealin's their way. They know it's risky, but to them it ain't wrong."

Geech spat a line of sticky brown spittle, wiped his chin with the back of his hand, and nodded to Cole's right. "You best git your wife gone from here."

Cole turned in surprise and frustration. He hadn't realized she'd followed him on foot. He didn't want her there. It raised the stakes. His own fledgling concern for the Indian was nothing to hers, and if they failed . . . He returned his gaze to Stokes, obviously the hothead of the bunch. "Did you get your goods back?"

"Sure did, with a bit of hide thrown in." Stokes laughed.

"Then why don't we call it square?"

Stokes' brow lowered. "Cuz we ain't square. We was wronged."

Wronged? With all the wrongs on both sides they could cover the land in blood. "What do you reckon he's worth to you?"

Geech and Stokes shared a glance. Geech spat, smeared his chin, and grinned. "I reckon fifty dollars easy."

Cole eyed him. Greed was already cooling Geech's bloodlust.

"Fifty each." Stokes palmed the grip of his gun.

What did Stokes think he was made of? Cole shifted in his saddle. He'd bluffed his way into this, now he'd bluff his way out. "Well, I don't reckon I value him so high." He felt Abbie stir and prayed she'd keep silent.

He read the immediate disappointment in Stokes' face. He'd like to get him at the poker table. He'd fleece him quick and no regrets.

"Fifty," Geech repeated. "Split."

Cole waited a long minute. Long enough to see them sweat, then shook his head. "Reckon you'll have to be about your business after all." But he'd cooled them down so they were thinking about it. It was harder to kill that way, though he didn't doubt they'd do it.

Miller drew the rope tight, as though just recalling that he held it. Cole heard Abbie's breath catch and willed her to silence with a look. The three men turned, as one, to face the Indian. Cole unfastened the leather strap on his Navy-issue Colt revolver. He'd have to be more than quick. He'd have to be perfect.

His throat cleaved. *Lord, now would be a good time.* Miller fastened the rope securely to a bare branch and stepped back. Stokes raised his gun to the sky with a defiant glance Cole's way. Cole felt the beads of sweat rise up on his forehead. The brave met his eyes and Cole could feel his tension. It hadn't been so long since his own thoughts had dwelt on a rope choking his breath away.

He caught the tightening of Stokes' jaw, the quick sharp breath, the twitch of his finger. He drew, and his gunshot and Stokes' sounded almost as one. Cole's bullet severed the rope even as the horse leaped forward, and the Indian dropped in a heap. Cole spun, fired again, and the gun flew from Stokes' hand. Stokes hollered and gripped his bleeding palm. Cole turned the gun on the others. Geech and Miller raised their hands wide. If they were armed, they made no move toward their weapons, and Cole saw no evidence of such.

"H-h-hey . . ." Geech stammered. "Go ahead an' take him. We were just funnin'."

Cole looked down at the Indian. He had gotten to his knees in the dust and looked ready to bolt. Cole pointed the gun at him. "Don't move."

The Ute froze, and Cole relaxed only slightly. He nodded at the cowboys. "Cut him loose, then git."

Geech cut the ropes that bound the brave's hands behind his back and slipped the severed noose from his neck, then he and Miller mounted clumsily. Eli Stokes wrapped his palm in his kerchief, pulled himself into the saddle, and followed the others with a final dark look Cole's way.

Cole held the smoldering eyes. He'd made an enemy there and registered it. It was good to know your enemies. He waited until they were gone, then waved the gun toward the brave. "On your feet."

The brave stood, exhibiting steadier legs than Cole would have credited him. Cole opened his mouth, but before anything came out, Abbie rushed to the Ute.

"Are you hurt?"

Cole tensed. "Abbie, get back!"

But the brave seized her neck in the crook of his arm and flashed a knife from his legging.

Cole felt a surge of fear and fury as he lowered his gun. He flattened his voice and held the brave's gaze. "Let her go. We won't harm you."

The Indian stayed unmoving, the knife inches from Abbie's throat. If he so much as nicked her . . .

"Let her go." Cole gave his voice an edge of authority, then spoke the words in the trade language of the tribes. He saw the brave falter. "Go back to your people," Cole added in words the Indian knew.

The brave stood unmoving but for the quick ventilating of his rib cage, then suddenly he released her and stepped back. He held his right hand flat in front of his chest, making the sign for "go." His eyes flicked to the shaggy horse standing some ten yards away. With a sudden dash he gained it and swung up in one motion. He kicked his heels and lay flat as the horse bolted.

Cole felt his innards untwist and glared at Abbie. He raised his finger pointedly, but again she beat him to it.

"Oh, Cole, you were wonderful."

He kept his scowl. "And you were downright half-witted." He holstered his gun and swung down from the saddle. "Don't you know better than to run at a brave?"

But she came to him with the same fervor, wrapping her arms about his waist. "I was so relieved and worried and— How did you do that? How did you hit the rope at just the right instant? Oh, Cole, I'm so proud of you. I know it wasn't easy with . . . your painful memories. But I knew you would. I knew you wouldn't let them do it."

Her face shone with such praise it both shamed and angered him. Would he have stopped the hanging if she hadn't forced him? Would he have looked the other way, given in to his own vicious desires? He couldn't take Abbie's eyes.

He gripped her arms and shook her. "Don't you ever pull anything like that again. You hear?"

"You may scold me all you like, Cole Jasper." She slid her hands to his chest. "I know your heart."

Doggone. He hoisted her toward the horse. "Get up where you belong. Let's go." He swung up behind her. If she so much as spread the smile at the corners of her mouth, he'd tan her hide. It was bad enough word of this would spread without Abbie thinking him a hero for saving a redskin's neck.

Abbie rode before Cole in silence. She knew his anger was not solely due to her foolhardy behavior with the brave. What dark thoughts he had conquered, she could only imagine. His dealings with the tribes ran deep and painful. But as Pa had always taught her, the hatred had to stop somewhere.

Twice now, Cole had spared the life of an Indian brave. The other had been Gray Wolf. She recalled Cole describing his last encounter with the Comanche who had played such an integral and mysterious part in her life. Gray Wolf had tried to kill the man he knew as Death Rider. Cole had proved he was Death Rider no more.

And today he had proved it again. She leaned back into his chest. He might not be completely happy with the situation, but she was. She felt as though she were soaring on air. Not only was Cole brave and capable, he was good.

He might not believe it, but she knew he could never be like those men, making sport of another's suffering. She shuddered to think if they hadn't come in time. . . . Again her heart swelled, riding the peaks of her tumultuous relationship with this man behind her. Impulsively she turned and kissed his jaw.

Cole softened at Abbie's touch and felt the annoyance leave him. Her face was sweetly contrite, and no anger of his could stand against that.

She brushed his sleeve with her fingers. "I'm sorry about this morning, about getting angry."

"I reckon it took two of us."

"I shouldn't expect things of you."

He smiled sideways. "That's as likely to stop as the sun risin'."

She raised her chin. "At least I recognize my shortcomings."

He chuckled. "I've always admired that in you, Abbie."

"You might admit you have one or two of your own."

"I'll do one better."

"What?" She guardedly anticipated his words.

"I'll have that party you want." That dropped her chin in a right pleasing way.

"Do you mean it, Cole?"

"Course I do. Wouldn't have lined up the fiddler otherwise."

She reined in sharply. "Did you? Already? I mean before . . ."

"Yes, ma'am. First thing when I went to town."

"Oh, Cole." She threw her arms around him and nearly unseated herself to boot.

He caught hold of the reins in case the mare took off, as the spirited Arabian was wont to do. "Just one thing."

"Anything." Her face shone.

"I don't want any fussin' about the birthday."

She sobered dutifully but kept a distinct look of mischief. "I won't tell a soul . . . outside my family, my friends, and our guests."

He squeezed her. "I mean it."

She wiggled free, grasped the reins, and kicked her heels. The mare leaped to a gallop, and he knew that was as good as saying she had every intention of ignoring him completely. If this woman didn't beat the Dutch.

Sixteen

With the side of her bottom lip caught between her teeth, Abbie counted the days again. She took a short breath. It wasn't possible.

The stress and strain of everything, the turmoil with Marcy, with Birdie, with Cole, the hard ride ... All those could account for a disruption in her monthly cycle. She looked up as Cole strode into the room. He bent and kissed her with considerable swagger.

How easily his affection came, how confident his demonstration of it. But then, he'd always had the rogue's way when it came to courting. He nodded toward the things on the desk. "What're you doin'?"

She closed the calendar and laid out the lists she'd been making before other thoughts distracted her. "I'm deciding whom to ask to your party."

"It ain't my party." At her frown, he corrected himself with exaggerated diction, obviously mistaking her annoyance to be with his speech. "Is not."

She caught his hands in hers. "It is your party, Cole, but I promise I won't make a scene."

"That's as likely as—"

She put a finger to his lips. His thick mustache was soft to her touch like the fringe of mane on a new foal. "I'm simply planning menus and seeing to details that will make it a night to remember."

He bent close. "I could tell you how to make it a night to remember."

She breathed in the scent of sage and leather that always seemed a part of him, even though the smell of tobacco smoke was long gone. "Could you?"

"Yeah. But I'd just as soon show you." He clasped the back of her head in his palms and kissed her mouth.

Her heart hammered insistently even after he released her, and her thoughts returned to her calculations. Could a man like Cole . . . no, it was too much to hope. She wouldn't allow it yet, not even the thought. It had taken so long the first time, more than a year of waiting, wondering, and aching hope.

It couldn't be this easy, this soon. But when he brushed her lips again so gently, it was more mustache than kiss, and she melted against him. If anyone could have her with child already, surely it was this man who loved her so compellingly. Would God bless their union so?

Was it yet another sign that it was His will and purpose for her to be united to Cole? Why would it take more than a year to conceive before, and now—why, it would have to have been the very first time or close to. But no, she couldn't be sure. Not yet. It was too soon to know. Too soon to guess.

"What's the matter?"

She looked into his concerned eyes and realized she'd drawn back unconsciously. "Nothing." Her voice sounded breathless and tense. She knew he misread her, but she couldn't tell him her thoughts. Not yet. What if she set up hopes and expectations she could never meet?

Cole straightened slowly, rubbed his hair back from his forehead, and glanced from her to the papers. "Well, don't make the list too long. I expect to dance plenty with my wife. In fact, I ai . . . I *am not* sure I want anyone else havin' a spin with you."

She smiled, recalling the very first time she'd danced with Cole. He had fended off his cowboys with vim and vigor, then taken her outside and kissed her. And she had exulted only because it hurt Monte, who was dutifully attending his new wife, Sharlyn. How wicked she was. How could she think God would now bless her with so much?

He raised her chin with a finger. "You're a thousand miles away."

"No. Just another time."

She saw his concern, heard it in his tone. "What time?" he questioned.

"Do you remember the first time we danced?"

Cole's voice softened. "I remember every time we danced." He curled his arm behind her, pressing the flat of his palm to her back. He raised her to her feet and stepped her out away from the desk with smooth arching steps, then swirled her in widening circles before the fire in the brazier.

Abbie closed her eyes and allowed him to carry her on his arm to a rhythm and tune she nearly heard, so fleet and smooth was he. He had always danced well for a cowboy, but this silent waltz was more dreamlike and yet more real than any other time their feet had moved together. She hardly knew where he ended and she began. They were one.

She suddenly stumbled, caught her head with her palm, and gripped his forearm.

"What's the matter?"

"I . . . I guess I got dizzy."

"Are you feelin' all right?" His look held a healthy dose of misgiving.

She squeezed his hand. "Don't look surprised. You know quite well what you do to a girl, dancing like that."

"Well, it's been some while since I danced a woman dizzy." His mouth pulled sideways into a cocky grin. "But it's good to know I ain't—doggone it—I *haven't* lost my touch."

He finished with such ferocity Abbie laughed. "You don't have to stop saying 'ain't,' Cole."

"Well, I want to. I don't want anything in my example to set the children wrong."

"What, my Texas-born, rough-riding husband set the children wrong? Never."

"Laugh at me if you like."

Abbie stretched up and kissed him. "I'm not laughing." But she couldn't stop the giggle that followed.

"Like heck you ain't." His Texas drawl was as pronounced as she'd ever heard it.

✦✦✦✦✦✦✦

As Abbie carried a tray in to Marcy the next morning, she noticed that not only was her sister-in-law's strength returning, but her temper, as well. By the look on Grant's face, he'd just received a tongue-lashing.

"What is it?" Abbie asked, all innocence.

Grant turned and shook his head. "I only suggested that Marcy might be up to joining us at the table this morning."

It was three days shy of a month since she'd birthed, but with the hemorrhage and fever that had followed . . . And Marcy was not one to recover quickly, though the trouble she'd had was reason enough for that. Abbie turned to Marcy with inquiring brows.

But Marcy only sniffed. "He has no idea what I've been through."

Abbie swept forward with the tray and set it on the bedside table. "Of course he hasn't. He's a man." She turned and shooed Grant out with a wave of her hand. "Find Cole and tell him breakfast will be served shortly."

Grant scowled good-naturedly. He couldn't be cross with her for real, not when he saw the effort Abbie was making with his wife for his sake most of all. But he paused at the door and faced Marcy. "I expect tomorrow you'll be up to it."

"Well, I won't. You know I can't face . . ." Marcy flushed and yanked the covers up around her.

When Grant left the room, Abbie sat down on the edge of the bed and took Marcy's hand. It seemed natural now, she'd held it so often these last two weeks. But Marcy looked away, cross and ill tempered.

"What can't you face, Marcy?"

"I'm simply not strong enough. He can't expect me to do something I'm not ready to do."

"Of course not. But the doctor did say you might get up some this week."

Marcy huffed. "What does he know? He missed the whole ordeal—and for the Epperson twins, as though Pauline doesn't have enough babies as it is. Now she has to have them in pairs and make the rest of us suffer?"

Abbie held her tongue. She knew from experience the mood swings giving birth could wreak on a woman. And Marcy's had truly been an ordeal. She startled when Marcy suddenly gripped her hand. "You won't make me get up, will you?"

"No." Abbie soothed her brow. "But I think a little fresh air and maybe a walk, even just down the hall, would do you good."

Marcy closed her eyes and dropped her head back. "I can't. It would be so humiliating...."

"In what way humiliating?"

Again Marcy flushed, and her pale blue eyes sparked with a touch of anger. "Where's Wendel?"

"Zena has him in the nursery. You were sleeping fitfully last night."

"And is it any wonder? I'm stretched as thin as new milk, and now Grant thinks I should thank..." She yanked her hand away.

Ah. Abbie's thoughts caught up to Marcy's. So that was it. "Marcy, I assure you Cole expects no thanks. He only did what had to be done to save you and your child."

All the color left Marcy's cheeks. "How could you! How could you let him in here? Wasn't it enough you nearly killed me? Did you have to make it so I won't ever hold my head up again?"

"Nonsense."

"That's easy for you to say. You..."

"Have no reputation left to worry about?"

Marcy turned to the wall and tears brimmed up in her eyes. "How will I face anyone when word gets out that Cole Jasper..." She made a small gasping sound as though the very words choked her.

Abbie felt the dangerous stirrings. "Well, I doubt Cole's told more than a handful, and of course, Doctor Barrow is discretion itself." It had taken all of two hours for the doctor to relate to nearly the whole town how Abbie had helped in birthing Marcy's last breech baby. "As for the women, I'm certain they would never repeat something ugly about a friend."

Marcy's eyes kindled. "So that's it, is it? You're paying me back for telling them—"

"Telling them what, Marcy?"

"About Cole wanting Monte dead!" She clutched the covers like a shield, her knuckles whitened and stiff.

Abbie counted her breaths, forcing her words to wait. *Dear God, your words, not mine.* "I forgive you for that, Marcy. I hope one day you'll see how wrong you are about Cole, but I hold nothing against you."

Marcy's hands dropped limply to her lap. "Why are you saying that?" Her voice was scarcely more than a whisper.

"Because it's so. And I regret allowing it to provoke me to unkindness before. Please forgive me."

Marcy's jaw hung slack, like a pouch whose string was undone.

"There, now." Abbie pressed her hand. "Eat your breakfast while it's hot. Wendel will be coming any moment demanding his own."

She only wished he *would* demand it. The baby's worst tirades were scarcely more than listless baas. She stood and lifted the tray onto Marcy's lap. "If you need anything, ring." Abbie indicated the bell on the table. Then she left. As usual, she'd had the last word, but this time she hoped it healed rather than injured.

At the base of the stairs, she met Grant and Cole heading for the dining room. Grant stopped and took her arm. "What do you mean by sending me off like an errant schoolboy when you know I'm in the right?"

"Yes, you are right, Grant. Marcy is capable of some exertion now that the fever has broken. In fact, she'd probably be better for it. But emotionally . . ."

"It's not her emotions, but her sensitivities that are smarting."

"Yes, I know. She's mortified Cole saw fit to save her life."

Cole raised his hand. "Now, Abbie . . ."

Abbie halted his protest. "I'm not saying Marcy hasn't grounds for discomfort. But it's her poor opinion of you that keeps her from stomaching your part in her ordeal."

Grant hung his head. "I'm afraid she's right, Cole. I've tried to convince Marcy to express her gratitude . . ."

"That's not necessary."

"Maybe not, but we all know well enough what's due. Even Marcy, if she'd just admit it."

Cole shook his head. "It don't matter. She's gettin' well and that's all."

Abbie took Cole's arm and walked to the table between her two favorite men, outside of Pa. She released them to take the seat Grant held for her. Abbie noticed Birdie was already seated and sent her a smile.

Though she didn't receive the usual belligerent smirk in return, she could hardly describe the expression Birdie did send her way. Extinguished, maybe, like a wind blown out, a shadow faded by the clouds overtaking the sun. Birdie refused to come out of her room except for meals, and Abbie feared she would not come at all if they didn't insist.

She would try again to speak with her, perhaps after breakfast. But all her attempts since bringing Birdie home had been rebuffed by silence. She was truly at a loss and suddenly felt tired herself. Her near sparring with Marcy, her failure with Birdie . . .

Abbie watched Jenny pull Emily Elizabeth's hand from the sweetmeats, then caught Elliot's gaze and her heart brightened. His soothing presence, intuiting her ruffled nerves and sending her his love with a glance—was there ever such a child to tug her heartstrings? If she never bore another, at least she had Elliot, Monte's son.

But when she looked at Cole, she found herself wondering what a child of his would be like. Her folded hands rested on her belly as she lowered her eyes and Cole offered the blessing. She felt truly thankful for each person there at the table. Even Marcy would have been welcome.

She sat straight for Pearl to serve her and wondered where James was. Pearl read the question in her eyes and muttered, "His back so bad this mornin', Mizz Abbie."

"Oh dear. I'll tend to him later."

"Yessum. He sure is poorly."

Abbie lifted her fork to sample the plump buttery grits, but Zena hurried to her side. "I's sorry Mizz Abbie, but Mizz Marcy, she's got so worked up. She's a'cryin' an thrashin' so's to wake the dead."

Abbie laid her napkin beside her plate. "Yes, thank you, Zena. Please excuse me." She stood and hurried out. Had she so upset Marcy yet again? She scrutinized her words, but could think of nothing that would have set her off. *Lord, show me if I failed.*

Pausing outside the door, she heard Marcy's weeping. "Heaven help me," Abbie murmured under her breath and went in.

Marcy's distress was not feigned, and Abbie hurried to her side. "Stop, Marcy. For heaven's sake, you'll make yourself sick again." She removed the tray from the bed and dipped a cloth in the washbowl.

Before she could lay it on Marcy's brow, the sobbing woman covered her face and shook her head violently. "Oh, stop it. I can't bear it. How can you be so cruel?"

Abbie dropped the cloth to the bowl, at a loss of how to answer. She knelt beside the bed, resting her hands on the coverlet. "Tell me how I've hurt you, Marcy, and I'll beg your forgiveness."

"You only say that to hurt me more."

It was on her lips to argue, but Abbie stopped. Was she taking a high ground to show Marcy up? Did she want Marcy's forgiveness, or was she heaping coals on her head by returning kindness for cruelty? Did she want to hurt Marcy for betraying her to the women they both knew, the nasty insinuations, for the insults, for all the years of hurt on both their parts?

Her heart was duplicitous enough for that to be so, but she suddenly wanted it to stop. Sitting back on her heels, she dropped her forehead to the bed. *Dear Lord, let us put past wrongs behind us.*

"Marcy, there have been trespasses on both sides between us. I make no excuse for the things I've said and done, nor for the wrongs you've done me. I only want it to stop now." She raised her face. "I want friendship and peace between us."

Marcy calmed visibly, though tears still streamed from her eyes. She parted her lips, but no sound came. Then she sniffed and swallowed. "Why?"

What was she asking? What lay beneath that query? "Because you're my sister, and . . . and I love you." The warmth that rushed over her was surprising. She did love Marcy. These weeks of praying and caring for her, of nursing and feeding her, of stroking her hair and cooling her flesh . . . It had transformed her own heart.

Marcy sat mute a long moment, then asked, "How can you?"

Abbie smiled. "Oh, it's not so hard."

"Isn't it?"

"No. Not when I stop thinking of all the things that annoy me and see the gentle way you mother Wendel, your concern for Emily Elizabeth, the way your face shines for Grant, and how you spoke of the angels."

Marcy startled. "Was that real? Did I really say that to you, about the wings and . . . and the light?"

"Yes." Abbie nodded.

Marcy sank back into the pillows. "I thought I must have been crazy with fever."

"I don't know what you saw, but I know the fever had left you. In His goodness, the Lord saw fit to answer our prayer and deliver you from your distress."

Marcy faced her with eyes suddenly sharpened. "Will He do the same for Wendel?"

Abbie felt her throat cleave. So Marcy had noticed, too. Somehow the bond between them at this moment would not allow any false comfort. "I don't know. God's ways are above ours. I've known too many griefs to believe everything always comes out as we want."

Marcy closed her eyes. "Has the doctor said anything?"

"No."

She nodded slowly, eyes still closed. "Then maybe he's all right."

Abbie took her hand. "No matter what, he'll have your love and devotion. And ours, as well."

A tear slid through Marcy's lashes. "Will he live?"

Abbie felt her heart stagger and gripped Marcy's hand tightly. "For whatever time God has allowed him." She held Marcy's hand, offering strength and comfort . . . and love. She felt Marcy's fingers quiver, then tighten in hers. *Thank you, Jesus. Your mercy endures forever.*

Abbie went next to James and, crouching next to his bed, clung to that message. Pain had wizened the old Negro overnight, it seemed. She clasped his hand in hers and hushed his protests. "I won't hear it, James. You've been pushing too hard again, and it's time you admit it. There are enough hands around here to handle all the work, and you've earned your rest."

She glanced at the bottle of laudanum Doctor Barrow had left the last time the arthritis had flared up so badly. It was nearly empty, and she guessed James had nipped it in secret, not wanting them to know when he suffered. The dear old man had served her too faithfully.

"Listen to me, James. Monte's father freed you once, and I'm doing it again. This is your home and always will be. But you are no longer to raise a hand to anything but your own needs. It's time you let us serve you."

"No'm, Mizz Abbie." He shook his grizzled head.

"There's no use arguing. You've worked hard every day of your life. Lord knows you've been most diligent. I won't ask any more of you."

His eyes looked sunken and dry as he closed them and slowly nodded. "I jus' sleep a little now. Yessum, I will."

Abbie brushed his hand once again, feeling the fine parchment texture of his skin, the knots and wrinkles testament to his advanced years. She looked upon him with love and compassion, this old man who had come west with Monte and served in dignity and faithfulness even after Monte's death.

Here, too, was someone she loved, someone the Lord had given. She thought of the ways people had come into her life—James and Pearl and Zena and Nora, Sharlyn and Monte, little Jenny and Elliot, and now Cole. Though there had been pain and loss, how blessed she was by them all. Oh yes, Lord. How truly blessed she was.

Seventeen

Elliot crept along with the silent stealth he'd seen in the barn cats, rolling the bottoms of his feet until his toes splayed, then lifting them with a slow, deliberate motion and placing them down again softly. The space around him was filled with shadows and seemed strangely large, as though the ceiling had risen, stretching the walls up taut.

He clung to the rail as he went, feeling it solid and sure beneath his hand. He'd never been downstairs after all the house slept, never seen the rooms draped in night and full of whispering shapes waiting to leap from the corners at him. He almost turned back, but he couldn't. He had to go.

He could have wakened Jenny. She would be brave, but he wanted to go alone. It was as though the baby called to him. Every time he saw the little face and hands, he felt a tug inside as though someone gripped his shirt and pulled. The baby needed him.

He saw the looks on Pearl's and Zena's faces. He heard their clicked tongues and murmurings. He saw his own mama's concern. But when he looked at Baby Wendel it turned his tummy around inside, and he couldn't keep his finger from the soft, velvety skin or his thoughts from the little round mouth and eyes like the sky when the night stars first shine.

There was something different about those baby eyes than any he'd ever seen. A little like Mama's sometimes when she was remembering, and hurting. But he didn't think Wendel was hurting. He was just remembering. Angels?

Elliot turned the corner in the dark, thinking of the tall angel who brought the little carved pony. He didn't mind that Jenny saw it and he didn't. He would have been afraid if he had. And besides, he got the little pony that he loved, even if Cole did carve better.

But now . . . now the angels had brought Wendel. And Wendel was special. Elliot knew it. Jenny had heard James and Pearl talking. Pearl had said bright heavenly angels had brought Wendel, but a dark one would carry him away. They were afraid Wendel was damaged, but Elliot knew that wasn't so. Wendel just remembered the angels.

With his fingertips, Elliot pressed against the door, and it slowly granted him entrance. Uncle Grant and Emily Elizabeth had returned to town, but Aunt Marcy lay in the big bed. He looked closely at her face, almost glowing in the dim light of the lamp. Mama kept the lamp burning low so Aunt Marcy could see to Wendel when he woke in the night.

Elliot swallowed the lump that felt like dry bread in his throat. Aunt Marcy would be angry if he woke the baby. But he didn't want to wake him, only see him, only . . . touch him. Mostly Zena shooed him away. That's why he had to come at night when the baby lay cuddled up in blankets in the cradle.

Elliot almost remembered that cradle. When Mama had pulled it out from the attic, he'd had the strangest feeling. He was glad Wendel was in it now. Maybe it would help him get strong. Wendel needed to get strong, so the dark angel would see he didn't have to take him.

Elliot crouched down beside the cradle where Wendel lay sucking his lips. The motion moved them up and down, up and down with the crease between the bottom lip and his chin going in and out. Asleep, he didn't have that look that made him different. He just looked small and puny.

Maybe the angels had brought him too soon, before he was ready to leave heaven. Maybe that was why Wendel remembered. And that was partly why Elliot needed him now. There was one burning question he had to put to the baby before Wendel forgot. One thing he had to know.

The baby's eyelids fluttered, and Elliot leaned near. With his mouth almost to Wendel's cheek, he whispered, "Do you know my pa?"

He saw his breath moisten the baby's skin, then disappear. Wendel didn't stir. Elliot leaned back on his heels. He hadn't really expected an answer. Babies can't talk. But he had thought maybe Wendel could let him know somehow.

With one finger he petted Wendel's hand. It had a dusting of down like the fuzz along the ridge of his ears and the back of his neck. It was so soft Elliot wanted to touch him all over. But he didn't. That might wake Wendel, and he didn't want anyone to know he was there.

He just wanted to be near the baby. It made a warm spot inside him, and he liked it. It was like Mama's kisses, like Cole's arm around him, like Pearl's low humming when she made something warm and sweet to eat. It was nice. Baby Wendel was nice.

Elliot stretched his arm across the cradle and put his head down. Wendel was warm and cozy. His little breaths barely moved the covers. Elliot's own breaths slowed and lengthened. His eyes grew heavy, then closed.

◆◆◆◆◆◆◆

Marcy woke. Was it Wendel's sounds that had stirred her from her dreams? She leaned forward and peered over the side of the bed. Her heart jumped until she realized the dark head nestled next to her baby's was Elliot's. What on earth?

She shook the sleep from her eyes. Yes, it was Elliot sprawled across the cradle, his arm resting on the blankets that held Wendel secure. The two heads together were a picture of bliss and contentment, deep in slumber and lost in dreams. Did her baby dream?

The ache that had been growing stronger within her awakened. Could Wendel dream? Would he ever dream and think and be like other boys, like Elliot? He was so small, so . . . helpless. Every baby was helpless, but his helplessness seemed endless.

Where was the recognition she had seen in Emily Elizabeth? The way her eyes would follow, her face turn to her mama's voice . . . Wendel showed none of that. He had to be urged to eat and wakened to finish. When he opened his eyes, they were blank, though Doctor Barrow said he was not blind.

She looked at Elliot nestled beside her child. What had induced him to come here in the middle of the night? She felt a pang. Elliot was such a beautiful child. He had the look of his father, except for his eyes, which were all Abbie.

And he was bright, so bright and eager he amazed her with the things he thought and said. Just as Monte had done. Marcy sank into the pillows. Abbie was right. She had been insanely jealous that Montgomery Farrel had eyes only for Abbie. She had tried in vain to capture his heart and felt her defeat bitterly.

And now Abbie had this son, this offspring of that man ... Her eyes trailed to her baby. But she had Grant's son, and for the life of her she could not help but love him better. She would choose Baby Wendel over any other. She would fight for him, die for him. She almost had.

Marcy closed her eyes. She would have, except for Cole Jasper. Cole. Why did she despise him so? He had never harmed her. In fact, their paths had scarcely ever crossed. He, too, had eyes only for Abbie.

Her disdain was based on something more, something inside herself, something so insidious it ate at her without reason. It was who he was, how he was. He carried within himself a confidence, a capability that nothing deterred.

He was the kind of man she should have been, had she been born a boy as her parents so fervently had hoped. He was the kind of man she still wished she could be. And he had shown her up, even in this most feminine act. He had given life to her baby. And life to her.

Her breath became jagged. Why? Why was she deficient even as a woman? Why could she not bear strong, healthy sons? She had Emily. But that was different. Was it? Emily was a girl. *Oh, dear God.* She couldn't be like that. She couldn't disdain her own daughter as she had been disdained.

Marcy tried so hard, tried to atone, gave the child everything. But in her heart, she knew. She was vile, hateful. Yet what was it Abbie had said? The Lord had sent angels to minister to her distress. Why? Why would He care for her when she cared so little for Him?

Yes, she sat beside Grant at the mission church on Sundays. It was her place as his wife. It allowed her to wear her fine gowns and sit proudly beside her prominent husband where all the less fortunate could see her. But she cared little for the Irish priest and the Latin gibberish he mouthed for an hour and a half. And she cared less for God.

He had made her a girl. Marcy felt the scars of half-heard comments and retorts. *If you had borne me a son . . . If Marcy were a boy . . .* And some directed to her face. *How can you be so clumsy? I'd expect that of a boy, but you're only a girl. . . .*

And now her own boy . . . Oh please, let him just be sleepy. Maybe when he grew, maybe . . . She looked again at the two heads lying together. What had drawn Elliot down there in the dark? Wendel? Did Elliot know? Did he see? But would that not repulse and frighten him?

Perhaps it was natural curiosity, just wanting to see. But something in his pose, something protective, tender . . . Elliot loved her son, and Marcy felt the warmth kindle her heart. She hated to disturb them, but it was cold there on the floor with no blankets. Elliot might catch a chill.

She rose from the bed and gently touched his shoulder. He made no response. His sleep was that of the young—deep and routed only with difficulty. She shouldn't lift him, couldn't carry him far if she did. Instead she took one of the covers from her bed and tucked it around him in thick layers.

He sighed and sank down from the cradle, his arm slipping away from Wendel as he nestled to the floor in the wraps of blanket. Marcy smiled. This was something she would tell her son, how his cousin came and slept on the floor by his cradle.

She felt a sudden longing for Emily Elizabeth. She would insist Grant bring her back to stay for however long she remained here. She wanted her daughter close. She wanted her to love Wendel as Elliot did. She wanted her to know she was loved, too.

Marcy climbed back into bed. She was weary, so weary. Amazingly, Abbie hadn't pushed her, hadn't forced her to try more than she was able. Perhaps, perhaps what she said was true. Perhaps they could put the past behind them and be sisters. She blinked in drowsy languor. She would like Abbie for a sister. She . . . truly . . . would. She drew a long, slow breath and let sleep overtake her.

◆◆◆◆◆◆◆

In the tepid afternoon sunshine, Cole looked up from his perch outside the stable where he was repairing a worn horse collar. He watched the approaching horse, its long-legged shadow stretching across the yard, then jumping up the wall beside him and halting there, normal sized. Cole nodded to Sheriff Davis.

The sheriff swung down from his mount and returned the nod. "Fine springtime weather we're havin'."

"Not bad for March." Though the day was indeed clement, Cole was certain the sheriff hadn't come to discuss the weather.

The sheriff didn't disappoint him with chitchat. "Heard about that Indian incident."

Naturally. Now what?

Sheriff Davis rubbed his chin. "It's been some while since we had Indian troubles near town. The Utes aren't known for aggression, and they mostly keep to their place. Truth be known, there aren't many left wandering hereabouts."

Cole gave a slow nod.

"I'd hate to see anything gettin' stirred up. Guess it's lucky for all concerned you happened in when you did."

"I reckon." Cole rubbed the harness leather with his thumb.

The sheriff shifted his weight, no doubt settling in to the point of his visit. "That's the kind of presence of mind I could use."

"What do you mean?"

The sheriff twisted the reins between his fingers. "I'd like to offer you a job."

Cole half grinned. He couldn't help it. "Sheez. I'm bein' offered positions all over that I ain't asked for."

"I know you've been elected chairman of the Stockmen's Association. . . ."

"Vice chair."

"And I'm sure you're busy—"

"Yup. I'd like to oblige you, Sheriff, but I got my hands full with the ranchin' business." Cole shifted the collar to test the strength of the new stitches.

"If I could just count on you in case of an emergency . . ."

"Such as?"

The sheriff dug into his pocket and removed a telegram. "This came this mornin'." He unfolded the paper but recited its information without looking down at the words. "Seems Crete Marlowe held up a bank in Golden, then worked his way down to Denver. There's a deputy marshal on his trail, but a lawman up there sent word to all neighboring towns to keep a watch."

"Marlowe ain't stupid enough to come here. He'd be recognized for sure."

"I'm not so certain of that, and with all the men coming through selling this, that, and the other, I could use another pair of eyes."

Cole started to shake his head, but the sheriff raised his hand.

"Oh, I can deputize someone for that. It's in case things get ugly that I've come to you. His gang killed three men in Golden. One of them the sheriff. Seems to me, with your knowledge of the man . . ."

Cole halted his own refusal midbreath. The sheriff's request was valid. He did know Crete better than anyone else in town. "Well, sir, I don't have time to be keepin' rounds or anything like that, but if it comes to it . . ."

The sheriff reached into his pocket and retrieved a badge. He held it out.

Cole reached for the badge and eyed it in the palm of his hand. "This here's a sheriff's badge."

"That's right." Sheriff Davis tapped his own. "Only if this one's out of commission."

Cole slipped it into his pocket. "You keep your head low. If Crete knows what's good for him, he'll steer clear of Rocky Bluffs. If not, we'll be ready."

"Thank you, Cole." Sheriff Davis held out his hand. "I'll rest easier."

"Keep it under your hat, will you? I don't want folks thinkin' they can come here for all their troubles."

Sheriff Davis grinned broadly. "No, sir. But you're buildin' your own reputation. I wouldn't be surprised to see you governor one day."

Cole shook his head. "Not on your life. I'm as likely to involve myself in politics as an egg to fly."

"Even an egg can fly once it's found its wings." The sheriff tipped his hat and mounted. "Keep your ears open. I might be callin'."

Cole watched him ride away. The sheriff was a good man and not so thick in the head as some made him out to be. He was hiding his aces and none too soon, if Crete had folks running scared. Well, this was one man who wouldn't run.

Turning back, he saw Abbie heading his way and geared himself for her questions. Her blue skirts rustled about her legs like waves on a river and she came forward as inevitably. He set aside the collar and stood.

"Don't let me interrupt you, Cole. I know you're behind in your work."

"Not behind, just well entrenched."

"Was that the sheriff?"

He reached his thumb to her cheek and brushed the dusting of flour from her skin. "Yup."

"Why didn't he come in?"

"Don't know."

"Well, what did he want?" A strand of hair caught between her lips and she brushed it free.

"He thinks I should run for governor."

"What?"

Cole chuckled. "Don't worry. I told him I wasn't hankerin' after political office."

Abbie raised her chin skeptically. "What did he really want?"

"Just keepin' me apprised of somethin'."

"Am I to know what?"

"Nope."

She frowned. "Why is it men keep all their business to themselves?"

Cole cracked a wry grin. "Why is it women think everything is their business?"

Abbie swirled her skirt aside to perch on the upturned log he'd vacated. "I can't think what the sheriff would have to do with you that wouldn't in some wise pertain to me."

He hooked his thumbs in his belt. "Well, I reckon you have a point. He was askin' me to cover his back."

Her brow furrowed. "What do you mean?"

"Seems word got out about our Indian affair, and he thinks that makes me good material to stand in should he be rendered unable."

"Gracious, Cole!" She stood up. "What did you tell him?"

"What do you suppose?" He took her arm. "I sure do hope that flour on your cheek means there's somethin' hot and bubbly in the oven."

"There's a pie, all right, but you won't get a single bite until you give me a straight answer."

Cole reached into his vest pocket. Holding the badge for her to see, he watched her reaction. "It's only a temporary sort of thing and only if it's needed. I don't reckon it will be, so don't fret." That was like telling the wind not to blow.

"Honestly, Cole. Haven't you had enough trouble these last months without putting yourself in the way of it?"

"I'm not intendin' to."

"But you've agreed to."

He tucked her hand into his arm and started toward the house. "But that don't mean it'll happen."

Abbie studied his face with an intent gaze. "There's something you're not telling me."

He dropped his chin, considering his options. In the long run it was usually less painful to come clean with her. He figured it was best this time, as well. "Crete Marlowe appears to be headin' this way."

She stopped and spun. Her eyes danced between his faster than he could follow. He expected an outburst, but it didn't come. Instead, her hand went to her belly and she looked so stricken for a minute it actually pained him.

"Don't worry, Abbie."

"How can you say that? That man almost killed you. He did kill Auralee."

He didn't mention the others the sheriff had told him of. That would only scare her worse.

She went on without urging. "He tried to burn down my house, threatened and terrorized the servants . . ."

"He's a coward and a bully."

Abbie shook her head. "How can you stand there as though a good scolding would take care of things?"

"I'm not buyin' trouble, Abbie. If he shows his face in town, he has less sense than I credit him."

Her eyes ignited. "And what if he shows it here?"

"There's nothin' here for him."

"Nothing but revenge."

"Only a fool goes lookin' for revenge."

The tendons visibly tightened in her neck. Her voice came clipped and cool. "Then why did the sheriff come to you?"

Cole drew a long breath and released it slowly. "I reckon just in case."

◆◆◆◆◆◆◆

As Abbie watched Cole savoring the pie, she couldn't help think what a joy he was to cook for, his taking such unabashed pleasure in her efforts. She wished she could set aside her worry as easily as he appeared to have. But it gnawed at her. Crete Marlowe was a fiend. And he was Cole's enemy.

Would he come to settle up? Or would he steer a wide berth around the man who had stood up to him time and again? One thing was certain: Cole wouldn't back down. If he told the sheriff he'd stand with him, he would.

She glanced at Jenny and Elliot. They had survived the man's attempt to burn them out. Hidden in the wine cellar with Zena, they had escaped the smoke and fumes as Sam and Pearl put out the fire that decimated the parlor and porch. The parlor was still in shambles.

Abbie shook her head free from those thoughts. As Cole said, she shouldn't buy trouble. But looking over to Birdie and Emily Elizabeth, and thinking of Marcy in her room with Wendel, Pearl and Zena and poor ailing James, she was acutely aware of how many depended on her. She dropped her hand to her abdomen. Not to mention the one she had yet to acknowledge.

Eighteen

Vanity. What an insidious thing it was, sneaking in when you least expected. It didn't trouble her often, Abbie allowed, not like some women who were always fretting over their looks, but just now, sitting in front of the mirror, she felt an unhealthy satisfaction with the curves of her face and figure.

With Zena's nimble fingers finished with her hair, Abbie regarded herself. It had been a long time since Zena had transformed her mane into such a semblance of order. Not since Monte's death had she primped so. She felt a different twinge, one she hadn't felt for a small while, but familiar nonetheless.

"Don' you like it, Mizz Abbie?"

"Yes, it's . . . it's fine, Zena. As always." She made the feeling pass.

"You'll wan' them garnet earbobs with yo' burgundy dress."

Abbie nodded, then stopped. "No. I don't know."

Zena spoke over her shoulder. "Them's the perfect finish."

"Yes, but . . ." How could she put into words the sudden feelings that overwhelmed her? She gave Zena an airy smile. "Go ahead now and see who else needs you. I'll finish here."

"Yessum." Zena drew it out uncertainly, her head cocked.

Abbie knew she was questioning her condition. "I'm fine."

"Yessum. You is fine, considerable fine."

Abbie smiled. Zena had been telling her that since the first day she came into the room sloshing water down her skirt. "Thank you, Zena. You work wonders with my hair."

"I has a gift."

"Yes, you do." Abbie laughed.

When the door closed behind Zena, Abbie stood, walked staunchly to the bureau, and reached her hand to the small silver box. It was cold to her touch, and the fire's tarnish that had turned it black conjured too many memories. Did she not want to wear the jewelry because it reminded her of Monte? Or was it to spare Cole even a thought of her former love on this, his special night?

The feeling wasn't definite. Both the earbobs and the bracelet would be lovely with her gown. The elegant style of her hair all swept up would perfectly set off the garnets and pearls dangling from her ears. And the emeralds would contrast with the rich red, and yet . . .

Her fingers slipped from the box. No. This night she would honor Cole without Monte's jewels. She would let her respect and love for him be enough. She looked back over her shoulder to her reflection in the looking glass. At twenty-six, her figure in the dress was nearly as winsome as it had been years ago.

Cole would be pleased with her appearance. He always had been, even when he shouldn't have. But then, can one help loving? She hadn't stopped loving Monte when he married Sharlyn, though she'd tried to hate him. And Cole had never presumed on his feelings for her. It was not the feelings that mattered, but what one did with them.

Would they be married now if Cole had ever once tried to force his suit wrongly? She had known how he felt, but not because he wished it so. She didn't doubt for a moment he tried with all that was in him to keep his love hidden. It was that same disguised honor she had lately come to recognize. Well, tonight it was his turn to receive honor. Who deserved it more?

Abbie turned her back on the silver box. Nothing would detract from her esteeming Cole. She would show him just how much he meant to her, and not wearing Monte's jewelry was only the start. She swept across the room and out the door. It was time to oversee the myriad details of this event.

Though Pearl and Zena had no doubt managed everything she had directed, she nonetheless wanted to see for herself. Reaching the base of the stairs, she glanced down the hall toward the guest rooms. On his morning visit, the doctor had allowed that Marcy was strong enough to sit up in the drawing room with a quilt over her knees for the party.

Now, as Grant led his wife into the drawing room and settled her into the chair by the fire, Abbie felt it like a personal victory. Marcy's smile even held a measure of true warmth as she passed. Abbie sighed. If only she could coax Birdie from her room, as well.

But her efforts there had been nothing if not dismal. The child scarcely ate, refused any but the slightest response to her comments and questions, and adamantly repelled any return to the discussion of Jesus and His love for her. It was as though Birdie had slipped into a crack between light and darkness and could not see past the walls that held her trapped.

Abbie shrugged. Well, she could only keep trying. Her burgundy silk skirts swirled as she swept from the room, though thankfully the size of a bustle these days was scarcely more than a woman's own shape. She had gladly taken in the yards and yards of fabric required to cover the hoops and bustles originally purchased with this gown.

Most of it had been transformed by Zena's nimble needle into flounces and a train down the back, and Abbie did feel extravagant and giddy at being dressed in such finery. Surely Cole would enter into the spirit of it. He used to like a dance as well as any. With a hopeful heart on more than one account, she hurried down the hall and stopped outside Birdie's room. She whispered a prayer for wisdom before tapping the door lightly.

"Sí?"

Abbie went in. Birdie had not donned the elegant blue dress laid out on the bed for her. It was one of the early gowns Monte had purchased, and it had been remade and shortened to fit Birdie's figure. Abbie looked from the dress to Birdie sitting by the window. More often than not, Abbie found her sitting there, staring out. But at what, she did not know.

Abbie walked over and crouched down, heedless of her skirts, in order to be eye level with the girl. "What is it, Birdie? What do you watch out there?"

Birdie's voice came slowly as from a distance. "*Nada.*"

Nothing. Abbie knew too well the hold "nothing" could have over a person. She had dwelt there too long herself.

"Why don't you put on the dress and join us? Wouldn't you like to dance?"

Birdie turned slowly. Her eyes flickered. "Would you have me again take the hand of El Diablo?"

Abbie shrank in spite of herself. Just hearing the name spoken in Birdie's tongue seemed to give shape to the menace. "No. Never. But . . ."

Birdie returned her gaze to the window. "I cursed mi mamá. I hoped for her to die."

Abbie quailed inwardly at the cold manner in which the words were spoken. Birdie was fighting a battle inside, a battle of old thoughts and old wounds rising up to accuse and torment her. "You were a child, hurt and afraid."

"I took the devil's hand and danced. My feet flew, my skirts spun. The blood pumped in my veins and my heart burned, but my soul shriveled up and died." Her breath clouded the cold glass. "Now I have let go, and there is nothing."

Abbie rested a hand on Birdie's knee. "There is Jesus. He loves you."

"*Jesús?*" Birdie slowly shook her head. "He is a dream, forgotten with waking."

"He's real, Birdie. And He wants to show you."

"How?" She turned from the window. "How will He show me?" It was more challenge than question.

"Maybe through us." Abbie tightened her hold on Birdie's knee. "Birdie, Cole and I care for you and love you. We want you to be our daughter." Perhaps she spoke out of turn, but Grant had at last brought the adoption papers for the children, including Birdie, and they had only to be signed.

Birdie searched her face with little or no expression. "Why?"

"I believe the Lord put you in our care. I believe He wants to love you through us. Love you back to life . . . the life He intended for you, which for a time was snatched away. But no more."

Birdie raised her eyes to the ceiling. "I do not know Him."

"But He knows you."

Birdie returned her gaze to the window, and Abbie felt the cloak of nothing once again consume her. "I do not wish to be known."

As though gently but insistently repelled, Abbie's hands slipped from her knee. She could do no more. She stood, paused, then sighed. "Join us if you like, Birdie. You know you're welcome." She walked from the room.

Glancing up the hallway, she caught sight of Cole and stopped. Not only had he donned the black velvet frock coat, pleated white shirt, and gray-and-black-striped trousers she had laid out, his boots were shined, his mustache trimmed, and he looked . . . incredible. She felt her breath come short. How could that happen after knowing him all these years?

"Now, Abbie, if you're gonna gawk, I'm goin' right upstairs to change."

She rushed forward and grasped his hands. "I've filled my eyes and my memory, but my heart just can't get enough."

"Doggone it." He brushed the tear from her eye. "You are the cryin'est woman a man ever knew."

"I'm not crying."

"What, then?"

"Bursting. I'm so excited I'm sure to embarrass myself. I feel like a girl, dizzy and elated. Do you know if I wasn't wearing this dress, I'd run outside and climb to the top of the tallest tree and holler until the echo came back to tell me what I said."

He stood back a step and scrutinized her. "Well, I reckon that sort of excitement is all right as long as you direct it my way and don't be givin' off that shine in your eyes to any other gentleman comin' tonight."

"It's only there because of you. You're . . . oh, Cole, I couldn't bear for anything to happen to you." She bit her lip, sorry to have brought up the sore subject when she had determined this night would be free of all conflict.

But he didn't scold. Instead, he grinned. "Well, lucky for you, I'm too stubborn to allow trouble and circumstance to bear on me in any wise. 'Cept of course the considerable annoyance of this here celluloid collar." He stuck his finger in and tugged. "But I will endure it for the duration of this night's celebration. A man of my mature years should be able to handle that at any rate."

Abbie laughed. "For a man of mature years, you sound incredibly like many a complaining schoolboy."

"Well, given that I never had school to complain in, I reckon it's now or never."

"You look fine, Cole. So fine I hardly know you."

"And that's a sorry statement if ever I heard one. What good is it to a man if his own wife don't know him?"

"When I looked at you just now, you were so handsome I felt my heart jump and my breath stop, as though I were seeing you for the first time. How can that be when I've known you so long?"

"I don't rightly know. I've always been a shockingly handsome man, and I have never taken you for slow."

Laughing, Abbie pressed her palms to his chest. "Dance with me now, Cole."

"What, here?"

"Yes, anywhere."

He took one step back. "Mrs. Jasper, you are a sight too tempting for me to handle just now. If I take you in my arms we might not make it out to our guests at all, and this getup will be totally wasted."

"Not totally. I'll see you."

He cocked his head down, in as near a flustered state as she had ever seen him.

"Goodness, Cole. Can it be you're uncomfortable under a lady's scrutiny?"

"No, ma'am. But I feel a sight silly all duded up like this and—"

Abbie's laughter halted his words. "You look marvelous. It's amazing how nicely a shockingly handsome man can clean up."

"That does it." He started to turn, but she caught his arm.

"You can't go, Cole. I was coming to find you."

"What for?" He glanced past her to Birdie's room.

"Yes, it concerns Birdie. I told her about our decision."

He raised his brows slightly. "What did she say?"

Abbie shook her head. "So far she says little. She's not at all herself."

"Thank God for small favors."

Abbie pinched him. "It's not a joking matter."

"I know it . . . isn't. She just needs some time to figure things out."

Abbie sighed. "Maybe I'm not the one to talk to her. Maybe you . . ."

"Oh no." Cole shook his head. "Anything I'd have to say would only put her off worse. She's got some venom toward me that ain't likely to dissipate on its own."

"Why?"

"She blames me for Auralee."

Abbie shook her head in frustration. "I wish everyone would just let that business lie. Doesn't she know—"

"Sure she does. But she also knows the most fatal thing that can happen to a woman of her profession is to fall in love. Cuz with that comes hopes and dreams and things they can't afford to want. I was a death knell to Auralee before Crete ever pulled his knife. And that's somethin' I'll take with me to the grave."

Cole's expression was one of dismay and remorse. Abbie threw her arms around him. No words of hers would make his untrue. Even the unconditional love and forgiveness of Jesus didn't undo the consequences of wrongs committed.

He closed her in his arms and kissed the crown of her head. "Come on. All the folks you've invited to this folderol will be comin' any minute."

Shaking off the regrets, Cole took Abbie's arm and led her toward the drawing room that she'd done up all fancy with ribbons and bows and paper flowers. The floor shone with a mellow glow that made his feet itch to dance across it. The fiddler had arrived, and his wife warmed up the melodion that stood in the corner of the long majestic room.

The tall windows were draped against the cold night air, and fires burned in fireplaces at opposite ends of the room. Lamps were lit from one end to the next, and the furniture had been arranged to afford the greatest space possible for dancing while leaving clustered seats where folks could jaw.

Abbie had surely come into her own as mistress of the house without losing her spark. She could be as stately or as ornery as she chose. She was a true lady, but not so stiff she broke with a tussle or two. She was everything he'd imagined she'd be and more.

Now if she'd let him be what he was, they could forge a life together of lasting proportions. He looked down the black velvet vest he wore to the gold watch chain to the polished shoes. He swallowed hard. He felt like a peacock strutting around in another man's feathers.

He'd done it to himself, but he had done it to satisfy Abbie. More like head her off at the pass. She'd have set up a howling if he'd come down in anything less, with her all dolled up fine. Not that he didn't appreciate her own efforts. He had as much an eye for a pretty dress as the next man.

Still, he wished he could enjoy it without having to match. It was plumb foolish pretending. At any rate, he could handle a night of it if she'd just keep this birthday foolery to a minimum. He might even enjoy himself. He turned as the hollow knock announced the first guests.

James was laid up, but Cole didn't head for the door. Zena was admitting the guests, and he merely took his place beside Abbie in the hall. Of all the tight fits he'd been in, this squeezed the worst. And it didn't improve when Wes McConnel pumped his hand and wished him happy returns.

He recollected the one time his ma had made a to-do for his seventh birthday. Some of the town kids had come bearing gifts. That gesture had set his pa afire. They didn't need charity. Wasn't he up to seeing for his kin? He'd hollered and thrashed so to scare the living daylights out of them kids, and they'd never come back.

At least the McConnels hadn't brought gifts. The fine tooled saddlebag Abbie had presented to him earlier and the two pictures of himself that Jenny and Elliot had chalked were enough to fill his cup. He'd have been content to leave it at that, though he had to admit he wasn't averse to cutting the rug with Abbie tonight. The rest he'd just have to bear.

Nineteen

Staring through the glass, Birdie watched the long stripes of fiery clouds fade to pinkish lavender, then surrender to the coming night. The sharp edge of mountains below the graying sky looked dull and hazy.

In the same manner, she felt her own life fading. Soon it would be sucked away into darkness. *No.* She had turned from the darkness, rejected it. But she could not find her way. Mrs. Jasper had said she would see it, but she was stumbling as the blind seller of sombreros, who became sport for the boys.

How many times now had Mrs. Jasper spoken to her of Jesús, of His love? How many times had she listened, though her own responses were trapped within, like cats in a drowning sack? The light did not come.

Like the clouds void of color before her, she waited in the shadowland between night and day. She watched one fleeting wisp, perched just over the crown of the great peak, hold its blush. Its delicate pink was the shade of the inside of the great seashell one traveler had held to her ear.

He had told her she could hear the sea inside, but Birdie had known he was merely saying it to distract her, and the whispers of the shell had mocked her. *You are nothing, nothing, nothing . . .*

Now as her eyes clung to the cloud, she heard the whispers again. *You are nothing, nothing, nothing.* Then another thought, bleak and sinister, *"You are mine."* And she knew that voice. Her brow furrowed painfully as she watched the pink lose its warmth. *No . . .*

Her breath tightened as she set her teeth on edge. *No. No more!* Her throat closed painfully on a sob, and with the breath that squeezed through, she whispered "Jesús."

For one moment the thinnest edge of the cloud shone bright as flame, caught on a single ray shining white behind the peak. In three quick breaths it was gone, but Birdie held it in her mind. "Find me, Jesús. Find me."

A rushing peace like scented water filled the room. With it came a warmth inside her, melting away the silence within and filling her with joy. Birdie gasped, trembling, then sank to the ground, conscious of nothing but the presence.

How long she lay there she wasn't sure, but it was no sleep. She felt more awake than ever before, yet still and calm at once. She felt wrapped in love, and clean. Her lips moved, and though no sound came out, she spoke again and again the name that she could not refuse. *Jesús, Jesús, Jesús.*

◆◆◆◆◆◆◆

Abbie breathed in satisfaction. As the night wore on, the drawing room radiated with the magical glow of friendship and celebration. All the people she loved were here to honor the man she cherished. Cole had borne the congratulations and the "Jolly Good Fellow" with wry humor, and she watched him now across the room spinning one of his yarns, so animated and captivating he didn't notice her scrutiny.

Throughout the evening he'd found her with his eyes as they came together and drew apart as in some great dance within the dance. He hadn't been shy about skipping her across the floor, but neither had he been remiss to his guests. She could see well enough the pleasure he was taking in all this "tomfoolery," as he'd called it more than once.

The night was a success, and she approached him now amid the laughter of the young men assembled around him. Cole noticed her at once and held out his open palm. She rested her fingers on its callused surface and stepped close. "We haven't yet danced the Caledonia."

Cole raised his brows as the music started up. "Is that an invitation, Mrs. Jasper?"

The men around him laughed. Pa clapped his back. "See to it, Cole. Abbie's mighty impatient."

Abbie raised her chin and Pa tweaked it. Then Cole took her arm and they joined the dance. Cole was fleet and energetic, though the bullet wound in his thigh gave him a twinge now and then. He'd never admit to it, but she saw it in his face.

It had been a nasty wound, though thankfully it had done little damage to the bone. She could still recall the blood spurting from the artery and her own torn petticoat keeping it at bay. That had been her wedding night. Her first wedding night. A night of supreme joy and agonizing pain.

She trembled. Even then Cole had loved her. He alone had understood her heart. He alone had known her horror at the death she had caused, and he had sought to comfort her. He had known her better than Monte and had given her hope and courage.

Abbie relaxed into the motion of his steps, letting him direct her where he would. He gave her a sideways smile that bespoke his amusement. Let him smile. Her own wasn't far behind. But abruptly his gaze changed and slipped from her to something behind. What could have alerted and disturbed him so?

She turned swiftly and felt her own spirit leap. Birdie stood between the wide open doors in the blue dress laid out for her. Her hair was swept up simply and twisted at the back, and she looked fresh and young and vulnerable.

Suddenly aware of the many other eyes on the girl, Abbie gripped Cole's arm. "Go to her, Cole."

He met her gaze briefly. "And what?"

"Chaperone her in."

He hesitated, sucked in his cheek, then nodded. "All right."

Abbie watched him walk straight, but unhurriedly, over. She watched for the usual change in Birdie's features, the dark sultry look Birdie kept for Cole, but saw instead an awkward shyness. Why? And what had induced her to join them after all?

She saw Cole's head bow slightly as he spoke to her, and Abbie hoped he was not laying down the law in a way that would raise Birdie's ire. A moment later Birdie accepted his outstretched elbow, and he led her into the room. Abbie swept toward them, but before she'd taken three steps Grant caught her arm.

"You have to dance this one with me, little sister. Cole's been a good deal too stingy."

"Oh, Grant, I can't, I . . ." But when she looked back over her shoulder, she saw Cole take Birdie's hand in his and rest his other at her waist. Abbie stared, dismayed. The fact that he danced in a perfectly chaste manner scarcely dulled the jealous twinge in her belly.

She turned back to Grant. "Well, all right."

"That's hardly the best response I've had tonight."

"I'm sorry." Abbie flashed him a rueful smile. "It's just . . ."

" . . . that Cole has a stunning brunette in his arms."

She flushed deeply. Grant knew her too well. Whatever argument she might raise would be worthless. Yet wasn't it foolish to feel as she did?

"Unless I heard wrong, you sent him over."

Abbie stiffened. "Well, yes, but I didn't tell him to dance with her."

"Seems to me that's the best way to head off the stampede. Cole has some experience with that, I suppose."

"What are you talking about?"

"Come on, Abbie. You saw the attention she was getting. Cole is setting the limits, establishing his responsibility for her. You can be sure he'll only turn her loose to someone he trusts, and even then he's set the example for the manner in which she's to be danced."

Grant chuckled before continuing. "Reverend Shields hardly has more space between himself and his partner."

Abbie glanced at the minister dancing with Nora's sister Maggie, then returned her attention to Cole. Grant's words rang true. Was it a fatherly gesture? Was Cole protecting and validating Birdie for all to see?

"You two did ask to have adoption papers made up for her, or have you forgotten?"

"Of course I haven't. But . . ."

"Then stop dragging your feet and put some spring in your step. You're making me look clumsy."

She looked once more at her husband and would-be daughter.

Something in Birdie's expression caught her heart again, and she responded powerfully. It wasn't jealousy this time, but wonder. Birdie looked . . . new, vibrant . . .

Abbie couldn't take it any longer. She broke Grant's hold and left him standing alone. Cole nearly swung Birdie directly into her but caught the girl before they collided.

"Birdie." Abbie clasped the hands Cole had dutifully released. "I'm so glad you've come out. You look lovely."

Birdie's eyes shone. "I am."

Abbie raised her brows in surprise. Was this some game Birdie was playing? But her heart said no. Something had happened to lift Birdie's gloom.

Cole lowered his head and spoke softly. "Remember—it's your choice, Birdie. You can say no." With a quick wink at Abbie, he left them.

"I do not want to dance." Birdie looked anxiously over her shoulder.

Abbie followed Birdie's nervous gaze and saw Will and several others making their way over directly. "Then come and talk." Abbie hooked their arms together and drew her to the alcove behind the melodion. She then caught Birdie by both arms and held her squarely. "Something's happened."

"Sí." Bright tears sparkled in Birdie's eyes. "I have met Jesús. And it was as you said."

"Oh, Birdie!" Abbie felt her heart leap again. This was more than she had expected, but no more than she'd hoped and prayed for.

Birdie's face was serene and beautiful. "I do not dance with Diablo. It was a lie."

"Yes. A terrible lie."

A shade of sorrow colored Birdie's joy. "But it has left wounds." Her gaze flicked to the room.

Abbie nodded gently. "They will heal, in time."

"Maybe."

"Trust Him."

"Sí. But I do not wish to dance."

"And you don't have to." Abbie looked quickly around. She didn't want to send Birdie back to her room. She had made this step, had returned to the living. Now she needed to stay free, yet protected. She saw Mama on the settee with Mary McConnel. Yes. If anyone could fend off the young bucks, they could.

Though her heart was singing with joy at Birdie's revelation, she understood the girl's feelings, her uncertainty, her insecurity. Did she know how to behave with propriety? Did she have even an inkling of the ways of decent society? And were her scars too deep to allow any desire to learn? They would deal with that, but tonight was not the time. For tonight she need only watch from a position of safety.

"Come with me, Birdie. Mama will see that no one bothers you." She drew Birdie from the alcove to the place where Mama sat. "May Birdie join you? She doesn't wish to dance."

She gave Mama a telling look, and the two women made room for the girl. Though Mary McConnel did not, Mama knew Birdie's story as far as Abbie had been able to share it. And Mama was wise. She would watch over the child as even the angels had.

Abbie turned and found Cole at her side. He bent to murmur low in her ear. "Do you think it's wise to have her stay? Will's likely to bust his buttons."

"He'll have to bust them, then. Birdie's not dancing."

Cole hung his head a moment, considering, then glanced once at Birdie, shielded on both sides with matrons. "You reckon she's on the level?"

Abbie smiled. "I believe she's more level than you know. She's given her heart to Jesus."

His brows came together in a frown. "Right here and now?"

"Is it any less believable here than on a dusty trail beside the Rio Grande?"

"I had the aid and urging of a man of God."

Abbie closed his hands in hers. "Birdie had God himself." She watched Cole take that in, then slowly nod.

"Well, if anyone deserves divine intervention, I reckon it's that one."

Abbie felt the warmth and concern in his voice like a summer breeze. "If God stands for her, who can be against?"

"You got a point there."

♦♦♦♦♦♦♦

"Mrs. Jasper?"

Abbie turned at the soft voice outside her door. "Come in, Birdie." She wrapped herself in a dressing gown, having removed the burgundy silk and laid it across the bed to be brushed and hung.

"I am sorry to disturb you."

"Nonsense."

Birdie stood awkwardly, her hands clenched together in a double fist.

"What is it, Birdie?"

"I fear to tell you, Mrs. Jasper."

Abbie rested her hand on Birdie's shoulder. "First off, call me Abbie. And second, whatever it is will be better out in the open."

Birdie slowly unclenched her hands and raised one, palm upward. In it Abbie saw her emerald bracelet. She raised quizzical brows, not comprehending.

"I took it when I ran away. I thought to use it for my escape."

Abbie fought a surge of indignation as Birdie faltered. How could the girl have stolen from her? And something so precious? Not that Birdie could know the bracelet had been a gift from Monte, yet still Abbie felt violated. She had opened her home, risked her life for this girl. . . .

"Ever since you brought me home, I had thought to replace it secretly, as I had taken it. But I could not let it go. I did not wish to steal from you, but I thought it would help me gain my freedom if . . ." Her throat worked. "I could not see my way."

Again her anger flared, and Abbie prayed, *Your heart, Lord. Let me see her as you do*. She released a slow breath. "Why bring it to me now? Why not replace it without my knowing?"

Birdie dropped her eyes. "I wronged you. I could not make it right without . . ." Her voice broke and a single tear caught on the lower lashes of her eye.

The bracelet glittered in her hand. Staring at it, Abbie softened. What a temptation it must have been for Birdie. Not only the value of the emeralds, but what their price could mean in her life. Her heart rushed with sudden love and understanding.

She reached out and closed Birdie's fingers around the bracelet. "You may keep it."

Birdie looked up, stunned. "No."

"It's my gift."

Birdie shook her head, more tears falling down her cheeks. "You are kind, but ... I cannot keep it. It would always remind me of ... what I was."

Abbie met her eyes, their brown awash with tears, the lashes standing out in spears. She saw there the urgency and understood. Slowly she extended her hand to receive the bracelet Birdie held.

"Thank you for returning it. It was a gift from my first husband. It is dear to me more for that than for its worth."

Birdie sniffed and nodded. "I am sorry."

"I'm not. I'm thankful you trust me now."

Birdie smiled through her tears. "It is Jesús."

Abbie returned the smile. "Yes."

Twenty

The next day dawned balmy after the evening's chinook winds banished the cold to other regions. Abbie knew better than to expect it to stay for long, but it was such a whisper of the promise of spring, she had to be out, alone and one with the land, the sky, and the wild things. As she rode beneath the blushing sky, she lifted up the praises that filled her heart, the hope she felt for Birdie, the love she felt for Cole, the expectant joy that would not be suppressed for the child growing within her.

The queasy stomach and light head told her better than Doctor Barrow that her calculations were correct. When they signed the papers today knitting together their hodgepodge family, she would tell Cole of the other. She pressed her hand to her belly. Her child and Cole's, the result of their union. Given swiftly amid their turmoil, this child fulfilled all the promise of joy her heart could hold.

Oh Father, how good you are, how everlasting your promises. My heart sings your praises for you alone are worthy. Abbie closed her eyes to the warmth of the sun burning away the morning haze. *For I will repay the years of the locust, sayeth the Lord.* And how truly He was doing just that.

From his perch on Sirocco, Cole watched Abbie riding alone on the barren brown plain. His stallion's hooves made a dull thud on the dry bristly sod, but he held the animal in check. He wasn't aiming to get close enough to spoil Abbie's privacy, but he wasn't about to let her wander the range alone, not with Crete Marlowe within the state borders and seemingly working his way south.

Though he'd made light of Sheriff Davis's concerns to Abbie, Cole didn't take them lightly himself. He knew well enough the power of a grudge, and Crete wasn't one to let it go lightly. Like Cole's own pa, Crete believed in getting even. The fire he'd set to Abbie's place was evidence enough of that.

Cole turned back over his shoulder and scanned the new porch on the fine house sitting like a picture way down beyond the piece of open land. He hadn't yet repaired the damaged parlor, its windows blackened and grim, though it was on his list. Frankly, he was stretched a mite thin. As it was, he'd have to take on additional hands come spring.

He turned back to see Abbie riding the mare at an easy lope toward him. He crossed his wrists on the saddle horn and waited, enjoying the current sight as much as anticipating her arrival. Her hair was none too tidy, especially compared to its taming the night before. Truth be told, he liked it better with the wind's handling.

"To what do I owe this scrutiny?" The breeze had colored her cheeks, and a strand of hair caught in her lips until she dragged it away.

"Just enjoyin' the view."

She brought Zephyr in beside him, rear to fore. "Am I needed?"

He gave her a wry smile. "Have you ever questioned that?"

"I mean, is there some urgent business that brings you out after me instead of to your chores?"

"No urgent business, Abbie." Except the urgency of keeping her safe. "But I think if you take off before daylight you ought to let me know."

"You were washing. And I didn't intend to go so far. Once I was out, I'm afraid I let the wind carry me."

He grinned. How that had troubled Mr. Farrel, her propensity to wander. Farrel had ordered more than once for a watch to be kept on her. All through the trouble with Captain Jake it had been wise, but Cole had often wondered if it just didn't sit right with the aristocrat to have such an untamed wife.

If it weren't for Crete, Cole would let her ride to her heart's content. He knew what she was capable of. Sure, she found her share of trouble, but trying to corral her was like harnessing the sun, a good sight more trouble than it was worth. Besides, he loved that part of her.

"I imagine Pearl's waiting breakfast and—"

"Is it so late?"

"Have a gander at the sun's position, Abbie. You know as well as I do how to read it."

She shielded her eyes and blinked at the brightened sky. "I guess I wasn't thinking."

"What, then?"

"Praying. Counting my blessings."

He hunched over the saddle horn, resting his forearms. "Well, I won't dissuade you from that. But I know two of them blessings that'll set up a howl if breakfast ai . . . isn't there when they come lookin'."

Abbie laughed. "Especially Elliot. He must have grown two sizes overnight. I looked in on him before I left, and his legs looked half as long as yours."

Cole looked down at his leg, bent at the knee and resting in the stirrup. "Maybe not quite, but it won't be long. His pa was no midget and—" He looked up quickly to see if his words had brought that flicker of pain to her eyes.

She leaned forward in the saddle. "And neither am I."

Seeing no sign of grief, he relaxed and surveyed her. "Now, that all depends on yer perspective. In my mind you're a mite small to be talkin' so big."

"Oh yeah?"

"Yeah."

Her face took on the taunting look he knew only too well. "I don't believe stature is measured in inches alone."

"Well, I ain't done much arithmetic, but that was my understanding, ma'am."

"Stature is much more than size, Mr. Jasper."

"That so?"

"Yes, it is. Stature involves spirit and cunning and ability."

He rubbed his jaw with the back of his hand to hide the grin.

"Then I reckon you're near giant proportions. Throw in sass and sparkle, and I'd be knee high to you."

She pouted. "I know a twisted compliment when I hear one, Cole Jasper."

"I meant every word of it."

"I'm sure you did." She raised her chin. "Well, it just might please you to know there's more to me than you suspect."

"That right . . ." He drawled it intentionally.

"Yes, it is. In fact, you might say I'm twice the person you are." Her hand went to her middle and rested there oddly.

He wasn't sure where she was going with this. "I have never doubted your prowess. Nor . . ." He paused when she reached for his hand and brought it to her belly.

"You won't feel anything yet, but soon."

"Abbie, what are you goin' on about?" Cole leaned over close enough to circle her with his other arm.

"Only your coming son or daughter."

He jolted up in the saddle and eyed her sternly. Was she playing him some trick?

"Of course a great big strong man like you isn't concerned with a small, insignificant woman and a tiny unseen—"

"Just hold it right there." Cole gripped her shoulders. "Are you tellin' me in this short a time I have you with child?"

"I believe that to be the case."

He threw back his head and let out a whoop. "Now how's that for stature, Mrs. Jasper?"

She huffed. "Leave it to you to take all the credit."

He folded her into his arms, careful to keep hold of Sirocco, should their tight quarters concern the horses. "I've never known of a man lovin' a woman without that love bein' inspired by his woman."

"No?"

"No, ma'am."

"Then do you suppose together we've done something wonderful?"

He grinned more broadly than he could help. "I don't reckon I could put it any better myself."

She turned up her face, and he kissed her with all the ardor and respect due her stature. There was nothing that could compare to the woman he loved carrying his child inside. But he had a sudden thought and paused in his affections. "Abbie, I wonder if we shouldn't keep this to ourselves a bit."

"What do you mean?"

"Well, with the signin' of the papers and tellin' the kids of our intentions an' all, maybe we ought not to mention this new one comin'." She searched his face, and he headed off her doubts. "Sorta let them have their day in the sun, so to speak, without stealin' the thunder."

Abbie dropped her head to his neck. "How is it you know so much?"

"It ain't so much knowin' as . . . well, supposin', I guess. I know what it's like not to feel wanted, to be outshined in any number of ways. I don't want Jenny, or Elliot even, feelin' like they're second best to this one we've made between us."

She shook her head, but he laid a finger to the argument on her lips. "I'm not sayin' that's how it is, just how it might seem, especially to one who hasn't had a real ma or pa for too long. In case you haven't noticed, Jenny's a mite possessive of me."

"Really?" She gave him doe's eyes that belied the innocence in her question.

"Really."

"How *do* you bear it, all these ladies—"

"Don't say it."

She laughed. "I won't, then. And you're right about not mentioning the baby to the rest. I should have thought of that myself. I don't know why I didn't."

He knew. It was because she'd been a cherished child from a solid family with no inkling what it was like to die inside for want of a parent's love. And that was also why she didn't understand Jenny's need. But he did. And once the papers were signed he would do his utmost to be the best pa to those children that he could. *And Lord in heaven, a child of my own . . .*

♦♦♦♦♦♦♦

Abbie listened while Cole explained in his own words why they were adopting the children as their own. She had decided it would be best coming from him, since he was the one with no natural connection to any of them. Now she gauged the reactions, looking from face to face.

Birdie had told her simply, "I cannot think of you as mi mamá, nor Cole as mi papá. But I will submit to Cole's guardianship. And I will accept your friendship, which is worth more to me now than family." And Abbie had hugged her with all the warmth she could.

Jenny looked at Cole now as though nothing else existed, and Abbie wondered for a moment if such devotion was healthy. But then, Jenny had never had much male attention until Cole came into her life. Would it be unhealthy if he were her natural pa?

Abbie knew she had to stop thinking of them in any other terms. From now on they were a family. She looked at Elliot, his small face moving from Cole's to hers and back. She caught his eye and smiled. He beamed back a smile, but she wondered how much of this he understood.

To him, Cole was a hero, bigger than life and a lot more fun. How would it be when Cole disciplined him and took on his training, as he no doubt would? How would it be to think of Elliot as any but Monte's child? But no. He was no less Monte's son, even though he now bore Cole's name.

Grant laid the papers on the desk. "I just need a signature from you both."

Cole made his name, then handed the pen to her. She signed below his manuscript letters with her flowing script.

Grant gathered up the papers. "I'll file these and see that everything's in order."

Cole clasped Grant's outstretched hand. "What do I owe you?"

"This is family, Cole."

"It's your livelihood."

Grant cocked his head to the side, his brown eyes both serious and determined. "Well, as far as I'm concerned, I'm deeper in your debt than I can ever dig out."

"Nonsense."

"No, Mr. Jasper, it isn't."

Abbie turned in as much surprise as Cole to Marcy, who spoke as she entered the room with Wendel in her arms and Emily Elizabeth at her skirt. "And my gratitude is overdue."

"Marcy, you shouldn't be walking alone." Abbie hurried to her side.

"I'm well enough." But she allowed Abbie to ease her into the brass-studded leather chair across from the desk.

Cole looked uncomfortable under her gaze.

Marcy tucked the edge of the cover down away from Wendel's face. "The fact is, I've hidden behind my false modesty too long and . . . it's time I thanked you in person for saving my life and bringing my son into the world. Whatever Grant or I can do to repay you—"

"That ain't necessary."

Elliot jumped to his feet. "Pa said ain't."

"It doesn't matter." Jenny stood and walked to him.

Cole rested his hand on her head and shrugged toward Grant. "Let's just call it all square and have some grub."

Jenny looked up at him with shining eyes. "I'm as starved for grub as a polecat that ain't seen food in a month of Sundays."

Abbie bit back her correction. Jenny was incorrigible, but she had a pa now to take her on. Though, if his amused smirk was any indication, there was work to be done on all fronts.

Cole bent slightly at the waist. "And my belly button's sayin' howdy to my backbone."

"And my belly's growlin' like a griz in springtime." Jenny rubbed her hand over her pinafore.

Elliot jumped to them in awkward one-footed leaps. "I'm hungry, too."

"Run and wash." Cole tousled his head, and the two of them raced for the door.

With a laugh Grant gathered up the papers. "We have impinged on your hospitality long enough. I'll be taking my family home now and letting you get used to yours." He nodded toward Cole with that.

Cole held the chair for Marcy to rise. "I don't reckon it'll take too much adjustin'."

Grant smiled. "You wait." He gave Marcy his arm. "You just wait."

Abbie caught Grant's elbow. "You're not leaving immediately?"

"I've brought the wagon out. We'll just gather our things. Come on, Emily Elizabeth."

Though she never thought she'd see the day when she was sorry to have Marcy go, Abbie felt it now. Then she glanced at Birdie and realized she still had plenty to do. She brushed Marcy's sleeve. "I'll come see you in a day or so."

"Thank you. For everything." Marcy held her eyes a moment with a poignant searching.

Abbie kissed her cheek and watched her go. Who would have thought? Who would ever have thought?

"Abbie?"

She turned to Birdie, hiding the unfamiliarity she felt with the address, though she had told Birdie to refer to her so. "Yes, Birdie."

"I, too, want to thank you."

"You're welcome. Cole and I are so happy you agreed to stay with us." She looked to Cole for confirmation.

He nodded. "That's right. I reckon it might take some gettin' used to after all, but we got us a start now."

"A start." Birdie nodded back, but her eyes shaded. She half smiled. "I'll wash for dinner now."

After Birdie left, Abbie released a hard breath and leaned into Cole. "I certainly hope you're up to all this. Because I am not riding herd on this bunch alone."

"Well, I've bossed a trail or two."

"Then you might remember that when a certain seven-year-old heifer calf needs a crack of the whip."

He only laughed. "That certain heifer calf has a good deal of her ma in her. And I don't mean her natural ma, either."

✦✦✦✦✦✦✦

"Mrs. Jasper?"

Abbie turned from the clothesline where she was checking the linens Zena had hung. "Yes, Will?"

He circled his hat in his hands, and she knew instantly what subject he wanted to broach. "Well, ma'am, I was wondering . . . that is, I thought maybe . . . Could I have your permission to walk with Birdie sometime?"

Abbie let her hands fall to her sides. She supposed it was natural Will would come to her. After all, they were the ones who had sprung Birdie free from her old life. He probably felt she would help him as he'd helped her. But she knew Birdie's feelings were too fragile to even consider a romance, however gentle Will might prove.

The difficulty would be convincing Will. She could only try. "As for permission, Will, you'd need to see Cole for that. But as you've come to me, I'll ask you a favor."

"What favor?"

"I want you to wait."

He sniffed and shifted his weight to his left foot, rubbing the side of one hand against the seam of his jeans.

"She's not ready to consider a relationship, not even a friendship with a man. Especially a man who can hardly keep his affection from showing in his face." Abbie saw him color, the red rushing up the sides of his neck. "She needs time, Will."

He nodded slowly at that, then turned to look across the clothesline, then back. "Okay." He replaced the hat on his head. "But if you think there's a chance, I mean if she's ever . . . ready . . ."

"I can't think of anyone I'd sooner have her keep time with."

He flushed again. "Thank you, ma'am."

Abbie brushed the sheet with her hand. When she turned, Will was ambling back toward the bunkhouse. She couldn't help but think of him as the somewhat sullen, unimpressive stableboy he used to be. She smiled. One never knew what lay beneath the surface, just waiting to be inspired.

Twenty-One

When the smoke cleared from the blasting of his gun, Crete eyed the old man and woman who kept the miserable inn at the crossroads. Probably they wouldn't have posed a threat—not much gumption in either one, to his mind. But when the old man started making remarks on his looking familiar, he'd had to see that their mouths were closed for good.

In a little way station like this, someone like that might tell the next fella, who'd tell the next, and before you knew it, the law was close on your hide and you were running for the border. The old woman? Well, she was a casualty on account of her taking it personal when he shot her husband.

"Crete!" Finn burst inside.

Crete turned slowly, holstering his gun.

Finn looked from one body to the other. "What happened?"

"They got nosy."

"There's a rider coming. I think he heard the shots."

"How far?"

"Just up the bend."

Crete turned to Washington. "Take your rifle to the roof. Soon as you got a clear shot . . ."

Washington nodded, turning immediately for the door. Crete jabbed a finger at Finn. "Clean out the larder. Take anything that ain't nailed down."

◆◆◆◆◆◆◆

In the mellow lamplight of Monte's library, amid the book-lined

197

walls, Abbie sat on the carpet with her small son nestled in her lap while somewhere outside Cole and Jenny savored the brisk April evening. Abbie could only hope Cole wasn't filling Jenny's head with tales to make her hair rise or adventures better suited to a boy twice her size.

For a moment, Abbie had a keen understanding of how her own mama must have felt watching her run about wild with Blake Mc-Connel for a companion. While she still held that a woman had a right to know things like woodcraft and self-protection, even shooting and tracking, she knew Jenny could easily get carried away. And she knew full well how easily Cole's better judgment crumpled under Jenny's wiles.

Abbie smiled in spite of herself and shook her head. Carefully she moved the pencil tightly gripped in Elliot's hand. Together they formed the letter *e*, drawing the lines slowly to keep them straight and even.

Perhaps it was early for penmanship. But though his hands were small, his muscles young, and his control shaky, Elliot was eager to do whatever Jenny could. And his mind was quick and curious. With his lip caught between his tiny pearly teeth, Elliot smiled up at her. "Now let me try it myself."

Abbie placed his hand beside their model, then released the pencil. Slowly he drew it down as she had shown him. The line wobbled, but he tucked his tongue to the side of his lip and stopped the pencil just short of the edge. She saw his uncertainty. "Come out from the top."

"I know, Mama."

She smiled to herself. He was not precocious in the same way as Jenny, but he certainly believed in his abilities. She placed his hand down a bit to start the middle line, then looked up abruptly from the slate as Zena hustled to her side. The look of the woman's face sent fear to her soul. "What is it?"

"It's James, Mizz Abbie. Pearl says come quick iffen you can."

Her heart plummeted. She had looked in on him earlier, but he'd been asleep. Had the pain increased? Did he need the doctor? She tried not to jump ahead of herself as she set Elliot on the floor with a quick reassuring pat, then swept swiftly out with Zena on her heels.

The room that housed the ailing man was as comfortable as the others. There were no slave huts, nor even servants' quarters. Monte had allowed no discomfort for the faithful pair who had served him since his youth. They had not even been expected to sleep upstairs these last years with James' condition worsening, but were given one of the lower guest rooms.

The bed for the old man was deep, the covers warm. But the hand she grasped was chilled and feeble. Abbie's fear quickened. Why had they not called for her sooner? Pearl sat hunched, eyes closed, in a ladderback chair beside the bed, rocking slowly side to side and humming a low, soulful tune. Abbie had never seen her so. She always bustled about, working, bossing, doing something. Now she seemed ... dazed.

"Pearl?"

Pearl opened her eyes but kept humming and rocking.

Abbie dropped to her knees beside the bed, clutching James' hand to her cheek. "What is it, James? Are you in pain?"

His eyes fluttered weakly, then partly opened. "No pain ... now ... Mizz Abbie." His voice came slowly, the intermittent breaths like dusty wind from his throat. "The chariot's ... a'comin' ... for to carry ... me ... home."

Abbie noted the gray ring around the brown of his eyes, the yellow hue of the whites. She looked for some sign of pain or fear, but saw neither. He seemed removed already from the husk of flesh that had bent and pained him these last years. Pearl hummed.

Abbie swallowed the ache that filled her throat. She had hoped this was only another episode that would ease with rest and give him back his strength. But looking at him now, there was no denying the truth.

Pearl sang low, her words hardly discernible. *"I looked over Jordan and what did I see, comin' for to carry me home ... A band of angels comin' after me, comin' for to carry me home ..."*

Angels. Abbie pictured them as she felt the song vibrating inside her, the longing in Pearl's voice for the joys of heaven, the release from earthly bonds. She knew the song was doing more for James than anything she could offer. She had tried to summon Doctor Barrow for him two days ago, but Pearl had refused. "Leave him be, Mizz Abbie. He don' want no fuss."

Now Abbie felt the barren helplessness of time slipping away. What more could she have done? What could the doctor have done? Where was Cole? He should be here, but then, maybe not. Though Pearl had warmed to Cole, James had kept his distance. Not from spite, but out of faithfulness to the previous master he had loved.

Did James know how much Monte had thought of him? Did he remember the esteem Monte had afforded his old servant, even against his upbringing? No, not entirely against. Monte's father had been an honorable master, not like Kendal and those of his ilk. Monte had never viewed his servants as objects, never treated them without respect.

Yet James had kept his place, not overstepping his bounds, obeying a law of propriety scarcely enforced. He had loved his young master. As they all had. *Oh, James, you'll be with him soon.* She stroked the wizened hand, blotched and gnarled, the veins like windblown spider webs bursting across its surface.

"There is a balm in Gilead ... to make the wounded whole ..."

Abbie looked across the bed to Pearl. As she sang she seemed transported to another place. Why had she called for Abbie? She felt deeply honored, yet somehow unworthy to share the last moments James had on this earth. These two had seen so much, borne so much, so many things she would never understand. Yet they had called her in.

She returned her gaze to James, lying still now, a slight but perceptible smile on his lips. Her heart beat with love for him and sadness ... yet the sadness was not so great she couldn't bear it. This was as it should be. A long, valiant life, an honorable life, waning even as the winter surrendered to spring. James would have his spring sooner than they.

On her knees beside him, Abbie kept silent vigil. Pearl's songs wove in and through her thoughts, leading her from peace to mourning to hope and back again. Sometimes Zena joined her voice to her aunt's. Abbie was content to lift her thoughts in silence to the Lord.

He knew. He saw. He awaited a faithful servant, a humble servant. A man who had once been treated as less than a man. A person who might have been sold as a thing. What a great wrong had been done to his people! But the Lord saw. He knew. And He waited to welcome James with a crown of glory.

"*Oh brothers, you ought t'have been there. Yes, my Lord. A sitting in the Kingdom to hear Jordan roll...*" Zena joined Pearl in a harmony. "*Roll, Jordan, roll. Roll, Jordan, roll. I want to go to heaven when I die ... To hear Jordan roll.*"

Abbie closed her eyes, remembering the waters of the Rio Grande as they had pulled and tugged her with an irrepressible force. Even so, death tugged now at James. She felt the slightest tremor in his fingers as he drew his last rattling breath and slipped into silence.

At last she allowed the tears, dropped her head to the quilt, and stroked the dark papery skin of his hand. "Be at peace, James, free of suffering." Her breath caught jaggedly. "Our Father, who art..."

Pearl joined her voice and Zena, too, though Pearl's words were choked with wails of sorrow. Though she hadn't before, Pearl now looked old and weary of life's trials. How much had she seen of its ugliness? But surely also its goodness. She must know how Abbie loved her. What would she have done without Pearl and James through the dark times?

Abbie went to her, took the great, thick shoulders in her arms and held her while the old woman wept. The heartrending sobs freed her own tears once again, and they held each other against the pain. Zena, too, wept, and Abbie clasped her hand, drawing her in. She placed Zena in Pearl's embrace and stepped back.

She had rejoiced at the new life within her. Now Abbie grieved the loss of this old one. No. Not loss. Only passed beyond to the great thanksgiving with a brush of God's hand, laying to rest the old and awakening the new.

Abbie raised her face and murmured, "The Lord giveth and the Lord taketh away. Blessed be the name of the Lord."

Roll, Jordan, roll. Roll, Jordan, roll...

◆◆◆◆◆◆◆

Abbie and Pearl had James laid out with candles at his head and a clean white shift covering his old bones when Cole and Jenny came in. Abbie hustled Jenny upstairs with Elliot as Zena and Pearl, and now Cole, held vigil.

"Is James very tired, Mama?" Elliot slipped his hand into hers, his sensitive nature probing her grief.

Abbie stooped down and gathered him into her arms. "No, my darling. James has gone to heaven to be with Jesus."

"Did the angels come for him?"

She drew a tentative breath. "I think so, Elliot. Someone did. He left very peacefully." She saw Jenny's throat move, but the child didn't speak. Abbie released her son and drew Jenny close. "What is it, Jenny?"

"Nothing."

Abbie stroked Jenny's hair. How many people had she lost already? Her mama and pa, Uncle Monte, and now James. And Abbie knew James wasn't the least of them. He had dandled her more often than her own father, Kendal, had. James had often secreted peppermints in his pockets for her to root out, all the while pretending he knew nothing of their presence and acting so surprised when she found them there.

"He's in heaven, Jenny."

The skin between her eyebrows creased and her nostrils flared with the effort, but still she didn't speak.

"Run and change, Elliot. I'll be in shortly." Abbie sent him off, more concerned now with Jenny than with Elliot's questions.

She felt the stiffness in Jenny's shoulders when she tried to hold her. Why wouldn't the child allow her comfort? "I know you loved him, dear. But he was old, so old that each day was more difficult than the last. You wouldn't want him to stay here in pain, would you?"

Jenny pulled away, the tendons in her jaw tense and tight.

"Think, Jenny. He's in heaven with . . ."

"I know. But I don't like God and I never will." She pronounced every word as though it were ice in her mouth, then turned deliberately and stalked to her room.

Abbie sat back on her heels, dismayed by her inability to reach the child. The words concerned her less than the hard anger behind them. She wanted to follow Jenny, to make her understand, but how? Instead, she went down to Cole.

He looked weary from the day's work. She could see it in his stance. Somehow the ten years between them seemed more just now than usual. "I'll dig the grave for him tomorrow. The ground's softening up some."

She nodded. It had been a dry winter without even the March snows thus far.

"I'm sorry, Abbie. I know he meant a lot to you."

"He's better off." She sighed. "But I'll miss him." She knew the ache in her heart was only the beginning. One thing she had learned, though: Grief had to happen. Holding it back only made it worse. She hurt again for Jenny. But what could she do?

Cole led her up the stairs, his arm solid beneath hers. Then he held her until she slept. Somewhere in the night, she woke to find him gone. But Jenny's sobs and Cole's voice, low and soothing, came through the night's stillness.

✦✦✦✦✦✦✦

They laid James in the family plot atop the hill where the graves for Sharlyn and Kendal and Monte lay. Abbie hated to see the grave-yard fill, the stones rising up from the ground like an unnatural growth. The angel above Sharlyn's grave smiled her sweet, benign smile and beckoned with delicate fingers.

The gray marble of Kendal's stone and the black marble of Monte's stood like monoliths amid the new spring growth of pale green grasses. The ponderosas that overshadowed the graves waved gently in the breeze. Pearl rocked as she stood with Zena beside the fresh earth mounded up over the coffin purchased by Cole that morning.

Abbie rested a hand on Jenny's shoulder and one on Elliot's head as Reverend Winthrop Shields read the Twenty-third Psalm, James' fa-vorite piece of Scripture. With his head bowed low, Cole held his hat to his chest, as did the ranch hands gathered around him. Mama and Pa and Tucker had come, though who had sent for them, Abbie didn't know.

Their little adopted orphan, Tucker, stood solemnly beside Pa, though his eyes took in everything around him, no detail too small. Maybe he would become the journalist Pa hoped he would. Tucker gave her a small smile when he hugged her, then left with Pa after the ceremony.

Mama stayed for the day, overseeing the thin stream of friends and neighbors who brought baked goods or stews that could be warmed without fuss. Only the close friends came, those who would understand the place that James had held in their hearts. Winthrop Shields stayed several hours comforting Pearl and Zena, his words rich with the promises of Scripture.

Abbie had never urged the servants to switch allegiance from their Methodist roots, and Winthrop Shields had overseen their spiritual needs with no eye for skin color. Nor had he allowed any in his congregation to do so in his presence. He spoke now with gentle surety.

Cole went out to work. Abbie held the children and told them stories of fairy kingdoms where everyone was immortal. It would never be so, and perhaps it was foolish to fill their heads with such fantasies. But right now she needed to. She knew all too well that life went on, and with time the hole would fill even as the mounded earth would sink and grass over.

Twenty-Two

Three weeks after burying James, Abbie opened the door to a stranger. He stood on her porch with slightly hunched shoulders, his ball-shaped head capped by a nubby mat of black hair and his chin outlined by a closely trimmed beard that was almost a shiny black.

Tiny drops of perspiration gave a sheen to his smooth skin, the color of strong coffee, but his fingernails were pink ovals at the ends of short, tapered fingers. He stood nearly her own height and looked at her with large expressive brown eyes. She couldn't gauge his years, but he seemed about Cole's age or younger.

Though his beige cotton coat was worn at the seams with the lowest button missing, it was clean and well fitted. Even with the stoop of his shoulders, this man's bearing was different from that of James as he switched his weight to his left leg, waiting.

Realizing she had scrutinized him longer than she might, Abbie caught herself. "May I help you?"

The man's gray flannel hat was already pressed to his chest, but he pressed it closer now, which did little for its worn and crumpled condition. "Yes, ma'am. I heard you might be needing a man." He did not speak with the southern dialect James and Pearl and Zena used.

She scarcely disguised her surprise at his words. "A man?"

"A houseman, ma'am. I heard your man passed on."

Abbie drew a comprehending breath. "Oh. Oh, well, my husband isn't in at present. But . . . won't you come inside?"

In all her time in this house, Abbie had never hired a soul. Monte had brought Pearl and James and Will out with him and had sent for Zena. He and Cole had hired on and let go the hands as needed by the season. She had on one occasion dismissed Cole, then of course taken him back on. But never a stranger.

How did one judge a person's character and determine his suitability? How would it be to have a new man in place of James? The wound was too fresh, yet . . . here was a man, willing.

"Have you only just come to town?"

"Two days, ma'am."

"May I offer you tea or coffee?"

He looked surprised. Likely that wasn't his usual treatment. "No, ma'am. Thank you, but . . . I'm more trained to serve, you understand."

Abbie folded her hands at her waist. "Well, come into the study. As you see," she waved her hand to the right, "the parlor is in disarray."

"You had a fire, ma'am?"

"Yes. Thankfully contained in that area alone. My husband has re-built the porch."

"Fine construction, ma'am. The boards are well seated and planed."

"Yes . . . thank you." Abbie motioned him to the chair across from the desk.

He took the seat, but he perched on the front edge with knees apart, one forming a rest for his hat, the other his free hand. "I could see to that front room. I've done my share of carpentry. I also cook, and I've served as a gentleman's valet, besides which I can draw and paint and write poetry."

Abbie laughed. How could she not? "Well, Mr. . . ."

"Grimm. Hezekiah Grimm. I go by Zeke."

"It certainly sounds as though you're well qualified."

"Oh yes, ma'am. I can't say I've put my hand to everything, but everything I put my hand to, I learn."

"Do you know much about ranching?"

"I'm a city boy. Hail from Massachusetts."

Now she placed his diction. "That's a long way from here."

"Yes, ma'am, it is. But maybe not far enough to separate me from the grief of that place. I lost my whole family to cholera. My wife of thirteen years and three little ones."

Abbie heard the pain in his voice, but he said it plainly, as though actively exorcising the pain. "My former employer, Mr. Cecil Ellington, is a man of small compassion, and I felt no compulsion to remain with him. I hope that in no way reflects poorly on me, ma'am. I'm just telling it the way it is."

Abbie was taken aback by his straightforward ebullience. But surely here was a valuable man, a man Cole would approve. "My husband is out with the herd. I know he's looking for hands, but it seems your experience lies elsewhere."

"I'm certain I could fill the spot left by your manservant." He scanned the room floor to ceiling. "Your husband must need a valet."

Abbie bit back her giggle. "What exactly does a valet do?"

"Dress the gentleman, of course, see that his shoes are shined, his coach is ready, see to his personal needs, and manage his schedule. That sort of thing."

Again the giggle tickled her throat. She dropped her eyes to hide her mirth. "Mr. Jasper will have the final word, of course, but I feel we'd be foolish to pass up your services, Zeke. If you're agreeable, I could turn you over to Pearl at least for the day. I know there are tasks building up that James wasn't able to do in his infirmity."

"You just point me in the right direction, and I'll begin at once." He stood again, holding his hat to his chest.

Abbie led the way to the kitchen. Seated at the table, Pearl was methodically plucking the brown-striped feathers from a pheasant hen. Beside her a cock lay on the floor, the long colorful tail feathers catching the sun from the window. Abbie opened her mouth to introduce Zeke, but he brushed past her.

"And that, dear woman, is a chore of which you should be relieved."

Abbie bit her lip as Pearl looked up, surprised. It was true that before his passing James had done the plucking, but this young stranger waltzing into her kitchen and asserting himself was not something to which Pearl was accustomed. Abbie read the emotions as clearly as if she had spoken them.

Again she fought laughter. "Pearl, this is Zeke. He's here at least for the day, until Cole comes in, which, as they're branding, might not be until dark. I told him you'd have chores that needed seeing to."

Pearl puffed her cheeks and looked him up and down. "Where you come from?"

"Massachusetts."

"I thought so. Well, no Yankee man is a'goin' to come in my kitchen an' have his say on what I is an' what I isn' a'goin' to do."

Zeke looked totally abashed. "Oh no, ma'am."

"Humph. Then if you's ichin' to, you can pluck dese here pheasants an' wash 'em at the pump."

"Yes, indeed." Zeke held out his hand. "And I am pleased to make your acquaintance. Pearl, is it?"

"It is." Pearl folded her arms across her ample bosom. "And I don' have all day to wait for dem birds."

Zeke laid his hat on the counter, then jumped when Pearl hollered and hung it on the hook instead. Abbie left before her laughter could no longer be constrained.

◆◆◆◆◆◆◆

Only the lamps in the entry and in the bedroom upstairs were lit when Cole came in for the night and hung his Stetson on the hook in the cloakroom. His back ached and his arms were sorely griping. Branding was just plain hard work. Maybe he shouldn't have pushed it so hard or so long, but he always felt too far behind. Losing the months in El Paso on top of the years when Breck was running things had left the ranch in a sorry state.

Not that Breck hadn't done his best, Cole reckoned. But running the place shorthanded and meagerly funded was a chore for anyone. Retiring Abbie's debts had pretty near used up Cole's savings, and he had to make the herd pay soon. He didn't doubt he could do it. The Lucky Star was a gold mine in the right hands, and he knew well enough his own were prime.

Cole made his way to the washroom beyond the kitchen. He knew more about running a ranch than most men, and a good sight more about cattle than anyone else he knew. But there didn't seem to be enough hours in the day to accomplish all that needed doing. He hadn't seen Abbie or the children since breakfast, since he and the men had taken a chuck wagon out with them for the other meals.

Curtis could cook passably, at least without burning the grub entirely, and the men were now bedded down at the camp. He would join them at sunup, but he'd been reluctant to leave Abbie to sleep alone, with her grieving James and all. Truth to tell, he didn't sleep so good anymore without her at his side. Funny how a few months time could undo all those years alone.

The water in the bucket was cold, but he stripped off his shirt and vest and bandanna and plunged his hands in, sloshing the water over his arms and chest, neck and face. He lathered and rinsed, then reached for the towel. Rubbing the back of his neck dry, he hoped Abbie was awake yet and hadn't merely left the lamp burning for him.

He laid his dirty shirt on the laundry board and tossed the vest and bandanna over his arm. Then he made his way through the dark kitchen, around the table, and . . . his boot struck something soft and heavy, and his instincts jumped at the motion on the floor. He felt his lips curl, and his hand had the gun at his hip free before the scant moonlight showed the whites of a man's eyes.

"What in blazes . . . On your feet!"

The man staggered up and Cole saw, by the contrast with his eyes, that he was dark-skinned. With the gun held steady, he dug a match from his pocket and lit the candle on the table. The man stood shoulder high without his boots, his hands held wide and eyes even wider.

"Who are you, and what're you doin' here?"

"H-Hezekiah Grimm. The missus said I should wait for Mr. Jasper. I . . . I just curled up a bit by the stove there to wait on his coming."

Cole felt the fire leave his blood. He holstered the gun and opened his mouth to speak, but the sudden appearance of his nightgowned wife cut him off at the pass.

"Good heavens, Cole. What are you doing?"

"I might ask you the same."

The stranger looked from one of them to the other, then settled on Abbie. "I'm sorry, ma'am. I was resting a bit there on the floor, waiting on your husband, when this man . . ."

Abbie walked into the room. "This man is my husband, Zeke." She pulled a coat from the hook and covered herself. "From the sound of things, I thought a gang of outlaws had broken in." She glanced up, and Cole recalled he was shirtless.

Well, hang it all, he hadn't expected meeting someone in his kitchen in the dark. "Anyone mind tellin' me what this is all about?"

Abbie raised her face sweetly. "Cole, this is Zeke. Your new valet."

He sucked in his cheek a moment while he studied her, reining his roiling emotions, then turned to Zeke. The man had apparently recovered quickly from his fright, as his hand was extended already.

"I'm pleased to meet you, Mr. Jasper. And I do apologize for this unfortunate mishap. I've been traveling a long way, and your woman, Pearl, kept me running today. I thought I'd just rest by the warmth of the fire and—"

"I'm afraid you're working on a misconception here, Mr. ..."

"It's Grimm. Hezekiah Grimm. But I go by Zeke." He flashed a white smile.

"Well, I have never had, nor been in need of, a valet. As you see, I can wash and dress myself." He almost glared at Abbie, but that would come later.

"Oh. Well, as I told your wife earlier, I'm sort of a jack-of-all-trades. I'm most suited to work about the house, but I think you'll find I'm highly trainable. Though I have no experience with livestock, I heard about the opening you might have with the passing of your manservant and availed myself of the opportunity."

"James was not my ..." Cole closed his mouth. "A'right, listen up. You can bed down here for the night, in a bed, not the floor where folks are walkin'. In the mornin' we'll talk about what you can do." He couldn't help the glower he turned on Abbie.

She apparently was blind to it. "There's a room in the attic, Zeke. Zena made it up for you earlier. Last door at the top of the back stairs."

"Thank you, ma'am." Zeke caught up his hat and coat from the hook and hustled off.

Cole waited as Abbie slipped the coat from her shoulders and rehung it. Then he caught her arm and headed up the stairs, wife in tow. Once inside their own room, he turned her square on. "You care to explain yourself?"

"I don't know what you're so worked up about. If I had thought you'd be coming in at this hour, I'd have sent Zeke to bed already. As it is, I dropped off waiting to catch you before you found him."

Cole held rein on his temper. "And why exactly would I be needin' a valet?"

"Oh, you heard him, Cole. He's quite amazing, really, what he knows and what he's done. He's very capable, and what he said about Pearl is true. She kept him at it all day, though he never complained."

"And why do you suppose he found it such a surprise that I was your husband?" Now he clearly caught the mirth in her eyes, though she tried to mask it.

"Well, I'm sure I don't know."

He closed on her. "And I'm sure you do. I reckon you made little effort to set the fella straight on what was and was not required in this house. And if you think I'm gonna stand still while some valet . . ."

She bit her lip against the laughter.

He grabbed hold of her arms. "Cuz if you want some namby-pamby gentleman who cain't blow his own nose . . . oh, go ahead an' laugh, why don't you. I'm sure all this is great sport."

She did laugh, but stifled it quickly. "I couldn't resist, Cole. When he said my husband must need a valet . . . it was simply too rich."

"I can well imagine."

She rested her hands on his chest. "Besides, he's exactly what we need."

"How do you figure?"

"Well, he can repair the parlor, for one. He's a skilled carpenter. It would relieve you of that. He says he can cook, Cole, and best of all . . . he writes poetry." Her laughter followed close on his exasperation.

Times like this he wondered why he'd ever found riding herd so tiresome.

Twenty-Three

Abbie waited without speaking while Cole eyed the man who wrote poetry in the light of the tall burned-out windows of the parlor. The room had been closed off and sealed tightly enough to preserve the smell of smoke in the outer portieres and charred woodwork. Only now had Cole removed the boards from the windows and allowed the sunshine in.

He watched the man, Zeke, turn slowly on the charred carpet, his round head pivoting as he surveyed the damage. Abbie tried to stay still and quiet at his side, also watching Zeke as he turned, hands in pockets. He came around to face them. "Yessir, there's possibilities."

Cole merely cocked his head, resting his hip to the doorjamb.

"What do you mean, Zeke?" Abbie spoke for him.

"Well, ma'am, the way I see it, the room is configured to take advantage of the glorious daylight. The size and shape of the windows, the layout of the space, the location of the fireplace . . . Mmm, this will yield some fine things."

"What did you have in mind?" Cole sounded skeptical enough for both of them, unsure of this man who appeared so confident of his abilities.

"Well, for starters I wouldn't go with mahogany as originally done. This room cries out for something golden. Fiddleback birch, I'd say."

Fiddleback birch. She didn't know what that was, but Cole seemed to. She saw in his quick glance about the room that he was picturing it in his mind. And Zeke was right about the configuration making the most of the light, though Monte had all but stifled it with the heavy velvet draperies he'd hung at the windows.

212

Abbie had removed them at Cole's urging, when he'd been shot and spent days on the sofa in this very room. She had climbed onto the desk there, flashing petticoats as she removed the rich velvet drapes. She had wanted them gone from the first time she entered the room, but it was Cole's comments that had bolstered her to actually do it, even against Monte's desires.

Abbie sighed. They had so often been at cross-purposes, trying to meld personalities that by nature conflicted. At least with Cole . . . She stopped the thought. Was it disloyal to Monte's memory? Could she even entertain the fact that she and Cole were better suited?

"See, we'd coffer the ceiling and match the pattern in the floor, then bring the beams up around the windows and fireplace there." Zeke motioned as he spoke, and she saw that Cole had left his position and stood in the center of the room beside the shorter man. "And on the walls, something pastoral."

Abbie stirred. "You mean you'd paint the walls?"

Zeke turned his earnest eyes on her, eyes large and melting as a calf's. "Canvas, ma'am. I'd paint it on canvas, then adhere it to the walls." He swung slowly, trailing his hand around dramatically. "One continuous scene. Like one I saw in the Louvre."

"You've been to the Louvre?" She felt the wonder fill her. This man, this manservant, had been to the Louvre.

"Yes, ma'am. Traveled the world with Mr. Ellington several times over."

She felt the old longing, the desire to experience exotic places, to see with her own eyes the things she'd read about and studied. She hadn't wanted any place but home for so long it felt foreign. "And you could reproduce what you saw?"

"In my own style, after a fashion. I wouldn't want to copy too closely another man's genius."

Where he stood on the burned-out carpet, Cole shifted his weight. "Sounds a mite pricey." His words brought her back to earth. She'd spent too many years watching the money dwindle, then scrapping for whatever she could to really consider Zeke's proposal.

Zeke turned to him. "The wood would run high, that's true. Especially out here where it isn't readily available. But beyond that—give me a room and something to do with my hands, Pearl's fine victuals, and a living wage . . ." He spread his hands wide. "I'll be a happy man."

Hope flickered as Abbie watched Cole's expression. He was as good a judge of character as any man she'd known, her pa included. What did Cole see when he looked down nearly on the top of Zeke's head? Did he consider the possibility, or would he reject Zeke's offer?

He glanced at her expectant face, and she tried to appear submissive. Whatever he decided, she would accept, but wouldn't it be wonderful . . .

Cole turned back to Zeke. "Where would you get the lumber?"

"I have a source out east. We'd freight it over."

"How long?"

"I can't say for sure. I'm not familiar with the trains in these parts."

Cole fixed him with a stare. "What'll you do in the meantime?"

Again the man spread his hands. "I'm a house servant, Mr. Jasper. For a decent wage."

Cole scratched the side of his head. "Well, I don't know much about that. I take on hands for running the ranch, but . . ."

"Whatever you pay your men will sit fine with me, sir. I've wandered far enough, and I'm ready to settle in."

Abbie held her breath at the words. How strange they must sound to Cole, unused to the house help as he was, as she'd been. She realized with a start that she'd already accepted Zeke as naturally as though she'd been raised as Monte had. He could assume James' place with little disturbance to her.

That did not detract from her devotion to James, but merely showed how truly she had acclimated to the life-style Monte had given her. Perhaps the hardship she had suffered after his death had forged even deeper ties between herself and Monte's servants. She recalled James' deathbed and the deep honor she'd felt being included there.

Yes, she could take this Hezekiah Grimm into her home, but could Cole? She sent him a questioning glance, read his indecision. His words came, slow and measured. "A'right, Zeke Grimm. You can come on into the study and I'll sign you on. Least until we set this parlor in order."

"Yes, sir." Zeke flashed his wide white smile, the skin creasing at the sides of his eyes.

Cole only nodded and returned a half smile. Nothing was sure yet. She could see that. Cole would watch, wait, and see. But she knew Zeke would win him. And she could almost picture the walls with a pastoral mural like one in the Louvre.

◆◆◆◆◆◆◆

Zeke proved such a willing worker, even Pearl softened somewhat. Abbie noticed the approving glances Pearl sent, even if the woman would never admit it aloud. It was true that whatever Zeke took on, he learned. He had a quick wit and good humor. And he'd brought an air of refined dignity to the house that had been lost somehow with Monte's passing. Not that Zeke put on airs. On the contrary, he was so meek he made everyone else feel elevated.

The only one who didn't seem to appreciate it was Cole. He didn't say so, but she could tell he wasn't sure what to make of the man. It was almost as though he didn't trust him or saw some ulterior motive in Zeke's actions. It was almost as though he felt threatened somehow.

Maybe Abbie shouldn't have made the joke about the valet when they first met. Maybe that set Zeke in a bad light from that moment. Maybe Cole just wasn't sure what to do with a man who rushed to his side and removed his coat the minute he came inside, who saw to his bath whether Cole ordered one or not, who waited with a towel, face turned discreetly away. No matter how often Cole told him he didn't need the help, Zeke still waited on him like royalty.

But Zeke was proving invaluable to Pearl, being young enough to shoulder tasks that she had taken on to relieve James. Zeke chopped and ground and scoured without a word of complaint, and the men had never been so happy with a chuck-wagon cook as they were with Zeke. The two weeks that he'd been with them were nothing short of halcyon, at least to Abbie's mind . . . and one other.

She looked now at Zeke and Zena walking in the garden. She had thought of Zena as part of the family so long that it had hardly occurred to Abbie that the young woman might have thoughts and desires of her own—thoughts of marriage and children. Abbie wouldn't say there was anything serious between them yet, but when they stole these moments alone together, she couldn't help but wonder. And hope. If Zeke developed a fondness for Zena, wouldn't he be that much more likely to stay?

Abbie looked around the bare walls of the parlor where she stood. Cole was working beside Zeke to remove the burnt rubble, peel away the damaged and blistered plaster from the walls, and replaster it to a thick, smooth finish. The plaster was dry now, thanks in part to the gaping window holes that allowed the cool spring air to flow freely.

That was all they could do until the lumber arrived, and that wouldn't come for some time yet. Though Zeke's source in the east was highly reputable, the fiddleback birch he wanted for the job had to be specially milled. It was just as well since Cole's hands were full this time of year with branding the new calves and repairing the winter damage of fences and windmills and pumps and all the other things that kept the ranch working as it should.

She half suspected Zeke could handle the parlor job himself, if Cole would allow him, though there were parts that took both their strength. The coffered ceiling would be a chore, surely. Zeke had drawn it out for her to see what it would look like, his precise lines a testament to the drawing ability he'd mentioned on arrival. Now she looked at the bare ceiling and pictured it formed in the boxwork pattern, with a flat repetition of the pattern on the floor.

With the walls painted and the wood gleaming, this room would keep the tongues wagging more than Monte's original construction. She recalled back to the time she had first heard of the southern gentleman who'd come to town and was building a mansion fit for a queen. She was probably the only girl who hadn't dreamed of living there.

Her mind and manners had not yet been tamed, nor her heart captured by the gentleman himself. What would Monte think of this parlor with the wood gleaming golden instead of the dark reddish mahogany, with the walls painted a pastoral scene and the windows letting in the light? What would he think of Zeke?

Her stomach twisted suddenly. Monte would have felt perfectly at ease with all of Zeke's ministrations. Monte would have been the gentleman Zeke expected Cole to be. For a brief moment she felt disappointed in Cole. When had her mind so changed that she, Abbie, could disdain his ways, so like her own had been?

Was it the course of life, of maturing, that made her value things she had taken no stock in during her youth? Or was it living here, amidst the gentility of servants and the ease of wealth, that had turned her head? How much harder must it be for Cole, who'd come from such humble beginnings?

Abbie shook away the webs of doubt. It was only mood swings, these moments of bliss turning to worry. Another proof of the life growing within her. Yet ... She scanned the room, picturing the beauty that would soon fill it. Why did she feel such foreboding?

Was it simply the memory of what happened here when she was away, what might have happened to her children? Was it knowing somewhere in the back of her mind that Cole carried a badge in his pocket? Was it recalling Crete Marlowe's hollered threat that she'd live to regret her interference? Or was it the tone in Cole's own voice when he'd spoken of Crete selling the whiskey to the Comanches, who then burned his mother?

Would Crete Marlowe come gunning for Cole? The fear that had once been her companion returned to her door. With the least effort she could welcome it in, again fall victim to its driving force. *Oh Lord, don't let me take my eyes from you. Nor Cole either.*

Elliot rushed in and grabbed her skirts. "Mama, I want to see Wendel."

She smiled, her heart lightening at once. She was hardly amazed by his words anymore, their coming on such a regular basis these days. She checked the watch pinned to her dress. "Well, it's nearly time to fetch Jenny from school. We can stop in on the way and pay cousin Wendel a visit."

Elliot jumped up and clutched her waist. "Thank you, Mama."

"Ask Tucker to harness the buggy."

That was another way Abbie was feeling her age. Little Tucker with the missing teeth now came over regularly to muck the stalls and do whatever other work Cole had for him. At twelve, his limbs were starting to lengthen and he'd lost his little boy's softness. Just in the two months since James' funeral, Tucker seemed to have outgrown his pants again.

Abbie had carried him in her arms to the back bedroom the day the Franciscan brothers moved away from the mission and left the orphans in her care. How happy she was Mama and Pa had taken him as their own. She sighed now, watching Elliot through the open window hole.

He skipped like a pony for the stable. One day he, too, would be going off to work. Too soon, she knew. She would never be ready for it. Never be willing to see him go. She placed her hand on her abdomen. Would this child fill and tug at her heart as extremely as Elliot did?

She shook off the shadows. She only prayed the baby would be healthy and whole as she watched Elliot reach the stable doors and fling open the left one. How eager he was to see his little cousin, little Wendel who still couldn't follow with his eyes, nor make the normal movements a baby his age should make.

Abbie passed into the cloakroom across the entry. She took her shawl from the hook and called to Birdie, who enjoyed riding into town with her. Then she followed her little son outside. Marcy would be pleased to see them, Abbie knew. Of all the townswomen who pandered to Marcy because of her husband's position, she alone sought Marcy for herself.

And her son adored the little baby. How that must warm Marcy's heart.

Twenty-Four

Elliot held Wendel's tiny fingers. Although they now had little puckers of fat at the knuckles, they still seemed awfully small, almost too little to be real. He felt the papery edge of one fingernail with the pad of his thumb. Wendel pulled the finger back, and Elliot laughed.

"Wendel's fingernails are ticklish."

"No, they're not." Emily Elizabeth settled to the floor beside him.

"Watch." Elliot stroked the nail again, and Wendel curled the finger up and away.

"He just does that." Emily shrugged.

Elliot ignored her. He knew from Jenny that girls liked to be right. And he didn't argue because Aunt Marcy was watching him with that happy look she got when he played with Baby Wendel.

"I like his hair." Elliot stroked a finger over Wendel's blond hair that sprouted straight up from his head like a dandelion seedball.

"He doesn't like it petted." Emily tried to push his hand away, but Elliot pushed back just enough to keep his hand in the baby's hair.

"Come here, Emmy." Aunt Marcy patted the couch beside her. "Show Aunt Abbie the picture you made."

Emily Elizabeth scrambled up, and Elliot dismissed her from his thoughts. She wasn't nearly as wonderful as this baby. As he stroked, Wendel's eyes opened. They weren't the dark blue they used to be. Now they were getting paler, but they still had a rim of dark blue around the edge. They came to his face and went past, then came back again.

"Hello. Hello, Wendel. It's me, Elliot."

"He doesn't understand you," Emily called from the couch.

219

"You have little bitty fingers and fuzzy, fuzzy hair. I think you must be a duck, 'cause you're so fuzzy."

Wendel kept his eyes on him, and his mouth made the smallest *o*. Elliot touched the *o* with his fingertip and Wendel opened wide. Elliot felt the baby's tongue and let his finger go in just enough that Wendel closed his lips around it and sucked. "He's sucking my finger. He thinks I'm food."

"He always does that." Emily Elizabeth dropped from the couch to Elliot's side again. She tugged on Elliot's wrist and his finger came free of the baby's mouth. Then she put her own finger to the baby's mouth and Wendel sucked it, too. "See, he always does it."

Elliot sat back on his heels. He wished he could push her aside the way she did him, but Mama didn't like it. She said a gentleman never pushed girls, and he must be a gentleman like his pa, his first pa. She had even let him see the picture of his pa, the one in her dresser drawer.

And he wanted to be like the man in that picture. He looked so nice and . . . fine. Mama had said he was fine, and he looked it. Cole was fine, too, but different. And Cole was his pa now. Cole never pushed ladies. He was a gentleman, too. But as soon as Emily got tired of Wendel sucking and took her finger away, Elliot replaced it with his own.

As he felt the tug and pull of the baby's mouth, he knew Wendel was giving him something, something Emily Elizabeth didn't feel. He kept the thought to himself, carefully stroking the soft downy hair with his free hand and letting Wendel suck the other. "I know, Wendel," he whispered under his breath. "I know."

◆◆◆◆◆◆◆

Cole paused on his way to the stable as Jenny jumped from the buggy, dumping her leather strapped books onto the gravel yard, and ran for him. "Did Blondie have her calf?"

Cole caught her by the shoulders and stopped her from crashing into him. "I'm a mess, Jenny. You'll muss your dress."

"I don't care. Did she, Pa?"

"No, and you'd better care. Your mama works hard to keep you sharp." He looked over her head to Abbie, standing beside the fallen books with a look of vinegar. "Go fetch your things up from the ground."

"Why hasn't she dropped?"

"I don't know."

"Jenny," Abbie called.

Jenny frowned. "They're just a bunch of stupid books."

"Don't sass your ma."

"I'd rather work the ranch with you than go to school. I don't need to read and write. I don't care about the old presidents and wars and laws. I want to see Blondie drop her calf," Jenny stated.

"Go fetch your books up, Jenny."

The child sent him a look of pure despair. "I thought you'd understand." She spun, stalked to the buggy, and snatched up her books, then took off running across the yard and around the house.

He waited for Abbie to join him. "What's got into her?"

"She got caned at school today."

Cole felt his blood rush. "Caned? What for?"

"She slapped Billy Peel."

Cole frowned. "Then he had it comin'."

"Mr. Ernst could not convince her to share her reasons."

"Mr. Ernst has all the warmth of a toad."

Abbie sighed. "Nevertheless, Jenny was wrong. If she had reason to slap the boy, she should have shared it."

"Before the whole class? You know his tactics. That would have served Billy Peel's purpose better than anything."

Abbie shook her head. "Cole, you weren't there. You can't assume Jenny had no fault in this."

"I ain't sayin' that. I'm sayin' she prob'ly did the best she could. I got half a mind to keep her out o' there."

Abbie's face jutted abruptly. "What do you mean?"

"Just what I said. I won't have my little girl caned in no school-house in this county."

He watched Abbie's chest rise and fall sharply twice before she spoke. "So you'd have her unschooled instead?"

"Is that so bad? You could teach her."

"That isn't the point."

He spread his hands. "You got enough books in the house to fill her head with nonsense to last a lifetime. I could teach her a thing or two myself."

"What? How to lasso a steer?"

He narrowed his eyes at her sarcasm. "That and a few other things."

She spun, speaking over her shoulder. "There are three weeks left in the term. I hope you think this through before we take it up with Jenny. The last thing she needs to hear is you defending her actions."

Cole held his tongue. Maybe that was so, but he'd have a word with Mr. Ernst on the subject—and put the fear of God in him if he ever laid hand to Jenny again.

He found the child nestled in the clump of oaks clustered behind the house. The books lay scattered on the dry bristly grass where she sat, her knees caught up under her skirt and pinafore. "Come on out of there, Jenny. Let's talk."

Jenny didn't move, nor did she look up at him.

"It's real hard for me to climb in under them low branches."

Her shoulders raised and dropped, but she still wouldn't look.

"A'right, then. Better make room." He pressed into the scrub oaks, still bare of leaves, but starting to soften and bud. The gnarly branches caught at his hair and snagged in the armholes of the leather vest he wore over his cotton shirt.

He settled down next to her and pressed into the small space between the crooked trunks. She merely vacated a portion of the space without taking her knees out or unloosing her arms from her shins.

"Suppose you tell me what Billy Peel said."

"I don't want to." She still wouldn't look at him.

"Why not?"

"I just don't."

Cole let his breath out sharply. "Then I'll have to let the caning stand and suppose it was deserved."

Jenny's cheeks flushed crimson through her velvety skin, but she didn't take the bait.

Cole sighed. "Whereas it might've been right and proper not to tell it to Mr. Ernst, I cain't rightly see how you should keep it from me."

"Because . . . because . . ." Her color heightened.

"Cuz it's about me?"

She looked at him now, her eyes burning, and nodded.

"Then let's have it out."

Jenny sniffled, her voice getting tight and pinched. "He said you were a golddigger."

"What's that?"

"Someone who . . . he said you married Mama for her money. And that you killed Uncle Monte so you could marry Mama for her money."

Cole drew a long, slow breath. He supposed that sort of speculation was to be expected, though it was his money that had bailed Abbie out. Still, he'd kept that quiet, and on the surface there was no good reason Abbie should have married the likes of him. But the part about killing Mr. Farrel . . . Well, even Abbie had thought along those lines.

He dropped his chin to the kerchief at his chest. "Sometimes folks think crazy things, Jenny. Mostly it comes from what's in their own hearts. Billy Peel prob'ly heard a careless word and spoke it to you out of spite. I ain't sayin' you should've slapped him. It's always better to walk away, to not dignify the lie with your anger. But as you did do the slappin', I hope you slapped him good enough to pay for your canin'."

"I slapped him so hard he had my hand print on his face a long time."

Cole felt his mouth quirk. "As for Mr. Ernst, if he had a brain in his head, he'd see why you didn't repeat what was said to you."

Jenny nodded painfully. "I saw Billy Peel smirking and . . ."

"I know. But here's another thing. You had a weapon even better than your hand. You know what it was?"

"My foot? Should I have kicked him, too?"

Cole fought a grin. "No, miss. You had the truth."

"The truth?"

"That's right. If you know what someone says is a falsehood, you can simply stand on the truth. You don't even have to say it out loud. Just knowin' it in your heart is enough."

"You mean I should ignore it when he says bad things about you?"

Cole nodded slowly. "If you know in your heart what's true, then nothin' else matters. The truth will come out one way or another."

Jenny looked down at her knees. "I don't want to go back there. Mr. Ernst had never caned a girl before—not ever."

"And he was wrong to cane you. But you cain't let that keep you away."

"Why not?" Jenny's gaze was fixed upon him. "You never went to school, and it hasn't hurt you any."

Cole measured his words. He wouldn't tell a falsehood, but he had to be careful. "I don't know if it's hurt me or not. I know a lot of things no schools teach, and I've got my own sense to boot. But it seems your mama sets a huge store by book learnin', and it might just be there's a value there I don't know about."

"Aunt Abbie—I mean Mama—doesn't understand."

"I know it seems that way sometimes. But she loves you, and she wants to do right by you."

Jenny's eyes dropped from his. She worked her finger back and forth over the gathered fabric on her knee, flattening the ridge with the tip of her finger. "Do you want me to go?"

Cole swallowed hard on the lump that filled his throat. He knew she wasn't just asking if he thought she should be schooled. He cleared the emotion from his throat. "I'd like nothin' better than to have you at my side all day. But there's a time and place for things. And right now it's time for you to learn all you can from Mr. Ernst."

Jenny scoffed, and he half joined her before he cut it off. "You fill your head with all the book learnin' you can, then when it comes time to learn about life, it'll be that much easier."

"But I want to see Blondie drop her calf."

Cole drew a long breath. Blondie was Jenny's favorite cow, named by her for the yellowish lock of hair on her forehead. "I tell you what. If Blondie decides to drop while you're away, I'll send a man right after you and get you here as quick as I can. But you know as well as I, she'll likely drop come nightfall."

"But you'll get me otherwise?"

"I will."

"Then we can tell Aunt . . . tell Mama I'll go back."

"I think that's wise." Cole stroked her hair and smiled.

◆◆◆◆◆◆◆

Abbie worked the pump up and down, filling the bucket for her bath. It was strange the way the bottom seemed to shrink up as the water rose inside it, making the bucket look half as deep as it was. She looked up at Cole approaching. "I'm glad you saw fit to set Jenny straight."

Cole joined her at the pump and took the bucket from her. "Straight on what?"

"The importance of education."

"Is that what I did?"

"Well, it came to me that way." She cocked her head, but he didn't elucidate. Abbie stopped pumping and let the stream finish filling the bucket.

Cole held it to his shoulder and started for the house. "I saw plans the other day for an attic cistern by which water can be run down inside the house to all the sinks and even indoor privies."

She turned to him, surprised. "Where did you see that?"

"A man in town was showin' plans for all kinds of things. Seems he wants to start a gasworks."

"Here in town?"

"He's not sure where yet, but there were plenty of folks persuadin' him what a nice place this is."

Abbie stared at the house before her. "Imagine that, Cole. Gaslights in every window."

"Heat, too. And hot running water if we installed a coal burning boiler like the steamships have."

She shook her head, a little amazed by his dreaming. "I can't even imagine." She took his free arm. "What a time we live in."

"Yes, ma'am. And no end to what you can do given a little ingenuity and know-how."

"That's exactly what I told Jenny. Why, if she could just see the good of learning to read and write and cipher and understand history and know basic physics and—"

"I don't know about all that," Cole said, shaking his head. "Seems to me a lot of these inventor fellas happened on their discoveries without all that learnin'."

"Nonsense."

"No, it ain't. There's a whole world of learnin' outside the school, Abbie."

She suppressed her argument. "Well, I'm glad you didn't tell Jenny that. Just now she'll take any excuse not to go back."

"Can you blame her?"

Abbie stopped and freed her arm. "I can certainly expect her to do the right thing."

"And what's that?"

"Face up to her humiliation and let it keep her from making the same mistake again." She stood firm under Cole's slow gaze.

"You sure have forgotten things."

"Like what?" She raised her chin.

"Like how it is to be different, to have that wild streak that just won't let you sit still. To want to know and experience more than you can. To be so alive it hurts."

Abbie stared at him.

"Tell me that isn't how it was for you."

"I loved learning, in school and out. And I loved teaching. Jenny is a brilliant and imaginative child . . ."

"And Mr. Ernst is doin' his level best to destroy that."

Abbie expelled her breath. "I don't believe it."

"Yes, you do."

"He may not be very energetic—"

"A toad on a cold rock comes to mind."

Abbie spread her hands. "What would you have me do? He's the town's choice. He's been there three years now."

"Teach her yourself."

"I do teach her."

"I mean all of it. The way you teach Elliot."

Abbie shook her head. "When Elliot's old enough he'll go to school, too."

"I wonder how you'll be when he's caned in front of the class."

Abbie felt her cheeks burn. The very thought sent fire to her spine. "He won't be." The words were out before she thought.

Cole just eyed her, then shook his head. He started back toward the house.

"Besides, you're a fine one to speak of my teaching. I offered to teach you, and we saw how readily you accepted."

"That's not the same." He kept walking.

"Yes, it is."

"No, it ain't. I'm a full-grown man with too many years behind me to learn readin', writin', and 'rithmetic."

"It's never too late."

He half turned. "This song is gettin' old, Abbie."

She sighed. "Let's not argue."

"Fine by me."

"Cole." She stopped at the door. "Thank you for handling it with Jenny."

"You're welcome. If Ernst canes her again, I'll personally see to it he never sits behind a school desk or anywhere else again. I didn't work a whip all those years for nothing."

Abbie bit back her objection at the look in his eyes. After all, would she want him any less protective? And she had to admit there was truth to his words—she *had* forgotten how it was to ache with life so real it burst from you. Little Jenny was fighting her own battles. She felt ashamed that it took Cole to show her . . . again.

At dinner that night, she watched Jenny. The child was understandably subdued. Abbie could hardly imagine the shame she must have felt being caned in front of the class, though she'd seen Blake endure it often enough in their school days at the mission. She tried to see through Jenny's shell to the real little girl, but it seemed only Cole could do that.

Jenny had informed her matter-of-factly that she and Pa had decided she'd go back to school, but she'd had nothing more to offer. Now Abbie watched Jenny's small jaw chew deliberately while she stared at the center of the table. A sudden thought occurred to her and Abbie mulled it over.

Why not? It was one of the rare times the family dined alone, as

Birdie had begged off with a headache. Abbie figured it would soon be difficult to hide her condition, and the news would take Jenny's attention off her own disgrace.

"Jenny, Elliot, your pa and I have some news for you." She glanced at Cole to see if he guessed her intent.

He held his fork poised, his look both quizzical and cautious.

Abbie felt her determination waiver, but she turned back to the children. "It's a wonderful thing being a family. And . . . well, Elliot, you've seen how special it is for a family to welcome a new baby."

"Like Wendel?"

She smiled. "Any new baby." She had Jenny's attention now. The child's sharp mind had made the leap, and Abbie saw her look to Cole with guarded eyes, almost accusing. Maybe this hadn't been the time.

Abbie folded her hands with a falsely bright smile. "This fall we'll be welcoming our own baby." No, that didn't sound right, as though Jenny and Elliot weren't their own. "A new brother or sister for the two of you." That was better. It stressed their importance in the relationship.

Jenny looked down at her plate and poked a green bean with her fork.

Elliot dropped his fork and dashed his napkin across his face. "Will he sleep in my cradle like Wendel?"

"Yes."

"And suck on my finger?"

Abbie nodded indulgently. "Only if you're clean." She'd certainly pleased Elliot with the news, but Jenny made no response. "Won't it be nice to have a baby to play with, Jenny?"

Jenny raised the bean and eyed it. "I suppose."

"I'm sure you'll be a wonderful help."

Jenny took the tip of the bean between her teeth and nibbled down its length. She knew better than to display such manners, and Abbie tensed at her blatant display. But she held her peace, glancing Cole's way. He was staring at his plate with a look of discomfort.

Abbie frowned. What was it with those two? This was his child she was discussing. Couldn't he show a little joy in the prospect? He looked up, as though feeling the heat of her thoughts, but said nothing.

"I want to play with the baby." Elliot raised a bean to follow Jenny's trick.

Abbie rested her eyes on her small son, who of all of them was the most understanding. She wanted to run around to him and squeeze his neck and thank him for being happy. Instead she said, "Elliot, you have a knife for that."

She had wanted to cheer Jenny and share the wonderful news and give them all something to look forward to. Now she was simply chastising her sweet boy. "Well, if you've finished your dinners, you may be excused for your baths."

Both children left their plates. Elliot scampered, and Jenny walked straight and solemn past Cole at the end of the table. Their eyes met for a moment, then she passed. Abbie sat, tensely waiting until Cole's gaze turned to her.

He raised the napkin to his mouth, catching the mustache and rubbing it clean, then dropped the napkin and leaned back as Zeke cleared away his plate. He rubbed the back of his neck, but still didn't speak.

Frustrated, Abbie expelled her breath. "I thought it would cheer her up, give her something to look forward to."

"It might have," he said, "if she didn't already feel inadequate."

Abbie closed her eyes and rested her fingers on the table. She felt excluded and ignorant, unable to understand or penetrate the relationship Cole had with the child of Monte's sister. How could that be? She heard the chair creak and scrape, felt Cole's hand warm and strong on her shoulder.

"We can't force it. She'll come around when she can."

Abbie said nothing. Part of her wanted to blame Cole. But inside she knew he was Jenny's best hope.

Twenty-Five

The wood that came from the lumberyard in the east was like none Abbie had ever seen, its grain and pattern beautiful even in its unfinished state. When it lay stacked in the parlor ready to be cut and fitted to the floor and ceiling, she drew a breath of deep satisfaction.

Was it that she could more easily put the violence of someone like Crete Marlowe from her mind when all traces of his presence were purged from her home? It had been nearly two months since Sheriff Davis suspected Crete was on his way to town. Cole must have been right to assume Crete Marlowe would not show his face where it would be known.

With the clear summer sunshine shining through the new glass in the parlor windows, the gentle June breeze swaying the cottonwoods outside, and the clouds like tufts of cotton, Abbie could almost believe it herself. She rested a hand on her growing belly. Maybe, just maybe, this baby would never know the trouble the world could hold.

"Abbie?"

She turned. "Yes, Birdie."

"I do not understand this word."

"Show me." Abbie reached for the book and followed Birdie's finger to the trouble. "Panacea." She looked up at Birdie's face. "Well, that's like a remedy for all evils, all difficulties. A cure for everything."

Birdie dropped her eyes to the page. "I do not understand. Does such a thing exist?"

Abbie shook her head. "Not really. Some have said love is a panacea, others faith. But I've found difficulty in both. I don't think there's such a thing as a miracle cure unless it comes from God himself, and those are few and far between."

Birdie nodded slowly, her own wounds tenacious in their hold.

Abbie smiled, gently clutching Birdie's hand. "Just because God allows hardship, it doesn't mean He loves us less."

"No." Birdie's voice was soft. "But I could wish . . ."

Abbie clasped the narrow fingers in her own. "I know." She cleared her throat. "Birdie, there's something you should know."

Birdie gave her a questioning look, but one that held concern, as well. Nothing came to Birdie without cost, it seemed, and she had learned too early to guard herself.

"Will came to me the other day. He'd like to walk with you, to get to know you."

Birdie turned to the window as though she would see him materialize there before her eyes. And by her stiffened demeanor, Abbie knew the thought was not comfortable.

Abbie reassured her with a squeeze of her hand. "I've asked him to wait, and it's up to you how long. But you could do worse."

For a moment Birdie displayed the sullen, caustic look she'd worn so often before. Then she sighed. "I have already done worse, and I do not wish to know a man again."

Abbie nodded. "I understand that. But Will would not be the same. It's you he cares about, not . . ."

Birdie scoffed. "It is always the same. Even the ones who claim unending love."

Abbie knew better than to push it. She had put forward Will's request, but it was Birdie who must decide. She alone knew her heart. She and God. But as the girl swept from the room as graceful as a young antelope, Abbie found it impossible to recapture her hopeful spirits. She pressed her hand to the child in her womb. In this world ugly things happened, and she was a fool to think otherwise.

✦✦✦✦✦✦✦

In the dwindling light of the stormy August night, Crete Marlowe jabbed at the joint of elk meat on the spit with the tip of his knife. It was tough still, and his stomach was rumbling. The cave they huddled in was hardly more than a scoop from the rocky cliff on the side of the bluff, the shelf that hung out from its base a rough rusty edge scarcely wide enough to hold them all.

He heard the horses stomping and snorting below, skittish and jumping at every flash of lightning, every crack of thunder. He looked to the sky, the inky blackness seared by the next flash, then tensed for the boom that followed less than half a minute later. As though the lightning had torn open the sky, the rain rushed down, pelting the cliffside like stones. Crete stepped back, though the ceiling above caught the bulk of the onslaught and the fire only spluttered with the drops the wind gusted inward.

He thought of the animals below, out of reach. If they were rushed, they'd break their necks just trying to gain the horses. But the cave offered the best protection from the rain to be had up in the foothills on the eastern slope of the Rocky Mountains. The wind blew a wet blast at him, but he refused to give ground. The hair on his arms and neck stood up with the storm. What kind of weather was this anyway?

He missed the dry heat of the Texas plains, the wet heat of the Texas coast. He didn't like the sharp blinding sun of the high country and the cold nights that followed. He missed a warm summer night with a jug of whiskey. He missed a bed and a roof over his head. And most of all, he missed sleeping without listening for pursuit.

The only thing that made him feel better was knowing that the derned federal marshal was also out somewhere in the storm. They'd glimpsed him once, this lawman who'd been trailing them like a hound. But so far as he could tell, they'd never given the marshal even so much as a glance at them. He was no seasoned veteran, hardly more than a whelp and, Crete guessed, more than a little scared of what might happen if he did find them.

The wind gusted and he spit against the sparks and ashes that flurried in his face. He heard the men grumbling, knew their grumbling had grounds. They should quit the state, head for the territories, lose themselves in empty country—and they would. But not yet. No, he had one more thing to do before they left Colorado for good. One man to see; one score to settle.

Finn came to the fire, banging his arms. "You suppose this blow will keep up all night?"

"Don't know."

Finn hunched down beside the fire's warmth, shielded by the rocky outcropping of one wall. Like a shadow, Washington emerged from the hollow to join them at the fire. Its light harshly planed his broad face. "The wolves howl this night, chief."

"It's the wind. The derned wind."

"The spirit of the mountain is not pleased."

Crete grunted. "Whatever you say, general."

Finn poked the fire with a branch of scrub oak. "Wonder where the posse is."

"Somewheres less comfortable, I reckon." Crete formed a cold smile. He heard Dooley, MacComb, and Speer mumbling behind him. Funny how the cave chased their whispers out as though they spoke in his ear. Well, let them grumble.

Speer and MacComb had joined up with them in the slums of Denver, already wanted for petty theft and assault. They were a motley crew, but necessary if he was going to pull off the final job in one little town called Rocky Bluffs. He still wasn't sure in his mind what it would look like, but he had two days to work out the details. Beyond that, he only knew one objective: Put an end to Cole Jasper, once and for all.

The fire faltered, diminishing, then fighting back, then succumbing again to the watery onslaught. Crete reached over and cleaved a hunk of meat from the bone, then sat back with it gripped between his hands. It was the color of raw liver inside the charred edges and tasted gamy. Must have been an old antelope. He bit in again and nodded to the men to do likewise. "Best you're gonna get tonight. May as well have at it."

As he watched the men eat, he wondered how each would prove when it came right down to it. So far the jobs they'd pulled had carried little risk to themselves. Except the bank in Leadville, they'd kept to the smaller banks, trading posts, and inns without guards. Rocky Bluffs wouldn't prove so easy.

He only hoped it wouldn't prove a fiasco like Golden, Colorado, almost had, putting that federal marshal on their tails. They'd miscalculated that one badly. But in a town like Rocky Bluffs there would be no room for error, and they'd make none. Rocky Bluffs called for drastic measures. And with what he'd found in the back room of that little inn, he had exactly the drastic measure he needed . . . if they could shake the posse loose long enough to get it done.

After the others had turned in, Crete lay down on his blankets at the front edge of the cave, boots toward the opening on account of the persistent rain. Only the spray from the wind reached him, and he reckoned he could sleep through that. The snores of the others showed they were having no problem. Maybe it was his age that made him wakeful.

He punched the sack of dirty clothes he was using as a pillow and settled his head in place. Then he lay there, listening to the night noises. Below, the horses were restless from standing in the rain. Every crack of thunder made them jump and stomp. Little else stirred, but the horses had no choice.

Crete hunched his shoulder and yanked the blanket around. He closed his eyes and made them stay closed. He thought about the money he had, the money stuffed into the packs at the back of the hollow. He carried the lion's share himself, having promised they'd distribute it all once they hit the territories. He couldn't have anyone running out before this next attempt.

Attempt? What kind of thinking was that? His eyes were open again. He sounded like an old woman. Rocky Bluffs would be no attempt, nor would his confrontation with Cole. He shifted on the blanket, rolled his weight to his left hip, and turned his back to the cave wall.

Thunder again rumbled across the sky, but the rain had subsided and now descended as a drifting mist carried on the wind. Crete touched the cold metal of his rifle lying at his side, then closed his eyes again. The night would pass soon enough and they'd be up and moving. He needed to be sharp. He needed . . .

A sharp smattering of stone outside the cave caught his ear. Rain runoff? Maybe. The pile of stones down the steep slope outside the opening revealed frequent rockslides. He strained his ears. Nothing.

He drew a long breath and settled back. This time Crete forced his eyes closed and held them there with grim resolve. He would not be found bleary-eyed in the morning. Gradually he felt the slackening of his muscles, the settling of his bones. His breathing slowed and the faint drumming of the rain faded.

All at once his senses erupted, and he lurched up, rifle ready. He hardly thought before drawing bead on the shape at the mouth of the cave and firing. The man tumbled backward from the edge as his bullet winged the wall near Crete's head. Crete turned and fired to the other side of the opening and heard the thunk of a bullet finding flesh.

Now Finn was at his side, firing blindly at any sound or movement. Speer and Washington had scrambled to the other side near the mouth. Washington shot twice down the slope. A horse screamed, and he fired again. Crete moved forward on his knees, gained the opening, and searched the night.

One man scrambled low down near the horses. Crete took aim and fired. The man went down, sprawling almost at the horses' hooves. The animals shied and strained at their ropes. Crete scanned through them for shapes and shadows, for men using the beasts as cover.

Once the animals settled there was nothing. No noise, no movement except the pounding of his heart in his ears and the dull buzzing from the magnified gunshots inside the cave. He rubbed his right ear with his shoulder, felt a wetness, and raised a hand.

The edge of his ear was bleeding, probably from a rock shard when the bullet struck behind him. Or maybe the bullet itself had grazed his ear. It didn't matter. That bullet hadn't worn his name. He glanced quickly at Finn, then Washington, then turned to see Speer and MacComb and Dooley.

He felt the grin start and let it go, then leaned back on his haunches and expelled his breath. Finn returned the grin. Washington did not, but Crete could see it in his eyes, more a bloodlust than a pleasure at being alive. He was a hard son of a gun.

MacComb scuttled to the edge and looked out. He kept his head low as he searched the slope beneath. "Sure looks clear."

"How many bodies you see?"

He shook his head. "Four close, maybe one by the horses. They're keepin' shy of somethin' down there."

"That's five. There were seven trailin' us."

"Could be they fell where I can't see them," MacComb stated.

"Could be they're still out there." Crete dumped the spent shells from his rifle and replaced them with fresh. These new casings sure beat the old powder and ball method for getting the job done.

"What do we do now?" Finn spoke into the fine, steady rain.

"Wait and see." Crete sent his own gaze out the opening.

Speer shifted his position. "Could be those two are positioned, waiting for us to creep out as soon as it's light."

"Could be." Crete nodded. "Could be they're putting as much distance between us and them as they can before it's light."

"We should get to the horses."

Crete looked at Washington, surprised. The man rarely spoke to any but him and on occasion Finn. For Washington to air his thoughts before the whole assembly meant he felt strongly about it.

"What—and break our necks going down those wet rocks in the dark?" Speer made a scoffing sound in his throat.

Crete stood and joined Washington at his perch by the opening. "You think they'll try for the horses?"

"I would."

Crete looked out into the night. "You suppose those two are down there somewhere?"

The barely perceptible nod was answer enough. Crete swore. "Could be they'll pick us off as soon as we show."

The half-breed made no answer. Some instinct, some native wisdom controlled his thoughts.

"All right, Speer, you watch our backs. Anything moves besides the general and me, shoot it."

Speer cocked his gun and moved into position, his sneer gone. Crete nodded to Washington, who eased out of the cave almost soundlessly. Crete followed with as much stealth as he could manage, alert for the whirring of a bullet that would come before the report.

With one free hand and both feet, he felt his way down the broken slope, keeping low to the ground. The rain, though scarcely more than a wet drizzle, was cold and diminished his view, blurring the trees around the spot they'd staked the horses. He could see the animals milling and chafing their restraints. But beyond that he could tell nothing.

Washington crept on ahead. Crete followed, then paused and took up a position just above the horses. He saw Washington reach the base of the slope and start in toward their mounts. A sudden gunshot dropped Washington, and Crete spun, firing at the bright flash of light that gave away the shooter's position.

Then he lunged and rolled as a shot from the other side glanced off the stone he'd crouched on the moment before. The sharp edge of a rock sliced his knee as he rolled, but he wedged himself into a gap and waited. To the side, about halfway up the slope and a little around the bend, he saw the man crouching.

His plan had probably been to provide cover for the one below who meant to free the horses and chase them off. Crete tried to get a look at Washington, but when he raised his head, the other man fired. The binging ricochet splintered the rock and Crete took the fragments in his face.

Focusing above him, he gripped the rifle and fired. For a moment it looked as though his shot had missed entirely, then the muted shape slowly sagged and sprawled head first down the slope. One more. Crete raised to one elbow and saw Washington, lying prone and motionless.

He scanned the woods behind him. Crete made his way to his knees, then climbed out of the gap. From the corner of his eye he saw movement and spun. He raised up and pulled the trigger, but the rifle jammed.

He saw the flash of fire and rolled. Then, even before he could reach for his sidearm, Washington rose from the dead and put a bullet in the last gunman. The man buckled at the waist, staggered, and fell. Crete cackled. Never believe a dead Injun. He leaned back against the stone, chest heaving, and laughed again.

Twenty-Six

Resting on one elbow, Cole stretched out on the blanket spread flat in the center of the library floor. With the day's festivities rained out, Abbie had done her best to keep the mood cheerful. Though they hadn't gone outside for the picnic they had planned in celebration of the sale they'd made on the beef herd, Abbie had prepared a feast in the library. There they'd enjoyed the fried chicken, deviled eggs, boiled potatoes with mustard greens, and apple pie Pearl had prepared for the occasion.

Now Cole sprawled, sufficiently full and satisfied. He smiled indulgently as Jenny recited a portion of Patrick Henry's famous speech with a heartfelt "give me liberty or give me death." How well he could imagine she meant those words, now that she was facing the upcoming school term with Mr. Ernst again retaining the position.

Following her patriotic vein, Elliot stood and placed his hand over his heart. In his child's voice with a hint of lisp still attached to his *s*'s, he said the pledge of allegiance. He was an accomplished little dickens, and Cole gave him the same approving smile he'd sent Jenny.

Now Zeke shuffled to his feet from his chair against the wall. "With your permission, I'll recite a little piece I wrote some years back."

Cole couldn't control the twinge he felt inside. What was it about the man that bothered him? It wasn't his color. Cole had never judged by the skin. And he couldn't fault the man his work ethic. Zeke worked as hard as any of them. No, it was something else, something he couldn't lay hold to.

But as he listened to Zeke's poetry filling the room with hushed tones and bringing expressions of awe and delight to his listeners'

238

faces, Cole felt as close to squirming as he'd felt since he left his youth behind. Pearl and Zena, the children, and especially Abbie all looked as though they'd been transported to heaven.

Abbie's hands came together in a rousing clap. "Oh, Zeke, that was wonderful!"

Was it over? Cole hadn't attended too well. He hoped Abbie wouldn't ask him to comment, but she never looked his way.

"Give us another one, Zeke. I haven't heard such poetry in so long." She was fairly gushing, and Cole dropped his chin to his chest to hide a disagreeable frown.

"Well, ma'am . . ." Zeke dipped his head, taking the praise humbly. One thing couldn't be denied—the man was as meek as they came. So much so it made one uncomfortable.

"I have one—something I wrote concerning my family—of which I spoke to you, Mrs. Jasper."

Cole saw Abbie nod sympathetically. She obviously knew more about the man than he did. Probably had his whole family history by now.

With hands clasped before him like an encore singer Cole had seen once in a San Antonio saloon, Zeke started in on another poem. Cole listened this time, so as not to be caught if Abbie questioned him. When Zeke finished, a collective sigh hung in the room, then vanished with the words of praise heaped on the man's head.

Cole raised an eyebrow and Zena took the cue, herding the children off to bed. Like as not, she was eager to spend some moments with Zeke in the kitchen before they, too, turned to their respective rooms. Cole frowned. This Hezekiah Grimm was making inroads quicker than a jackrabbit in a wolf's sights, and marrying Zena would give him a permanent place in the household.

With a last sad smile directed Abbie's way, Zeke left, head bowed. The rustle of Pearl's skirts fading behind him told Cole he was alone with his wife. But she might have been all by her lonesome, so wrapped up was she in her own thoughts.

She turned at last with a small sound, part sigh, part tremble. "That's how it must have been to hear Sir Walter Scott or Keats or Lord Byron or even our own Henry Wadsworth Longfellow. Why, Zeke is as accomplished as any. Don't you think?"

Cole knew his blank expression told her all. He suspected the men she listed were some sort of famous, but if they fell into the category of Zeke's prowess . . . not that he knew or cared. He held a hand up to ward off her next words. "Don't say it." She'd harped so on the reading subject these last months, he could see it coming before she opened her mouth.

"But, Cole, if you learned to read . . ."

"So I can carry on like Zeke?"

"He has a gift." The firelight played on her hair.

Cole looked down at the glow in his wife's eyes, the same glow he'd seen there when he'd stopped the lynching of the Ute brave, when he'd faced down Pablo's threat at the Rio Grande, when he'd saved her from the rustler. How could Zeke's flowery words compare to that?

She almost pouted. "Surely you heard it. I don't know when I've experienced such moving poetry."

Cole frowned. "Seems to me plain speech is more effective. What does he need with all those descriptions and fancy phrases?"

She half turned from him, her profile stark in the shadowed room. "You're only saying that to be obstinate. I saw you taking it in."

"I was bein' polite."

"You were swept away."

"Abbie, I have never been swept away in my life. Leastwise not by some silly words about love's finest flower."

"That was only a small part of it. The rest was noble and—" She shook his arm. "Stop trying to look bored."

"Abbie," Cole said as he stood and stretched, "I ain't feignin' nothin' I don't feel."

She glared, and he realized he had crossed the line. He should have agreed that Zeke's poetry was everything she thought it. He would have, too, if he hadn't seen her so wrapped up and carried away it made him jealous—jealous of a man who could move his wife by words alone. What was it with Abbie and words?

He looked around the room, lined with these books full of words. She spent as much time in this room, losing herself in the pages of these books, as anywhere else. And for what? To imagine herself somewhere else, someone else, to delve into thoughts and images that stretched the mind away from all reality?

Reality was here, in his person. He was the man who loved her, who supported her, who saw to all the chores and tasks that made her life work. Here was the man whose hands had built this ranch, all but the house and buildings. He had made it run, made it successful, brought her life back into control.

But there she sat, all worked up by Zeke's poetry, expecting him to say it was some kind of wonderful. As though it took considerable effort to think up fancy words, string them together, and then speak them with too much emotion. The man had looked like a woman, his eyes big and watery, speaking his lines in a voice all whispery and soft.

And here Abbie was, caught up like a branch in the current, carried into some foreign place where a man can't go without being less a man. She actually looked hurt that he hadn't seen fit to dab the tears from his eyes and sniffle right along with her. Cole felt a growl rising up that would get him in trouble. "Come on, let's go to bed."

She raised her chin defiantly. "Do you know what I think? I think you're jealous."

"Jealous of what?"

"Of Zeke's abilities. I heard you mumbling as you walked through the parlor examining his work. I think you're jealous that he can actually do the things he said he could. You felt the woodwork, saw the quality. And you felt the power of his words tonight, deny it as you will."

"Abbie, I am not jealous of a man who talks like a woman."

"Oh?" She stood, and he could see the bulge of her abdomen. "And how does a woman talk?"

"All teary and emotional."

"Cole Jasper, it's men like you that make women want the vote."

"What's the vote got to do with anything? We're talkin' here about a man who uses purty words and tears up like a girl. And you got your hackles up cuz I won't say that's how it should be."

"Well, maybe if you'd ever expanded your mind beyond the backside of a herd, you'd appreciate the genius of a man who thinks beyond his next meal."

241

If she had taken a dagger to his ribs she could hardly have sunk it deeper. There it was—exactly what she thought of him, exactly what he was. The growl grew within him until he could have bit her head off. Instead, Cole turned and stalked out. He didn't head up the stairs but took his duster from the hook in the cloakroom and went right out the door.

Abbie stood, shaken. What had caused those cruel words to come from her? She put a hand to her breast at a sudden pain as real as any physical ache. She hadn't been angry, hadn't been hurt. She had been moved to tears by Zeke's poem about the family he'd lost, and yes, it had surfaced her own losses, her old pain.

But that wasn't Cole's fault. What kind of wife was she to strike out at him that way? And the set of his shoulders as he walked out into the night . . . Maybe he just needed a moment to cool down before he faced her and made peace.

He was always one to measure his words, to consider before he spoke. He was so much better than she at that. So much wiser. The thought surprised her, but it was true. Who was she to insist he learn the things she knew, when he already had greater wisdom and self-control than she could hope for?

Her tongue was as unruled as always, no matter how many books she'd read, how beautiful her script, how knowledgeable her mind. She went to the entry, hoping to see him standing there on the porch. But she caught a motion at the stable, saw a horse taking off in the darkness fully laden.

Her heart sank. Though the rain had passed, the sky still hung heavy. Surely he couldn't mean to stay out all night. But it was in him to do just that. *Better to sleep on the corner of the roof than remain in the house with a contentious woman.* Maybe Cole hadn't mounted the roof, but for him he'd done the next best thing.

She sagged against the doorjamb. What could she do? Upstairs the house was quiet. She could go up to bed, sleep in its warmth, and let Cole work out his own temper. But Abbie knew even as she thought it that she wouldn't sleep a wink. He was her husband, and she had driven him away.

She paced the library, rushing every ten minutes or so to peer out the front window of the entry hoping to glimpse his return. When a full hour had passed, she drew up her shoulders. He was not planning to return. He was angry enough to stay out the whole night, and deservedly so.

She walked to the cloakroom, wrapped herself in her riding cape, and followed him out. Most likely he'd taken Sirocco and headed east—not toward town, but out to the empty land where the herd grazed.

She kicked herself again. How could she? Her fingers fumbled as she saddled Zephyr and led her out. The night was dark, the moon through the clouds not quite at the half. How would she find him?

She pulled herself awkwardly astride, sitting back into the saddle to make way for the baby, then started out. It was crazy. The last thing Cole wanted just now was her. But she had to take back her words— or at least try.

The night air was rare. Though tomorrow would likely be as hot as any summer day, this evening's temperature dipped low, the air at this altitude thin enough to dissipate all the day's warmth. And with the rain, it had hardly any warmth to start with.

She searched the darkness before her. Would Cole light a fire? But even if he did, he would build it where it would not attract attention, his old instincts kicking in any time he slept out. He could be anywhere.

She rode on, scanning the land. They rarely kept a watch on the herd since they fenced in the nearly three thousand acres that comprised the ranch. So Cole would be out there alone, licking his wounds. She hung her head. Zephyr's hooves thudded in the softened ground, the day's rain adding to its marshy depth. In the clouded darkness, the straw-colored thatch was all gray.

But where would Cole have gone? He could have headed any direction after leaving the yard to the east. Had he turned down toward Templeton Gap? That place held bad memories, memories of her shooting the boy, of her being held by the rustler, and of Cole's near brush with death for her sake. But it would be a sheltered place from the wind.

She turned that way. The gap began as a mere dip, then dug and plunged down some thirty feet deep. It ran for miles. She kept to the near edge, realizing as she did how ludicrous it was to think she'd find Cole out here on the land. As she shook her head, her eye was caught by something.

There ahead was the uneven flicker of a fire in the draw. Cole. She drew a long breath for courage, then headed for its light. Yet even before he might have heard her, Abbie sensed something was wrong. There was not a lone man by the fireside but several milling around, a dark patch of horses tethered in the gap.

Had Cole sent the men out after all? Had he gone to join them? Silently she slid from Zephyr's back, tethered the mare with a rock on the reins, and crept forward. The brush offered little cover, but she kept low, allowing the ridge of the gap to shield her from sight.

Gathered in the firelight, their night sight would be limited. She had the advantage of darkness about her, and light to illuminate them. Still, she kept low and crawled as she approached the edge of the draw. A gaping crevice to her right had allowed the firelight to pour out into the night and catch her eye.

Abbie carefully avoided sending even the slightest earth down the slope, but she wanted to see what manner of men were there on her land. Rustlers? They'd had little trouble with that these last years. Her brand was too well known. She crouched.

The firelight sent the men's shadows up the sandy wall of the draw, black wraiths leaping and waving above them. Their discussion was animated, played out on the wall of earth like a puppet play on strings. One man stood, his back to the far wall. He put a finger to his partner's chest, speaking harshly, and raised his face enough for her to see beneath the brim of his hat.

Abbie's spine went cold. She remembered that face from the trail to El Paso, the red of his long johns showing even now through the collar of his shirt, his boots back on his feet where they belonged. *Crete Marlowe.* Her breath caught in her throat, twisted by tissue suddenly tight and clinging.

And Cole was out here somewhere alone.

✦✦✦✦✦✦✦

Cole dropped the bedroll to the ground and kicked it out flat. His temper was taking hold and gnawing his gut. Who did Abbie think she was, talking him down that way? Maybe what she said was true. Maybe he was just an ignorant cowpoke. But couldn't he expect a little respect from his own wife?

No, he wasn't the learned, genteel Montgomery Farrel. Cole clenched his hands at his sides. And he never would be. He was Cole Jasper, son of the drunken fool, Asa Thomas Jasper. And he hadn't gone to school one day in his life because his pa couldn't read and he wouldn't have his sons knowing something he didn't.

The first years when he was small, his ma had pleaded to teach the boys herself, but his pa wouldn't hear of it. He wouldn't be shamed by his own sons. The next years Cole had defended his own ignorance with his fists. Then he'd discovered how to learn without schooling. He'd picked up all the know-how he could and gleaned more than most people suspected.

He was not stupid. Even Brother Lewis had seen that. But when Sam taught himself to read and write, Cole refused. Maybe in some warped way he followed his pa's footsteps. Maybe by then he'd spent so much energy convincing himself it didn't matter that he couldn't go back on it.

Whatever the case, he'd thrown himself into learning the practical things, the daring things, the useful things that had gotten him where he was today. Why couldn't Abbie see that? Why couldn't she accept him as he was?

Cole uncinched the saddle and pulled it from the stallion's back. He left him bridled and tied him to the scrub. Pulling open the canvas sack, he pulled out kindling and chunks of pine, dry and seasoned for campfire use. He built a fire ring and arranged the tinder.

Striking the match, he felt a quiver in his chest just at the base of his sternum where the ribs met. It had been some time since he'd desired a smoke, but he felt it now, imagined himself drawing the tobacco into his lungs and breathing out the smoke. He shook his head. He was better off without it.

The flames began to lick up the small branches and dry pine needles, the tips glowing like shooting stars. He watched the chunks of pine catch and suck the flame into their roughhewn layers. The bark of the single log smoked and red sparks popped from the sap.

Settling down onto the bedroll, he didn't pull the cover over. It felt good to be out and alone. Maybe he should have stayed that way. Maybe he had too many years of solitary riding to make a successful marriage. Maybe Abbie knew better than he how ill equipped he was to meet her expectations.

He should have left well enough alone. He could have let her go. Down there in El Paso they could have parted ways. But he'd needed that one last try, that one fatal question one more time. Why had she said yes?

He pictured her standing before him in the windy yard of his rundown shack, saying she loved him, saying she'd be his wife. Then he pictured her standing before him in the glow of the library saying he knew nothing but the backside of a herd. Maybe she was right.

Cole drew a weary breath. Maybe he'd closed the door on things he shouldn't have and grown as stubborn and set as his pa. If so, he'd done it to survive. Nothing hurt you bad if you could spit in its face. But he'd been spitting a long time now. Thirty-seven years. He'd come into the world spitting without even knowing why.

He dropped his head in his hands and closed his eyes. It would be different for his child—son or daughter, it didn't matter. His child would not have to kick and spit through life. His child . . . and Abbie's.

What if she wanted things for the child he didn't agree on? What if she guarded this baby as she did Elliot? What if she kept Cole out, believing him an ignorant fool? The thought hurt, hurt bad. All his life he'd disappointed those who wanted something from him, wanted things he couldn't understand, much less accomplish.

Here he was again, letting down those he loved. Cole couldn't be what Abbie wanted. He should never have tried. But his child was growing inside her. He couldn't walk away from that. And he'd never been a quitter.

He ran his hand through his hair, lay back, and looked at the stars. How long had it been since he sat out under a night sky and listened to the loneliness? Not as long as it seemed. Seven months ago they'd been on the road home, sleeping with the stars for a blanket amid a symphony of night noises.

Blanket of stars and symphony of night noises. He'd turned a poetic phrase in his head. His own thoughts had run into words such as Zeke had used. He sucked his cheek. Is that what Abbie wanted? A man who could turn her head with a poetic phrase?

He crossed his arms behind his head. Did she really think he'd ever be anything but a hard-riding cowboy? He closed his eyes. Time would tell. Now he needed to feel the open country around him, the night air sucking away his warmth, hear the wind in the grass and the throaty call of an owl somewhere in the night.

Twenty-Seven

"Mama?" Jenny crept softly into the dark room. With only the dim light from the window, she couldn't make out any shape in the bed. It looked smooth and empty, and when she came forward to its side, she saw that it was.

"Mama?" She turned and glanced around the room, expecting movement in the shadows. None came. Mama must be downstairs with Pa.

Jenny shivered in the wake of the dream that had jolted her from sleep. At least she thought it was a dream. Why else would she have the bad feeling? She didn't often come to Aunt Abbie—to Mama—with her fears. But this time ... Jenny squared her shoulders and walked out of the room, along the hall, and down the stairs.

The house was dark and silent as she crept to the library where she'd left Mama and Pa after Zeke's reading. Maybe they were there still. But the library was empty, a lone ember glowing like a small red eye in the fireplace, and suddenly she was afraid. As afraid as the dream had made her. Where were they?

She walked back into the hallway and nearly jumped out of her skin. A thin white figure moved toward her, and as she drew air to scream, a hand reached.

"Jenny? What are you doing?"

Jenny's heart dropped out of her throat and returned to beating. Birdie. It was Birdie there in the hall like a ghost come to haunt her. Birdie, whose touch was warm instead of the frigid breath of death she'd expected.

"I can't find Mama." She sounded like a baby.

Birdie looked up the stairs.

But Jenny shook her head. "She's not up there. Neither is Pa."

"They must have gone out somewhere."

"In the middle of the night?" Jenny quirked an eyebrow skeptically.

Birdie made an odd face. "You do not know everything."

Jenny sagged. "But where would they go?"

Birdie was quiet. She drew in a breath and sighed. "What did you want with her, your mamá?"

Jenny didn't want to admit her bad dream, didn't want Birdie to know she'd gone creeping to Mama as Elliot might. She drew herself up, but before she could speak, Birdie took her hand. "Come. There is room in my bed for both of us."

Jenny held back a moment, reluctant to accept Birdie's offer. Would it show she was scared, needy? Why wasn't Pa there? Where was he? Where was Mama? She pushed aside her questions and followed Birdie.

They entered the dark room and Birdie released her hand. "I will light a candle, and the angels will watch over us."

Jenny heard the scratch of the match and saw the tiny flame sputter and fall. The wick of the candle took what it needed and glowed in place of the match extinguished by Birdie's puff. Jenny looked around the room, unsure what to do next.

"Come." Birdie held up the coverlet.

Jenny slid in and curled into a ball. Birdie wrapped the cover over her, then climbed in the other side. Their backs just touched, but Birdie's warmth was like sunshine to the earth. Jenny snuggled closer.

"Birdie?"

"Sí?"

"Can I tell you my dream?"

"Sí, *cara*."

Birdie rolled and put a hand on her shoulder. Jenny rolled, too. She started to speak but no details of the dream formed on her lips. The feeling was still there, but she couldn't find the dream. "I guess I just got scared."

"Sí. Sleep now. It will be morning soon."

Jenny drew a long breath and curled up again. It wasn't so bad to admit she was afraid. Maybe sometime she could tell Birdie the other things she felt. Maybe.

◆◆◆◆◆◆◆

Abbie felt frozen in place. *Crete Marlowe.* He'd come after Cole. In spite of Cole's denial, he'd come. What else could he be there for? What other reason did he have to be on her land? She closed her eyes and forced her breath to steady.

What should she do? Move from there, that was first. She had to get back without being seen or heard, back to her mare, to the ranch— no, to Cole. But how? How could she find him? What if he happened upon Crete unawares as she had? She looked down again and counted heads. Six of them. And Cole was alone. As was she.

Slowly she backed away from the edge, creeping slowly, until a stick cracked under her boot. She froze. Abbie couldn't see into the gap, but she saw the shadows. One man had risen to his feet, a large man with a ten-gallon hat. She stayed still, perfectly still as their voices rose to her indistinctly.

The tall shadow moved, bent, then dropped from sight. Had he left the fireside or resumed his seat? Either way she couldn't wait. Slowly and with great care she turned, then hurried away, crouching low to the ground. Zephyr raised her head as Abbie approached.

Don't whinny, she silently pleaded, reaching for the reins. She freed them from the stone, then swung astride. Looking back over her shoulder, she saw the glare from the fire but no motion. She walked Zephyr until she was certain the sound would not reach those in the gap. Then she kicked the mare's sides and rushed for the ranch.

Maybe Cole was home, but even if he wasn't, she had to alert the men and her family to the danger. She wouldn't be able to find Cole in the dark, and too much could happen while she wasted time searching. Zephyr was winded when she pulled up at the house, but Abbie didn't stop to care for her.

She slipped down and ran for the stairs, then burst into her darkened home. No lights burned, no sound reached her ears. She rushed up the stairs. Her bedroom was empty. She went next to the room adjoining, the room she called Cole's, though he'd not spent one night there. He knew too well how she needed him beside her.

It was empty, of course. She took a step toward the door, then dropped to her knees instead, her heart aching. With the earnestness of rising panic, she beseeched the Lord on her husband's behalf. Feeling no calmer but filled with renewed confidence, she lit a lamp and made her way to the children's rooms.

Elliot slept blissfully, soft and rosy amid the thick quilts. But when she passed into Jenny's room, she saw the bed rumpled and empty. *Jenny.* Her breath seized and she pressed a hand to her chest. Had the child somehow followed Cole, the two of them so akin Jenny knew his distress? She spun, but Birdie's form in the doorway arrested her flight.

"She is safe."

Three small words, but Abbie felt their powerful reassurance.

"She had a fright and searched for you." Birdie's eyes flickered in the light of the lamp. "When you were not to be found, I put her in my bed."

Abbie expelled her breath. "Thank you, Birdie. Now I must fetch Zeke and the men." She paused only a moment before adding, "Crete Marlowe is out there."

Birdie's eyes went wide, her hand came to her throat. *"O Dios."*

"Yes, Birdie. Pray."

"But where is Cole?"

Abbie felt the constricting in her throat. "I don't know. He went out . . . alone."

Birdie rushed to her and caught her arm. "Crete will kill him. There is bad blood."

"I know, Birdie, I know." As the girl collapsed in her arms. Abbie held her, this girl-woman who was now legally her charge. She drew strength even as she gave comfort, then pulled away. "I must get the men."

Birdie clung to her hands only a moment. "But . . . it is not only Cole he seeks. He swore to kill me if I told, if I—"

"Don't you worry. He won't come near you." Abbie squeezed Birdie's hands with more confidence than she felt, then hurried up the small stairs to the attic, where Zeke slept in relative comfort, his snores soft and rolling. She tapped the door, then knocked full out. The snore cut off with a snort, and she heard the bed creak.

"Yes? Who's there?"

"It's me, Zeke. I need you at once." Abbie didn't wait for him to dress. She hurried back down the stairs and went outside, the night air off the mountains colder than before. Wherever Cole was, he must be chilled to the bone.

She ran for the bunkhouse. Maybe . . . maybe he was there. Maybe he'd come in while she looked for him. Maybe sleeping in the bunkhouse was statement enough of his displeasure. But when she opened the door, she counted only Curtis, Matt, and Will.

She fought her disappointment and went first to Will. Though the youngest of the three, he was the one she trusted with her life. And she knew his loyalty to Cole. She shook him awake and gasped, "Crete Marlowe is here."

He scrambled up as though shot. "Where?"

"Templeton Gap. With five others."

Will looked over her head. "Where's Cole?"

Curtis stirred and sat up. "What's going on?"

Abbie shuddered. "Trouble, Curtis. The kind that's going to take every one of us. Wake Matt."

She briefly told them that Cole was out on the land somewhere, but that he didn't know Crete was there. If her eyes told Will more than he needed to know, it couldn't be helped. "Someone's got to go to town and tell Sheriff Davis."

"I'll go," Curtis said.

"Do you think Crete'll try anything tonight?" This from Will made her turn.

"I don't know. I wouldn't put anything past him. Though it is odd they camped in the gap. Almost as though they intended to make for town instead of the house."

"Maybe they do." Curtis reached for the gun that hung at the end of his bed. "Maybe it's just coincidence they're on your land."

Abbie shook her head. "I don't believe in coincidence." She realized Curtis was waiting for her to leave before he stood and dressed. "Be careful, Curtis. Come straight back and let me know what the sheriff intends to do."

"Yes, ma'am."

"Will, you and Matt meet me at the house."

Will shook his head. "Matt can go with you to the house. I'll find Cole."

Abbie hesitated, then agreed. "All right. But be careful, Will." She headed back to the house, unconsciously searching the yard for Cole. The night was less deep, the first paling toward dawn giving breadth and substance to the shapes around her, the sullen moon illuminating the gravel at her feet. She swallowed her aching fear. *Where are you, Cole? Where are you?*

Birdie had roused Pearl, and Zeke waited in the entry, perched on the bottom stairs, his knees up and spread. He stood when she came in. "Any sign of the mister, ma'am?"

She shook her head. Birdie must have filled him in, too. "I've sent Curtis for the sheriff. Matt will be here in a moment and I'll have him keep watch. Zeke, I want you to guard the children. You and Zena. They've hidden in the wine cellar before. If it comes to that . . ."

Zeke nodded. "Don't you worry, ma'am. We'll keep the children safe. It's Mr. Jasper I'm concerned for."

Abbie felt her chest constrict. "Yes, Zeke. That's my concern, too."

◆◆◆◆◆◆◆

Curtis rode hard through the darkness. He knew Mrs. Jasper was not given to overreacting, and he'd heard enough about Crete Marlowe from Cole to keep his pace sharp. He'd wake the sheriff and hightail it back to the ranch before Marlowe stopped snoring. If indeed men like that slept.

He hunkered down into the saddle and urged more speed from the gelding. One second too late he saw the rut gashed through the road by the rain. The gelding went down with a violent twist, hooves splaying to the side. Curtis reached to brace himself, then felt the bone of his arm snap. His head struck hard, shooting pain down his spine. Then nothing more.

✦✦✦✦✦✦✦

Something nagged. Something that wasn't temper and wasn't sore. Something inside that wouldn't let him sleep. Cole rolled inside the blanket. What did he expect, stretched out on the ground on a late summer night that felt more like December, when he had a bed and a roof and a wife to curl up with if only he'd been less touchy?

He pressed an elbow to the ground. But no, that wasn't it. This nagging had substance. He didn't think it was something he'd heard in his sleep. He hadn't been deep enough to miss a sound.

This feeling was different, like the one he'd had when Mr. Farrel rode to Captain Jake's hacienda. Mr. Farrel had gone alone, but he'd followed, and found the man thrashed and left for dead. Now the feeling intensified, growing inside him until the hair at the back of his neck stood out.

Trouble. He could almost smell it in the air. And he'd left his family unguarded. Cole sat up and searched the night. Everything was calm, silent. Not even a cricket song. He pushed the blanket aside and stood. The holstered gun slapped his thigh and settled into place. The moon had set, but enough dawn was coming to allow some sight. Sirocco stood undisturbed by any scent or sense of danger.

Cole waited, listening. The tiny rustle of a rodent, a breath of wind, nothing more. Was he imagining things? Even so, he had to act. He rolled and tied the bedding, then loaded and saddled Sirocco. He would go home and eat crow, but at least he'd know his family was safe.

Twenty-Eight

Abbie waited. The early dawn was turning the land to silver and still Curtis had not returned with the sheriff. Nor had Will returned with Cole. Had they encountered Crete Marlowe? Had Curtis been intercepted? She shuddered, then with sudden resolve turned from the window where she watched. "I'm going to town."

Birdie's eyes met hers, then Abbie turned away to instruct Zena. "Wake the children and take them to the cellar. Try not to frighten them, but keep them there till I return."

Pearl puffed her lips but didn't argue. "I'll fetch them their vittles."

"Thank you, Pearl. Zeke, you stay in the kitchen by the cellar door. Can you use a rifle?"

"Well, ma'am, I'm a bit of a crack shot, if you'll believe it."

She half smiled. She'd believe anything of him. She took the Winchester down from over the mantel. "The shells are in the drawer of the desk there. Keep it loaded and ready. If Crete Marlowe shows his face—"

"You needn't elaborate, ma'am."

"Matt, you'll watch from here?"

He nodded.

Abbie drew a quick breath. "Very well, I'm going now."

"No." Birdie stepped forward. "I will go."

Birdie's words took Abbie by surprise. She had meant to keep Birdie safely hidden in the cellar with the little ones. "No, Birdie."

Birdie stood firm. "If it were not for me, for my lie, Crete Marlowe would not have left El Paso. He would be hung already for Auralee's murder."

"That doesn't matter now."

"It matters. I will ride to town for the sheriff. I will not have you risk—"

"Birdie, you can't—"

"Perhaps if you both went." Zeke's calm, reasonable voice broke in. "It's safer for two."

Abbie swallowed her apprehension. Maybe that was wise. Maybe she could even leave Birdie in Sheriff Davis's charge, at least until Crete was gone or apprehended. He knew where to find the ranch, but he might not look for Birdie in town. "All right, Zeke. Please harness the buggy."

Even before the sun's appearance, Abbie could tell the day would be fair. The night's cool was quickly dissipating as she set out with Birdie beside her. But the chill within her body was not so easily dispelled. She kept Lady Belle prancing, the reins tight in her hands.

Had Curtis misunderstood? Had he remained with the sheriff instead of coming back to report? Had he . . . Her jangled thoughts were interrupted by the sight of Nightstar standing lamed and empty saddled beside the road. The gelding held his right forehoof gingerly and hung his head.

Abbie reined in, toed the brake, and jumped from the buggy. Her skirt snagged and she yanked it free, then hurried to the horse's side. The sweat had cooled on his neck, matting the hide, and she could tell he'd been standing for some time. But had he been lamed going to or from town?

He was facing homeward, but she searched the road ahead. She took in the newly formed ruts across the low dip, then saw Curtis lying in a heap a dozen feet from the road. She snatched up her skirts and rushed forward. He lay without moving as she crouched beside him. "Curtis?"

She touched his cheek with the back of her hand. He was chilled, but his pulse throbbed weakly in his neck. Abbie shook his shoulder and he stirred, mumbling, but didn't open his eyes. Reaching for his hand, she noticed the bone of his forearm protruding through both skin and shirt.

A wave of nausea passed through her more acutely than it might without her pregnancy to magnify it. She put a hand to her stomach and willed it away. Quickly she felt his bones for any other damage. The side of his head where it had struck the rocky ground had a rude swelling that gave beneath her fingers, and again her gorge rose. But she could find nothing else damaged.

Standing, she turned and motioned for Birdie to bring up the buggy. As soon as the wheels stopped beside her, Abbie spoke. "Help me get him up. We'll leave him with Doctor Barrow."

Birdie climbed down. "Should we move him?"

"Probably not, but we can't leave him lying here. Not with . . . No, I think we have to take him. He moved his head himself, so I believe his spine is sound."

Birdie nodded, then slipped her hands beneath his waist and shoulders. Abbie did likewise and together they heaved with all their strength. Curtis was not a small man, and his dead weight seemed more than they could manage. Abbie clenched her teeth against the strain in the small of her back. Her arms burned, and she winced as she pushed to the limits of her strength and lifted him to the back of the buggy.

Birdie cradled his head as they eased him down. Abbie tugged a blanket from beneath the seat and wrapped it over him. Then she laid his broken arm atop where it wouldn't bang the side. "We'll have to go slowly."

Birdie nodded again. "I will sit back here." She huddled into the corner of the floor between Curtis and the back of the seat, holding his head steady. Abbie pulled herself up to the seat, released the brake, and started the mare slowly toward the deep ruts in the road.

The wheels of the buggy were large and well formed, the whole contrivance expertly built thanks to Monte's fastidious tastes. Nonetheless, as they dipped down into the first rut, she felt the jolt and heard Curtis moan. The wheel turned, rode the ridge, and banged down into the next rut.

A third time the buggy rose and fell, and then they were past the worst of it, though the rushing water from the torrential rain had made rough work of the entire road. Abbie glanced over her shoulder. "Okay back there?"

"He is starting to wake."

"If he gains any semblance of consciousness, ask if he made it to the sheriff."

Abbie felt bad disturbing him so, but her own urgency drove her, rising to fever pitch with each rut and bump that slowed them. She chafed the delay Curtis was causing. Was the sheriff even now laying plans to apprehend Crete Marlowe? Or had he not yet heard of the impending danger?

Curtis moaned, the sound reminding her of the last time she had driven him to town, sick and reeking from typhoid. She gripped the reins tighter, her nerves pulling the tendons in her fingers taut, the muscles in her shoulders knotting. Here he was again, helpless and injured. She didn't want to consider that it was her order that had sent him out, her fear that had driven him.

And now that fear grew as the sky paled and the day warmed. Would Crete make his move with the dawn? Was he even now starting for the house—or perhaps for town? What was he planning? And where was Cole?

The first glow of sunlight kindled the eastern sky as she rode in among the outermost buildings of Rocky Bluffs. Not too many were about yet as she drove the buggy down Main Street to the turn at Fourth. Mr. Simms was tying up the awning above his dry goods store, and several shop owners swept the walks before their establishments.

A few horses were tied at the hitching rails, two at the hotel restaurant, and several beside the smithy. Abbie yearned to keep straight on and find the sheriff, but her first responsibility was to see Curtis safely to the doctor. His injuries and the exposure he'd suffered needed immediate attention. She made the turn and drove the three blocks to the clinic.

She climbed down and knocked impatiently at the doctor's door. The clinic was silent, but she knew he might still be sleeping in one of the back rooms. She knocked again, praying he was not out on a call. She spun around, realizing that every minute spent standing there was keeping her from reaching the sheriff. "Birdie, climb down and wait here for the doctor. I'm running for the sheriff."

"But—"

"You can meet me there after you've seen to Curtis." Abbie didn't wait for an answer but picked up her skirts and ran. Her belly felt like a cannonball as she held tightly with one hand to the child inside. Maybe Crete was only passing through. Maybe he would skirt the town and leave them in peace. Maybe even now he was heading south to ... to ... Even her imagination would go only so far.

The sheriff was not at the office, a bad sign, she knew. He would hardly be lying abed if Curtis had reached him. She ran across the street to his cabin and hammered the door with one hand while pressing the other to her side, where a stitch was making her hard breaths painful. She banged again and the door gave under the onslaught.

"What is it? Mrs. Jasper?"

"Crete Marlowe ... he's ... camped at ... Templeton Gap. Or at least ... he was last night."

Sheriff Davis scowled, stepping halfway through the door. "Where's Cole? Why didn't he ..."

Abbie shook her head. "He doesn't know. He was out ... last night. Please, I don't have time ..."

But even as she spoke, the street behind her erupted with a terrible explosion. It rocked her from her feet, and she staggered against the sheriff.

He caught, then dragged her down. "What in blazes!"

Another explosion sent shards of wood and glass and clouds of dust billowing to the sky. Abbie felt the percussion of the blast in her chest. It winded her as she clutched her ears with her hands. Dazed by the deafening noise, she shook her head.

Sheriff Davis was already pulling his gun from its holster. He must have strapped it on before opening the door to her. That was likely something a sheriff learned to do. He staggered up and reeled toward the street, his balance shaky from the deafening blasts.

Abbie watched him go, his broad back and hefty shoulders hunched, knees bent and gun ready. Even as he advanced, another explosion threw him off his feet, and she lost him in the smoke and rust colored dust. She choked on the cloying air.

Sheriff Davis staggered up, but a volley of gunshots buckled and tossed him back like a scarecrow in the wind. Abbie's hand clamped her mouth against the cry. Figures moved in the swirling haze, men on foot, two on horseback, other horses in tow. She pulled herself to her knees, stunned to see only rubble and one brick wall where the Rocky Bluffs Bank had been.

Half the Dry Goods and Mercantile was blown away, and along the street every window she could see through the smoke was shattered. More gunfire broke the morning stillness and a woman screamed from down the block. Already five bodies lay in the dust, one of them Sheriff Davis. Abbie couldn't tell if there were more. As she stood, searching for shelter, a figure rushed toward her from the side. She recoiled, then recognized Birdie.

The girl collapsed against her, shaking. "I thought you were—"

"Hush, Birdie."

But already one of the men turned, the large man whose shadow Abbie had watched on the gap's wall. Cringing, she pulled Birdie tight against her. Maybe he would . . . But he waved them forward with the gun. She had no choice but to leave the shelter of the sheriff's stoop.

The man was Indian, or at least part. His height suggested some white blood, but she didn't have time to ponder it. Birdie's legs scarcely held her as they stopped at the edge of the street. Another man approached, masked by the whorling dust. Abbie's heart faltered when his face came clear.

She held his eyes defiantly, eyes as cold as ice beneath the steel gray brows. Though his hair had grayed substantially, his beard still had stubborn streaks of brown. Bits of debris clung there. A tendon twitched on the side of his face as he licked a trickle of blood from the corner of his mouth.

Behind him two men hurried from the vault, which stood naked and out of place amid the ruin. Their arms were full of bags, and she knew the bags held money, her money and Cole's, and all the people of the town's. "It's clean," one of them said, and Abbie recognized the one who had ridden with Crete when he came for Cole. Was it Finn? Jackson Finn.

"Load the horses." Crete spoke without taking his eyes from her. "Y'all listen up!" he hollered.

Abbie didn't dare look to see who else was on the street to hear.

"You tell Cole Jasper I'll be waitin'! If he don't come, I'll be back."

She felt her breath catch jaggedly. He had hollered it to the town, but it was to her his eyes were pinned. Slowly he turned, grabbing the reins offered him by a scraggly youth, and mounted. He drew the horse's head up and around, and Abbie waited for him to kick his heels and be gone.

Instead, he passed slowly, so slowly she never anticipated the swift rise of his hand, the gun muzzle flashing, and Birdie slumping in her arms. Abbie screamed, catching Birdie's full weight as the girl's legs collapsed.

"You tell your husband I'll be waitin'."

Abbie staggered. Something warm and wet filled her hand as she lowered Birdie to the ground. Her whole being quaked as she turned her face to the speaker of those cruel words. He looked briefly down at Birdie's bleeding chest, then turned away and rode.

Abbie pressed her face to Birdie's lips, feeling the faintest breath of life. The girl's eyes fluttered open, and her breath rasped on the blood trickling from her mouth. She looked from Abbie to the sky above, and her lips trembled, the sides turning ever so slightly upward.

"They are here...."

Abbie held her, feeling the tears stream down her face.

"He calls me by name. Bernadetta..." The breath faded and stopped. Her lips almost closed, but her eyes remained fixed on the sky over Abbie's head, though they no longer saw.

Abbie stared, waiting for something, something more from this child she had known so briefly. This child who had trusted her, trusted God ... and for what? Abbie swallowed painfully and closed the lids of Birdie's eyes. Her own chest heaved suddenly with aching sobs.

She did not weep alone. Others had gathered in the street filling the new day with cries and curses. Rocking Birdie's head in her lap, Abbie joined theirs with her own.

◆◆◆◆◆◆◆

Cole reined in briefly, rocked by the thundering booms and eyeing the rusty cloud over town. What on earth? "What do you make of that?" he threw back to Will.

Will shook his head.

Zeke pulled the mare he rode nose to nose with Sirocco. "If I didn't know better I'd say it was blasting."

Cole narrowed his eyes. "Blasting?"

Zeke nodded. "Sounded like dynamite to me. Heard plenty of it around the mines when I was small."

"Dynamite." Cole looked harder at the reddish smudge rising to the sky, the sun's early rays making it redder still. Then he looked at Zeke and wondered. What would a man who dressed up another man and wrote poetry know about dynamite and mines?

When he'd left Matt in charge of the ranch half an hour ago, Zeke had begged to ride along. Cole had growled his assent, more concerned with Abbie's absence than anyone's presence. The children were hidden in the cellar, but where was Abbie? He noticed now that Zeke carried Mr. Farrel's Winchester. Will had only a six-shooter.

Cole looked down at his own Colt .44 revolver and the Springfield rifle in the scabbard. If Abbie was correct and Crete was carrying five extra men, they'd be hard-pressed meeting up with them in the open. But just now he was more concerned with getting to town and fetching Abbie home, and Birdie, too, from what he'd heard.

Why hadn't Abbie waited? Why did she get it into her head to handle things on her own as though—as though she hadn't a husband to do it? He looked back toward the ranch. Though it was long out of sight, he felt a tightening inside, hoping he'd done the right thing.

He couldn't second-guess it now. The children and servants were locked in the cellar. Matt was on guard in the front entry with orders to shoot on sight anyone fitting Crete's description. Now, if only Abbie and Birdie had stayed put ... But he knew it was his own fault. He hadn't been there when they needed him.

Never mind that Abbie wouldn't have known of Crete's presence if she hadn't been out searching. The thought of her creeping up to Crete Marlowe's camp made him shake. The woman was ... He spurred the horse. "Let's go."

They smelled the ruin before they saw it, Zeke confirming with a nod that his dynamite theory was correct. Cole felt his heart quicken with fear as they entered the street ringing with angry cries and sobbing. He hardly recognized what he saw. Buildings torn apart and . . . gone. The bank was missing altogether but for one wall, heaps of brick and splintered wood where it should have been.

The crowd parted to let him pass. He searched frantically for one thing only. And he found her, huddled in the street with . . . Birdie's head in her lap. *Dear God.* Cole caught her eyes with his, saw there all he needed to know. The fury burned a hole in his chest, and his jaw tightened, the muscles hard as rock as he dismounted. His breath came in tight heaves.

"Cole Jasper."

He turned to the voice. Oscar Driscoll, the banker. The man looked like death, one cheek gashed, the rest of him covered in dust.

"Cole Jasper, I hold you responsible for this." He waved a finger that shook badly. Murmurs started around them.

Will stepped between him and Driscoll. "What are you talking about?"

"He said he'd be waiting for you, Cole." This from Hank Thorne.

Cole scanned the faces. "Where's the sheriff?"

Two men stepped aside, and he saw the mound covered with a blanket. Blood seeped into the wool like dye.

"Eight more dead." Judge Wilson came forward. "Some from the guns, some the dynamite." He swung an arm toward the demolished buildings. "They came in here with full intent to wreak destruction. And wreak it they did." His white goatee bounced up and down as he spoke, and a vein in his temple stood out blue against his pale skin.

"So what are you gonna do?" Eli Stokes stepped forward from the crowd. From the looks and smell of him he'd spent the night in the saloon, a long way from the Lazy Y.

Cole saw the strong disdain the man felt for him. Well, he'd shown him up and caused him injury besides, though the hand seemed to have healed. He looked around at the other faces filling the street. He looked down at Abbie, her tears streaking the dust on her face like war paint. He swallowed the sawdust in his throat and reached into his pocket.

"No!" She laid Birdie down and jumped to her feet.

Cole tensed, knowing without a doubt she was going to make a scene.

Abbie stalked toward him, arms tight at her sides, eyes raking the crowd. "This is no more Cole's doing than anyone here."

Men shuffled uncomfortably, but none offered agreement. They knew this was his fight. They'd heard Crete's own words, or heard them repeated a dozen times in the clearing of the dust. Cole drew out his hand, and the badge glinted in the sunlight.

She turned her eyes on him. "No, Cole."

"I got to."

Her chest heaved with her effort to stay calm. He could see she was on the verge of hysterics. Why had they all left her sitting there with Birdie's dead body? Did they blame her, too? Had everyone lost their minds?

He heard a sound from Will, who appeared to have just noticed Birdie. His voice came out hollow, like a wind off the desert. He walked to her, then bent as though someone had punched his middle. He dropped to his knees and lifted her into his arms, cradling her there.

"No, Cole. I won't let you." Abbie's voice was low and all the more forceful for it.

"I gave my word."

"Your word. Your honorable word." She almost spat it, though scarcely louder than a whisper. He saw the venom in her eyes. She blamed him, too, if not in the same way as the rest, enough to put the fury in her gaze. But it wasn't him. It was Crete.

Cole looked away, searched the street, the blown-out windows. He felt the tension, the fear, the need for revenge, his own not the least. Birdie. His heart wrenched. Little Birdie with all her wiles and her hope to put her life right. The rage flared up. And it might as easily have been Abbie. Crete was a cold-blooded killer, and a man who could shoot down a woman was . . .

He moved the badge to his chest and pinned it there, hearing the murmurs of assent and relief.

"You think that makes it right?" Abbie's hiss halted the voices around them. "You think because you put on that badge it gives you a right to revenge?"

"Abbie . . ."

"He's a killer. Look what he did!" She swung her arm in a wide arc. "Look." She pointed down at Birdie in Will's arms. "He has no soul. And you think you can bring him to justice?"

"I gotta try."

"He'll kill you."

Cole held her in his gaze. Didn't she see? Didn't she know? There was no other way.

Her lips trembled, and he could see a change in her eyes. The fury passed and a strange, blank glare took its place as though she'd shut a door inside her mind. Her voice was calm, almost passionless. "If you go, don't bother to come back."

"Abbie . . ."

"I mean it, Cole. I've been through enough."

"This isn't about you."

"Isn't it?" She began to shake. "And who will be crying at your grave?"

With his gaze fixed on her face, he fought the need to give in, to take off the badge and go home. He'd live the rest of his days shamed by it, but he'd live them with her. He looked past her to Will, who came up behind and laid Birdie gently beside the others.

Will straightened. "I'll ride with you, Cole."

Cole saw Abbie's knuckles whiten, her teeth clench. Davy Mc-Connel came and stood beside him. "And I."

Abbie closed her eyes.

"I'll ride with you, too, Mr. Jasper."

Cole turned. "No, Zeke. I need you to stay with my wife." He looked for a reaction from Abbie, but there was none. Though she opened her eyes, they were as expressionless as the painted eyes of a doll. He looked around the crowd, but no one else came forward.

"Take what you need from my store." Samuel Peterson indicated the hardware and tack store behind him. Though the windows were gone, the building was intact. "Weapons, ammunition . . ."

"You can get your other supplies from me," Jack Smythe added. "No charge."

Nora pushed forward. Cole hadn't noticed her there, and for a moment he thought she'd light into him on Abbie's account. But she turned and faced the crowd. "Will no one else go with them? Three men against six? Killers all?"

Cole saw the eyes shift, the gazes drop. It wasn't that they were unwilling, it was that Crete had made it personal with him. They believed it was his fight. He put a hand on Nora's shoulder. "Are you willin' for Davy to come?"

Nora turned to her husband, and for a moment Cole saw Abbie's eyes flicker. Did she hope Nora would take up her cause? Nora licked the dust from her lips. "Aye. He'll not see you go alone."

Abbie turned away, her hand resting on her belly as though shielding the child from him. Cole felt the ache clear through him. Maybe if he had the right words, she'd see. . . . But he knew what he lacked.

He turned to Zeke. "Take Mrs. Jasper and . . . and Birdie home. Send Matt with fresh horses. I want a remuda of six. He'll go back directly and help you with the buryin'." Cole looked at Abbie once more, but she refused to return his gaze. He dipped the brim of his hat and walked into Peterson's Hardware.

◆◆◆◆◆◆◆

Though she kept her head down, Abbie watched Cole walk away. She felt empty, all emotion gone. The fear, the aching need . . . the love . . . gone. There was nothing inside her. Nothing. She felt Zeke beside her, saw the hat twisting in his hands like a dog circling its bed before flopping down.

He cleared his throat. "Mrs. Jasper?"

"The buggy is at Doctor Barrow's. Please fetch it. And inquire of Curtis's condition." Abbie's voice might have belonged to someone on the street, so distant from her mind it seemed.

"Yes, ma'am."

"Abbie." Nora stepped forward.

She turned to Nora, but her look must have silenced her friend, for she only stood there without words. That was good, because she wanted nothing Nora had to offer by way of explanation or consolation. Nora half turned as Davy touched her cheek briefly, then followed Cole into the store. Nora watched him go, then cleared her throat. "I'll send Father Paddy over . . . for Birdie."

"We'll take her out to the ranch," someone said. A man, but Abbie didn't look to see who or if he even spoke to her.

Zeke answered something that was lost in the mutterings, then started up the road to fetch the buggy.

Abbie glanced at Birdie lying beside the other bodies. She indeed looked like a fallen bird, shot from the sky. She was gone. All that remained was her shell, the body that had been used and paid for. Birdie's spirit had fled. Bernadetta. The Lord had called her name. As He did again and again to the people Abbie loved.

She made her way through the crowd and started up toward Fourth Street. She would not wait for Zeke to bring the buggy down. The sooner they started back, the sooner she'd release her children from the cellar and begin putting things to rights. She was only glad neither Grant nor Pa had been in town—Grant was in Denver on law business, and Pa was not yet in from the homestead to the newspaper office.

Abbie met Zeke halfway up to the doctor's and climbed into the buggy silently, then inquired about Curtis in a voice more poised and controlled than she felt.

Zeke answered in kind. "Mr. Curtis is staying at the clinic. His arm is set in plaster, but his head is bad. He's not yet fully conscious."

She nodded. "Take me home."

A shard of pain seized her when she passed Birdie, lying beside the other dead. She didn't want it, didn't want to feel the wrongness of it. It wasn't like James. It was violent, cruel, and evil. It was Satan unleashed, and for a moment she wondered if El Diablo had not triumphed after all.

Bernadetta. Birdie. The shock and sadness overwhelmed Abbie, and she dropped her face to her hands and wept. There had been no remorse in Crete's face. He had shot her down without conscience, without thought. Killed her as easily as Auralee. And now Cole was paying again, as willingly as he had the last time.

She allowed the tears to flow for Birdie, knowing full well the penalty of holding them back. Knowing also that her grief for Birdie kept away the bleak emptiness that filled Cole's place in her heart.

Twenty-Nine

With the horses loaded and the remuda in tow, Cole set out with Davy McConnel and Will at his back. He didn't know how either would be in a fight, though he'd seen Will show some mettle at the river against Pablo. But that was different from taking on armed men hand to hand and being the one to press the fight.

He didn't know much about Davy at all, besides the fact that his brother Blake had loved Abbie before he was cut down by outlaws. Maybe it was his need to see justice done that made Davy willing to ride now.

Cole thought of Abbie's words. *"He has no soul. And you think you can bring him to justice?"* But that wasn't true. Every man had a soul, if indeed a damned one. He pictured Birdie lying in Abbie's lap and felt the pain of it. That pain, added to all the other Crete had caused him, would keep him firm in purpose.

He had etched in his mind the memory of his ma hanging burnt from the tree, by Crete's hand as much as the Comanches who did it. Crete knew what whiskey did to some men. He knew and he didn't care, because he couldn't win for himself the wife of his drunken friend, Asa Jasper, couldn't win her even though her husband had long run off. He might have even planted the thought in the Comanches' heads. But Cole had no proof of that.

He only knew what Crete had done—and it was bad enough. Cole wished now he'd finished Crete when he'd had the chance. One more blow, maybe two, and the man would never have raised his head again. How much misery would have been prevented? Too late for his ma, but what of Auralee and Birdie?

Two no-account saloon girls, some might say. But Cole didn't see it that way. He thought of Brother Lewis. Where was he now, and what would he say to all this? Cole frowned. Would he think Crete Marlowe worth saving? Would he ride unarmed beside that one, speaking of man's need for God and repentance being the cure?

Cole shook his head. There could be no repentance for a man like Crete. Maybe Abbie was right to say he had no soul. More like he had no conscience. And what need had a man with no conscience for repentance?

But that was not the point of this excursion. Bringing Crete to justice had nothing to do with the man's soul. It had only to do with stopping the killer from killing again—and keeping from being the next target on Crete's list. As well as those he cared for.

Cole frowned. Crete Marlowe knew he would not ignore the challenge. That's why he made sure the whole town heard it.

Will rode in silence behind Cole, scarcely aware of Davy beside him. It wouldn't have mattered if twenty men surrounded him, he felt so alone. For months now he'd longed to take Birdie in his arms, to feel her shape, breathe her scent, touch the softness of her hair. All of which he'd done when he lifted her from the street.

But she hadn't been warm and responsive, hadn't turned her fiery eyes on him even to cut him with her words. No breath had come from her lips when he pressed his cheek close. She was gone.

All the words he'd wanted to say, all the feelings he couldn't share were wasted now. She was gone, cut down by Crete Marlowe. Had a stray bullet found her? No. It was no glancing wound. It had come from close range straight for the heart and passed clear through, leaving a larger wound behind.

He looked ahead at Cole. Why had Marlowe chosen this way to challenge Cole? Why couldn't he have called him out, or tried to back shoot him, or anything but slaying Birdie? Cole rode staunchly, keeping a strong lope. If anyone could bring down Crete Marlowe, it was Cole Jasper. But at this moment, Will wished he wouldn't. He wanted to do it himself.

◆◆◆◆◆◆◆

Having dismounted the buggy and entered her home, Abbie made her way to the cellar. Matt and Zeke shouldered the cupboard from the door and released the hiders. In a voice shaking with pain and fury, Abbie told them what happened.

She dreaded the look she saw in Jenny's eyes, the stunned reaction not only to Birdie's death, but more so to Cole's leaving. She had not thought beyond her own fury to what the children would suffer. In the terror of the morning's events, she had dealt only with the immediate.

Now she saw the depth of pain Cole's departure was bringing to her children. How could she ever forgive him for that? Inside herself she still felt nothing, nothing for him. But a great wound for her children opened up.

There was little chance Cole would survive this showdown. And whereas this lack of emotion within her might have carried her through yet another loss, it would not sustain her children. Elliot was young and resilient. In time his hurt would pass. But Jenny . . .

Abbie stooped down and took the girl in her arms. "We must be brave." She felt the child stiffen. Jenny always rejected her comfort.

Then suddenly the child's fists were against her. "I hate him. I hate him. I hate my pa!" She fought free and ran, crashing through the door and tearing outside, hair streaming behind.

Abbie rushed to the open doorway. Should she follow? What words could she use to dissuade such thoughts when they were buried in her own heart, as well? She felt Elliot press into her skirts and turned.

His small face was creased with worry, one hand fiddling with his hair. She stooped and swung him up into her arms, pressing him close to her heart. He was all she had. How many times had she thought that? How many times had she filled her grief with him, this son, this child of hers? Indeed he was all she had. A kick from the child within protested Elliot's weight and reminded her otherwise.

She stood there, locked together with her son and Cole's child inside her. Try as she might to win her niece, Jenny would always be foreign to her. And now Cole was lost, as well. But she had Elliot, and Cole's baby to come. And somewhere, when she was ready to admit it, she had God. But His ways . . . His ways were not her own.

✦✦✦✦✦✦✦

Three days later, Abbie sat beside the newest mound, smelling the fresh earth and ruing the scent. She had not ordered a marble or granite stone for Birdie. Instead, she had set up a red chalky stone, cut from the rock of the ranch. Zeke had chiseled her name and the date of her death, but Abbie hadn't known the day and month of her birth.

Why had she not asked? How could such a simple and obvious question have never been broached? If they had adopted her, it would have been on the papers, but Birdie had chosen the informal guardianship instead. Abbie looked at the stone. BERNADETTA.

And there it was again, the burning guilt. Not even a surname. And the name engraved only learned through the child's dying breath. *Who were you, Birdie? I would like to have known.*

Abbie sighed, then slowly rose to her feet. She could spend no more time there. She felt an urgent need for her children.

✦✦✦✦✦✦✦

Cole shook his head over the gory scene. The solitary trader shot through the neck, his place cleaned out of all but the rats and vultures that had come to feed on his body in the yard. Crete was leaving a sure and definite trail. When had the man turned so bloodthirsty? Or was it the pack he ran with?

Was it a message for Cole to find? And how many lives would be taken to make Crete's point? Cole took the hat from his head and slapped the dust off on his thigh. "Will, you reckon you can find a shovel in that shed?" He could see the lump rise and fall in Will's throat as he nodded and turned.

Cole turned Davy from the sight with a hand to his shoulder. "See what you can hunt up to wrap the body in. I'll keep the buzzards off."

He saw Davy walk stiffly to obey. None of them had anticipated this sort of thing. It turned his stomach to think of Crete riding free. The man was more animal than human, more demon than man. And he had let him live—all those years ago he had kept himself from finishing Crete off and had let him live to become this.

Cole eyed the tarp Davy returned with, then nodded. Davy laid it on the ground beside the body. As Cole rolled the days-old corpse over the edge, Davy lost his breakfast in the dirt. Cole pulled the tarp up and around, then rolled the shape tightly with the edges free to grasp and carry. Then he relieved Will of the shovel and worked out his own horror through sweat and labor.

◆◆◆◆◆◆◆

Elliot poked the stick up at the squirrel on the yellow-leafed branch above him. He watched the animal's furry cheeks puff and slacken as it chattered at him, dipping its head and showing tiny teeth. Its eyes were like black marbles in brown skin pouches that opened and closed without string.

The muscles bunched in the back hind legs, and the squirrel leaped to a higher branch to continue its chatter. It was teasing him to go higher. Elliot didn't want to. It was scary enough climbing into the lowest thick branch of the cottonwood from the lean-to roof.

Jenny had shown him how to mount the roof from the log pile, and from there to climb onto the overhanging branch. But he didn't want to go higher in the tree. Already the ground looked too far away. If Jenny were up there with him, she'd coax the squirrel with a nut, or trap it between them and make it jump to the roof.

But she was in one of her tempers and had hidden from him. He should tell Mama, because she'd ordered them to stay together outside. But Jenny would be furious, so he'd climbed into the tree, hoping to catch sight of her somewhere. Instead he'd found the squirrel.

Elliot looked up at the animal making its darting way back toward him. It enjoyed the game, just as Jenny did. Neither one cared that it wasn't much fun for him, being littler and unable to catch them. A streak of fire shot through him, and he pouted his lower lip with determination.

That squirrel would not get away this time. Elliot pulled himself up standing on the branch. It was so large he could have both feet together on it sideways. But the next branch was high. He could hold it with his hands, but how could he get on it?

He could swing up and hook his leg like Jenny did. He knew he could if he were just not afraid. He felt the rough bark against his palms as he pressed them tighter. Gathering all his courage, Elliot swung his leg up, but it was a halfhearted swing and his heels grazed the branch, then fell.

He came down on the branch with his hands still tight to their hold. This time he would kick harder. He kicked, and his heel caught, his free leg clawing toward the branch in wild swings. He would get it. He almost . . . had it.

Suddenly his hands slipped. His legs followed in a tumble of bent knees and scraped shins. He struck the branch and rolled to the side, came down on the shed roof and slid. Crying out, he scrabbled for a hold, then felt the air beneath him. He hit the ground so hard he couldn't cry at all. He couldn't even breathe.

Elliot rolled into a ball, making awful gasping sounds, but no air would come. His tummy hurt, and his hands and legs hurt, and he let out his hurt in a sudden wail as his lungs at last filled with air. Mama was running for him, bursting from the back door, and all he could think was that she would hold him and somehow the hurt would go away.

Abbie gathered her son against her chest feeling the violent pounding of her heart. *Oh, God, oh God, dear God! Please let him be all right.* "Elliot! Talk to me, Elliot."

"Mama." He could only cry.

But he was breathing and moving and no part of him seemed broken. She remembered her own tumbles from trees, climbing with Blake when she was no bigger than Elliot. He was all right. She could tell that, but somehow the knowledge didn't stop the fear from rising up and engulfing her.

Be still, and know that I am God. Hadn't she just read that this morning? Hadn't she been reading it when the children slipped out to play? Couldn't she trust that they were in God's hands? No. Not with Cole gone and too many graves on the hill. She must increase her vigilance. She must not let Elliot out of her sight.

And where was Jenny? She didn't care if she smothered the child's adventurous spirit. She must protect her at all cost. She pressed Elliot's head to her neck and buried her cheek in his hair. "Elliot, where's Jenny?"

"Hiding." He sniffed and started again to cry.

"Well, she won't hide again. I will keep you both in my sight every moment." *Once I find her.* And find her she would.

◆◆◆◆◆◆◆

As the days passed into weeks, the weeks to a month, Abbie kept watch over her house like a mother eagle guarding her nest. No action of Elliot's, no word of Jenny's passed without her knowing. She would even govern their thoughts if she could.

In the midst of her vigil, Zeke brought the parlor back to life. The beauty of the wooden panels that outlined the walls, the coffered cubical honeycomb on the ceiling, and the patterned floor shone when the wood was finished and gleaming its rich amber hue. The plume and feathered grain of the birch ignited under the polish in the sun's rays from the tall glass windows.

Zeke had not yet painted the fresco, but the walls stood ready to receive the canvas when he did. Even without the pastoral mural, the room was stunning as Abbie led Nora in. She had not spoken with her friend since their husbands left, not sought her out, nor responded to the overtures Nora had made.

But today, with Nora planted on her doorstep, Abbie could hardly refuse her. She motioned to the settee, which had been returned to the parlor with the completion of the woodwork. As Nora sat, Abbie settled herself stiffly into the wing chair across from her.

Abbie knew Pearl had seen Nora arrive, so she didn't bother to ring for tea. These last weeks Pearl, Zena, and Zeke seemed to have bonded together into something of an army, their efficiency and will taking on everything outside the needs of the children, upon which Abbie had fixated.

Each morning Matt checked in for his orders. And each day she told him the same. "Do whatever you think needs doing." Though it was impossible for him to run the ranch alone, she knew. The thought added to her bitterness. Cole had abandoned them, kept his word to a dead sheriff as more important than his duty to her, to the Lucky Star.

But she didn't care. As long as the children were safe, the world could fall to shambles around them. They were all she cared about, the only ones to whom she poured out her heart. Day and night she kept Elliot beside her, and she had refused to send Jenny to the new term of school in town. Rather, she worked with her in the library herself, opening the child's mind and diverting it from the pain she saw there when Jenny was free to consider her loss.

She made it a crusade to keep Jenny's mind occupied, challenged, distracted. She thought up games for both children, activities to enjoy in the mellow September days. She allowed them to profit from their small tasks, setting up a store in the back shed for their handiwork. Her heart nearly faltered when she placed a penny in Elliot's palm in return for the carving he'd made with his own small knife.

She glanced at Nora, now, and realized that her thoughts had carried her away. How long had she sat there brooding? "Forgive me, Nora. I'm distracted."

Pearl came in with tea, and the serving of it gave her a chance to gather herself. When Pearl left, Abbie took up her cup but didn't yet sip. "How good of you to come. It's a beautiful day for a ride."

"Aye."

"The changing leaves are glorious."

"I dinna come to speak of the leaves, Abbie."

"I know that." Abbie straightened. "But I don't wish to discuss what you came for."

Nora brushed back the coiled strand of red from her temple. It had come loose from the twist at the back of her head. Abbie noticed the fresh lines at the corners of Nora's eyes. Her fair skin, born to a moister clime, did not take well to the dry Colorado air.

Nora fixed her gaze frankly. "You're a bitter woman, Abbie. Bitter and wrong to send your man off without your blessin'."

Abbie stiffened. Even from Nora that was direct . . . and cruel. Didn't she see how well she was coping? What an effort she made with the children? She refused to answer.

"Och, Abbie. Ye think I don't know what it is to fear? My own Davy is gone away with him."

"With your blessing," Abbie snapped.

"Aye. Because I wouldna have it different. I sent Jaime to his death a dozen times with only my fury to hold him as he fought his rebellions. Each time he returned less than he'd been for it."

Abbie turned away. Why was Nora bringing this up now? What right did she have to open a wound safely closed? What business of Nora's was it how Abbie felt about Cole? "What do you want from me?"

"I want to know that when your Cole Jasper comes home you'll have a welcome for him."

Abbie surveyed the wood pattern of the beam climbing the wall to the ceiling, the grain like rows of sideways trees and their reflections, one atop another. "He won't come home." She said it so softly she wasn't sure if she had actually said it.

"You dinna know that. You shouldna have him dead already in your thoughts, Abbie. You canna abandon him so."

"Abandon him? Is he not the one who left us?"

"Nay. He hasna left you, not for good. Where is your faith? Your hope?"

Abbie turned to her. "My faith has never once saved someone I loved. I told Birdie to trust the Lord. She surrendered her heart only to take Crete's bullet right there."

"And she's now with the saints in heaven. Surely ye haven't turned your back on God?"

Abbie shook her head. "I know full well that God exists. I know His will is paramount. But I don't understand it, Nora. Nor do I understand how Cole could sacrifice his life and ours to have vengeance on Crete Marlowe."

"Ye think that's why he went?"

"I know it is."

"Then ye dinna know your man."

"And I suppose you do?" Abbie raised her chin mockingly.

"He's an honorable man, Abbie. A God-fearin' man. There was nothin' else he could do."

"He could have told them no." But even as she said it, she knew it wasn't so. Honor, her lifelong enemy, it seemed, would not allow him. She closed her eyes. "It doesn't matter now, anyway. I told him not to come back."

"He won't listen to that."

"Yes, he will. He's too proud to beg my love again. He said as much in El Paso." She sighed. "Besides . . . I'm not certain I have any more love to give him."

"How can ye not?"

Abbie shrugged. "It's just gone. Everything I felt for him."

"Och. That's feelin's, Abbie. They're not worth the pain they cause ye. Your love has to come from here." Nora pressed the side of her head. "From knowin' who he is and why ye love him. And from decidin' you'll love him no matter what, for all your days. It's not about how he makes ye feel. It's not about you at all. It's a pledge ye made before God, Abbie."

It's not about you. Cole's own words. Was that why she felt nothing? Because her whole focus was on herself and what she would suffer without him? What if she thought of Cole? Turned her care to him?

A crippling fear washed over her, a pain so real, so present she staggered beneath it. *Oh, Lord God, how could I bear it?* The cup dropped from her fingers, drenching her skirt in tea and shattering on the wood floor.

Nora rushed to her side. "Aye, it hurts. But that's our part, Abbie, to bear the pain of it."

Abbie pressed her face to Nora's shoulder. "What if he dies? What if this baby, like Elliot, should never know his pa?"

"Och, *aroon* . . . I know. I know how it is."

Abbie allowed the tears, feeling now the depth of her distress. Why could she not have kept the dull emptiness? *Oh Lord, keep him safe. Bring him home to us, I beg you. Yet . . . not my will, but yours.*

Thirty

"You know this land, Cole?"

Will's question brought Cole's head up, and he surveyed the vast stretches of cactus-covered landscape, the boulder-strewn arroyos, bluffs, and hillocks waving in the desert heat. They'd drifted to a stop, beaten down by the midday sun and the dry that tapped your bones.

Cole cleared his throat. "I know it some. This is Apache country."

Crete had led them southwest, giving more of a chase than Cole had expected. He was no doubt heading for the Mexican border, but if the man wanted a showdown, why didn't he pick his spot and stand? Cole knew even as he thought it that Crete was doing just that. He'd wanted out of the States and into a territory, where the jurisdictions were different and most disputes were settled with a gun.

They'd kept a steady pace, could have made forty or fifty miles a day, even through the rough country by using the remuda and keeping the horses as fresh as possible. But Davy wasn't hardened to the saddle as he and Will were. Blacksmithing didn't afford the hours riding leather that working a herd did. He didn't even wear spurs.

And now they were in the desert, where pushing an animal past its strength meant certain death. Crete hadn't stopped when he reached the Arizona territory. He'd kept on all the way to Tucson, then turned west toward Yuma. And now he was leading them to hell by way of the Gila trail, this section known as *El Camino Real del Diablo*. The Devil's Highway.

Saguaro cactus stood in the sweltering sun with their arms up as though at gunpoint. Pulque cactus and ocatillo grew around them, as well as creosote scrub and, in patches, poor desert grass. But little else.

The climbing sun dwarfed all their shadows and formed silvery lakes in the distance from heat and the yearning of the mind. The bluffs wavered under the brassy sky.

Cole looked to his right. A horseshoe hollow of limestone rocks afforded some shade and the feeling of shelter. He started his horse that way. "We'll hold up there a bit. Let the sun pass over some."

When they reached the hollow and dismounted, Cole nodded for Will to water the horses. He knew to go sparingly even though they could refill their water bags at any of the way stations of the Butterfield stage line. It was best to let the horses go easy, though a man survived longer by drinking his fill, then going without, rather than by sipping regularly.

Cole hunched down and checked the ground inside the hollow. It had been recently trampled, which didn't mean anything, as plenty of travelers, including whole regiments of cavalry, used the road along here. This was as good a place as any to pull off and shield yourself from the midday sun. Likely it was used regularly for such.

Since striking the road he'd relied more on word from the stationmasters concerning Crete's progress than any tracking the stony ground would afford. The men who lived in the desert outposts kept a line of communication through the stage drivers and other travelers along the way, and Crete hadn't been keeping his head low, though he hadn't killed another man.

He knew there was too much traffic to risk that. As long as he merely passed through, there was little chance a territorial lawman would set up chase, even if they had a poster on him. But the way-station *hombres* were savvy. They remembered a face, a voice, even a gait. And they passed the word at every opportunity. Crete knew this well. And he was keeping his trail fresh for Cole to follow, leading him on.

Cole settled in against the limestone wall. The sheriff's badge still pinned to his shirt meant little down here. But he kept it there as a reminder of his true purpose. Because no matter what Abbie said, this wasn't about revenge. He was angry, yes, and he didn't try to deny it. But this anger was directed—what Brother Lewis would call righteous wrath. Cole kept the badge there to remind him. He was not here to settle a personal score, but to bring a man to justice. Or die trying.

◆◆◆◆◆◆◆

With the smell of camp smoke in his nostrils, Crete held the gun muzzle to his lips, signaling silence to Finn and Washington crouched beside him. Below, the four Apache squaws laughed and chattered as they bathed in the brackish water hole just this side of their camp. The smoke from the ocatillo branches that burned beneath their cooking pots rose in thin wisps against the purplish tops of the bluffs behind.

Just past the bathing squaws, three old women slept with a handful of small children in the scant shade of the boulders, their skin browner than the chalky earth they threw their blankets on. They were napping away the worst of the day's heat while the younger women cooled themselves in the water. Not that the water would be cool, even with the rocky overhang providing shade.

Those natural water tanks heated up like cooking pots this time of year, and the dry breeze off the desert cooled the moisture from the skin almost immediately. Even your own sweat evaporated the moment it rose to the surface. Then there was nothing but the sun, the cursed sun beating down.

Crete narrowed his eyes, watching the squaws fouling the water he'd intended to use. Since leaving the road early this morning, he'd headed for this hole, knowing it was one of a bare handful he could count on in September. It was time to put an end to Cole Jasper, but he wanted to do it here in the naked desert where no court and jury could interfere.

So he'd left the road and the chance of soldiers and lawmen behind. Crete knew this land well enough to stake a spot where Cole would be disadvantaged. But these squaws were putting a kink in his plans. And it wouldn't be long before their men returned. It was now or never.

He crept back the way they'd come, hearing the others follow. "We'll circle around and shoot 'em." He saw Washington's eyes stir. "You got a problem with that, Washington?"

The tall half-Sioux drew himself up. "It be a shame to kill them too soon, chief."

Crete looked from face to face of his men, then back down at the camp. It wouldn't do to stand in the way of the men's wants. He saw a young boy, no more than six, splash water at one of the women. He frowned. As he looked, the eyes of an old woman, rheumy with age, rose to his. Her skin was a parched and rutted landscape. But he saw there that she knew. She was looking at the face of death, and she did not blink.

Crete felt a rush of rage and disgust. "Let's go."

✦✦✦✦✦✦✦

The small boy huddled in the limestone hollow where the old woman had shoved him. It took all his courage not to scream and scream and scream. He knew when the shooting stopped that he was alone. It was a long time before he dared leave his hole.

✦✦✦✦✦✦✦

Cole caught sight of the paper flapping in the wind just before the sun's rays passed behind the ragged edge of land. It was some twenty feet from the road, held down by a rock, but unnatural to the land-scape. That's why it had caught his eye. He reined in. "Hold on a bit."

He rode for the paper and looked down from his view atop White-sock. Then he swung down and retrieved the paper from under the rock. It was a money band stamped First Bank of Rocky Bluffs. He slowly shook his head, looking now at the ground and seeing the tracks heading off from the road, two, maybe three days old.

"What is it, Cole?" Davy McConnel rode up and dismounted.

Cole held up the money band. "A little message from Crete that this here's the turn."

"He's leaving the road? Heading into the desert?"

Will also joined them, sliding from his mount and scrutinizing the band in Cole's hand.

Cole nodded. "I reckon he's ready to stand now. Wants a place free of commotion."

"Do you think he's just heading for the border?"

"He's headin' that way, but I doubt he'll cross—not before he meets with me. This here's my invitation."

Will rubbed the sweat from the ring where his hat met his forehead. "What are we gonna do?"

"Follow." Cole saw Will and Davy exchange a look. "We've got full water bags. I don't think he'll go far."

Will swallowed. "It's not that, Cole. It's what do we do when we find him?"

"I'll let you know when we get there." He turned to Davy. "You know how to shoot?"

"Well enough . . . though I've never aimed at a man."

"You're right to know there's a difference. I hope it won't come to that."

Again Will and Davy shared a look, but this time Cole didn't answer. They'd ridden this far with scarce enough conversation. The land hereabouts did that, dwarfed you and made thinking a chore. It dulled the senses and closed you in on yourself until anything you might say seemed unimportant anyway.

It occurred to Cole that he hardly knew either one of these men with him. But he knew well enough that neither was prepared for what might happen. Neither had seen a man die by his own bullet, and neither had faced his own death at the end of another man's gun. If he had his druthers, he'd see that it stayed that way.

Cole looked up and around him. They had enough daylight to make some distance, and the riding was best with the sun down, though the air chilled fast in the desert. He swung into the saddle and took up the reins. "Let's go."

◆◆◆◆◆◆◆

The sun the next day was as unrelenting as the day before, drumming down on their heads and burning any uncovered flesh they gave it. The water bags were running low, what with the remuda, their mounts, and their own needs. Cole was unfamiliar with these parts, but he figured Crete's tracks would take them to water—the man had the same needs as they. Even he could not cross the desert without water. So they rode on through the waving heat, watching the lizards and scorpions skitter from the horses' hooves, the occasional rattler coiled and licking the air for scent, and the buzzards circling in the harsh sky.

They came on the camp unexpectedly, though the smell should have warned them. But the horses had caught the scent of water, and Cole just figured something had died at the water hole with the flock of buzzards circling and landing, then lofting again, glutted. It was not uncommon for a predator to stalk the watering spot. With the number of buzzards around, it would be a fresh kill, no more than a day or two.

But as they rounded the curve of rocks and took in the scene, he swayed in the saddle. The bloated bodies half picked of flesh gave off a stench he'd never borne before. Will hung his head to the side and retched, losing his lunch and likely all desire for supper. Davy's oath and strangled breath confirmed his distress.

Fighting the need to flee, Cole dismounted, though his legs were shakier than they'd been in years as the memories rushed over him of other Indian camps, camps decimated by his own bullets. But not women and children! He walked forward, willing his legs to move, leading the horse.

The animal came unwillingly, balking at the smell of death, then overcame it and rushed for the water tank, drowning its muzzle in the still water. Amazingly the tank was unfouled by the carnage. Whoever did this had herded the women away from the water before opening fire. Cole pulled the horse's head up, refusing it more water than it needed so it wouldn't over-drink. He ground reined the horse with a rock, then made his way toward the bodies.

The buzzards flapped and hopped about and screamed, then reluctantly lifted to the air to circle once again. With his eyes, Cole searched the corpses, but found no men among them. Why had the braves of this encampment not seen to their dead? Would they have pursued the attackers without first honoring the dead?

Or had they not yet discovered the dead? If that were the case, they were in imminent danger. The braves would not wait to ask questions. He turned, saw Will and Davy still frozen in the entrance. Before he motioned them in, he searched the ground and found what he expected. The tracks of shod horses.

He freed the reins of his bay and led it back to Will. "Take this one. I'll water the rest. Keep a lookout for the braves who belonged to these women and children."

Relief at not having to come any closer turned to fear in Will's face. Cole shook his head. "Just watch. I'll be quick."

"Is the water good?" Davy's voice was shaky but clear.

"I reckon so. This wasn't the job of poison."

Will's chest heaved. "Was it Crete?"

"The horses were shod." Cole rubbed the back of his neck.

Davy straightened. "We can't just leave them here, the way they are."

Cole turned back and scanned the camp. "Ordinarily I'd agree. But their men are gonna come this way sooner or later, and I don't have to tell you how they'll be."

Davy dropped his head. "It goes against the grain."

"Yes, it does. But if we buried them, we'd hide the evidence of what happened here. The braves deserve to know." Cole reached for the reins of both their horses, then the rope of the remuda. "I won't be long."

Davy nodded. He and Will backed out to make room for the horses. Cole tugged on the balking animals torn between thirst and the scent of death. Their thirst, like that of his mount, won out. He gave the animals freedom at the tank for as long as it took to fill the bags. Then he pulled up their heads and led them out. With one last look behind him, he left the circle of rocks, the weight of death like an iron chain around him. Where would it end?

Thirty-One

Abbie sat perfectly still beneath the yellow branches of the cottonwood as the sun sparkled off the brilliant green feathers of the hummingbird paused in midair before her. Its wings fanned on each side, no more than a blur, making the high-pitched buzz that had alerted her to its presence. Beneath the lancelike beak, the bird's throat glowed red as an ember under a bellows.

She narrowed her eyes to slits and watched, so as not to allow the bird a chance at her eyeballs. Their blue could attract a misguided dive that would produce no nectar for the hummer, but serious injury for her. Yet she couldn't close them entirely and miss the antics of this creature.

The bird hovered in the brisk autumnal air, turned to the left with a quick dart, then to the right, then swooped upward almost faster than she could watch. Abbie breathed in the faint scent of woodsmoke and damp leaves, resting her hand on the pages of the Bible open across her lap, Monte's Bible. She glanced down at the printing across the page, the words telling the story of Esther, and the line she had just read vibrated in her mind.

Had God truly placed Esther in the position of queen just so she could risk her life to save her people? Abbie ran her eyes over the page again, thinking how she'd pushed Cole to learn the meanings of those symbols so that he, too, could read the words on the page. But maybe that had never been God's intent.

Maybe God had merely intended Cole for such a time as this. Maybe even now his bones lay parching in the desert. But he had kept Crete from returning, had done his duty in such a time as this. The thought brought both pain and worry. They had heard nothing from him since the last wire he'd sent to Grant from Tucson in the Arizona Territory. The wire had simply said that they continued to pursue but had not overtaken Crete and his men.

Had they met since? Had one destroyed the other? Would she not have heard something if it were Cole who survived? She sighed and leaned back into the hills and valleys of gray bark on the cottonwood trunk. The roots spread about her like arms of an octopus, and she sat in the fork between two of them.

Abbie closed her eyes and lifted a silent prayer for Cole and Will and Davy as she often had since Nora's visit. Maybe she would never know, never see his remains. Maybe he would be lost to the desert where he had been called for such a time as this. She prayed, but beyond that she could do nothing.

She had finally come to realize that she could not strive against God's will. She could not saddle up and strike out, seeking to change what was set up before the dawn of time. Her action, as Nora said, was to bear it. And so she tried.

The baby stirred and gave a healthy kick to her ribs, and Abbie pressed a palm to her side in acknowledgment. She could feel the baby's strength and determination. She smiled. Between her and Cole, this child was likely to come out sparring. If only . . .

She stopped the thought. As Nora said, she could not abandon Cole in her thoughts. She must believe in him until time proved its futility. If only Jenny could do the same.

Abbie shook her head. She had reluctantly put Jenny back into the town school under Mr. Ernst. Her decision was based more on the hope that removing Jenny from the ranch for at least a portion of the day would keep her thoughts that much more from Cole's absence. She couldn't tell yet whether it helped or not.

◆◆◆◆◆◆◆

Jenny watched Mr. Ernst's mouth move up and down as he talked, his lips like caterpillars she'd poked with a stick to make them crawl, scooching up their middles then stretching out again. His voice droned like a wasps' nest deep in the mud, caked and dried. And when his eyes landed on her, she felt their sting.

She brought up her chin and refused to look away, though she knew he wanted her to. He wanted her to break, but she wouldn't. Nothing could touch her, nothing hurt her. She wouldn't let it. He blinked slowly and sent his gaze to another as he read on and on.

Jenny fixed her eyes again on his lips and kept them there until he stopped talking. Then she opened her notebook like all the others and took up her pencil. She hadn't heard a word, but she had read the story herself twice and knew it as well as any. She swallowed a smug smile at the thought and waited for the first question.

Aunt Abbie was right to send her back here. As much as she hated it, it was better than roaming the ranch with Cole gone. Yes, Cole. She would not think of him as Pa. Never again. He was not her pa, and he never would be. Never, never, never.

◆◆◆◆◆◆◆

Cole rode alone in the gathering dusk, the sun having just set behind the distant edge of hills to the west. He had told the others he would scout ahead, ordering them to stay put in the camp they'd nooned at and giving the horses a much-needed rest. With a band of Apache warriors out there somewhere looking for blood, it was best to get this ended swiftly if at all possible.

They were now so near the Mexican border, the outlaws could cross over to relative freedom any time they wished. After a month in the grueling desert sun, Cole didn't much care if they did. All except Crete. Crete Marlowe had a date with destiny—whether on this side of the border or the other.

Cole caught the scent of smoke and slowed from the easy lope to a walk. If he knew Marlowe, he'd have a watch set, but likely with orders not to kill. No, Crete would want that pleasure himself. And that's what Cole was banking on. If he could keep it personal between the two of them . . .

A horse whinnied from a shallow arroyo, and Cole reined in, hushing his own mount's response. Less than a heartbeat later a coyote howled far off to his right. Good luck, that. The men would think it was the coyote scent that disturbed the horse. He dismounted and ground-tied his gelding. Hopefully he'd have need of him again. Then he removed the spurs from his boots. No sense announcing his entrance with their jingle.

With his hand slipping over the horse's mane after a calming caress, Cole started forward on foot. He felt the weight of the revolver at his hip. He'd never been a shootist, never practiced a fancy draw or spins or anything more than it took to stay alive in a hostile land. But his reflexes were prime, his instincts sharp. Even years of cattle work hadn't dulled what he'd developed from his natural strengths.

He stood a good chance against Crete Marlowe one on one. It was the one on six that had him worried. But he'd come to the decision that he couldn't let Will and Davy lose their lives in a fight that wasn't theirs. If they rode in all three together, it would be one bunch against another, and there was no way Davy and Will could take two hardened men each.

On foot he made stealthy progress to the edge of the arroyo, scarcely more than a gash in the land with a dry creek bed at the base. The fire burned under an overhang of rock about sixteen feet from the ground. The overhang caught and dissipated the smoke, giving little away.

The men milled about, and Cole counted heads. Only five present. One must be on watch as he'd assumed, but that didn't matter, because the head he sought was there, silver in the mellowing daylight. Cole scanned the land within sight. It was broken and gashed with piles of lava rock, and cacti paused mid-conversation to watch him, arms up and waiting.

He saw no sign of movement except for a gray-streaked horned toad that fled to the shelter of a rock when he crouched. Slowly Cole lowered himself over the edge, and keeping to the boulders that choked the path of least resistance, he crept down to the camp. With his eyes he took in the positions of all the men present.

Then, when he knew he could get no closer without alerting them, he stepped into the open, gun at the ready, and spoke. "Crete Marlowe, tell your dogs to lie down."

Crete spun, took in the gun barrel leveled at his heart, and raised his hands. His eyes narrowed and his mouth jerked sideways. "I got six to one. You ain't gettin' out of here alive."

"This is between you and me."

Slowly Crete's hands lowered, but he kept them well away from the gun at his hip. Smart man. Crete might have him outnumbered, but that wouldn't stop the bullet to his chest, unless one of them was willing to take it in his stead, and somehow Cole doubted Crete inspired that kind of loyalty.

"All right." Crete took a slow step to his left away from the fire, then took another.

Cole kept his eyes on the man, watching for any sign—a twitch, a tightening of muscle or sinew.

Crete grinned. "I've been waitin' for you."

"You could have stopped any time."

"I wanted to see how far you'd go to have your revenge."

And now that Cole had him face-to-face, he knew both Crete and Abbie were right. Justice and revenge were inbred. "I'd go all the way to hell. You've been nothin' but misery to me and my family. What my pa ever saw in you, I can't say."

Crete's grin took on a devilish twist. "He liked me for my whiskey, poor drunken sot. Never realized I only hung around to spend time with his missus."

Cole showed none of the fury Crete's words caused within him. "If I cared to defend him, I'd break your jaw for that."

Crete laughed. "No, I don't suppose there's any love lost between you and Asa."

Cole said nothing.

Crete wiped his mouth with the back of his hand. "Guess you never wondered why."

"What my pa thought or felt is none of your business."

Crete spat. "Asa Jasper ain't no more your pa than I am."

Cole kept the surprise from showing . . . barely. What game was Crete Marlowe playing?

"It's true. Your ma, see, she thought Asa'd died. Guess she heard it somewheres, maybe from me." His eyes narrowed distastefully. "He'd run off for so long after Sammy's birthing, you see."

Cole made no answer.

Crete swallowed, the tendons in his throat working. "She wouldn't have none of me. But she took to a nice young fella right off. Married him even, though it didn't count for much once Asa came back. Yessir, he hightailed it back when he heard his woman was with child again without his bein' there to do the honors."

Cole felt sick. He couldn't hide it now.

Crete gloated. "Asa made quick work of that one."

"You mean he killed him?"

"With his bare hands. I helped dispose of the body myself. Then he set about trying to rid her of you, as well. You should be glad I stopped him short of beatin' her to death."

Cole's chest heaved, and he almost lurched forward to take Crete with his own bare hands.

"In a sense, I guess you owe your very existence to me." The grin was purulent.

Cole's throat was like bleached bones powdering in the sun. "What was his name?" He hated himself for asking, but couldn't stop it.

"Heck, I didn't stop to ask 'fore I went to find Asa. After that, it was too late."

Crete. Crete had fetched his pa back . . . no, not his pa. Asa Jasper had murdered his pa, a man his ma had loved and married, probably believing her hardship and ill use was over. But his had just begun.

Now he understood why he'd come into the world spitting. Had he somehow known the man had tried to kill him in the womb? Was that why he'd never trusted his pa . . . that and the beatings? Had Sam known? Was he old enough to understand? Why had his ma never told him?

Cole shook his thoughts free. He couldn't let this dull him, distract him from Crete's threat. They were here to fight. The past was the past. Now they were only two men with hatred between them. It was him and Crete alone in the world.

But the crack across the back of his skull told him otherwise. He tried to spin—did spin in his mind's eye—but none of his limbs would work. He felt his fall, then nothing more.

✦✦✦✦✦✦✦

Beneath the shady cottonwood, Abbie woke with a start, trembling. She could not shake the image of Crete Marlowe's eyes. *"Tell your husband I'll be waiting."* She shook her head to clear away the memory, but still the vision remained, the words spoken low and deadly.

A single golden leaf had landed on the pages open in her lap. She lifted it, taking in the myriad tiny veins in its yellow flesh, then tossed it aside. Her eyes fell to the page where it had landed, and she read there Esther's response, how she fasted and prayed for the strength to save her people.

Abbie's trembling increased. Cole. She swallowed the bitter taste in her mouth and felt the child inside stir. Awkwardly she rose to her knees and clasped her hands at her chest. She closed her eyes and started to beg, then stopped. No. It was God's will that must be done.

Softly she murmured words of honor, of praise and thanksgiving. Over and over she glorified God until the trembling stopped. Then Abbie thanked Him for all the ways He had blessed her life and for every person in it whom He had given either to love or challenge her, or both. She smiled with the thought, then couldn't stop the tear that followed.

Monte had made her grow up, even as Mama and Pa had. But Cole ... he called her to the wisdom and maturity God wanted for her. Could she find it without him? She would have to. Learning from life as Cole had, she would have to find it alone ... if he didn't return.

Now she prayed in supplication. *Ask, and ye shall receive ... Ye have not because ye ask not. Whatsoever ye shall ask for in prayer, believing, ye shall receive.* Well, she would ask, knowing that God would accomplish whatever He willed. But she would ask. She would ask for Cole's life.

She thought of little Birdie and her candles. Maybe there had been a lesson even in that. She couldn't light a candle for Cole, but she could ask for angels, angels to guard and protect him wherever he was.

◆◆◆◆◆◆◆

Will slumped under the shade of the rocky ledge. With the setting sun the heat had become bearable, though the night's cooling had not begun. The tops of the mesas looked purplish red, and the sky was more rosy than brass.

In the distance, the heat waves settled to a flat silver sheen across the land, glinting like water until you drew close. It was a horrible land, yet somehow awesome, as well. But he didn't want to stay there, not any longer than he had to.

Will stood and walked over to where Davy was scouring the frying pan with sand. They'd heated a can of beans and a can of tomatoes for supper, but Cole hadn't returned to join them in the meal. The plate they'd dished for him sat drying and congealing on the flat rock where they'd set it.

Will took a step and stood over it. "You suppose he'll want this still?"

Davy looked up from his work, then continued scouring without answer. Will glanced his way, waiting.

Davy shook his head. "He's not comin' back."

"What do you mean?"

"I mean he's handling this himself."

Will stared. "You think he's goin' in alone?"

Davy shrugged. "I don't think we'd be much help to him."

"Like heck!" Will clenched his fists. "What can he do alone against six men?"

Davy sat back on his haunches. "What can he do with us against them? Besides, if he was scoutin', he'd be back by now."

Will searched the land with his eyes. Could it be true? Would Cole leave them out of it like that? Would he? Will felt the rage boil in his belly. He wanted a strike at Crete Marlowe himself. He wanted to take out the man who killed Birdie. He wanted to do something to take away the terrible feeling inside.

Davy stood and tucked the pan in the saddlebag, then turned. "So the question is, what do we do now?"

Will looked back over his shoulder. "You need to ask? He's had three hours. It's time we caught up."

Davy drew a long breath. "I suppose it is."

Thirty-Two

It was the throbbing in his head he noticed first. The next thing was the braided rawhide rope that cut into the skin of his neck and made breathing difficult. Cole felt a tug on the rope and opened his eyes. Judging by the lingering evening light, not much time had passed. He reckoned only enough to get him trussed up and astride his own horse beneath the rocky overhang to which the far end of the rope was attached.

He noticed a big Indian fella who hadn't been among them before. That was the one who'd clocked him from behind. The men were ranged out before him with grins like they'd have for a show, and he realized he was the show. He swallowed against the rope.

"Well, now." Crete hung his thumbs from his belt. "Seems you're right back where you should've been months ago."

Cole held his piece. No sense making more sport of this than need be. If Crete meant to hang him, there was precious little he could do about it. He tugged against the rope that held his wrists behind his back. New hemp, by the feel, and plenty strong.

"What have you to say now?"

Cole slowly moistened his lips. "Guess I was mistaken."

A man to Crete's right cackled and spat, but Crete held Cole's eyes. "Mistaken how?"

"I thought you were man enough to face me alone."

Crete's face hardened, then he shrugged. "Now why would I do that when I have my friends here?"

Cole hadn't an answer for that. He'd walked into the trap, blinded by some misguided thought that Crete would honor a fair fight. Why he should have thought that, Cole couldn't say. The man was a back-stabber and a wife stealer. Only he hadn't succeeded in that one.

Was that why Crete hated him so much? Because the woman he wanted, the woman he lied to about her husband being dead had still chosen to spurn him and marry another. And Cole was the offspring of that union, a bastard really, though that couldn't be held to his ma's account.

He felt an absurd relief at the thought, the knowledge that he was not Asa Jasper's son, though he bore the man's name. He was glad he would die with that knowledge, even though Crete had used the tale only to distract him from the Indian's approach. He looked over into the big man's face.

Half Indian, he guessed. The other men were as dirty and crooked as any he'd laid eyes on. They'd have to be to do the kind of work they'd done at the Indian camp. Woman and child killers.

Cole cocked his jaw to the side. He tried not to think about Abbie, but her face came to him suddenly, as clearly as though she stood before him. It hurt, hurt bad. But she was in God's hands, and she was a survivor. She'd find a way. And she'd see the children through.

Cole glanced at the sky. He'd nearly had a gallows conversion. Maybe it was fitting he went to see his maker the same way. Cole drew a long breath, maybe his last, then felt it catch halfway out, arrested there by the shape that appeared at the edge of the arroyo.

Rock That Sings looked down from his perch where he lay on his chest beside his small son, Half Moon. In the dimming dusk, he smelled the sweat of the men below, the men who had murdered his woman, his Running Wind. He could always smell the white man. His scent was feral, toxic, unnatural. As were his ways. Hatred filled Rock That Sings as the rain surfeiting the sand until it was in all of him. He drank of it and felt the strength it gave him.

It was like the sweetness of cactus juice that became bitter to the tongue. Too much hatred could sap his strength, yet the sight of the white men brought fresh waves to his being. He took in the scene below, as he knew the boy beside him did.

With a silent glance he saw the boy's distress, though the child did not allow tears to his eyes. His son was a man now, inside his mind if not in his small body. He had seen death and knew its bitter sting. He alone the gods had spared. Rock That Sings was thankful for that.

Without moving even his head, he sent his gaze to the left and right to see his brothers and friends lying like himself in readiness. Each would become a weapon with the avenging medicine of the gods. This night the white men would know the shadow world. Even now he hungered for their blood.

But before he gave the signal, he felt a halt inside him, something contending with his will. He put his mind to it. It was dangerous to ignore a sign. What was it that made him reluctant? He looked at the white men, tried to guess what was happening among them. One, on the horse, was captive to the others. He could feel the animosity between them. What did it matter?

But Rock That Sings narrowed his eyes to scrutinize that one. He was a warrior of middle years and much courage. He did not beg for his life, nor tremble at death. He held his head tall, defiant. Rock That Sings battled inside himself. That one was white, too, yet . . .

As softly as the air through the grass, Rock That Sings asked his son, "The one on the horse. Is he one of them?"

Half Moon stared at the man his father indicated. Already his eyes had been drawn there. It was difficult to see him through the feathered wings of those that surrounded him. The brightness hurt, yet his eyes would not stray. As he looked, one of the tall, shining eagle-men turned aside and drew the wing away. Half Moon looked at the man and felt the man's eyes on him, as well.

He knew he had not seen him before, and his medicine was strong. His father must know it, too. The eagle-men who surrounded the white man closed in again, and Half Moon replied, "He was not with them."

●●●●●●●

In the fading light, Cole watched the Apache fit an arrow to his bow. It was as likely that one was aimed at him as not. Those braves would not be in any mood to pick and choose. He only hoped they shot to kill cuz hanging was mild compared to their methods of ending a man's days.

The first arrow took the big half-breed through the throat. He stood a long moment staring straight ahead as though unaware he'd been hit, then his knees crumpled and he fell. Crete jerked to his left, reaching for his sidearm even as he spun. Rifles and handguns exploded from inside the arroyo and down from the edge.

"Steady," Cole rasped, putting the spurless heel of his boot to the horse's shoulder, holding it there to keep the horse from jolting forward and ending his life sooner than might be, though he expected a bullet or the bite of an arrow soon enough.

With animal shrieks, the Apache warriors stormed downward, rifles blasting and death in their eyes. Cole felt himself cringe. Was he impervious to their onslaught? Surely one would aim his way, but they all seemed intent upon Crete and his men hiding in the rocks, where they now sought protection. Cole was the best target the Apaches had, yet they didn't shoot.

Cole's breath quickened and sharpened as the horse strained forward, and he held the boot tight to its flesh. "Whoa, there." He was not eager to hang, but if the Apaches meant to take him alive, he would kick that horse to high heaven.

He counted four of Crete's men dead, one of them Jackson Finn. Only Crete and another returned fire, and even as Cole watched, Crete buckled with a bullet to his side. He reached up to fire his revolver, but the warrior was upon him and kicked the gun aside. The knife flashed out and carved a chunk of gray hair from the front of Crete's scalp.

But Crete was still fighting. He brought a fist into the Apache's face, though blood streamed into his eyes and blinded him. Two other braves landed beside the first, and Crete bellowed like a bull as they tied his arms behind. The other man was likewise trussed, and the braves in charge of him had thrown him over the back of a horse and tied him neck to ankles under the animal's belly.

Cole guessed they'd head for him next and readied his heels on the horse's sides. But the Apaches paid him no mind as they mutilated the bodies of the dead, then took the two they had alive and started down the arroyo with them, both men helpless across the backs of the Indian ponies. As the men passed before him without even a look, Cole glanced up to the edge and saw the small boy running.

His legs pumped, and he held his arms over his head. For one moment their eyes met, then the little one quickened his pace and disappeared from the side. Cole waited, counting the seconds as the dust cleared. The rope was taut on his neck and his spine ached. He tried to get the animal to back up, but the horse was as tense as he.

Forcing himself to relax, he tried to swallow. For whatever reason, he seemed to have survived the attack, but his predicament was none too appealing. The remaining light was quickly fading and the evening growing cool. Tomorrow would find him in much the same position. He might not die of sunstroke beneath the rock shelf, but he'd sure not last long on account of other things.

Cole closed his eyes. *Well, Lord, if it comes to it, I'd as soon go quick as slow. But you know best, I reckon.*

◆◆◆◆◆◆◆

Will halted at the sight of the dust cloud rising up ahead. He wasn't sure if it was his eyes playing tricks on him in the last of the light, or the distance itself. He blinked and strained. "You see that dust out there?"

Davy squinted. "I see it."

"Let's go." Will raised the reins to switch the horse.

Davy caught his arm. "Wait a minute. We don't know what that is. Could be a twister or horsemen or a stampede of whatever lives out here."

Will tugged his arm free. "Could be Crete Marlowe makin' for the border."

"Or the Apache braves Cole talked about."

Will paused, swallowing the dryness from his throat. "Whatever it is, it'll be gone if we don't get there quick."

"Will." Davy laid a hand on his arm. "One rider can't make that much dust. If Cole's dead already, it won't matter when we get there."

Will clenched his jaw. "Then I'll cut Crete Marlowe down myself." He spurred the horse and fit his motion to the beast who carried him.

If Cole was dead, it was up to him to see this through. For Birdie.

Davy joined him and they rode hard, but the dust was fading into darkness. Will could no longer be certain they followed the right path, so he slowed his mount to a walk. No sense riding blind. Whatever had kicked up the dust could no more go on without light as he and Davy could.

Maybe they were making camp. Maybe he and Davy should do the same and wait for daylight to deal with the bunch ahead. He glanced at Davy riding doggedly beside him. Though the man was several years older, he seemed ready enough to follow Will's lead.

Will squinted toward the arroyo cut roughly along the direction he was moving, a darker gash across the dark land. Maybe he and Davy could hole up there until morning. He felt the heat of the chase fading. He didn't want to give in, but with the light all but gone and his eyes straining to see four horse lengths ahead . . .

Will jabbed his chin toward the gap. "Let's go down there for the night. I'll wager the others are holing up, as well."

Davy nodded. They led the horses carefully down into the arroyo, the darkness swallowing them among the rocks. When they reached the stony bed, Will led the way along its base. "See any place a man might stretch out without a boulder in his back?"

Davy half grinned. "It looks like it widens out up there a ways."

Will nodded. "Kind of an overhang, too, I think. Can you make it out?"

"Let's just hope there's a flat spot in there somewhere."

Will stopped abruptly when he heard another horse whinny just before them. "What the . . ." Will pulled out his six-shooter. "Who's there?"

"If I'd been a Mexican *bandito* I'd've shot your throats out by now."

"Cole!" Will rushed forward.

"Hold it! Whoa."

Will froze, just making out Cole's shape on horseback. "What? What's the matter?"

"I'd prefer it greatly if you approached slow and easy."

Will glanced at Davy, then walked forward slowly. He wondered why Cole was sitting there astride under the ledge like that. "What are you doin', Cole?"

"What's it look like?"

Will stopped short of Cole's mount, noticing now the stiff way he was sitting, leaned back enough to give any man a backache. "What . . ." He looked up, just making out the rope strung from Cole's neck to the rock above. "Jumpin' Jezebels! Who's got you all strung up?"

"Will . . . cut the rope."

Cole waited while Will let go of the reins he held and took hold of the horse he was on. He felt the rope slacken as Will backed the animal some and listened as Davy hacked at the rawhide with his knife. It would have cut easier with more tension on it, but given that it was his throat holding one end . . . The rope fell free and Cole felt the weight of it tug on his neck from behind.

His voice rasped. "Would you mind freein' my hands, too?"

Davy angled the knife in between his hands and sawed the hemp. "It's a real puzzle here, Cole. I can't quite figure it." He pulled the pieces of rope free. "I'd almost expected to find you dead, but . . ."

Cole pulled his arms forward with a groan and loosened the rope from his neck. "Ahhh." He grimaced, tossing the rawhide braid to the ground, then put a hand to the back of his head. It was sporting a lump the size of a walnut. "Well, I ain't dead yet," he said, easing himself down from the saddle. "Though I'm not sure my explanation will go a long way toward your puzzlin'."

Will took the horse's reins and led it out to the others. "Did Crete hang you up there?"

"Yeah. I was a sight unconscious at the time, but I reckon he'd be the one to put the rope on my neck."

"Then how . . ."

"Apaches." Cole saw Will's face sober.

"Then it was Apaches we've been trailin' hard this last hour?"

Cole rubbed his throat. "That'd be my guess, and you're derned lucky you didn't follow 'em any closer."

Davy shook his head. "I told him as much. But he was set on puttin' an end to Crete Marlowe."

Stepping back, Will stumbled, fell over backward, and cried out.

Cole grabbed him with one arm, yanking him up from the corpse of one of Crete's men. "Careful there. It ain't a purty sight, though given my druthers I'd be him right now instead of Crete and the other one they took alive."

Will shook under his grasp, rubbing the blood from his palm where he'd reached out to catch himself. Cole struck a match to show them. The man's face was slashed, the front of his hair gone. His eyes were open to the stars shining out now above.

Cole blew out the flame. "Got a shovel in the pack?"

Davy turned and fetched the folding shovel. Cole made a torch of an ocatillo cactus bush, and by its light they took turns shoveling the stony ground until they had a shallow grave wide enough for four bodies. They rolled the dead men in and covered them with stones thick enough to keep the wolves out.

Will wiped the sweat from his forehead with his sleeve. "You gonna say somethin' over them?"

Cole looked down at the mound, thinking of the bloating bodies of the Apache women and their young. "No, I don't reckon so."

Davy put his hat back on his head. "Should I make camp, or do you want to move out from here?"

Cole looked up at the edge of the arroyo visible against the stars. "If we were campin', this would be as good a spot as any."

"But?" Will's voice held more than a little trepidation.

"I cain't leave things as they are."

"What do you mean?"

Cole turned to face the young man. "I'm goin' after Crete."

Will's jaw dropped with his expelled breath.

Davy stepped up to Cole's side. "I thought you said the Apaches had him. Surely you don't think he can get away from them and go free."

"No, I don't think that." Cole started for the horses.

Davy surprised him by blocking his path. "Then why? Are you as crazy set on being the one to do him in as this youngster here?"

Cole felt a twinge. "It ain't that either." He stepped around and made his way to the spare horses. "This one fresh?"

"Yes, but . . ." Davy caught his arm as Cole pulled the rifle from his pack and checked the loads.

He slid the gun back in, then moved the saddle to the bay's back. "You two can stay here."

"No." Will stepped forward abruptly. "We ride together."

"I appreciate your sentiment, but frankly, the two of you make enough noise to alert the whole country."

Will gripped his forearm. "What do you mean to do?"

"That'll depend." He eyed Will a moment, then cocked his jaw. "Take him if I can. If not . . . give him a quick end."

Will's throat worked. "He doesn't deserve it."

Cole nodded slowly. "Likely not. But it ain't about deservin'. It's about doin' what's right. Have the horses grained and watered and saddled. We might need to beat a hasty retreat. Might be best to stake them out above."

"We'll be up there, too." Davy pulled a box of cartridges from his pack and stuck it into Cole's. "We'll be waiting."

Cole gave a curt nod, then started out. After a handful of steps he stopped and half turned. "Oh, by the way, thanks for happenin' along when you did."

He led the horse up the side, then mounted and started into the night. The Apache camp wasn't far as the crow flies. By the light of the rising moon, he got within three hundred yards with an hour's ride. Dismounting, Cole took the rifle from the scabbard and closed another hundred yards on foot. No one in the camp was listening.

They'd heaped brush up around a giant saguaro and it burned like a torch lighting the camp well enough to show him what he needed to see. The body of Crete's man was tied to the saguaro and already burnt beyond recognition. He must have died already.

The memory of his ma's body in flames flashed through his mind, the stench of human flesh kindling the old primeval rage. Cole pressed his eyes shut, but the fire stayed behind his lids, reflecting purple until he opened them again. He looked from the fire to the dancing, chanting warriors.

In the midst of them, tied naked to another saguaro, his back no doubt lanced by a thousand thorns, was Crete. His ankles were staked out and his arms wrapped the cactus behind, tied there to hold him standing. But that wasn't the worst of it.

Cole looked away, fighting his gorge at the sight of Crete's entrails. Yet Crete wasn't dead. He still screamed when the red-hot probes touched his eyes. He writhed when the knives flayed the layers of flesh. His screams took on an animal tenor.

Slowly Cole cocked the rifle, though he needn't really have worried over it being heard. Was it murder to end Crete's life for mercy's sake? Mercy. Was it mercy he felt or vengeance? Now he wasn't sure. He looked back at the fire, the charred body hanging there ... the memories of his own haunting pain. He felt the trigger with his finger.

He'd come a lot of miles to put an end to Crete Marlowe. He'd risked his marriage and his life. Would Crete have shown mercy if the Apaches hadn't come when they did? No way in this world.

He could leave him to the Apaches. Crete wouldn't last out the night. It was his just dues for what he did to the braves' women and children, to Birdie and all the others. Cole felt his finger twitch. But was it right?

Where was the line? Should he take life and death into his own hands and give Crete the mercy he didn't deserve? Or should he walk away, knowing he couldn't rescue the man alive? Even if he could have taken him, it would only be to hang him. He sighted down the rifle barrel.

Crete had stopped responding. He must have passed out, but he would revive. The braves danced about him, bent and prancing, waiting for him to return so they could once again add to his suffering. Now was the time, but was it right? Cole caught his breath sharply, but didn't shoot.

Could he be sure of his motive? Could he know it was mercy to pull the trigger—and was mercy enough? Something Brother Lewis had said stuck in his mind. Men are quick to end life, but can even one of them give it? It is God's alone to give or take.

Cole's finger cramped, held there tensed as it was. Sweat trickled into his left eye and burned. He swiped it with his shoulder and returned his cheekbone to the gun, then pressed both eyes shut in frustration. *Lord, show me what to do. I don't know what's right.*

He waited in the silence, then opened his eyes and saw the men piling kindling around the base of the cactus. It didn't make sense. They wouldn't burn until . . . As he watched, they drew fire from the one already burning and thrust the flaming brand into the pile. Crete made no move. The fire licked upward, igniting cactus and man. It was over. Somehow, without his doing, it was done.

Cole lay quiet, gun still in place, mixed emotions stirring in his gut. He'd been saved the decision, but he'd never know now which need had driven him. Maybe it was better not to know. He hadn't pulled the trigger for mercy or revenge or even justice. He was through with killing. It was over.

Slowly he crept back, then hurried for his horse. The warriors would not be so oblivious now. He led the gelding with a hand to its muzzle to keep it quiet. When he was far enough from the Apache camp, he mounted and rode back to where he'd left his partners. Neither Will nor Davy was asleep, though the night was quiet around them.

They stood immediately as he rode in. He read the questions in their eyes, then saw them find their own answers. He didn't bother to mask it. He felt the adrenaline leave him, and a bone-deep weariness settled in its place.

"Let's go. I'd just as soon have some miles behind us when those braves wake up come mornin'."

Thirty-Three

Sitting in the nursery with the Indian summer sunlight sending shafts across the reds and golds and greens of the carpet, Abbie felt the cramping again, pulling more insistently across her belly. She drew a deep breath and waited for it to pass.

Elliot looked up from the lead soldiers he was lining up. "Do you have a tummyache, Mama?"

She smiled. "A little one, Elliot."

He returned the smile, showing the tiny hole where he'd lost his first tooth on his fifth birthday. It was too soon. Too soon for him to be losing his baby teeth and the lisp that went with them. Many of the words he'd struggled with were now unconsciously coming right, and it gave her a pang. But there would be a new baby soon, a new mouth with no teeth at all that would suckle and cry and coo.

Watching Elliot put the commander in place at the front of his regimental line, Abbie thought of Wendel. She had dandled him that morning, surprised and pleased to see him hold his head up. No one could deny his progress was painfully slow, but each tiny step was greeted with such enthusiasm from Grant and Marcy that Abbie knew whatever his struggles, he would be well loved. As would her baby.

She rested a protective hand on the enormous bulge of her belly. It felt enormous, though Pearl pestered and fussed that she'd hardly fed well enough for one, much less two. That wasn't true. She had done her best for this baby, though the strain of keeping the children constantly cared for had drained her. She looked at Jenny brooding on the floor with the firelight flickering across her face.

What were her thoughts? Her imaginings? Did they mirror her

own? Abbie sighed. Still no word had come from Cole. Try as she might, it was getting more and more difficult to pretend, even for the children's sake. How long would she wait before she once again put on widow's black?

And then the horrible thought came again. What if he lived, but didn't return? What if he had succeeded in bringing Crete to justice but not come home, not come because she had told him not to? What if he believed he had no place here with her?

She shook her head. She knew Cole better than that. Then why had all the telegrams gone to Grant? Why had he not directed the correspondence to her? Oh, why had they not heard for so long now?

She felt the pain start at her sides and wrap across her front. She caught her breath sharply and tried to stand. "Jenny, Elliot, run along now and ask Pearl for a sweet. Tell Zena I need her." She smiled through the sharp tightening that squeezed her abdomen. Though she had scarcely any recollection of her labor with Elliot, she guessed well enough what this pain was.

Jenny guessed, too. Her face wore a sharp, knowing look, though she obediently led Elliot out. Abbie watched her son's innocent retreat. Soon he would have another baby to adore, to shower with tenderness. But would Jenny? She had hoped to labor while Jenny was at school, but here it was Saturday and Jenny far too sharp to miss the signs.

She wished she could have shared the anticipation with her, but every mention of the coming baby had brought a sullen look to Jenny's face or a hasty declaration of disinterest. Clearly, Jenny was not pleased with the prospect of a new sibling. Why?

The new pain came swiftly, though not as strong. The pains were erratic still. Abbie breathed deeply and made it to her feet. She felt as large as a horse, though in truth she hadn't gained much weight with all the worry.

She met Zena at the door. "Will you send Matt to town for Doctor Barrow? Let him know it's not an emergency this time."

Abbie started up the stairs, feeling the vague start of another pain, but it never materialized. She had time yet. She climbed the stairs and went to her room. There, she changed into her bedgown, but she did not get into bed. Soon enough she would be relegated there for the duration.

Right now she wanted to be on her feet. She felt restless and fussed with the blankets in the cradle, patting and smoothing the tiny pillow. She walked to the window and looked out. The morning was bright, the sky clear. But this time of year that meant little. They could have rain or snow showers or Indian summer all in the same week.

She held her belly as a real pain seized her. Dropping her head to the window sash, she closed her eyes. *Oh, Cole. Where are you?* Unlike the last time, her query was not the result of grief-driven delirium, not like when she had called for Monte, knowing, yet not knowing he was dead.

What was it this time? She had passed so many times through the emotions of loss and of fear for Cole. Now she just wanted to know. Was he out there somewhere, or did he look down from heaven awaiting the birth of his child, maybe knowing already who it would be? She turned from the window and paced the floor. She couldn't be still.

Her body was taking on a regularity of pain and relief, a rhythm over which she had no control. She must try not to fight it; it came easier that way. Abbie crossed the room and back, then stopped again at the window. How she would prefer to be out there, walking through the October sunlight beneath the last of the cottonwoods' gold, along the creek to the special place Monte had first taken her.

If she had her way, she'd stay outside until the baby's coming was imminent, but Pearl would be scandalized, and after seeing what could come of a traumatic birth, Abbie sighed resignedly. She must not do anything to hinder this little one's coming. Not even grieve Cole's absence.

But how could she not? *Where are you, Cole? Oh Lord, where is he?*

♦♦♦♦♦♦♦

Cole reined in when the house came into sight. Its pink stone blushed deeper in the sunset hues from the sky, and where the long western porch wrapped the corner, the last of the season's climbing roses meandered up the edge. The yard was strewn with cottonwood leaves under a dappling of sunlight coming through the giant canopy above. It looked so calm and peaceful it brought a lump to his throat. Home. He was home.

Will turned on his mount with a questioning glance. "You worried, Cole?"

Cole brought his eyes from the house to Will's young face. It was as dirty and trail-worn as he'd ever seen it, and he reckoned his wasn't much better. They'd left Davy in town to an ecstatic Nora and ridden on with spurs engaged. Now he tried to catch Will's drift. "Worried?"

"About your welcome."

Cole looked back at the house, the yard, the outbuildings. He'd stopped to just take it in, the way you savored the aroma before the first bite. Will had taken that for hesitance to face Abbie.

In truth he'd been less sure of his welcome this time than ever before. But the Lucky Star was home, and Abbie his wife. He had a ranch to run and a family to feed, and he meant to do his honorable best at all of it. He made a half smile. "No, I ain't worried."

He'd won her before. He'd do it again if necessary. He touched the horse's side with his spur, tugged on the lead rope of the remuda and started forward again. But his heart staggered when he caught sight of the doctor's buggy in front of the stable. Was someone ill? Jenny or Elliot . . . Abbie?

"Take the rope, Will." He tossed the lead to Will and spurred his horse in earnest. He reined in at a gallop before the house and sprang from the saddle as though bucked. He ran for the stairs, knowing Will would see to the animal, but far more concerned with what was happening inside. He flung open the door, and Zena jumped with a squeal, sloshing the pan full of water all over her skirts.

"Oh, Mistuh Jazzper, you like to scare the breath clean out of me!"

"What's happening? Why is the doctor here?"

"Well, now, it is his custom to attend the births."

Cole stared up the stairs. Birth? Was Abbie in labor with his child? Could it be that time already? How had the months slipped past? He felt hands on his shoulders and turned to find Zeke removing his duster. So the man was still there. He looked down into the soft brown eyes and felt satisfied. He might work out after all.

Cole started for the stairs, but Pearl blocked his way coming down. "Ain' no place for you up there. The missus doin' fine without you." Her look was not angry but determined.

He didn't care how determined. He'd taken on bulls meaner than her and come out on top. "All the same, I mean to see my wife."

"Ain' fittin' you bargin' in there. She workin' too hard to face you jus' now." Hands on her hips, Pearl fully blocked half the staircase.

But Cole pressed past her anyway, not caring what invectives she'd throw at his head. Abbie was birthing his child, and he didn't want her to do it alone. He gained the door and reached for the knob. A twinge seized him.

What if she didn't want to see him? What if she'd meant it when she said don't come back? What if he made it hard for her at a vulnerable time. He recalled the painful terror he'd driven her to with Elliot, making her come out of her trance and fight to live . . . and invoking her rage and hatred.

What if the sight of him was enough to do it again? His breath came quick and sharp. Well, he'd know soon enough. He turned the knob and walked in.

Abbie panted and strained, gripping the bedclothes and gasping for short breaths. She felt Mama's hand soothing her forehead and opened her eyes. "How much longer?" Her words were clipped, taking as little energy as possible.

"It won't be long. . . ." Mama turned and her eyes widened.

Abbie raised up in sudden concern, then expelled a soft cry. Cole stood in the doorway, rough and dusty from the road, but whole and strong and alive. She felt a new pain begin, seize her belly like giant tongs and squeeze. She moaned and gasped for breath, but never took her eyes from Cole.

"Good heavens, man. What are you doing here?" Doctor Barrow thrust his arms at Cole. "Get out. You're wearing enough dust to contaminate the whole room. Go on, get out."

"No." Abbie strained again to rise. "No, please."

"Don't you worry, Abbie. I'll be right back up."

The door closed behind Cole, and Abbie wondered if she had imagined it all. Had he really been there, or was her mind playing tricks of need and desire? Was she delirious as the last time? She didn't think so, but the pain and fatigue . . .

The next pain brought a new need, and she strained with it, pushing hard. She kept her eyes on the door as pain after pain brought the need to push. She clenched her teeth and bore down. The door opened, and he was there again. Real and determined and clean.

He must have scrubbed like a whirlwind, his skin was so red. His hair was wet, but he hadn't shaved. His mustache hung like a burly walrus and his cheeks bristled. It made her want to laugh as he came to her side and took her hand, but she wailed instead with the terrific effort that produced the baby's head. Cole's eyes filled with tears, and a moment later the doctor held a squalling baby daughter up for inspection, then clamped and cut the cord and wrapped her in the warmed blanket.

Abbie's chest heaved with relief and ecstasy as Cole took the baby from the doctor and laid her across her stomach. Abbie studied the baby's features, ran a finger over the dark, wet hair that would fall out and come in again dark or blond, saw the eyes already seeking. "Oh, Cole . . ."

She felt him caress her hand. He was there; he was home. And they had a beautiful daughter.

"Now I want everyone out." Doctor Barrow nodded toward Mama. "Take the baby and bathe her. I'll check her over when you're done. Cole . . ."

"I'm goin'."

Abbie felt his grip tighten as he bent to kiss her forehead. His lips were dry and scratchy, but Abbie didn't care. He was home. She closed her eyes, feeling the weariness settle in. She wanted to stay awake, to savor Cole's presence, to hold and suckle her baby. She would only close her eyes for a moment. . . .

◆◆◆◆◆◆◆

Jenny sat with Elliot on the floor of the nursery, biting her lip against the emotions churning inside her. The minute she'd seen Cole ride in, she'd known she hadn't meant a single thing she had said and thought.

He was her pa, and he'd come back to her. Only she hadn't yet had one word from him with the baby's coming. He hadn't come looking for her; he'd gone straight to Mama, closed the door, and not even thought of her. She and Elliot had to stay in the nursery, and she felt cross and frightened.

Elliot wrapped his knees in his arms. "I hope it's a boy baby like Wendel."

"It's a girl."

"How do you know?" He screwed up his forehead.

"I just know." Jenny worked her finger into a split in the seam of her pinafore ruffle.

"You only want it to be."

No. With all my heart no.

Elliot stretched his legs out and tapped the toes of his shoes together. "I hope she looks like me. Mama said I look like my pa. My other pa in heaven."

"Then she won't look like you." Jenny felt the knot tighten. *She'll look like Cole, her real pa.* "Come on." She jumped to her feet.

"What are we doing?"

"Going to see the baby."

Elliot raised his brows. "Is it here?"

"I don't know. But it might be."

Jenny opened the door and scanned the empty hall. "Come on, it's clear." She felt Elliot close behind her. He probably thought this was all a game. But she knew better. This baby could spoil everything. She jumped when Pa sprang to the top of the stairs and caught sight of them. Yes, he was Pa, her pa, always, always.

"I was just lookin' for you." He held out his arms, and they both ran to him.

Jenny pressed in, smelling the scent of him, masked now by soap and clean clothes. She felt his scratchy chin against her cheek and burrowed deeper. "I'm glad you're home, Pa." She couldn't begin to say how glad.

"Me too," Elliot piped.

"Neither one of you's so glad as I am."

"Is the baby here, Pa?" Elliot's question spoiled the joy of the moment.

"She sure is."

"It's a girl baby?" Elliot's eyes opened with wonder and respect for Jenny's abilities.

Jenny wished she cared, but she just sniffed. "I told you it was."

Pa's arm tightened. "And how did you know that, sprig?"

Jenny shrugged. "I just did." But inside she hurt.

"Would you like to see her?"

Jenny wished she didn't. But there was a small part of her that couldn't resist.

Elliot turned his face to Pa's. "That's where we were going. To find the baby."

"Then come along, and I'll show you." Pa took each of their hands, but Jenny felt as though he were leading her to her death. She didn't mind seeing the baby herself so much as she knew she'd hate Pa seeing her.

He pushed the door open, and they crept in softly as Pa held a finger to his lips. Mama was asleep and Jenny tiptoed close to the bedside. She looked at the soft, downy baby nestled in her arms, studied the tiny fingernails of one hand, the mouth like an upside-down heart, the little specks of eyebrows. Her heart felt like glass.

Elliot reached a hand to pet the baby, but Pa shook his head and whispered, "Not just now. We'll let them sleep a bit since your ma's all tuckered out."

Elliot's lip trembled. "I want to cuddle Mama."

Jenny suddenly realized he might be having a hard time, too, though it hadn't seemed so.

Pa's voice stayed soft. "All right, but be still."

Elliot walked around and climbed into the bed beside his mama. Jenny saw Pa's questioning look, but she didn't want to join them. She wanted Pa, wanted him so much it started deep in her tummy and climbed all the way to her throat.

He led her to the doorway, but Jenny turned back. "Is she the most beautiful girl baby you ever saw?" Her voice came from the cave inside her, from the hard knot, hidden in the hollow place.

"She's awful small." Pa's voice had a lilt to it, as it did when he was real tired or soft about something. "More your size than mine." He stooped down and curled her into the crook of his arm. "You reckon you could help your ma and me raise her up?"

Jenny snuck a quick glance at him. He must mean it. His eyes were truly concerned. She felt the flush burn her cheeks as the knot eased just a bit. She looked again at the baby curled into Mama's arms. Jenny felt a twinge. Mama liked to hold her, too, when she'd let her. And Cole's arm was strong and sure.

That baby might need her arms, too. She felt a tiny bit of ownership. "We won't spoil her, will we, Pa? Not like Emily Elizabeth?"

"Not on your life. I want her to be just like you."

The knot softened again. "Do you mean that, Pa?"

"You bet I do." He tightened his arm. "Though I reckon she'll be herself. She might not be quite so quick or so brave. But that's where we'll help her, see."

Jenny nodded slowly. "What if she doesn't like roping and riding and stuff?"

"Oh, I reckon we can teach her to. It might not come natural, but she'll learn."

"Do you wish she was a boy?"

He was quiet a moment. "It's kinda hard to say. Now she's here, it's hard to imagine her different."

"But if you had a boy . . ."

"Then it'd be the same, the other way around. I reckon since I already got one of each, this one's just a little bonus. It doesn't matter one way or the other."

The knot melted away, and Jenny felt the pain give way to joy, the kind of joy that sometimes carried her up like wings. "I love you, Pa." She turned in his arm and wrapped his neck tightly.

His arms closed around her. "I love you, too." His scratchy chin pressed her forehead with a kiss. "Don't you know it?"

Yes. Oh yes. At that moment, with his arms squeezing her just too tight and his voice as scratchy as his chin . . . "You won't stop, will you, Pa?"

"Never. Nothin' in this world or the next could make me."

Not even this baby. Not even his own baby.

◆◆◆◆◆◆◆

Abbie slept through most of the next day right along with the baby. It frustrated her because she wanted to be with Cole, to speak with him, to learn what happened and why he'd been gone so long. But her body would not cooperate, and the brief times she saw him, Pearl and Zena and Mama were always about, fussing over her or the baby or both.

With another sigh, she gave in and slept, biding her time until she could really welcome Cole back. She felt her strength returning and knew within a day or so she'd be chafing the bed. She startled awake at the touch on her face and looked into Cole's eyes in the dim lamplight. "The baby?"

"She's sleepin' as she ought to."

"What is it, then?" She looked out at the blackened window. What was he doing waking her in the middle of the night?

Cole wrapped her in the quilt and caught her up into his arms like a baby herself.

"What are you doing? Where—"

"Hush, or you'll have all your attendants after me like coyotes on a cottontail."

Abbie hid her smile in his shoulder.

He carried her down the stairs and through the back hall to the kitchen. Working the knob awkwardly with the hand beneath her knees, he got the door opened and stepped out into the night. "Cold?"

"Just a little."

He tightened his hold and carried her across the yard. "I got somethin' for you to see."

"What?"

He bent and laid her gently on a heap of straw covered by a thick woolen blanket. Then he lay down beside her and pointed upward.

Abbie followed his finger. "The stars?"

"That's right. A sky full of stars, and they're all ours for the lookin'."

Abbie smiled again. "Why, Cole. How romantic."

"Yes, ma'am."

Abbie nestled close, smelling the sage and horse and leather of him. He'd shaved the second growth of beard and his chin was smooth and hard, the mustache trimmed but full. She looked up at the brilliance of stars. He was right. The night was clear, the moon set, and the stars theirs alone. "Look, Cole, there's the constellation Cassiopeia. See it there? It looks like a *w*, or . . . I mean . . ." She hadn't meant to bring up the reading—not now, not ever.

"A *w*, eh?" There was humor in his eyes.

"Or an *m* if you look at it the other way. Two mountains or two valleys. The *m* is the mountains, like the first sound in m-mountain. The *w* is valleys like two *v*'s."

"Shouldn't it be double *v* then?" He was teasing, but she went along.

"I've always thought it should, but someone named it double *u*."

"What's its sound?"

"*Wuh*, as the first sound in we."

"Mmm." He nuzzled her neck.

"What?"

"First sound in mountain."

She laughed. "And in man and moonlight."

"And maybe."

She turned. "Maybe what?"

"Maybe I'll consider it. Readin', that is."

She caught his face between her hands with a rush of excitement. "You won't regret it."

"I said consider."

"I know." She made her face suitably subdued, but she couldn't contain the smile that stubbornly deepened the corners of her mouth.

"You suspect that means I will."

"Um hmm."

Cole pulled a wry smile. "I reckon there's likely some use to readin' I've missed these last years."

Her eyes shone like the stars above them. "You can't begin to know."

"Well, seems we've made a start."

Abbie could hardly believe what he was saying. "It'll come so quickly for you, you'll be astounded you didn't tackle it before."

"Takes inclination."

"And you were busy learning other things, learning them well."

"No sense goin' by halves." He ran a finger down her cheek.

"Then you'll be reading Virgil before the year is out."

He rose to his elbow and wound a strand of her hair on his finger. "I don't know this Virgil fella, but by the look in your eyes I reckon you're joshin'."

Abbie laughed. "Only a little. I know your nature well enough to guess you'll jump in with both feet."

"We're two sides of the same coin, Abbie."

"Yes." She looked up again at the majesty above them, and marveled at the truth of it. She and Cole Jasper, whom she couldn't see for the stars she'd had for Monte. Yet they were suited, so suited it amazed her.

Cole settled in and followed her gaze to the sky. "Cassiopeia, eh? What do you think of that for the baby?"

"Cassiopeia?"

"Just Cassie."

She toyed with the sound of it. *Cassie Jasper*. Cassie. How wonderful to have Cole home to name his daughter. "Cassie Bernadetta Jasper."

"Bernadetta?"

"After Birdie. Her real name."

He nodded slowly. "A'right." His hand warmed her cheek.

Abbie turned to him. "So did you get the reward?"

He crooked a brow. "What reward?"

"For bringing Crete to justice. You did do it, or you wouldn't be here now."

Cole's eyes trailed down the length of the blanket and back. "I didn't go for any money reward, Abbie. I went cuz I had to. Honor's its own reward."

The irony was not lost on her, but this time she had to agree. Would she want it different? Would she want him less than he was?

Her heart filled to aching. She tipped her chin up. "I thought I told you not to come back."

"I'm a stubborn cuss." Cole's mouth pulled crookedly.

Abbie smiled and reached for his lips with hers. "Thank God."

Acknowledgments

This series was only possible with all the help and encouragement I received from my family, my husband, Jim, my daughter, Jessica, my sons Devin, Stevie, and Trevor, from my friends, brothers, and sisters in the Lord, and the people at Bethany House Publishers who worked so hard to bring it to fulfillment.

I must express my gratitude to you, my readers—especially those of you who have written your encouragement. Thank you for your prayers.

It is by God's grace alone that I accomplish anything. So now I must thank my Lord and Savior, Jesus Christ, and the Holy Spirit who empowers me. Glory!